The
Outsider

ALSO BY CHRIS CULVER

The Abbey

The Outsider

Chris Culver

GRAND CENTRAL
PUBLISHING

NEW YORK   BOSTON

Grand Central Publishing
Hachette Book Group
237 Park Avenue
New York, NY 10017

www.HachetteBookGroup.com

Printed in the United States of America

RRD-C

First Edition: May 2013

10 9 8 7 6 5 4 3 2 1

Grand Central Publishing is a division of Hachette Book Group, Inc. The Grand Central Publishing name and logo is a trademark of Hachette Book Group, Inc.

The Hachette Speakers Bureau provides a wide range of authors for speaking events. To find out more, go to www.hachettespeakersbureau.com or call (866) 376-6591.

The publisher is not responsible for websites (or their content) that are not owned by the publisher.

Library of Congress Cataloging-in-Publication Data
Culver, Chris.
    The outsider / Chris Culver. — 1st ed.
        p. cm.
    ISBN 978-1-4555-2601-7 (trade)—ISBN 978-1-4555-2600-0 (ebook)—ISBN 978-1-61969-649-5 (audiobook)   1. Suspense fiction.   I. Title.
    PS3603.U629O88 2013
    813'.6—dc23
                                                            2012033724

The
Outsider

I

There were two armed men in his backyard when Detective Ash Rashid came home from work, and neither looked happy to see him. The first man was an inch or two under six feet tall and had a slight build and a wisp of a goatee on his chin. He sneered as soon as Ash came into view, clearly trying to look menacing but just as clearly failing. He centered his weight on his heels, which meant it would take him at least a second and a half to remove his weapon from his shoulder holster and pivot into a shooter's stance. He would have been dead twice over by the time that happened. He wasn't a threat.

The man's partner, though, was a different story. Ash didn't know his name, but in his internal monologue, he called him the Hulk. They had run into each other about a year earlier, after Ash shot the man's son in the chest and shoulder during an investigation. His son lived, but the Hulk didn't seem to be the forgiving sort. He stood at least six-five and had to be pushing three hundred pounds. Someone that big could take a lot of damage before going down, and Ash doubted his department-issue, forty-caliber Glock would cut it.

He slid his hand from the firearm inside his jacket to his

side and closed the gate to his cedar fence before stepping deeper into the yard. As soon as he did, he spotted the real threat. Konstantin Bukoholov. The skin on Bukoholov's neck was loose and jaundiced, and fresh liver spots marked his hands. His eyes were as Ash remembered them, though: cold and unfeeling. The old man had tipped him off to a drug-smuggling ring operating out of a nightclub in one of the city's suburbs a year ago. Ash investigated and ended up bringing down one of the largest drug suppliers in the region; in the process, he unwittingly eliminated one of Bukoholov's biggest competitors and likely doubled the old man's market share. Why Bukoholov sat in his backyard now, Ash didn't know.

He crossed the lawn, eyeing the guards. Bukoholov sat at Ash's teak outdoor table under a cedar pergola. The table had been set with three coffee mugs, all of which held a thick, black liquid. Bukoholov stood as he approached and held his hand out as if he wanted to shake. Ash ignored it.

"What are you doing here?"

Bukoholov gestured at the chair opposite him. "I'm enjoying your wife's very interesting coffee. Please sit. We have business to discuss."

Very interesting was one way of describing Hannah's coffee. It was so black and acidic it could have doubled as drain cleaner. If Hannah had made Bukoholov and his men coffee, she must be okay.

He nodded toward the Hulk. "Tell the goon squad to go back to your car. Call it a good faith gesture."

Bukoholov barked an order, and the two men slipped through the gate, exiting the yard. Ash pulled out a chair and sat down.

"You look good, Detective Rashid."

Ash leaned back and crossed his arms. "What do you want?"

Bukoholov took a sip of coffee but dropped the cup as a fit of coughing wracked his body. Hannah's coffee had a tendency to do that to the unprepared. Ash remained silent as Bukoholov regained his composure and ability to speak.

He stared at his spilled drink. "Excuse me. Your wife's coffee is quite strong."

"Yes, it is. I'll ask you again, though. What do you want?"

Bukoholov tilted his head to the side and shrugged. He managed to appear almost grandfatherly.

"It's always business with you, Detective. You should learn how to make small talk. We haven't seen each other in almost a year, and yet you dive right into business. How is a friend supposed to react to that?"

"We're not friends. We worked on a project once, and I've regretted it ever since. That project is now over, as is this conversation. Get out of my yard."

Bukoholov held up his hands in a placating gesture. He closed his eyes. "Just give me a moment," he said. "I want to talk to you about a job. You need to hear what I have to say."

Ash leaned forward. His eyes felt dry, and he wanted to blink, but he forced them to stay open. A shiver traveled up his spine as a late-fall breeze sent leaves skittering across the blue stone patio.

"I've already got a job, Mr. Bukoholov. A good one."

At least he had been truthful about part of that statement. Ash was the highest ranking sworn officer assigned to the investigative unit of Indianapolis's prosecutor's office. In most units, Ash's status as detective sergeant would make him a supervisory officer with privileges and responsibilities in accord with his rank. His actual unit was so small and specialized, though, that rank rarely mattered; everyone simply did whatever the prosecuting attorneys needed. It was a good job, usually. The pay was steady, and the work was interesting and varied. But with an election coming up, things were changing, and not for the better.

"This is a special sort of job. At four this afternoon, there was a car accident about two miles from here. A woman was killed. Did you see it on the news yet?"

Ash shook his head.

"It was a hit-and-run," Bukoholov continued. "The woman who was hit died on the way to the hospital."

"We'll pray for her family," said Ash, glancing at his gate. "If that's all you came to tell me, you can leave now."

"The woman's name was Cassandra Johnson. She had a daughter named Lisa. I believe you know them both."

Ash blinked several times, sure that he had misheard him.

"Cassandra and Lisa Johnson?"

"I believe that's what I said."

Ash felt as if he had just been slapped in the face. Lisa was his daughter's best friend. They rode the same bus; they played T-ball together; they had sleepovers. They were together so often in the summer that it felt as if he had a third kid; Lisa even called him Uncle Ash. Hannah and Cassandra, while perhaps not as close as their daughters, talked regularly and went to the same all-women's yoga class. Bukoholov stared at him knowingly.

"Is Lisa okay?"

"I'm sure she's fine."

Ash inhaled deep enough that he could feel his chest rise.

Indianapolis wasn't generally big enough to have organized crime like Chicago or New York; instead, it had loosely affiliated gangs, most of which came and went after their leaders killed each other in disputes over women or turf. Bukoholov was the closest thing the city had to a real crime boss, and he wouldn't risk being in a detective's backyard without damn good reason.

"Why are you really here?"

Bukoholov smiled. "I have only the best of intentions, I assure you."

"Bullshit. Get out of my yard."

Instead of leaving, Bukoholov reached into his jacket. Instinctively, Ash reached into his own and pulled out his firearm. He rested it on the table, a finger hovering over the trigger guard.

"Carefully reconsider your next move," said Ash. "I want to see your hands right now."

Bukoholov did as he was told and pulled his arm back, exposing a brick of hundred-dollar bills in his hand. He dropped the money onto the table and pulled his hands back slowly, showing his palms as if he had nothing to hide.

"For any expenses you may come across in your investigation."

Ash knew detectives in the narcotics squad who could look at a bundle of money and estimate its value to within a couple hundred bucks without batting an eye. Stacks of cash were just another part of their world. Ash didn't live in that world, though. He crossed his arms, trying not to stare.

"Take your money and get out of my yard."

Bukoholov stared at him for a moment, but then broke eye contact and sighed audibly. "I'm sorry we couldn't come to an arrangement," he said, pushing himself upright. "I'm sure someone will eventually discover what happened to her."

"Get your money and get out of my yard."

Bukoholov waved him off before turning to leave. "Put it in your kids' college savings accounts. You need it more than me."

Ash followed him out of the yard with his eyes before taking out his cell phone. He didn't trust Bukoholov, but the old man didn't make a habit of lying to him. Something was going on. He searched through his contact list for Cassandra Johnson's cell number. Her phone rang six times before going to voice mail.

"Hi, Cassandra, this is Ash Rashid. When you get this message, can you call me back either on my cell phone or at the house? Nothing is wrong, but it's important that you contact Hannah or me as soon as you can. I'd really appreciate it."

As soon as Ash finished that call, he called Cassandra's home number and left a similar message when no one picked up. It was probably a waste of everyone's time, but he also called IMPD's dispatcher and asked if there had been any accidents near Cassandra's home. The dispatcher hadn't heard of any, but Ash requested she send a squad car by Cassandra's house for a resident safety check anyway. No one would go in the house without cause, but officers would knock on the door and peer in a few windows to see if they could find anything untoward inside. Hopefully Cassandra and Lisa went out somewhere and left her cell phone at home.

With his immediate concerns quelled somewhat, Ash picked up the money from the table. Fifty one-hundred-dollar bills. As much as his family needed it, he'd sooner beg than accept a gift from Bukoholov; his money was dirty no matter how many times he washed it. He holstered his firearm before slipping the bundle of money into the inside pocket of his sport coat. If nothing else, the food bank at his mosque would have a nice donation.

Inside the house, Hannah stood at the sink with a cast-iron skillet in one hand and a green sponge in the other. She smiled at him as he walked through the door, a loose pink scarf covering her hair and neck. Its religious implications aside, Hannah said wearing the hijab around men other than Ash or her father made her feel comfortable in her own skin. She didn't have to worry about strange men hitting on her or staring at her. That was worth well more than a yard or two of silk.

"Look what I drew, *Baba*."

Ash mouthed hello to his wife before sitting across from his daughter at their breakfast table. As far as he could tell, Megan had drawn an abstract.

"That's a beautiful drawing," he said. "When you're done, we'll hang it on the fridge."

"It's our house," she said.

Now that he knew what it was, Ash saw the resemblance. Megan had drawn a series of brown squares with amorphous green shapes in front. Much like their actual home, Megan's roof sloped unnaturally to one side and her bushes had branches that veered off in every direction. He kissed her forehead and told her that her drawing was very realistic before walking toward his wife at the sink.

"You want me to take over?" he asked, nodding toward a pile of dirty dishes.

"No, I'll finish," said Hannah. "Are those men outside coming back?"

"No."

"Good," she said, pulling the scarf from her head. Her straight black hair was pulled back into a lopsided bun, exposing the nape of her neck. "Who were they?"

Ash didn't say anything for a moment as he considered his response. He never liked lying to his wife, and not just because it was a sin. She put up with him, she loved him, and she stayed with him, despite his faults. She deserved the truth; it was as simple as that. At the same time, he didn't want to upset her without cause. Bukoholov, as bad as he was, would never hurt a cop's family. The attention wouldn't be good for business. On balance, it seemed that a white lie in this situation was the best approach.

"It was a couple of guys from work. They wanted to ask me about a case."

Hannah nodded and stared out the window as if she were watching the conversation replay itself. "And what did that man hand you?"

Ash coughed and shifted on his feet. "Some money, but it's not for us. I'm going to give it to charity."

Hannah dropped her sponge and set down the dish she had been scrubbing. She put her hands on the edge of the sink and leaned forward, keeping her gaze riveted on the window. "Why couldn't he donate the money himself?"

On a lot of levels, Ash understood her trepidation. Hannah may not have known Bukoholov, but she still carried the scars—both literal and figurative—from the last job Ash had done for him. He leaned in, catching a whiff of the rose oil she had put on earlier that day.

"When was the last time you talked to Cassandra?"

"Yesterday, I think. Her car's in the shop, so she asked

me to pick her up for yoga tonight at the YMCA. You didn't answer my question."

Ash nodded toward the back patio. "That man just told me Cassandra may have been in a car accident. Before you get worried, I called my dispatcher, and she didn't have any records of it. I also tried to call Cassandra but couldn't get in touch with her. Our guest wants me to look into things. The money was a bribe."

Hannah looked confused. "Why would he tell you Cassandra was in an accident if she wasn't?"

"I don't know, but I plan to find out."

"Maybe we should go by her house right now and see."

"I already sent a squad car," said Ash. "If they find anything, they'll give me a call."

"Did he say anything about Lisa?"

"He said she's probably fine. I'm concerned that Cassandra's not answering her phone, though. Would she leave her cell at home if she was on a date?"

Hannah's voice faltered. "I...I don't know," she said. "She's not seeing anyone, though. I think she would have told me if she had a date. I live vicariously through her."

"Okay," said Ash, feeling his worry start to build. "Could you make me a sandwich? I'm going to go back into work and see what I can find out."

"Sure," she said, nodding. "Can you check on Kaden while I do that?"

"Of course," he said. "And I'm sure everything's okay with Cassandra. I'm just going to follow up."

"Yeah. Okay."

Ash squeezed his wife's shoulder before walking to his son's nursery. Kaden slept in his crib, his arms raised above his head victoriously as if he had just kicked the game-winning field goal in the Super Bowl. His skin was light brown, and his brown eyes sparkled whenever he smiled. He was a good baby, and he seemed to like his father. At least he had stopped peeing on him whenever he changed his diaper.

Since Kaden was asleep, Ash stayed outside the room, watching. After finding out that Hannah was pregnant with a boy, Ash had converted his old home office into a nursery by replacing the dingy carpet with oak hardwood and painting the walls a cheery, pastel yellow. Hannah had then drawn bumblebees near the ceiling. Islamic tradition was to sacrifice a pair of animals and have a party for friends and family when a boy is born. Since Ash was reasonably sure his neighbors would object if he slaughtered a pair of sheep on the front lawn, he and Hannah had instead donated money to Heifer International. Heifer used the money to purchase bees for poor families in Africa; Ash thought the décor fitting.

He watched his son for another minute before joining his wife and daughter in the kitchen again. It was time for *salat al-Maghrib*, dusk prayer, but nobody made a move to grab their prayer mats from the living room. Ash's mind was focused on his conversation with Bukoholov. At any given time, half a dozen government agencies had open investigations on the old man, and he still managed to conduct his business with relative impunity. He didn't get that power by nosing into other people's business, and he didn't act without thinking first. He expected to get something from his trip to the Rashid household. What, though, Ash didn't know, and that left him unsettled.

As soon as Hannah handed him a sandwich, he kissed her and hugged his daughter good-bye for the evening. In general, traffic accidents were handled by uniformed patrol officers from the various precinct houses around town, but hit-and-runs that ended in death or grave injury went straight to the homicide squad. Ash had spent six years in Homicide, so he knew a good number of the detectives assigned to the unit; hopefully someone would talk to him. He ate his sandwich on the drive but stayed in his car for a moment upon parking and called the dispatcher for an update on the safety check he had requested for Cassandra's place. A pair of officers had swung by the house, but no one answered the door. Unfortunately, without signs of forced entry or other problems, that was all they could do. He'd go by later to see if he could find anything himself, but in the meantime, he'd try another angle.

Ash left the car and went to the homicide squad's floor. As he should have expected at that time in the evening, the office was deserted. He took a few tentative steps inside and weaved his way around desks and stacks of cardboard file boxes, hoping to find someone but knowing he probably wouldn't.

When his suspicions came true, Ash took the elevator to the lobby and walked to the watch sergeant's desk. IMPD's headquarters had been built when public buildings were a source of community pride. Its white marble floors and granite walls had seen more than their share of abuse, but it was hard to deny the craftsmanship of the ornate crown moldings and perfectly straight joints on the floor. For all its aesthetic appeal, though, it was hardly adequate for a modern police department. Deep cracks in the granite walls ran from the floor to the ceiling, and the entire first floor smelled like laundry that had sat soaking in a washing machine for several nights. Ash didn't envy the officers who spent considerable amounts of time there.

He coughed, getting the attention of both the sergeant behind the front desk and a couple who were sitting and holding hands in the lobby. Ash didn't recognize him, but the sergeant looked to be in his late fifties or early sixties. Police work was taxing, both mentally and physically, so a lot of officers hoped to retire by that age. About a decade ago, that was a real possibility for a lot of people. But now that the world's economy was in an extended and seemingly never-ending slump, more and more officers kept plugging away until they were pushed out the door at sixty-five. At least those guys would have a pension and Social Security to fall back on; the way the economy was going, Ash and his family wouldn't even have that.

He leaned against the counter. "You got a minute?"

"If it's important."

Ash removed the badge from his belt and held it up. "It is important. I'm Detective Sergeant Ashraf Rashid, and I'm an investigator with the prosecutor's office. I've got a couple of questions that you might be able to help me with."

The sergeant slowly closed the magazine he had been reading before lacing his fingers together and leaning forward so he was only about a foot from Ash's face. Ash glanced at his nametag. Robert Doyle.

"And for what reason are you gracing me with your presence, Detective Rashid?"

It smelled as if the sergeant had eaten something with garlic for dinner. Ash forced himself to smile and took a quick step back, glad for the fresh air. "Have you heard anything about a woman named Cassandra Johnson tonight?" he asked, clipping his badge to his belt. "She may be a hit-and-run victim on the north side."

Doyle broke eye contact and picked his magazine back up. "If she was a hit-and-run, patrol has it."

"Someone told me she died at the scene, so Homicide might have it. I'm trying to find out what happened. Cassandra is a family friend."

Doyle stared back with a pair of dull, expressionless eyes. "Since someone told you about her, why don't you talk to him and stop wasting my time?"

Doyle was evidently quite a charmer. Had Megan been so charming, he would have called her Miss Grumpy Pants and made her sit on the naughty chair until her attitude improved. He doubted Doyle would respond well to the same sort of treatment.

"I did consider it, but I haven't had the opportunity yet. When'd your shift start?"

Doyle stared at him a moment, unblinking. Eventually, he must have figured out that Ash wasn't going to leave because he sighed and closed his eyes.

"Six. Anything else?"

"If there had been a call at four, would you have heard about it?"

"It depends."

Ash waited for Doyle to continue. He didn't.

"On?"

"Any number of things. Look, Detective, I don't know anybody named Cassandra Johnson. We didn't get a call about her, and I didn't hear about a hit-and-run. I don't have any clue what you're talking about, and I've got things to do." He opened his magazine again. "So unless there's anything else?"

Ash held up his hands in front of him, palms toward the desk. "That's it. Thanks for all your help."

"Anytime."

The sergeant had buried his face in his magazine. Doyle must have been on a complex case; *Sports Illustrated* didn't often make it into investigations. The lobby had room for twenty or thirty people, but it didn't feel very welcoming. He walked through the front doors and exited onto the street. The night was cold, and the street was wet from a downpour earlier that evening. Thursdays weren't big nights downtown, so the area was empty save the occasional passing car.

Ash buttoned his jacket and rubbed his arms for warmth, considering his options. There were two or three bars within walking distance, and chances were high that at least one would be quiet enough for him to make a couple of calls from. He considered going but decided against it. Even a quiet bar would be more distraction than he needed. Besides, he had been trying to stay out of bars after someone from his mosque spotted him walking into one about a month ago. That had been difficult to talk his way out of. Islam forbids the consumption of alcohol; unfortunately, drinking was one of the few activities that allowed Ash to sleep soundly at night and forget about the things he saw at work.

He stepped into the glow of a nearby streetlight and thumbed through his cell phone's directory until he found the entry for IMPD's dispatcher. News sometimes took a while to trickle through a bureaucracy, so if Cassandra had been in an accident, it was possible that Doyle just hadn't heard about it. The first officer on the scene might have even skipped the regular channels and called the homicide squad directly. Patrol officers weren't supposed to do that, and it screwed up normally clear lines of communication, but it did occasionally happen.

The dispatcher picked up after two rings and transferred Ash's call to the watch sergeant at the Northeastern Precinct house. Unfortunately, she knew as little as Sergeant Doyle. In the off chance the calls had gone through them, he called the two precincts bordering the Northeastern Precinct as well but got the same story both times. Nobody had heard of Cassandra.

Ash paced under the light, considering his next move. Bukoholov might have lied to him about the accident, but Ash couldn't figure out what he would get out of that. Moreover, despite having fewer moral scruples than most of the men and woman on Indiana's death row, Bukoholov hadn't ever lied to Ash before. Something else was going on, and he needed to find out what. He dialed the gangster's number and waited through two rings for him to pick up. Ash spoke before Bukoholov could.

"I just asked around, and nobody's heard of Cassandra Johnson. Tell me what you know."

Bukoholov paused. "I'm fairly old and I know a lot of things, so that may take a while."

"Cute. Tell me what you know about Cassandra Johnson."

"I've already told you everything you need to know."

"No, you haven't. No one has heard about the accident, and I can't find Cassandra. You know more than you're telling me. Where is she?"

"By this point, I would presume she's at the morgue."

"No, she's not. If she was killed in a hit-and-run, my department would know about it and they would have told me."

"I assure you, Detective, the accident did occur, and Ms. Johnson is, unfortunately, deceased. If you're half the investigator I think you are, you'll find out why. Just follow the evidence."

Bukoholov may have been a criminal, but he had his finger on the city's pulse better than anyone alive. When something in town was rotten, he knew it even if he wasn't always willing to share his information.

"What's really going on here?"

"You need to find out on your own. It will be better that way."

"Better for who?"

"You'll find out that, too."

"Okay," said Ash, hoping his growing frustration didn't seep into his voice. "If you're not going to tell me anything else, tell me this. If I keep going, what am I going to step into?"

Bukoholov chuckled. "You wouldn't believe me if I told you. If you're still stuck in a couple of days, give me a call. Otherwise, rely on your instincts and you'll do fine."

The Russian hung up before Ash could say anything else. Rely on your instincts. Follow the evidence. It wasn't the most helpful advice he had ever received.

Ash paced the empty sidewalk, thinking. If Cassandra were dead, her body would still be around. Finding that would answer some of his questions. More pressing than that, though, Lisa would still be around. He needed to make sure someone was taking care of her. He thumbed through his phone's contact list until he found the home telephone number of Julie Sims, the assistant director of Marion County's Department of Child Services.

The phone rang twice before she picked up.

"Julie, this is Ash Rashid. I need a favor. I've heard rumors that a family friend has been in a car accident, and I want to find out if you guys have her daughter."

Julie rattled what sounded like a drawer full of silverware.

"I'm at home. Did you call the information line?"

"Why would I need to call the information line when I've got good friends like you?"

Julie grunted. Good friends do that sort of thing when they're asked for favors.

"I guess my date with Ben and Jerry can wait, then. I'll see if she's in the system. What's her name?"

"Lisa Johnson. She's Megan's best friend."

"Give me five minutes."

Ash slipped his phone back into his pocket after hanging up. It was cold, but he was so lost in thought that he barely felt it. Julie called back within two minutes. A uniformed patrol officer had brought Lisa in a few hours ago, but Child Services hadn't placed her with a family yet. She agreed to a meeting if Ash met her downtown; he didn't need to think before saying yes.

As soon as he hung up, he glanced at his watch. It was a little before eight, and Julie would take at least twenty minutes to drive into town. For the second time that night, he considered going to a bar, and for the second time, practical concerns overruled his desire. He couldn't show up to the Child Services office with liquor on his breath. Instead, he went by a diner and grabbed a cup of scorched coffee and a slice of cherry pie. Neither improved his mood, but at least they distracted him for a while.

At the appointed time, he met Lisa and Julie in the Child Services office. Lisa brightened when she saw him, and he forced himself to smile in response. If her mom was dead, she evidently hadn't been told. Lisa had dark hair and dark brown skin. She had been Megan's best friend since the day they met almost three years ago. Now they spent more time in the principal's office than any other kids in school. They were both good girls at heart, just too rambunctious for their own good. Megan got that from him, and if he was any guide, they'd grow out of it.

"Hi, Uncle Ash."

"Hi, sweetheart. I'm going to talk to Miss Sims, but I'll be right back, okay?"

Lisa nodded, so Julie led her to a nearby playroom with a two-way mirror for observation. Once the door was shut, Ash slouched against the wall and put his hands in his pockets, one eye on Lisa and one eye on Julie.

"You guys have a file on her yet?"

Julie nodded and opened the tabbed manila folder she was holding.

"An officer brought her in at approximately six this evening. She's six years old and weighs fifty-three pounds. We don't have her medical records yet, but we ran her through Riley Children's Hospital. The attending physician said she looked healthy and couldn't find any signs of abuse or malnutrition. Lisa said she's not on any medication, but we'll check to make sure."

Ash nodded. It was nice to hear that she was healthy, but the rest was background information he already knew.

"What do you have on her mom?"

Julie's lips moved as she scanned the form. "My information says she died in a car accident, but IMPD had her house on a regular rotation. She was thirty-two years old at the time of her death, and according to our files, she had a history of mental illness. I have a report from a patrol officer requesting we send somebody by the house to check on things because he suspected Cassandra was manic and posed a threat to her daughter. I don't think we had time to follow up yet."

Ash narrowed his eyes and dropped his chin. "Are you sure you have the right file?"

Julie nodded.

"Unfortunately, yes. It looks like Lisa's mom hit the trifecta. Drug use, mania, and probable prostitution while her daughter was at school. If we had the manpower, we would have pulled her out of the house months ago."

Ash straightened and crossed his arms. "How old is this information?"

Julie skimmed the file and then shook her head before looking at him again. "There's no date listed."

"Something's not right," said Ash, turning his attention to Lisa again. "Cassandra was a good mother. She wasn't a drug user, and she sure as hell wasn't a prostitute. You might want to double-check to see that you have the right file." He paused. "Has anyone told Lisa what's going on?"

"Not yet."

Ash considered his options. Lisa was surrounded by strangers and probably scared out of her mind. It wasn't just unfair; it was cruel. He didn't know what the county's policy was in that situation, but he knew what it felt like to be scared and alone. He looked at Julie.

"Give me five minutes. I'm going to tell her what's going on. I'll be right back."

"Hold on just a second," said Julie, putting her hand on his chest. "We have a counselor on staff who will talk to her in the morning. That's how we do things when a parent isn't around."

"And by *counselor* you mean a stranger, right?"

"By *counselor* I mean someone with the training to deal with a traumatized child."

"With all due respect, Julie, I've known Lisa for almost half her life. She calls me Uncle Ash and my wife Aunt Hannah. She doesn't need to talk to a stranger with a degree in psychology; she needs someone who will give her a hug and tell her that everything will be okay."

"And what happens if everything isn't okay? We need to prepare her for what's going to happen next in her life. Besides, we haven't even talked to her father yet. Don't you think he might want to tell his daughter what happened?"

"He's serving a life sentence in the Wabash Valley Correctional Facility for killing an off-duty police officer at a nightclub. After losing his last appeal, your department petitioned for and won termination of his parental rights. I was Lisa's advocate during the hearing. She's never met him, and God willing, she never will. If that's not in your file, it should be."

"I forgot you were a lawyer," she said, taking a step back and flipping through the contents of her folder. When she looked up again, her gaze wasn't quite as sharp. As much as he cared about Lisa, though, Julie was probably right. It wasn't his place to tell her that her mom had just died. That should come from a real family member.

"Lisa has a grandma on the West Coast. She flies in whenever she can afford the airfare. If anyone should tell Lisa about her mom, I think it should be her," said Ash. "They're a close family, so she'll probably be the one who gets custody anyway."

Julie stared at Lisa through the two-way mirror. "Where on the West Coast is she?"

"Seattle. I'll fly her in if I have to."

Julie's nostrils flared. "That should be fine. We can let her do it."

It may not have been what Ash wanted, but it was still a victory of sorts. He breathed a little easier.

"Do you have housing lined up for her for the next few days yet?"

"We'll put her in a girls' home until her grandma arrives."

"How about you let me take her home?" Julie started to protest immediately, but Ash spoke over her. "Hannah and I are registered foster parents, so we're already in your system. We take kids on an emergency basis, and this sounds like an emergency."

At first, Ash thought Julie would fight, but she gave in. While she filled out the paperwork, he called his wife to arrange things at home. Hannah didn't even miss a beat in offering to put Lisa up for as long as needed. Ash went into the playroom and told Lisa that she would be staying with Megan for a few days. Since Lisa didn't know about her mom, she thought it was a rare Thursday-night sleepover at a friend's house. It almost broke Ash's heart to see how excited she was. After twenty minutes of paperwork, he buckled her into the back of his cruiser and drove home. Megan met them at the door, and the girls immediately ran to the living room where Hannah had set up a cartoon about a princess and a frog. The girls would probably fall asleep in the middle, but it would keep them occupied until they did. Hannah stayed in the kitchen.

"What happened?"

Hannah had been able to hold back most of her emotion when Megan and Lisa were around, but her eyes were growing red now.

"I don't know yet. I still don't have any confirmation of anything, so I'm going to go back to work and see what else I can find out."

The girls giggled loud enough that he could hear them all the way from the back door.

"Come back as soon as you can."

"I will."

Ash kissed her before stepping out. Rather than drive to his office, he drove to Cassandra and Lisa's house. The windows were dark, and the front door was locked. He knocked hard and rang the doorbell, but as expected, no one answered. He was alone but for the crickets. On his way back to the car, he pulled out his cell phone and found the number for the coroner's office. That's when he got his first break; the morgue didn't have a Cassandra Johnson, but they did have a Jane Doe who matched her description. The victim of a purported hit-and-run, she had significant trauma to her chest, shoulders, and head. It fit the story Bukoholov and Julie Sims had told him.

He drove over. The coroner's office was housed in a two-story brick building south of downtown near the White River. As soon as he went inside, Ash covered his nose. No matter how many deaths he investigated, he could never get used to the smell. Dr. Hector Rodriguez met him in the lobby and gave Ash a moment to throw on a surgical smock before leading him to the refrigerated vault where the bodies were stored.

Ash could see the outline of a petite woman's body beneath a sheet on an exam table at the far end of the room. As soon as Dr. Rodriguez pulled the sheet from her face, Ash recognized Cassandra. The blood had already begun pooling beneath her, leaving her face pale, but it was definitely her. According to Indiana law, only an immediate family member could provide an official visual identification, but Dr. Rodriguez wrote Cassandra's name down anyway as a provisional ID.

Cassandra's mother or sister would have to come in and

do the official identification later. On television, that was a relatively easy process. A victim's spouse or immediate family member would stand at a window while a technician pulled back a sheet covering the deceased person's face. On TV, a simple nod of the head sufficed. In real life, it was harder, more invasive than that. Cassandra's mother would have to give details. She'd have to identify tattoos, scars, birthmarks, and other unique marks that Cassandra might have had. She'd have to stick around the morgue for a while and possibly identify her clothing as well as fill out copious amounts of paperwork. It was a lot more than a casual glance, and it caused a lot more pain than anyone deserved.

When he got back to his car, Ash stayed in the parking lot and allowed the reality of the situation to set in. Cassandra and Lisa were as close to his family as they could be without being related. This was going to be hard. Instead of driving home immediately, he put the car in gear and drove until he found an open liquor store. Practical concerns didn't hamper him anymore, so he bought a pint of bourbon and drove to a small city park about a mile from his house. He started with a small sip, but that turned into a mouthful and then a second in short order. After that, he rested the bottle in his lap and closed his eyes, praying that the world would be different when he opened them but knowing it wouldn't.

Ten minutes after parking, he screwed the cap back on the bottle and drove home. The girls were in pajamas now, but they were still up and watching TV. Hannah had her arm around both of them. Ash must have been wearing his emotions because she closed her eyes and inhaled deeply as soon as she saw him.

"Hi, *Baba*," said Megan, looking at him for the first time since he came in. "You look funny."

"I'm tired, honey," he said. "It's late."

"Why don't you girls brush your teeth?" said Hannah. "It's time to get ready for bed."

Lisa and Megan dutifully slipped off the pullout sofa and made their way to the bathroom in the hallway. Hannah stared at him, her eyes growing glassy.

"She's gone?"

Ash swallowed and nodded. "Yeah."

She inhaled deeply as a tear slid down her face.

"We're out of toothpaste, *Ummi*."

Hannah stayed seated for a moment, but she eventually got up to help the girls. Ash took the opportunity to slip into his bedroom's en suite bathroom to brush his teeth and cover the smell of bourbon on his breath. When he finished, Hannah was in the bedroom, crying softly. Ash didn't say anything, but he held her and she cried on his shoulder until the girls went back to the living room.

Hannah went to bed a little after midnight, but Ash stayed up. For some reason, Megan and Lisa both liked professional wrestling and were watching a match with rapt attention when he got back to the living room. Thankfully, they weren't boys or they'd be reenacting everything the wrestlers did; as it was, Ash had his hands full telling them not to repeat the more inappropriate phrases the wrestlers used. He probably should have turned it off, but he didn't have the heart. Lisa had enough rough days ahead of her; she deserved another carefree night with a friend.

2

Ash's back felt stiff and his head hurt when he woke up the next morning. Megan and Lisa had finally conked out at a little before one in the morning, giving Ash a few hours of sleep before dawn prayer. Hannah was already awake, so he was alone in the room. He swung his legs off the bed and peered through the blinds covering their windows. The sun hadn't risen yet, and the sky was gray and overcast, making it another gloomy, November day in central Indiana. He yawned and went by the restroom for some aspirin before joining his family in the kitchen.

Lisa and Megan sat at the breakfast table while Hannah scrambled eggs at the stove. Kaden lay on his back in a Pack 'n Play beside the back door, playing with a brightly colored wooden toy designed to stimulate his brain and improve the strength of his grip. Having been on the receiving end of several of his son's hair-pulling incidents, Ash didn't think the latter was much of a problem.

"Hi, *Baba*," said Megan, waving with a piece of toast.

"Hi, Uncle Ash," said Lisa.

Ash ran his hand across his wife's shoulders as he crossed the room. He kissed Megan's forehead and hugged both girls simultaneously. In ten years or so, Megan would be a smart-mouthed teenager who would more than likely pretend to be adopted rather than acknowledge his paternity, but for now, she and Lisa accepted hugs gratefully. Sometimes he wished his kids would never grow up.

He stood beside the girls for a moment. As happy as Lisa was that morning, she wouldn't be for long. Her mother was dead and nobody knew a thing about what happened. That wasn't just unfortunate; it was wrong.

Ash rejoined his wife near the stove and leaned against the countertop.

"Are you keeping the girls home from school today?"

She nodded. "At least for the morning until someone comes to pick up Lisa. I wanted Megan here so she would have someone to play with."

Ash glanced at the clock on the microwave. He had slept later than he intended, so he had to hurry to make it to work on time. He kissed his wife's cheek before getting dressed. Hannah put the girls in jackets and had them play outside while she and Ash had dawn prayer in the master bedroom. He left at twenty to eight and was in his office at five after.

The morning routine in a police department was usually simple. An officer went in and, depending on his rank, he'd either go to a roll-call meeting where schedules and other information were shared, or he'd meet with his commanding officer to discuss his assignment. The routine was a little different in the prosecutor's office, though. Instead of meeting with another sworn officer, Ash met with the prosecuting attorneys to find out what they needed. Most of the time, they asked him to track down witnesses, recheck alibis, or conduct interviews; a big portion of the work was dull, but it was always varied. He liked that. Aside from being surrounded by lawyers all day, it wasn't a bad job.

As soon as he arrived, Ash walked to the office of the acting prosecutor, Susan Mercer, and discovered that their morning meeting had been moved to the conference room. Ash walked through a maze of cubicles to the other side of the room and stopped in the conference room's doorway. Susan sat at the head of a long wooden table while an older African American man in a navy blue pinstripe suit sat near her, talking excitingly. Their guest that morning was Leonard Wilson, chairman of the city council's Public Safety Committee. He was an important, powerful man; unfortunately, rather than use his power to improve the lives of his constituents, Leonard used his position to further his own political aims and fortunes, the city's neighborhoods be damned.

As soon as Ash saw him, he was tempted to walk out; he stayed, but only because his boss already saw him. She gestured to the seat to her immediate right.

"Morning, Ash," she said, gesturing toward Leonard. "This is—"

"No need for introductions, Ms. Mercer," said Leonard, interrupting her. "Detective Rashid and I know each other well." He stood and stretched his arm out but hesitated and then sat down when Ash didn't move from the door.

The two did know each other, unfortunately. With a city budget deep in the red and a regional economy in the tank, IMPD found itself in the unenviable position of having to perform its duties with a declining budget and a rising crime rate fueled by the newly impoverished and desperate. To alleviate some of that tension, Ash, along with his local rep on the city council, had proposed installing a series of bright streetlights in high-crime areas in the presumption that criminals would be less likely to mug people or break into homes under a spotlight. Similar lighting had lowered property crime at a minimal expense in nearby cities, so they figured it was worth a shot. However, since Ash's local rep didn't have anything to offer Leonard in exchange for his support, he allowed the proposal to die in committee without it ever coming to a vote. The man was a venereal disease for which the citizens of Indianapolis had yet to find a cure.

"What can I do for you, Councilman?"

"Have a seat, Detective Rashid," he said, pointing to the chair beside him. Ash glanced at his boss before sitting down. "As I was telling Ms. Mercer, I'm worried about an increase in crime in our traditionally ethnic neighborhoods."

Ash raised an eyebrow, but Susan didn't move. He shrugged. "It's a valid concern. Representative Watkins proposed setting up lights—"

"Lighting won't do it, son. Crime is rampant in this city. We need action, and I need your help. I need you to be my eyes and ears in the Islamic community. Find out what they're concerned about so I can take it up with the city council. Now that Jack Whittler is out of the picture, we can get things done."

Whittler had been Susan Mercer's predecessor in the prosecutor's office; now he was a guest of the federal government in a medium-security prison. In retrospect, Ash had difficulty deciding if he or Leonard was more contemptible. If someone offered Whittler enough money, he'd lose evidence, harass people he knew weren't guilty, and even refuse to prosecute strong cases. The city would feel the effects of his misadventures for years, but at least he had been up front about himself. Everyone knew he was a crook. Leonard, though, managed to hide his venal nature behind a veneer of righteousness.

Ash looked at his boss for some sort of tell. Her chin dipped a fraction of an inch, silently telling him to continue.

"Someone broke windows in our mosque last month, and some redneck in a pickup truck drives by during Friday prayer every week blaring country music so loud people have a hard time hearing our Imam speak. I've asked for regular patrols on Fridays to catch him, but the patrol division is spread pretty thin already. They say they can't justify the resources for a possible misdemeanor."

Leonard nodded and smacked his palm against the table, rattling a pair of coffee cups on the other end. Susan jumped.

"That's what I'm talking about," he said, punctuating the air with his index finger. "I will do everything in my power to take care of your problem."

Sneering was inappropriate, so Ash held his breath to stop himself from doing it involuntarily. He nodded instead and thanked him.

"Of course, son," said Leonard, clapping him on the shoulder. "We've got to look out for our own in this world, believe me. And let me give you my business card in case you think of anything else."

Unless Leonard had converted to Islam without telling anyone, *our own* must have meant "members of the human race" because the two of them had little else in common. He reached into his pocket and handed Ash a business card before turning to Susan.

"And thank you, Ms. Mercer, for indulging me in this meeting," he said, standing. "I appreciate your time."

She smiled and nodded. If Ash hadn't known better, he would have thought her smile genuine. It wasn't. Susan didn't smile to express friendliness. Most of her nonverbal communication came in the form of middle fingers and scowls. Leonard left the room, leaving the two of them alone. Ash started to say something, but Susan held her finger to her lips, presumably waiting until Leonard was out of hearing distance.

"What was that about?" he asked.

Susan looked at the door. "Jack Whittler's screwing us from prison. Since his arrest, the city council's been pressing for more oversight and control of our office."

She probably should have expected that considering the previous prosecutor, but Ash didn't think reminding her would be good for their working relationship.

"Leonard is just after votes—he doesn't care what you do. As soon as the news cycle shifts, he'll hammer on somebody else's door."

Susan nodded absently as she focused on some spot over Ash's right shoulder. Eventually, she took a breath and leaned back from her desk, regaining her composure. "I hope you're right. You have anything for me this morning?"

"Yeah. I stumbled on a case I'd like to work. A potential homicide that occurred about a mile from my house. The victim is an African American female named Cassandra Johnson. I believe she died at the scene."

"Who's the primary on it?"

"I can't even tell if anyone is yet. The case is all kinds of screwed up, and I want to make sure it's straightened out."

Susan furrowed her brow and leaned forward. "What's wrong with it?"

"The victim died yesterday. I went to the morgue last night and saw the body myself. Officially, she's a Jane Doe until a family member can ID her, but I'm positive it's her. The thing is, a patrol officer brought the victim's little girl by Child Services and filed a report that included our victim's name. A lot of the stuff in the report was wrong, but at least it got the vic's name right. My guess is that somebody is getting his cases confused and screwing up the paperwork. I want to make sure that's the only problem, though."

Susan opened her mouth as if she were going to say something, but then closed it. Finally she said, "I don't know that I'm following. If the patrol officer knew the victim's name, why doesn't the morgue? And why don't we have a detective assigned to it?"

"That's what I'm trying to find out. I hope it's just a paperwork mistake."

Susan stood and poured herself a glass of water from a carafe that rested on the table. "That's the kind of mistake that can kill a prosecution. It makes us look incompetent. I've got a meeting with the deputy chief of investigations this morning. I'll bring it up with her and see if we can fix it."

Technically, the deputy chief was Ash's direct supervisor, but the two met only once or twice a year during performance evaluations. Like most of her subordinates, he tried to keep his distance from her. It's not that she was a bad administrator—by all objective measures, she was quite good. Rather, the problem was that she was ambitious, and like a lot of ambitious people, she wasn't too concerned about the men and women she stepped on in her ascent to the top of the department's food chain.

"Give me a day before we take this upstairs. I bet the correct paperwork is sitting on a desk in the homicide squad. I'd hate for somebody to get written up for being forgetful."

Susan pursed her lips and tilted her head to the side.

"If it's not resolved by Monday morning, I want to know," she said, reaching to her side and picking up a worn leather briefcase. "This is going to be a long weekend. We're going to trial with Thomas Rahal on Monday."

She would have a long weekend. Rahal was being tried for murder, something that always got a lot of local media attention. Two things had compounded to make Rahal's trial explode, though: His alleged victim was a cop, and he was a Muslim immigrant from Iraq. Right-wing bloggers had even started a rumor that he was a Syrian spy living in the Midwest in order to scout infrastructure targets for a terrorist-style attack. Ash was pretty confident that was a lie, though. Rahal hadn't moved to the U.S. by choice. During the second Gulf War, he acted as an interpreter for American troops in Baghdad. Somehow, a group of insurgents discovered his identity and threatened to kill his family, so the U.S. military moved them all to the United States. Rahal wasn't a spy; he was a Muslim on American soil, which apparently made him a convenient target in someone's crazy, political narrative.

"Good luck," he said. "Have you got anything else for me?"

"One thing. Keep your ears open for news about Carl Gillespie. I've heard he's disappeared."

Ash paused. "Why is that name familiar?"

"Because Gillespie is John Meyers's lead investigator. Before that, he was a lieutenant with IMPD. You have better contacts in the department than I do, so I'm counting on you to keep me informed if you hear anything."

John Meyers was Thomas Rahal's attorney, which meant

Gillespie's disappearance could cause a major delay in her trial. He could understand her concern.

"Did you check the drunk tank downtown?"

Susan smiled again, but there was little humor in it. "Yes, but thank you," she said. She paused and blinked, her posture softening. "It's just a trial strategy. Meyers is trying to throw us off and make us think he's weak. He's treating this whole thing as a game."

Ash wouldn't vocalize it, but Meyers wasn't the only person treating the trial as a game. Susan had already sent eight boxes of irrelevant documents to the defense during the discovery phase of the trial. Those documents may have been tangentially related to the case she intended to present, but in actuality, their entire purpose was to overwhelm the defense with information and force Meyers to waste time following up on leads that would never make it into a courtroom. It was a fairly common if underhanded tactic.

Ash stood. "If I hear anything, I'll let you know."

Susan glanced up from her paperwork. "Thank you. Have a good weekend if I don't see you again."

"You too."

Ash shut the door and then took the stairs to his floor. Unlike the men and women on Susan's floor, Ash and his colleagues didn't have cubicles. They had desks that had been pilfered from other office buildings, dead houseplants in the corners of the room, and carpet with so many stains it almost looked like a giant piece of bad modern art. Overall, it had a comfortable, lived-in feel to it.

Ash walked to Bertha, the heavy oak desk he had been given when he transferred into the unit several years earlier, and sat down. The textbook thing to do in his situation would be to call Mike Bowers, the lieutenant in charge of the day shift at the homicide squad, and ask him what was going on with Cassandra's case. He and Ash didn't get along terribly well, though; in fact, they had gotten into a fistfight just eight months ago. Calling him wouldn't get Ash anywhere; instead, he dialed the personal cell phone of Detective Eddie Alvarez, a recent transfer to the squad.

"Eddie, it's Ash Rashid. How you doing?"

"Busy. What's up?"

"I've got wind of a case, and I wanted to ask you something. Who's the dumbest guy in your unit?"

Alvarez chuckled. "I really don't know."

"How about this, then. Who picked up the potential hit-and-run homicide on the northeast side of town yesterday afternoon?"

Alvarez clucked his tongue for a moment. "Nobody. It's not on the board."

"The board" was a large whiteboard the squad used to keep track of victims, cases, and detectives. It was supposed to help the officers in the unit know who was working what, but it ended up becoming more of a scorecard than anything else.

"Is the name Cassandra Johnson on the board?"

He paused for a moment. "No. You sure she died?"

"Yeah."

"That's odd. We didn't pick up anything new."

"Are you sure? Cassandra is in the morgue, and her little girl was brought in by Child Services."

"Yeah, I'm sure. Lupo and Walters went out on a call last night about a shooting, but the victim survived. Aggravated Assault took the case. That's all we had."

So Homicide didn't even get the call. Evidently there was more wrong with Cassandra's investigation than he realized.

"Okay," said Ash. "Thanks for the help."

"Sure thing."

Alvarez hung up, but Ash didn't move for a moment as he tried to think things through. Try as he might, though, he couldn't make sense of what he had just found out. Something was wrong. He dialed Susan Mercer's office. After being put on hold by her secretary for a few minutes, Ash had his boss on the line.

"You wanted me to keep you informed about my hit-and-run investigation. The homicide squad was never called. It wasn't just a paperwork error."

"What's going on, then?"

"I don't know. We've got a body, and I know at least one patrol officer saw it because he called someone from the morgue to pick it up. He didn't call Homicide, though."

"I think you need to call Internal Affairs. This sounds like something they might be interested in."

On paper, calling Internal Affairs was the smart thing to do. Moreover, they got things done. Of course, the same could have been said of Joseph McCarthy. If IA came in, they'd be more interested in finding dirty cops than finding out what happened to Cassandra; she deserved better than that.

"If you want me to do that, I will," said Ash, closing his eyes. "Before we call the Grand Inquisitor, though, I'd really like to have a better idea of what's going on."

"If that's what you think is best, I'll give you some leeway," she said. "The moment you find something concrete, though, I want IA brought in." She paused. "If no one else has heard about this case, how did you?"

"One of my confidential informants told me yesterday."

"You think your CI's involved?"

"That's one thing I'd like to find out."

"Okay," said Susan, sighing. "Good luck, and keep me informed."

"I will, and thanks."

Ash hung up and spun around in his chair. All he had to go on so far was the word of a gangster and a report filed with the Child Services office. Ash knew how far he could trust Bukoholov—not very—but he had no idea about the report with Child Services. It was time to see what he could find out about that. He turned on his computer and called up the department's felon database.

The officer who brought Lisa into the Child Services office implied that Cassandra had an extensive arrest record. Ash typed her name into the search box and waited as his computer whirred, coughed, and did whatever the hell else it did to search. Four records eventually popped up, but two were almost twenty-five years old. He eliminated those from contention before opening them. A third file was for a Caucasian female, so that was out as well. That left him with just one possibility. He clicked on the record and then sighed when he saw what it contained.

The mug shot was old, but it was unmistakable. Cassandra and Lisa had the same almond-shaped brown eyes, the same cheekbones, and the same nose. Cassandra had been arrested half a dozen times since she turned eighteen. Five of those arrests were misdemeanors, but the sixth was for felony possession of narcotics. A big part of him had hoped the entire report to Child Services was false. Clearly it was exaggerated, but it had some grounding in truth.

Ash leaned back in his chair, thinking. The record was both good and bad. Cassandra never resisted arrest, nor were any of her arrests for violent offenses. Her last run-in with the police had been six years ago when she was popped with a gram of crack cocaine in her pocket. Since it was her first felony, the judge gave her a suspended sentence in exchange for attending a drug treatment program. Reading between the lines, she cleaned herself up, probably for Lisa. A lot of people try to do that, but very few succeed. Cassandra was one of the system's rare successes.

Ash sipped his bitter and now lukewarm coffee; the drink fit his mood well. Eventually he leaned back and took out his cell phone. He thumbed through the list of recently made calls until he found Julie Sims's number.

"Hey, Julie, this is Ash Rashid. I have a quick question if you have a minute."

"You're not going to tell me about another kid, are you?"

"Nothing like that. I wanted to ask you about Lisa Johnson's intake form."

Julie coughed and rustled papers on her desk. "Give me a moment." She hummed a few notes before answering again. "Okay, I found the file. What do you want to know?"

"Who brought Lisa in?"

"Officer Joe Cartwright. He's from the Northeastern Precinct."

Ash wrote the name down. "Great. He and I are going to have a conversation. Thanks."

"One thing before you go. We got a hold of Sheila Johnson after you left. She's Lisa's grandma, and she's flying in this afternoon. Do you want to meet her?"

Ash minimized his Web browser and opened his calendar.

"I've met her before, actually. She came for Thanksgiving two years ago," he said, resting the phone in the crook between his shoulder and neck. "You have her number?"

"Not yet, but I'll make sure she calls you before she leaves."

"Appreciate it," said Ash, leaning back and blinking sleep out of his eyes. "And thanks again. You've been a big help."

"Anytime," said Julie.

Ash hung up and opened the department's telephone directory on his computer. IMPD had almost two thousand sworn officers, and while none would be nominated for sainthood anytime soon, the vast majority were good people who did their jobs in a professional, courteous manner. At least one, though, had ignored a homicide. Maybe it was a mistake, but Ash doubted it.

He clicked through the directory until he found the name and number of Paul Murphy, a detective he knew in the Northeastern Precinct. He and Paul were in the same department, but they had yet to see each other at work. In fact, they only met because they happened to run into each other at a continuing education conference in Miami. Ash liked him, though, and had him on the phone within five minutes.

"Hey, Paul, it's Ash Rashid. I need a favor."

"Well, I'll be. Is this that famous Ash Rashid my wife reads about in the paper? It can't be. I'm just a simple detective. What could someone like me offer such a wise man after such a long absence?"

About five months ago, Ash's former boss, Jack Whittler, was prosecuted in federal court on public corruption charges. Ash didn't have anything to do with the trial, but the newspapers covering it mentioned him nearly every day for his involvement with the team that uncovered Whittler's illegal activities. Ash didn't miss the exposure.

"For you, I'll keep it easy. I want to get in touch with an officer from your precinct."

Paul must have shifted his weight because his chair squealed loud enough that Ash heard it over his phone's tiny speaker.

"So you're after information. As I'm sure you know, information isn't always easy to come by, and my beer stein hath not runneth over for many months, my friend."

Ash grunted. "I'm working a case now. When I close it, I'll give you a call. We can go out for a round or two."

Paul paused and wheezed, catching his breath. He had asthma and a dislike of all things involving physical exertion; it was amazing he hadn't plopped over dead yet.

"That could be acceptable. It might be even more acceptable if said round was purchased at a concession stand in Lucas Oil Stadium during a Colts game."

"Why don't we just take it slow? If we go to a game, we'll start drinking, and then one thing will lead to another. Before we know it, we'll be shooting our guns in the air and peeing on burning cars in downtown Detroit with no recollection of how we got there."

"Yeah," said Paul, his voice disheartened. "It'd be like Miami all over again. Good times." He brightened again a moment later. "Well, if the game is out, what can I do for you?"

"Joe Cartwright. What do you know about him?"

"He's a little turd that just won't flush. Why do you ask?"

"His name has come up in a case I'm working. Is he on duty today?"

Paul bellowed the question to his fellow officers before

answering. "Word on the street is yes. He works in a special unit under Lieutenant Noah Stuart, but he ought to be off at three or so. He usually works out at the gym down the street until four or five. I can club him in the knee to make sure he sticks around if you want."

Ash thought through his already tight schedule. "If Cartwright did what I think he did, I'm going to do a lot more than club his knee. I'd rather have him fresh for that. Do a lot of guys in your precinct use that gym?"

"I know of its existence only through innuendo and rumor. I'm afraid I can't say."

Ash didn't really need to ask that question. Paul's circumference and height were roughly equal. Exercise was not a big part of his life.

"Okay, appreciate the help," said Ash. "I'll call you next week."

He hung up and glanced at his watch. It was already nearing midmorning, which meant almost seventeen hours had passed since Cassandra Johnson died. The first forty-eight hours of a homicide investigation were the most important hours a detective had. After that, memories start fading away and evidence starts disappearing. If he didn't find something soon, there might not be anything left to find.

Cassandra Johnson's neighborhood was only a mile from Ash's house, but it could have been a different state. Neither neighborhood had ever been a center of wealth and prosperity, but time had been hard on Cassandra's. Sixty years ago, Indianapolis had been an industrial town, and many of the hardest jobs in those industries had gone to immigrants and their children. He and Cassandra lived in what had once been thriving neighborhoods for that working class; unfortunately, as the industries that supported those neighborhoods closed, the residents either sold out cheaply or simply left, creating a blight-ravaged landscape the city eventually forgot.

Ash pulled to a stop in front of Cassandra's house and took a look around. At least half the houses around him looked abandoned, and almost all needed serious repair. Rooflines sagged, porches had broken steps, and sheets of rotting plywood covered what had once been doors and windows. As bad as it was, though, he saw bright spots as well. One homeowner had planted bright yellow mums around a tree on her front lawn, the woodwork on another was freshly painted, and a Dumpster overflowed with construction debris in front of a third. It would be a multigenerational effort, but things were getting better. In another twenty years, the area might be vibrant once again. Sadly, Cassandra would never see it.

Her home was a single-story bungalow with a trim lawn and rosebushes beneath the front windows; it was one of the nicest houses on the block. Ash stepped out of his car and caught sight of an older African American woman eyeing him from her porch across the street. He had seen her before, but she had never been overly friendly, and this time didn't look to be an exception. She took a long drag on her cigarette and blew the smoke in his direction but otherwise didn't acknowledge him.

Ash ignored his audience and took his notebook from the interior pocket of his jacket. He wasn't much of an artist and he didn't intend to introduce the pictures in court, but he sketched the layout of the streets and surrounding homes, making special note of the location of Cassandra's house and the elderly lady across the street. According to Bukoholov, she had been hit at about four in the afternoon, probably right after work. Hannah said her car was in the shop, so there was a fair chance she had been walking home from the bus stop.

Ash jogged two blocks up the street, following the route Cassandra would have taken and trying to spot anything out of place. The area was just a city neighborhood like so many others, though. He found a couple dozen cigarette butts, a few broken beer bottles, and a plastic bag from Walmart, but nothing interesting. Cassandra's house was west of the bus stop, so she would have had the sun directly in her eyes as she walked home. She wouldn't have even seen the car that hit her; hopefully she wasn't scared when she died.

He traced his steps back to the intersection nearest Cassandra's home but stopped on the corner. As expected, he saw a pair of long skid marks on the asphalt. Interestingly, though, they were a good hundred feet from the point where Cassandra would have crossed. He added them to his sketch and snapped a picture with the camera built into his cell phone, an uneasy pit growing in his stomach. If the car braked that far away, there should have been ample room to stop.

The sun was almost directly overhead as he stopped beside a dark residue near the sidewalk. On any other day, Ash would have assumed it was motor oil that had leaked from the engine of a car stopped at the corner. It wasn't, though; he was standing over the spot where Cassandra was hit. He snapped a picture of the stain with his phone, and as he did, he noticed several shards of clear plastic near the sidewalk. He bent and moved one with his pen, exposing striated ridges on one side. They were pieces of a Fresnel lens, the same sort that covered the headlights on a car.

Bent over, he also noticed navy blue paint flecks on the street. In a normal case, paint flecks and fragments from a broken headlight would help narrow down the suspect pool considerably. In their present condition, though, they were useless. The crime scene had been open to the public for at least twelve hours, time enough for hundreds of cars to pass. The broken headlight and paint shards may have been from the car that hit Cassandra, or they may have been from the local minister's Cadillac. He had no way to know; everything there was a waste.

The more Ash thought about it and the more involved he became with the case, the angrier he became. Cassandra wasn't just dead; she was forgotten. More than likely, the first officer on the scene looked up her arrest record and decided she was just another dead drug addict in a neighborhood full of people who didn't matter. He didn't bother investigating because he didn't think anyone would care. Well, people did care. Cassandra's friends cared; her family cared; a little girl who lost her mother cared. Ash cared, and he was going to make sure others did, too.

3

Since he couldn't use the physical evidence, Ash was going to have to do some work. He crossed the street and walked toward the elderly woman he had seen earlier. As soon as he stepped onto the sidewalk in front of her home, their eyes locked and she took another drag on her cigarette. He expected her to wave him over or at least say something to him, but she didn't. She simply stared and smoked.

He stopped walking before reaching her lawn to see if she'd react. No such luck. He took another couple of steps forward and waved, hoping she'd return the gesture. Tree roots had split the concrete walkway in front of her house, creating a tripping hazard every four or five feet. The UPS guy probably loved that. Her house looked little better than her walkway. Someone had removed several bricks from its facade, and an animal had made a nest in her gutters. Ash stopped on the edge of her porch, and she took another drag on her cigarette. She exhaled in his direction again, but the smoke dissipated before reaching his face.

"What do you want?"

Her teeth were yellow, and her voice sounded raspy. Ash looked over his shoulder. If she had been outside when

Cassandra was hit, she would have seen everything from her vantage point.

"Morning," he said, pulling back his jacket long enough to expose the badge clipped to his belt. "I'm Detective Sergeant Ash Rashid with the Indianapolis Metropolitan Police Department. Are you free to talk for a few minutes?"

She blew another cloud of smoke in Ash's direction before coughing hard. "I've got plenty of minutes. What do you want?"

Judging by her cough and smoking habit, Ash wasn't sure how many minutes she actually had, but he wasn't going to correct her. He put a foot on the porch, causing the wood to sag.

"I'm looking into the death of one of your neighbors," he said, pivoting ninety degrees so he could see Cassandra Johnson's home again. He pointed to it with his index finger. "Ms. Johnson died from injuries sustained in an accident yesterday. I wanted to talk to you about it. You live here alone?"

She threw her cigarette over the porch railing and onto the scratch of dirt in front of her home. "Why? You want a date or something? I guarantee you that I'm more than you can handle."

"I don't doubt that, ma'am," said Ash. "I'm just trying to find witnesses to Ms. Johnson's death."

"I don't have anything to say to you. Get off my porch."

Ash stood straighter and, as requested, removed his foot from the porch. His charm and good looks weren't going to work, apparently. As he took a step back from the porch, it looked like the blinds in the house behind his potential witness moved, but it might have just been his imagination.

"Ma'am, Ms. Johnson may have been murdered. I'm trying

to figure out what happened. Cassandra was a good woman and a good mom. I'm trying to do right by her, that's all."

"Don't go around talking like you knew her. You people stopped caring about this neighborhood a long time ago."

"That's not true. You remember when Habitat for Humanity renovated Cassandra's house last year?" She looked away but didn't respond to the question. "I built the frame around her front door and helped pour the concrete for her back patio. My wife, my daughter, and Cassandra's daughter, Lisa, planted the rosebushes beneath her front window. Lisa is my daughter's best friend, and Cassandra was very close to my wife. They're important to me, and I need your help to find out what happened."

She scoffed. "Like I'll believe that. I bet you just looked that up. You've probably never even been here before."

He gritted his teeth and inhaled deeply. "Were you here yesterday afternoon when she was hit?"

The woman leaned forward. "I'm. Not. Saying. Anything."

Each word was a short, deliberate sentence of its own. Usually, that would have been Ash's clue to back off. He needed her, though. She had the best viewing angle of the site of the accident on the block, and if she had been outside, she would have seen everything.

"What would it take to convince you to talk to me?"

She smiled. "The Second Coming of the Almighty himself."

That would probably be a little tough to arrange.

"Is there anything—"

"Go away, Detective Rashid," she interrupted him. She waved him off with the back of her hand. "You're done here."

"Did you see—"

46

"I said you're done here," she said, interrupting him, her voice hard and strident. "I'm not talking to the police."

"Ma'am, I'm trying to solve a crime. A woman is dead, and she shouldn't be. I'm here to help."

Her face screwed up. "Trying to help? You people aren't trying to help. You already took everything I got, and now you want my house. I ain't going to help you anymore."

"I'm not here to take anything from you, least of all your house. If you don't think I'm here to help, let me prove it. If someone has been stealing from you, tell me who it is. I promise that I will do everything I can to put him in jail and get your stuff back. Okay?"

"Oh, Lord," she said, chuckling as she threw up her hands. "He wants to help me, but he doesn't know he's the problem." She looked at Ash again. "The police have taken enough from me. If it wasn't for Leonard Wilson, you people would have taken my house, too, and kicked me out a long time ago."

Ash took a step back, surprised. "You mean Leonard Wilson, the city council member?"

She puffed out her chest. "I sure do. He's done more for folks around here than you'll ever do. He tore up my tickets and said I shouldn't have to fix my porch or windows if I don't want to."

Now they were getting somewhere, and her hostility was starting to make sense. Her tickets sounded like violation notices from the city's Department of Code Enforcement. It was one of the ugly sides of up-and-coming neighborhoods. Developers bought run-down homes, fixed them cheaply, and then complained to the city about the dilapidated homes surrounding them. If the developers complained enough, the city sent a building inspector to drive by, and chances were good that he'd spot a broken window or a lawn that's reaching waist high and give the homeowner a ticket for being in violation of the local building code.

In an ideal world, a ticket would be all the incentive the homeowner needed to fix the issue. That wasn't usually the case, though. If a homeowner had the money to fix his broken windows or repaint his garage, he would have done it on his own. The ticket didn't do anything, but with the city involved, the expenses piled on. That homeowner who can't afford to repair his damaged home has to pay court fees, attorney fees, and fines. When he can't pay those, a lien is slapped on his house. When he can't pay that lien, the city repossesses the property, the homeowner is evicted, and the home is put on the auction block for another developer. The same thing had happened to one of Ash's elderly neighbors. The situation had made his stomach turn.

"If you're having problems with the city, there's a free legal clinic at..." He paused midsentence as the blinds behind the homeowner moved again. It wasn't just his imagination this time. Someone was watching them, and it looked like he had a camera. Ash turned to the side, minimizing his profile exposed to the house. He didn't like being filmed from cover. If someone could film him from cover, he could just as easily shoot him from cover. "I thought you said you lived alone."

"No, you assumed I lived alone. That's my grandson. You're not afraid of a little camera, are you?"

"Does he use that camera a lot?"

"Like it's glued to his eyeball. He heard everything you said to me."

She leaned back in a self-satisfied manner. Ash glanced at

the window again, but the boy with the camera was nowhere to be seen.

"Can you ask him to come out? I want to talk to him."

"You going to arrest him?"

"No, I'd like to see if he filmed Cassandra Johnson's murder."

She looked at the door. "Well ask him yourself, then. I ain't gettin' up."

Ash forced himself to smile before stepping onto the porch. The wood groaned again under his weight. Even though the homeowner was beside him, he knocked on the door hard so he wouldn't scare the kid by walking inside unannounced. As soon as he did, the house shuddered and he heard what sounded like a back door slamming shut. The interior blinds moved so much in the breeze that he could actually see inside as they swayed. The back door swung back open, apparently having been slammed so hard the latch didn't engage.

Ash sighed in resignation.

Why do teenagers always have to run?

He jumped off the porch and ran around the house. The backyard looked like the front, mostly dirt with a few tufts of brown and yellow grass. A teenager in a royal blue hooded sweatshirt climbed awkwardly over the chain-link fence of the yard next door, almost racking himself on the top.

"I just want to talk."

The kid looked over his shoulder, his mouth wide open as he dropped to the other side of the fence. Ash wasn't much for long distances, but he could outsprint almost everyone in his department. An overweight teenager wasn't even a challenge. As soon as he reached the fence, he pulled himself over in one smooth motion, his feet clearing the top easily.

Unfortunately, his landing on the other side wasn't quite so acrobatic. He found a soft spot on the ground, and his ankle rolled, knocking him to one knee.

Before he could stand, a pit bull emerged from an alcove beneath the porch of the house, barking and snarling. Ash scrambled back toward the fence while the dog sprinted toward him. The kid he was chasing just kept running toward the opposite side of the yard, gaining distance.

Before the dog reached him, the chain securing it to the porch snapped taut, giving Ash some breathing room. He backed up and pulled himself to his feet, using the chain-link fence before sprinting after the kid. The dog followed in an arc around the yard but never got close to biting him. As soon as he reached it, Ash pulled himself over the far fence but was more careful on the landing. The kid was maybe fifteen yards away by then. Ash sprinted as hard as he could, ignoring the growing road noise around him.

The houses blurred as his legs pounded against the ground. Rather than lose time by jumping over the next fence, the kid veered left around it and ran into an alley, his feet skidding as the terrain shifted from grass to dry clay and gravel. By that point, the kid's lead had decreased to ten or fifteen feet, and the noise of a nearby road grew louder. A bus or maybe a semitrailer—something with a big engine anyway—rumbled the ground in front of them, but Ash couldn't see it around the obstructing buildings and trees. The kid reached the sidewalk a moment before Ash did. He looked over his shoulder again, his eyes and mouth wide as if he were surprised that he was still being chased. He didn't see the bus speeding toward him on the street.

As soon as Ash reached the sidewalk, he lunged forward.

The kid was out of reach, but he got a couple of fingers inside the hood of his sweatshirt and pulled hard. Fabric ripped and stitches popped, but the kid's forward momentum stopped almost instantly, causing his legs to kick up in an almost comic book fashion. Ash caught his weight as he fell backward and nodded his thanks to the bus driver for slowing down. Some of the bus riders glared at him, presumably for being jostled by the sudden braking, but at least no one was hurt.

"Let me go, man," said the kid, squirming.

Ash partially released his quarry but maintained a hold on the hood of his sweatshirt. He breathed hard, trying to catch his breath.

"Are you all right?"

"Let me go," said the kid again, twisting. He looked to be about thirteen or fourteen, but he had a professional-quality video camera around his neck.

"If I do, are you going to run away?"

"Do I look like I can run anymore, man?" he asked, practically gasping.

"Good point," said Ash, releasing his grip on the kid's sweatshirt. He leaned forward and rested his hands on his knees to catch his breath. The kid laced his fingers behind his ears, creating an inverted triangle with his arms. "What do you say we go back to your grandma's house? We need to talk."

"I already did what you wanted," he said, dropping his arms to his sides and balling his hands into fists. "You said you'd leave my grandma and me alone."

Ash didn't understand the outburst, so he didn't say anything at first, hoping the kid would elaborate. But the silent treatment didn't work because he kept his mouth shut.

"What are you talking about?"

The kid glared at him but didn't say anything.

Ash waited for another minute longer before speaking. "What's your name?" he asked.

"Michael."

"You got a last name, Michael?"

"Yeah." Ash raised his eyebrows. Michael sighed disgustedly. "Washington."

"Michael Washington. Good. Your grandma said that camera of yours is practically glued to your eye. Did you film something you weren't supposed to see?"

Michael broke eye contact and started walking down the sidewalk.

"Did you see someone hit Ms. Johnson?" asked Ash, hurrying to keep up with him.

"Leave me alone."

"I can't do that until you talk to me."

Michael shook his head but kept walking. Ash kept pace, not saying anything, hoping Michael would do the talking for him. That didn't get him anywhere for about a block.

"You know Lisa, don't you?" asked Ash. "Cassandra's little girl?"

Michael nodded but didn't turn his head to meet Ash's gaze.

"Her mom is dead," he said. "Someone killed her. It could be someone you care about next. Your grandma, your mom, your brothers or sisters if you've got them. Think about that."

Michael walked another thirty feet or so in silence.

"You're not from around here. You don't know what it's like."

"You're right," said Ash. "This isn't my neighborhood,

which is why I need to talk to you. Did Cassandra have a problem with a gang or something?"

Michael snorted. "Wasn't a gang. She was killed by the police."

That was a little surprising, but Ash tried not to let it show. "Why do you think it was the police?"

"I don't think it. I filmed it. Two cops parked up there by Ms. Johnson's house and then hit her when she walked across the street. My grandma tried warning her, but Ms. Johnson didn't hear her yell."

"And you just happened to have your camera out when this happened?" asked Ash.

Michael hesitated but then nodded. "My friends and I film stuff and put it on a website. I thought the police were hiding to catch people running the stop sign. They do that, and sometimes people start fighting. Fight videos get lots of hits."

They walked for another few minutes in silence. Finally Ash said, "Are you sure Cassandra was hit by a police car?"

"Yeah. It looked just like yours."

That was a little more believable. Cassandra might have been hit by a Crown Victoria, but Ash doubted it had been driven by a cop. IMPD and the Indiana State Police both had public auctions every couple of months to sell their aging cruisers and other vehicles. Because the cars had so many miles on them, they sold cheaply and oftentimes ended up in neighborhoods like Michael's. Ash had seen two that looked almost identical to his on the drive from his office that day alone.

"Can I see the video you shot yesterday?"

"I ain't got it anymore."

"Why not?"

"They made me get rid of it."

Ash stopped walking and closed his eyes. "The police made you get rid of it?" he asked. Michael didn't say anything in response. "No matter what they told you, you're not in trouble."

"I don't care if I'm in trouble or not. They told me not to say anything, and I'm not going to."

"Who were these officers? Were they in uniforms or a suit and tie like me?"

Michael didn't answer. Instead, he started walking toward his home again.

"Talk to me," said Ash. "I'll protect you. That's my job."

The boy looked over his shoulder. "Then you're not very good at it. Just leave my grandma and me alone. We don't need your help."

Michael walked the rest of the way to his house in silence. His grandmother was still on the front porch with a haze of smoke around her when he arrived.

A lot of detectives would have gone after the kid again, maybe even going so far as to take him into custody. Ash was even reasonably sure that once he had a pair of handcuffs around his wrists in an interrogation room, he'd break and answer every question asked. Michael thought he was tough, but he wasn't. Breaking him wouldn't have been a problem; it also wouldn't have been worth it.

Unlike a lot of boys his age in that neighborhood, Michael didn't wear gang colors, he didn't curse at the police officer chasing him, and he didn't want to fight. If Ash broke him in an interrogation room, he'd break him for life. He probably wouldn't start a life of crime afterward, but he sure as hell wouldn't trust the police again. There was precious little goodwill in that neighborhood as it was; Ash wasn't interested in squandering what he had. He could find the information he needed elsewhere.

He walked to his car and pulled out his cell phone before thumbing through a stack of business cards from his wallet. Eventually, he pulled out the card Leonard Wilson had given him that morning. Michael wasn't willing to talk about it, but someone had scared him. If nothing else, Ash could at least get some more patrols in the area to make the family feel safe at home. He dialed the number printed on the card and waited for the city councilman to pick up.

"Detective Rashid," said Wilson's booming voice. "To what do I owe the pleasure of this call?"

"I'm calling because I'm in one of the neighborhoods you represent on the north side of town, and something is going on. It might be a good idea to put some pressure on the patrol division and get some cars out here."

The smarmy bastard paused before answering.

"I am always willing to help out one of IMPD's finest. Before I make that call, though, may I ask you for a favor of my own? I've scheduled a meeting of the Public Safety subcommittee of the city council tomorrow morning at eight-thirty. I'd love for you to tell my fellow council members about some of the concerns you voiced to me this morning."

Ash should have expected Leonard's response, but it pissed him off anyway. While most city council members would be more than happy to take care of their constituents, Leonard's first priority was himself. Apparently it took a personal favor for him to get off his ass and do his job. Ash coughed so he wouldn't say that aloud.

"Do you usually have meetings on Saturday mornings?" he asked.

"Oh, no," said Leonard, his voice upbeat. "We scheduled it around Ms. Mercer's availability. We wanted to speak to her on the record before she goes to trial against Thomas Rahal. Can I count on you to show up?"

"Fine. I'll be there."

"All right," said Wilson. "I'll call patrol for you. Where are you at exactly?"

Ash described a roughly four-block area around Michael's home, and the councilman promised he'd do what he could. Not that it would likely amount to much. Ash looked up after his call to see Michael and his grandmother on their front porch. He hadn't gotten as much out of them as he had hoped, but at least he got a description of the car that hit Cassandra. A Crown Victoria, navy blue if the paint flakes on the street were any indication.

He would have left, but Michael came bounding toward his cruiser a moment later. Ash leaned against his door, waiting.

"My grandma wants to know if you'd feed Miss Johnson's cat. I'd do it, but Grandma doesn't want me going over there by myself."

Before he and Michael had talked, his grandmother hadn't seemed to want anything to do with him. Feeding a cat wasn't much, but it was a start. It also gave him an excuse to go inside and look around. He nodded and took a brass key from the boy's outstretched hand.

"I don't think Garfield likes me too much, but I'll do my best."

"Garfield doesn't like anybody except Lisa and some other girl she plays with."

"I think that other girl might be my daughter, Megan. Can I keep this key for a few days? My wife and I are baby-sitting Lisa, and we wouldn't mind taking her by the house to get some new clothes. I'll come back later and feed the cat again, too. I'd hate to keep bothering you guys to get the key."

Michael looked over his shoulder at his grandma. She nodded.

"Okay," he said. "And I'm sorry for running. My grandma says I shouldn't have done that."

"That's okay," said Ash, reaching for his wallet. He pulled out a business card. "If the people who threatened you come back, give me a call. Day or night, I'll come out and take care of them. I live about a mile and a half away, so I can get here quickly. And if you want to tell me anything about them, you can do that, too."

Michael took the card but didn't say anything else before walking back to the porch. Ash turned toward Cassandra's home. It had been empty for a night, which in that neighborhood meant someone might as well have hung out a sign inviting looters. He walked around the home's perimeter, looking for broken windows or other obvious points of entry. It appeared secure, though; hopefully that meant he'd be alone once he went in.

He used the key Michael had given him to unlock the front door. It was a small but efficient house with most of the original, antique woodwork still intact. There was a living room to the right of the door and a hallway straight ahead that led to the kitchen. There were no toys on the ground anywhere, dirty clothes were all neatly placed into hampers in the bedrooms, and the kitchen was spotless. Cassandra and Lisa may have been poor, but they weren't desperate.

Lisa had decorated the kitchen with drawings and projects from school. She had even hung a macaroni mosaic on the fridge. Megan had made an identical one, so it must have been a class project. Ash leaned against the countertop beside the refrigerator. His family and the Johnsons weren't really all that different. They experienced the same struggles, the same triumphs; they shared some of the same laughs. In every corner, in every drawing, and in every room of that house, Ash saw what had been and the promise of what would have been. It wasn't fair.

He searched the individual bedrooms quickly but didn't find anything interesting. Lisa slept with a number of stuffed animals, while, from all appearances, Cassandra slept alone. He found two toothbrushes in the bathroom, but no birth control pills or other contraceptives. Hannah didn't think Cassandra had a boyfriend, so that wasn't too surprising.

Ash checked out the home office last. Cassandra had been a receptionist at a commercial construction firm for the past couple of years, but her company went bankrupt as the economy struggled. From what Hannah had told him, she did temp work after that but never seemed to stay in one place very long. It was surprising, then, to find a stack of white file boxes in her office. He opened the top one and put the lid on the ground. It contained a neat stack of legal documents, and interestingly, all of them were from the same criminal proceeding: the murder trial of Thomas Rahal.

That's odd.

He closed the box and opened the one beneath it only to find affidavits in support of search warrants for a number of different cases. The documents by themselves didn't advance his investigation, but they did beget certain questions. What was she doing with them, and how did she get them? He closed the box and stood still to think. Aside from the files, nothing in the house was out of place. No drugs, no guns, no notes from possessive ex-boyfriends. It was just the home of a woman trying to make it in a world that didn't seem to care if she did or not.

He snapped a picture of the file boxes with his camera phone before sweeping the room a final time with his eyes. He stopped upon seeing a black cord on the desk. One end was plugged into an electrical outlet on the wall, while the other end was buried beneath a pile of papers. He moved the papers aside and exposed a clamshell cell phone with the logo of a prepaid cellular carrier on its back.

He flipped the phone open and thumbed through the recent call history. Cassandra had called only a single number in the last ten days, but she'd called it several times. Ash typed the number into his own cell phone and hit the CALL button but was transferred to voice mail immediately. He didn't recognize the voice on the other end, but he did recognize the mailbox owner's name: Carl Gillespie, former IMPD lieutenant and currently missing investigator for John Meyers and Associates.

"Well, shit."

4

The phone calls to Gillespie were problematic. If Cassandra had gotten a job working for Gillespie or his boss, John Meyers, the files in her office likely contained confidential client information. Ash could get a court order to examine them, but an impartial mediator would have to examine them first to ensure they didn't violate a client's privacy, and that'd take time, possibly even weeks. Ash didn't have weeks; he had days at most before the evidence grew cold and suspects disappeared. That would complicate things, and he didn't have time for it. He'd just have to find the information he needed another way.

Before leaving, he filled two plastic bowls with water and a third bowl with cat food. An orange and white striped cat came bounding into the room as soon as the food hit the bowl. At least he had accomplished something. Ash locked the door on his way out but stopped on the front porch. A breeze whistled across the home's support beams, carrying with it the scent of roses.

Michael said Cassandra had been run down by a police officer. Ash doubted that, but he needed to discount it completely before he could move on. He sat on the steps out front and called his boss's office to tell her what he had found so far.

She advised him to step lightly. It was fair advice. With Susan informed, he called IMPD's dispatcher and was immediately transferred to Vehicle Services. Within about two minutes, he had the shift supervisor on the line. He seemed jovial enough; hopefully he'd cooperate.

"So what can I do for you, Detective?" he asked.

"I need a favor."

"You don't say," he said, his voice taking on a sardonic tone.

"Hate to put you on the spot, but I'm looking for a dark blue cruiser with damage to the front panel, maybe even a dented hood. You have anything like that come in lately?"

"And is this an official request?"

An official request required paperwork filed with the deputy chief's office. That'd take at least a few days, time he didn't want to waste. Besides that, if he got a match, he'd jam up some poor bastard who was probably hit on the wrong time on the wrong day. That would get ugly.

"This is a personal matter."

"Personal matter like you're going to go after this guy because he hit your car? Or personal matter like you saw a good-looking girl driving it and want her number?"

Ash hoped his voice sounded sheepish. "More of the latter."

The auto tech grunted. "Computer says we've got one match. You're not going to like it, though. Driver's name was Detective Dennis Walker."

Ash wrote that down. "What else do you have on him?"

"I thought this was about a girl."

"It's a long story. What else do you have on him?"

The auto tech muttered something. "Intake form says he's on the night shift out of the Northeastern Precinct. He brought in a navy Crown Vic last night with a damaged front panel. Said he hit a deer."

"You get many deer accidents in the city?"

"No," he said. "You want to tell me what this is really about now?"

"You don't want to know. Thanks for your time."

Ash hung up the phone and called the dispatcher to request Walker's address. He lived just a couple of miles east of Cassandra, so the drive didn't take very long. The neighborhoods, though, couldn't have been more different. The homes in Walker's area appeared uniformly neat and the street was clear of potholes or broken concrete. Ash pulled to a stop in front of Walker's home, a garrison colonial with white siding, black trim, and a bright red front door. Kind of surprising he could afford it on a detective's salary.

Ash jogged up the walkway toward the front door and knocked hard. A young girl in a yellow sundress answered, so he smiled and knelt down to look her in the eyes.

"Hi. My name is Detective Rashid. Is your dad home?"

"What's this about?"

Ash looked up as a middle-aged man in shorts and a T-shirt walked down a carpeted set of stairs about ten feet from the front door. Like the little girl, he had blond hair and blue eyes. Unlike her, though, no smile crept onto his lips. Ash stood and pushed his jacket back, exposing his badge.

"I'm Detective Sergeant Ash Rashid. Are you Dennis Walker?"

He nodded and put his hand on his little girl's shoulder. She wrapped her arms around one of his legs but didn't say anything.

"I'm Detective Walker, yeah. What's this about?"

Ash cleared his throat and glanced at the little girl. He smiled again.

"Nothing too serious. I just need to talk to you in private for a few minutes. It's about work."

Walker nodded and patted his daughter on the back before sending her to the kitchen to be with her mother. Once the girl disappeared, he joined Ash on the front stoop, pulling the door shut behind him.

"We're alone now, Sergeant. What do you need?"

"I heard you were in a car accident yesterday. I'm glad to see you're walking around."

"I wasn't in a car accident. I hit a deer with my cruiser. Is that a problem?"

Ash shook his head and frowned. "Of course not. I just don't see too many deer in the city. I read on the Internet that they're afraid of homeless people."

Walker shifted his weight slightly, no trace of a smile on his lips. "I was on a call near Crown Hill Cemetery. The deer hopped the fence and ran in front of my car before I could slow down. Do you have any more questions?"

That was actually plausible. Crown Hill Cemetery was bigger than a lot of state parks and had ample trees. Ash knew firsthand that at least one family of deer roamed its grounds, because he had almost hit one while driving to an early morning funeral a year ago.

"Do you know the name Cassandra Johnson?"

There was a flicker of recognition in his eyes for a moment, but that passed quickly. "No. Should I?" he asked.

"She died in a hit-and-run accident a couple of blocks from here. It's an unfortunate coincidence. Your accident and hers, I mean."

Walker took a small step back and crossed his arms. "Are you accusing me of something?"

"No. I'm just making an observation. Where were you yesterday at about four?"

Detective Walker's eyes narrowed. "Do I need my PBA lawyer here?"

"I hope not."

Walker's eyes took on a distant gaze. He looked over Ash's shoulder. "I was in a meeting with Lieutenant Noah Stuart and half a dozen Northeastern officers," he said. "Is that good enough?"

He wrote the information down, nodding. "For now. Thank you."

Ash closed his notebook but stayed still and stared at the detective. Walker's story about hitting a deer wasn't entirely implausible, but he was still hiding something. Ash put his notepad in a jacket pocket and looked down at his feet, remembering something Michael said.

"Do you like working in the Northeastern Precinct?"

Walker shrugged. "It's close to home."

"How do you feel about your colleagues?"

The detective squinted at him. "They're like family."

"Someone told me that officers from your precinct threatened a kid against speaking out about a crime."

"I sincerely hope you corrected that misunderstanding. None of my colleagues would ever try to intimidate a witness."

Ash raised an eyebrow. "None of them, huh? No bad apples in that bunch at all?"

"None," said Walker, drawing the syllable out. "Let me give you some advice, though. Instead of investigating my friends, look at the houses near Thirty-Eighth and Audrey

Avenue. You can see the sort of stuff we deal with on a daily basis."

"Are you trying to tell me something specific?"

"No. It's just that when things go wrong in the North-eastern, that's where we look first. It can be a rough neighborhood, though, so be careful. I'd hate for you to get shot for sticking your nose somewhere it's not wanted. And get off my walkway. If you want to talk to me again, call my lieutenant."

That friendly conversation degenerated quickly. Ash took a couple of steps back, holding his hands up defensively. "Thanks for your time. I'll check out that intersection."

He walked back to his cruiser with Detective Walker's eyes boring into him the entire time. Walker may have been telling the truth, or he may have been feeding him a line of bull. It didn't matter. Something was going on in his precinct, and it wasn't good. Ash glanced at his watch. It was just before noon, and his day was becoming more and more booked. He wanted to go to Friday prayer, but his schedule was too tight. He'd make it up somehow, but for the moment, he needed to see the intersection Walker mentioned.

He put the two streets into his cruiser's GPS and headed out. The neighborhood shifted from pretty to pretty ugly as he drove. By the time Ash reached the intersection, some of the houses around him were literally falling apart, the stone and bricks that formed their walls having been taken by thieves. Indianapolis didn't have the history of cities like New York or Chicago, but it was still his home. He had grown up there, and it saddened him to see its old buildings gutted for parts.

He parked about a block from the intersection. The street

was wide and paved with light gray asphalt that had cracked and crumbled over the course of the years. The sidewalks fared better but not by much. Weeds popped through cracks and small vials that had once likely held drugs dotted the concrete. Ash did his best not to step on any crushed glass as he walked, but it littered the sidewalks, making it hard to avoid. Thankfully, his shoes had thick rubber soles that kept the glass from cutting his feet.

He stopped walking three houses down from the intersection. Unlike most of the homes nearby, the wooden Victorian in front of him had intact windows and a plywood sheet over its front door. The temperature hovered around the forty-degree mark, but several of the building's windows were open and box fans blew air from the inside out, causing the area around the home to smell like ammonia mixed with sulfur and burning engine oil. Ash covered his nose and winced. Either the home's inhabitants were in the middle of a methamphetamine cook, or a chemical company had opened a factory in the basement. He leaned toward the former.

Ash backed off but not before spotting a navy blue Ford Crown Victoria with a dented front panel in the home's backyard. Walker's tip was certainly prescient. He couldn't see the vehicle well from his current position, but he made a mental note to check it out once backup arrived.

He walked back to his car, considering who to call. Meth houses were tough to deal with for a lot of reasons. Four out of five of them burned down before the city found them, and those that didn't burn were an even bigger pain in the ass. The cooking process released acidic vapors, making the air so toxic it caused permanent damage with very little exposure. Worse, the people who made meth usually partook of

their own product as they produced it, making them irratio-
nal, unpredictable, and impulsive. A meth house was a tactical nightmare under even ideal circumstances, and with an
active cooker inside, this was far from ideal.

Ash called the dispatcher but was transferred to the lieutenant in the narcotics squad downtown as soon as he mentioned what he found. The department moved fast when an
officer found somebody cooking meth because meth cookers
had a tendency to blow themselves up when left alone. The
lieutenant to whom Ash spoke planned to raid the house as
soon as possible, but it would take at least an hour to secure
a search warrant and get the necessary tactical units and
equipment into position. Luckily, few civilians lived in the
neighborhood, minimizing the potential collateral damage.
Until the raid occurred, the department dispatched uniformed officers to secure the home's perimeter and keep any
of the meth cookers from escaping.

Ash walked back to his cruiser to watch the front door
and wait. Within five minutes, a black-and-white Crown
Victoria pulled up behind him and two uniformed officers
stepped out. The first officer would probably be carded if
he tried to buy a dirty magazine, while his partner was a
middle-aged sergeant. A field training officer and his probationary student. Ash filled them in on the situation, and they
agreed to watch the front door while he watched the back.
It would have been nice to have more officers, but the two
were all patrol division could spare at the moment. Better
than nothing.

Ash let the patrol officers do whatever they wanted in
front of the home while he walked to the back and checked
out the Crown Victoria he saw earlier. The front headlight

was broken, and there were small red stains on the hood and window. It felt too convenient to be chance. Ash wouldn't be able to prove it, but he had a feeling Walker had known the car was there before he'd given him the tip.

He knelt down behind the car and removed his firearm from his holster before peering over the top of the vehicle. The home's windows had been covered with black spray paint, so he couldn't see inside. Hopefully that meant no one inside could see him. Ash couldn't be sure what they'd find in that car, but he did know one thing: Detective Walker was going to get another visit before he was done with his case.

A plan shaped up quickly once the tactical team arrived. Even though Ash was the first officer on the scene, he played little role in either planning or conducting the raid on the house. He was okay with that, though; the SWAT team had taken down meth houses before, so they knew what to do. As six officers in full tactical gear and gas masks breached the front door, Ash and a couple of uniformed officers with shotguns waited outside in case any of the home's inhabitants tried to bolt.

No one needed a radio signal to know when the raid started because the SWAT team pounded on the front door and announced themselves loud enough that everyone within a block radius could have heard them. Almost as soon as that occurred, two middle-aged men tried to run out the back. Both were thin to the point of being gaunt and both were missing several teeth. Thankfully, they both put up their hands as soon as they saw the barrels of four police-issue tactical shotguns pointing at them. The entire operation took less than a minute; it was as good a job as any Ash had ever seen.

While the uniformed officers took care of the meth makers and the tactical unit swept the house, Ash checked out the car in the backyard again. The paint chips he had seen on the road in front of Cassandra's home weren't admissible in court, but he wished he had taken some for comparison's sake anyway. The meth dealer's car looked roughly the same color, though, and it did have a broken headlight. Hopefully they could pull something usable off it.

He walked to the front yard and stopped near the porch. The home's front door was propped open and all the windows in the home had been pulled open as wide as they'd go to air out the interior. Detective Sergeant David Lee from the narcotics squad directed the scene from the porch, a gas mask around his neck. When he saw Ash, he nodded and started toward the lawn.

"This is a good find," said Lee. "These guys had a pretty big lab."

"I'm glad we found it before they blew themselves up. Once you're done with them, though, I'm going to need to talk to them. They may have been involved with a homicide I'm investigating."

Lee whistled and shook his head. "Not a good day to be white trash in Indianapolis, is it?" he asked, looking at the two suspects, now handcuffed and sitting on the curb in front of the house. He turned back to Ash. "I'll make sure they're available for you when you need them. We've cleared the house, but I haven't done my walk-through yet. You want to go with me?"

"As much as I've always wanted to walk through an active

meth lab, I'm going to decline. If you've got one to spare, though, I'd like to borrow one of your forensic technicians for a few minutes."

"Sure thing," he said, already turning and motioning toward a young woman leaning against the forensic technicians' van. She stepped forward diffidently and pointed to her chest. Lee nodded, so she walked across the lawn toward them. She had blond hair swept back from her face in a ponytail, and she was young enough that wrinkles had yet to grace her skin.

"Can I help you, Detectives?"

"Are you with the lab?" asked Lee.

She started to nod, but then stopped and tilted her head to the side. "I-I'm in college," she stuttered. "I'm an intern, but I can do a few things."

"Do you know what phenolphthalein is?" asked Ash.

"It's a water-insoluble compound of hydrogen, carbon, and oxygen that's oftentimes used as an acid-base indicator. When placed in a solution of—"

"Good enough," said Ash. "I have a substance on a car behind the house that I think may be blood, so get your kit and get ready to work."

"Okay. I can do that, I think," she said, already turning and jogging toward the van she had been leaning against. Lee's eyes never left her back. He looked at Ash again when she disappeared inside the vehicle.

"What do you think? You think a thirty-five-year-old narcotics detective and a college intern could make it in this crazy world of ours?"

"I think you'd have a heart attack trying to keep up with her," said Ash, walking toward the backyard. He turned when he reached the corner of the house. "And I think your wife would kill us both if she found out I encouraged you."

Lee seemed to accept Ash's wisdom because he stopped looking at the girl and walked toward the house. Fewer people crowded the backyard than the front, giving Ash a moment to think. With any luck, they'd be able to match the blood on the Crown Vic's hood to Cassandra Johnson and prints on the steering wheel to one of the meth traffickers. A blood match wouldn't be enough to guarantee a conviction in Cassandra's murder, but it'd get the prosecutor's office most of the way there. It almost seemed too easy.

Since he had a moment, Ash called IMPD's dispatcher and was patched through to a supervisor at Indiana's Bureau of Motor Vehicles. He gave the clerk at the BMV the VIN number from the Crown Victoria, and while she searched through the office's database, the forensics intern came to the backyard carrying a fishing tackle box. Ash put his thumb over his phone's microphone and pointed to the front of the car.

"The substance on the hood. I don't need everything checked, just the red stuff near the grill. If it's blood, I'll have the entire car taken in."

She nodded and bent down to peer at the hood. Her face was pale, and her hands seemed to shake slightly.

"I've never done this except in the lab at school," she said. "I don't want to screw up."

"I'm sure you'll do fine," said Ash, straightening. He would have stayed and watched her closer, but the BMV employee had evidently found his record because she started speaking. The Crown Vic's last registrant had been the Indiana State Police, and curiously, the BMV had no record of sale or other transfer of title. How a pair of meth users had it was beyond him.

Ash thanked the BMV worker for her time and hung up before walking toward the hood of the car. Cotton swabs littered the ground and a small, nearly empty bottle of phenolphthalein sat beside the car's tire. Detective Lee's crush held up a pink cotton swab and smiled.

"I forgot the peroxide at first, so I had some false negatives. You'd have to do something like an Ouchterlony test to determine if it's human, but this is blood. At least I think it is."

Ash nodded and snapped pictures of the car with the camera built into his cell phone. His pictures wouldn't help in court, but they might be helpful in an interrogation.

"I appreciate your help. If I need anything else, I'll let you know."

The girl gathered her things and walked to the front yard with Ash following a few steps behind. Detective Lee was doing his initial walk-through of the home, so Ash waited outside and called the state police. The sergeant in charge of the motor pool seemed genuinely surprised that they were missing a car. At first, he thought his coworkers were playing a joke on him, but then Ash sent him a picture of the dent on the Crown Vic's hood. He became much more cooperative after that.

The vehicle was supposed to be in a secured impound lot about seventy-five miles west of Indianapolis. The sergeant said he'd investigate its disappearance, but Ash held little hope that he'd find anything. After all, this was a man who had lost an entire car and then realized it was missing only after it had been discovered with blood on its hood in a town seventy-five miles away.

Ash put the phone in his pocket and glanced at the meth traffickers Lee had arrested. Their clothes were tattered, and dirt and sweat caked their faces. Meth was one of the most addictive substances on the street, and even with the best treatment, those men had only a 5 to 10 percent shot of going clean. Even handcuffed on the curb, they were probably thinking about ways to get high again. The thought nagged at Ash's gut. Meth users weren't the sort to drive to a neighboring town just to steal a car; if they needed something, they went local. Moreover, Bukoholov wouldn't have brought him in on a case like that. Something else was going on.

Detective Lee stepped off the home's front porch, grinning and interrupting Ash's thoughts.

"Meth, guns, and cash. These boys are making it easy."

For you, maybe.

Ash looked at the meth dealers again. Both fidgeted and looked around, but their gazes never lingered on any object long enough for them to actually look at anything. They probably didn't even know where the hell they were.

"Do me a favor," said Ash. "I need the vehicle behind the house towed to the lab. There's blood on the hood that needs to be protected, and I'm sure you'll find something in it worth your time. Might be able to add another felony for receiving stolen auto parts to the charges against your meth heads."

Lee furrowed his brow. "Not auto theft?"

Ash looked away before speaking. "These guys don't seem organized enough to steal a car."

Lee glanced at the drug users. "We'll look into them and see what we can find. You got a case number for whatever you're working on? I'll make sure the blood is logged as yours."

Ash had to think for a moment before answering. The department assigned a case number to every criminal complaint lodged in the city, usually before a detective began work. The detective would then include that case number on every report, every piece of evidence, and every scrap of information he came across that was even tangentially related to the case. It kept things organized for trial and allowed a supervisory officer to track what his subordinates were doing all day. Normally, Ash would have a case number before stepping out of his office door; this investigation wasn't normal, though.

"Do me another favor and keep the blood for now. I might have to borrow it later, but I want to keep my involvement here quiet."

Lee squinted at Ash thoughtfully but eventually nodded. "I'll do that, then. Good luck."

"Thanks."

Ash left the scene. It was after one, and he hadn't eaten much that day, so he went by a microbrewery on his way back to the office and had a vegetarian pizza and a beer. After settling his bill at the table, he stopped by the bar at the front of the restaurant and ordered a shot of bourbon. The liquid burned his throat on the way down. The effects would be short-lived, but for a little while, he'd feel normal. Precious few things in the world had the ability to bring him that sort of succor. He popped a mint in his mouth and headed to his office at a quarter to two.

As much as he wanted to believe he had Cassandra Johnson's murder solved, he had too many questions without even the beginnings of an answer. Why would a pair of strung-out meth dealers murder a single mother who hadn't been on drugs for years? And how would those meth dealers get the police vehicle they supposedly used in the crime? And then why would the patrol officers assigned to the case ignore it? None of it made sense.

Konstantin Bukoholov.

The more he thought, the more he kept coming back to that name. Even if he could answer every question he had about the meth dealers and their stolen vehicle, he couldn't explain why Bukoholov had become involved. Something bigger was at stake than a mere murder, and until he could figure out what it was, he might as well have been trying to put out a forest fire with a garden hose.

When he got back to his desk at work, he found a yellow Post-it note on his computer monitor requesting that he contact Susan Mercer. He groaned inwardly before crumbling the paper and throwing it into the garbage. Susan had a big trial in just three days, so she wouldn't interrupt her afternoon unless it was important. Rather than wait for the elevator, Ash took the stairs up. At that time in the afternoon, most of the prosecuting attorneys were either at lunch or in court, so the place seemed deserted. He walked directly to his boss's office. Pam, Susan's secretary, put down her sandwich and smiled as he approached.

He nodded toward his boss's closed door. "Is she in?"

Pam nodded. "Yes, and she told me to send you right in."

Ash reached for the doorknob but stopped before opening the door. "Any idea what she needs?"

Pam paused and shook her head. "Something to do with a delivery. I'm not really sure what she means, though."

"Okay," said Ash, shrugging. "Thanks."

He knocked on Susan's door and waited for her to call

out before opening it. Susan sat at her desk with a salad in a Styrofoam container in front of her.

"You had lunch yet?" she asked.

"Yeah. I had a pizza."

"Then you won't mind if I finish mine," she said, picking up her fork again and stabbing a piece of lettuce in her salad. "Congratulations on your meth bust, but I thought you were working a potential homicide."

News travels quickly within the department. Ash relaxed his shoulders.

"I still am. I just tracked a couple of suspects to the house and called Narcotics when I found it. David Lee is heading up the drug investigation."

Susan nodded and wiped her hands on a napkin before scooting her rolling chair to a small refrigerator built into the base of one of her bookshelves. Had anyone else in the prosecutor's office had a mini-fridge in his office, it probably would have been full of champagne and beer for post-victory celebrations. Susan filled hers with water bottles and one brown paper lunch sack. She pulled out the sack and rolled back to the desk.

"Lieutenant Noah Stuart from Northeastern brought this by for you," she said, resuming her lunch. "He said you'd know what it meant."

"Okay," said Ash, not quite sure what he was about to find inside. He opened the bag and reached inside only to feel something squishy and cold. It was a piece of meat. Susan resumed eating her lunch.

"Any reason why a lieutenant would deliver a steak to my office?"

Ash coughed. "One of his detectives hit a deer near Crown

Hill Cemetery last night, and I had a conversation with him this morning. Lieutenant Stuart is confirming his detective's story."

Susan arched her eyebrows. "And will I be receiving deer meat on a regular basis in the future?"

Ash shifted his weight from one foot to the other. "This is a one-time gift."

"Good," said Susan, shifting her attention to a manila file folder on her desk. She glanced up at him over the top of her glasses. "Let's see if we can keep our grocery shopping to ourselves from here on out, okay?"

"Yeah," said Ash. "If you've got a minute, though, can I talk to you?"

"I sincerely hope you're not going to pick now to confess your undying love to me. I'm kind of busy."

"Later, then," said Ash, taking a seat in one of the chairs in front of her desk. "You said Carl Gillespie is missing?"

Susan nodded. "Yeah, why?"

"I have reason to believe he and my victim were involved."

"What do you mean by *involved*?"

"I don't know," said Ash. "She called him a bunch of times on a prepaid cell phone."

Susan crossed her arms. "And how'd you discover this without a search warrant?"

Ash had to think quickly. He had a good reason to walk through the victim's house, but he doubted Susan would appreciate that. Better she didn't know for now.

"Our families are close, so Cassandra's little girl is staying with us until her grandma gets here. She mentioned the name last night."

Susan leaned her head back and stared at the ceiling. After

a moment of thought, she leaned forward. "Are you sure your vic is dead?"

"Yeah. She's in the morgue. Very few people go there for fun."

"Has the coroner confirmed the ID yet?"

"No, but—"

"We need official confirmation," said Susan, interrupting him. "Until we have that, our options are limited."

"I saw the body myself, Susan. It's Cassandra."

"I assume you just did a visual ID, right?"

"Yeah."

She nodded and leaned forward. "You're probably right, then. It probably is Cassandra. We have procedures and laws about victim identification for a reason, though. We can't start prying into someone's private life just because a detective thinks she's dead. We can't even get a warrant to search her house."

She was referring to something called a Mincey warrant. Until the late seventies, detectives and some lawyers commonly believed there was a "murder scene" exception to the prohibition against warrantless searches. That changed with Rufus Mincey, a suspected drug dealer who shot and killed an undercover police officer in Arizona in the midst of a narcotics raid. The police conducted a four-day warrantless search of Mincey's apartment after the shooting and found enough evidence against him to send him to jail for the rest of his life. The U.S. Supreme Court disagreed and held that there was no murder scene exception to the Fourth Amendment. Detectives on TV forget that one all the time.

"What do you want to do, then?" asked Ash, crossing his arms and hoping his frustration didn't seep into his voice.

"Once we get official confirmation that Cassandra is the body in the morgue, we'll open a death investigation. We'll secure a search warrant for her house, we'll start looking at her life, and we'll figure out what her relationship to Carl Gillespie was like. If she and Carl were seeing each other and if he stayed at her house often, it's possible he'll have Fourth Amendment protections there. If we don't do this by the book, anything we find will just be thrown out. We've got to do this correctly."

She was right about their need to do things correctly, of course, but that didn't mean Ash liked it.

"Cassandra's mother is flying in this afternoon. She'll make the ID."

"Then it sounds like you'll have a lot of work to do. And if you find anything else related to Carl Gillespie, I want to know."

"Thank you," he said, standing up. "I'll leave you to your lunch."

"Take your meat with you."

Ash grabbed the bag and left the office but stopped at Pam's desk. Her husband was a hunter, so she'd know what to do with deer meat. She even seemed pleased to have it. Ash considered bringing the meat home, but he wasn't sure if a Muslim could eat deer; it had never come up in conversation when he was in school.

Ash went back to his desk to think. He had held back with Susan; Michael Washington didn't just say that someone hit Cassandra. He said a police officer hid in shadows and then ran her down while she was in the intersection. If true, that made it murder with special circumstances, and a conviction would earn the perpetrator the death penalty. Moreover, the story fit the scene. The skid marks he had found weren't the result of someone trying to brake; they were marks from the perp's tires as he accelerated.

Ash glanced at his watch. It was half-past two. He wasn't sure when Cassandra's mother was flying in, but hopefully it wouldn't be too much longer. She'd ID the body, and then things would really start rolling. In the meantime, he had other issues to deal with. However Cassandra died, someone actively worked to keep her case from being investigated. Ash needed to find out who and why. A lot of people could answer those questions, but Ash trusted only one. He picked up the phone and dialed IMPD's front desk. As occasionally happened, he got lucky.

"What do you need, Detective?"

The voice was gruff, tired-sounding, and familiar.

"Hensley?"

"No, it's the tooth fairy. What do you want?"

That sounded like Hensley, at least. He was the watch sergeant on the day shift. He had his fingers in almost every unit in the department and knew more about IMPD's operations than God. Internal Affairs would have done well to recruit him. If there were any rumors floating around about Cassandra Johnson or the people who killed her, he would have heard them. More important, he'd know how to exploit them.

"You free for about half an hour? I wanted to buy you a cup of coffee."

"That's awfully sweet of you, but I'm on the desk for the foreseeable future."

"If you're going to be on the desk, I'll swing by. I've got something for your kid's college fund."

The old cliché that information is power was rarely truer than in a bureaucracy. Hensley and Ash both knew how things worked. Hensley could leave the front desk at any time and have a junior officer answer the phone. He was posturing to make sure Ash was willing to pay for his company.

"You know, now that you mention it," said Hensley, his tone lighter than it had been a few moments earlier, "I think I do have a break coming up. What do you say you meet me at Dunkin' Donuts on Washington in about five?"

"That sounds fine," said Ash. He hung up the phone immediately after speaking and locked the center drawer on his desk, unsure if he would have enough time after his meeting to return. Dunkin' Donuts was only a few blocks away, so Ash walked over. The nearby buildings funneled and concentrated the breeze like a wind tunnel in the middle of a storm, while steam rose from several nearby manhole covers as it wound its way around the city, heating offices.

Ash pulled his coat around him tighter. He didn't know how long Dunkin' Donuts had been in its present location, but it looked like a fifties-style diner. It had a large, orange awning and a sign on top that pedestrians could see for blocks. On most mornings, the line stretched around the building, but at that time in the afternoon, the place was nearly empty.

He walked in and looked around to see if he could find Sergeant Hensley. Like the exterior, the interior was vintage fifties. The booths were bright orange vinyl, and most of the chairs were chrome polished to a mirror shine. Hensley sat alone at a booth on the other side of the room. Ash nodded at him before ordering two cups of coffee and four glazed doughnuts at the counter. He sat at the table across from

Hensley a few minutes later and pushed one of the cups to the sergeant.

"No cream?"

"I didn't think your cardiologist would appreciate me indulging you," said Ash, taking the lid off his coffee. Hensley was in his early sixties and had a thick head of white hair and a paunch that would have made even the most authentic-looking mall Santa jealous. Their booth was tucked in a corner, giving them privacy and a clear view of the front doors. A couple of teenagers sat about ten feet from them, conversing in low, hushed tones, while the restaurant's employees bustled behind the scenes. "Have you heard anything about a woman named Cassandra Johnson?"

Before answering, Hensley raised his eyebrows expectantly. Thankfully, Ash hadn't yet donated the money Bukoholov gave him, so he pulled two bills from the stack and handed them over.

"Aren't your kids out of college yet?"

Hensley pocketed the money and smiled wolfishly. "Graduate school. They've got a couple of years left."

Ash grunted. "Back to my question. Have you heard of Cassandra Johnson?"

Hensley leaned back and shook his head. "Should I have heard of her?"

"Maybe. She was a hit-and-run homicide yesterday afternoon."

"If it happened in the afternoon, you need to talk to Robbie Doyle. He's straight, so if he knows something, he'll tell you."

Ash nodded and grabbed a packet of sugar for his coffee. "I did talk to him, and then I called Eddie Alvarez in the homicide squad for confirmation. They never got the call. I'm trying to find out why."

Hensley grabbed a doughnut and stuffed the entire thing into his mouth at once. It took about a minute of furious chewing for him to regain his ability to speak. He smiled and licked his fingers after finishing.

"My daughter won't let me eat these anymore. Says she wants me to stick around for a while so I can walk her down the aisle and all that. She even put me on some diet full of whole grains and vegetables. I love her to death, but I'm seriously considering knocking her off."

"As far as I'm concerned, you can eat as many doughnuts as you want," said Ash, nodding toward the plate in front of him. "You think Doyle or Alvarez would lie to me?"

Hensley took a sip of coffee and smacked his lips before shaking his head. "No. Doyle has a stick shoved so far up his ass I'm surprised he doesn't shit bark. He's not lying to you. He takes his job too seriously. Alvarez seems like he's shooting straight, too."

"Then what's going on?"

Hensley wiped his mouth with a napkin. "You sleeping with this girl or something? What's the angle?"

Ash shook his head and sipped his now-sweetened coffee. "The victim was a friend of the family. I'm trying to find out what happened to her and why."

Hensley closed his eyes and sighed. "Look, you know how this works. If Homicide wasn't called in, somebody's pulling a job on her case. IMPD has good police—our boys wouldn't do that without reason."

Ash waited for Hensley to continue, but he didn't. "I'm not sure what you mean," he said.

Hensley scanned the room before leaning forward and speaking. "You remember when John Garrison's daughter died?"

John had been a very well-respected detective when Ash first joined the force, but he retired after his daughter died in a car accident five years before.

"Yeah. She was hit by a drunk driver, wasn't she?"

Hensley nodded. "You remember what happened to the driver?"

"No."

The sergeant sipped his coffee and looked left and right before focusing on Ash again. "Officially, he was killed on impact. In actuality, John and some of his buddies took him to a cabin near Turkey Run State Park and whaled on him until he died." Hensley paused and shot his eyes left and right before speaking again. "Now, I'm not saying this is certain, but my guess is your victim was important to one of our boys. More than likely your killer is having a rough couple of days. It may not be pretty, but at least the guy will be punished. If he goes through the department, he'll be charged with vehicular manslaughter and be on the streets within two years. He might even plea that down. You never know what the prosecutors will do."

Ash leaned back, considering the theory. It fit some of the facts he had found, but not all, most notably Konstantin Bukoholov's involvement. If Bukoholov found out some detectives were doling out street justice, he probably would have taken pictures and blackmailed the cops involved to help him hide his illicit business ventures. He wouldn't have brought it into the open, at least. Not unless doing so gave him something.

"If I was on patrol and I wanted to keep a murder secret, how many people would have to be in on it?"

"Other than principal actors?" asked Hensley. Ash nodded, and Hensley pursed his lips, apparently thinking. "Just one, but it'd have to be someone with real power. Deputy chief, maybe a captain or a lieutenant if enough people owed him favors."

"So hiding somebody's death wouldn't take a big conspiracy?"

"No."

The thought gave him little comfort.

"You heard anything like that coming out of the Northeastern Precinct?"

Hensley chuckled and sipped his coffee. "You're shitting me, right?"

"No, and I'm pretty sure they'd kick us out if I dropped my pants in the dining room."

Hensley put down his coffee and straightened his lips into a line. "It's just an expression, Ash. Are you telling me that you're investigating officers from the Northeastern?"

"Sort of. My witness told me some cops threatened him to keep him from talking about what he saw. I'm trying to figure out what's going on."

"Stop."

"Stop what?" asked Ash.

"Whatever you're doing," said Hensley. He looked Ash straight in the eye, unblinking. "You came to me for advice, and that's the best I've got. If you're looking at stirring up something in the Northeastern Precinct, stop."

"Why? What did you hear?"

"Two patrol officers from the precinct died in the line of

duty in the past two years, and two others killed themselves. They may not admit it, but those guys are hurting in a lot of ways. Despite that, violent crime drops seven percent in a quarter? I don't think so. That doesn't happen."

Ash leaned back and crossed his arms. "What do you think is going on, then?"

"My guess is that some of those Northeastern boys have gone rogue. They may be just running drug dealers out of town, but I doubt it. More than likely, some poor hiker's going to find bodies in an abandoned cabin in Brown County in the not too distant future. Be smart, and back off. You don't need to get involved in that."

Ash sat still, letting that sink in. Bad cops were still cops. He could handle cops; he knew how they thought, how they were trained. He had gone against worse and still came out on top. He nodded and glanced at his watch.

"Thanks for the warning. I'll step carefully. Rest of the doughnuts are yours," he said, sliding out of the booth. "I've got another meeting this afternoon."

Hensley grabbed his forearm before he could leave the table. "I'm not bullshitting you here. Back off. This isn't worth it."

"I'll keep your advice in mind."

"See that you do."

Hensley released his grip, and Ash left the restaurant, wondering what the hell he had gotten himself into.

5

Ash focused on his case for the next fifteen minutes as he walked to his car, but neither inspiration nor revelation struck. It was about a quarter after three when he opened his door. Joe Cartwright, the Northeastern precinct officer who had brought Lisa Johnson into the Child Services office, would be at his gym in about forty-five minutes. Before talking to Hensley, Ash had planned to go over there, but now he wasn't sure if that was a good idea. Even if Hensley's gut feeling was way off the mark, something was wrong in the Northeastern, and it'd be nice to have more information before he did anything stupid.

He took out his phone and thumbed through its contact list until he found the number of Paul Murphy in the Northeastern precinct. Unfortunately, Paul didn't pick up and his phone went to voice mail. Ash left a message requesting a call back, but he didn't expect a quick reply. Paul worked auto theft, and the volume of calls to his unit increased as soon as the area high schools let out for the day. He probably caught a case.

Ash considered his options but then decided to stick with his original plan. As long as he was careful, he should be fine. Cartwright's gym occupied an old storefront about two blocks from the Northeastern Precinct house. Whoever owned the place now had removed the signs from the previous tenant, but the word LAUNDROMAT was still visible in the faded brick.

Ash parallel parked in front and pulled open the gym's door a moment later. The interior smelled like sweat, leather, and air freshener. There were no treadmills or elliptical machines in sight, just weights, a boxing ring, and heavy bags. He walked to the desk opposite the door and cleared his throat, getting the attention of the guy behind the counter. The receptionist was young and had blond hair with dark roots. There were tattoos up and down his arms.

"Can I help you?"

The receptionist dropped the clipboard he had been holding, allowing Ash to see the nametag on his chest. Dennis.

"You get a lot of cops in here?" asked Ash, looking around to see if he knew anyone. He counted ten people inside, but no one looked familiar.

"Membership is IMPD only."

Ash pulled back his jacket, exposing his badge.

Dennis nodded. "What can I do for you, Sergeant?"

"You know Joe Cartwright?"

Dennis nodded and pointed to the boxing ring. "Black trunks and white shirt."

Ash's gaze followed Dennis's arm to the center of the building where two men sparred in the ring. Cartwright looked to be twenty-five or thirty and stood roughly six feet tall. He looked trim, but more than that, he had fast hands and decent footwork. He wasn't a pro-level fighter, but he knew what he was doing. His opponent, even though he was heavier and taller, was badly outclassed.

Ash thanked Dennis and walked over to the ring to watch

and wait. By the time their sparring match ended, Cartwright's opponent had blood trickling out of both nostrils and the cheekbone beneath his right eye was swelling and red. He wasn't going to look pretty the next morning, but he'd be okay. Ash leaned against the ring apron near Cartwright's corner once both men left the ring.

"You've got a good jab. You do any fighting outside the gym?"

Cartwright looked up. He was sweating heavily, but unlike his opponent, he had escaped his previous match with little more than some abraded skin. He spit into a bucket.

"Only in bars," he said, laughing at his own joke. "You're not a promoter, are you?"

Ash unclipped his badge from his belt and held it up. "No. I'm a detective sergeant with IMPD. I wanted to ask you about a call you took last night."

Cartwright leaned against the ring. Sweat dripped from his brow. "Oh yeah? What call?"

"You took a little girl named Lisa Johnson to Child Services. I'm investigating her mother's death."

Cartwright wiped his face off with a glove. "Name is familiar. Do I need a lawyer for this?"

Ash shrugged. "You can call one if you want, but I had hoped to keep this unofficial. Besides, you'd only need a lawyer if you did something wrong. I don't think you did."

The statement was a ploy he used to keep a suspect from calling his lawyer. Cartwright was young, but surely he saw it for what it was. Still, he nodded.

"All right, then," he said. "I'm parked out front. I'll meet you when I finish getting dressed."

Ash nodded. "See you in a few."

While Cartwright went back to the locker room, Ash left the building and stood beside his cruiser. Cartwright had given in to the interview request easier than he had anticipated. Something was up. He called IMPD's dispatcher and requested the make and model of the younger officer's car. According to BMV records, Cartwright drove a late-model SUV. Unfortunately, there was no SUV in sight.

Ash walked around the side of the gym until he found a small lot behind the building, where, sure enough, he found Cartwright's vehicle. He was tempted to let the air out of his tires, but that was a little juvenile, even for him. Instead, he merely leaned against the bumper, waiting.

Cartwright walked out of the gym's back door a few minutes later, twirling his key ring around his index finger and whistling to himself. Paul Murphy had called Cartwright a turd that wouldn't flush. Ash could understand why.

"Did I say I'd meet you out front?" he asked. "I meant in the back. Sorry about that. Glad you could find the car."

"Yeah. Me too," said Ash, crossing his arms but not moving from the car. "Tell me what you know about Cassandra Johnson."

Cartwright squinted. "Remind me again why her name is familiar."

"She was the victim of a hit-and-run in your precinct yesterday. You drove her daughter to the Child Services office and filed a report."

Cartwright tilted his head back and hummed to himself. "Sorry, but you came out here for nothing. I didn't know the broad."

Ash squeezed his arms across his chest tighter. "I'm in a

really bad mood, and that's twice you've lied to me. Do it a third time. Let's see what happens."

Cartwright shifted on his feet. "I never met the woman, okay? It sounds like you're misinformed."

"Then dispel my ignorance."

Cartwright rolled his eyes. "I don't think I'm interested in having a conversation with you after all," he said, starting for his vehicle. Ash put his hand on the younger officer's chest, stopping him in his tracks. Cartwright looked at Ash's hand. "Don't touch me."

Ash stepped back and put his hands up, shrugging. "Fine. But if you don't want to talk to me, you're going to talk to Internal Affairs later. Susan Mercer in the prosecutor's office already wants them brought in. I came out here as a courtesy to see what you had to say."

"I haven't done anything wrong," said Cartwright, his face and throat turning red.

"You took the vic's little girl to Child Services, so I know you were at the scene. You can talk to me now, or you can talk to a board of inquiry later. I'm giving you the option. Don't be stupid."

Cartwright didn't blink. "Fuck you."

"Stupid it is," said Ash. "Get your affairs in order. I have a feeling IA will go for your badge for this."

"Bullshit," said Cartwright.

"No bull. You failed to report a homicide. That's not a procedural infraction—that's a class-A misdemeanor."

Cartwright's face turned a brighter shade of red, and his eyes narrowed as he took a step forward. He looked like a bull getting ready to charge. Normally, Ash would have backed down and called for additional officers from his cruiser, but Cartwright had him pinned against an SUV in an enclosed parking lot. There was nowhere to go. Ash brought his right leg back and put his hand in his jacket over his firearm. He didn't draw it, but Cartwright would have known what he was going for. The patrolman stopped moving and exhaled heavily through his nose, his nostrils flaring.

"I'm not your enemy," said Ash. "I'm trying to give you a way to get in front of this. Take a step back before somebody gets hurt. I saw you in the gym, so I know I couldn't take you in a fight. If you keep coming at me, I will interpret that as a lethal threat and react accordingly."

Cartwright might have seen something in his eyes because he took another step back. Unfortunately, as Cartwright backed off, Ash heard a squeal as the gym's rear door opened and then slammed shut a second later. The patrolman smiled smugly before meeting Ash's gaze.

"Are you sure this is what you want to do, Detective? You want to come into my place and threaten me in front of my friends?"

Ash felt a nervous pit grow in his stomach. He glanced over his shoulder. There were two fully dressed men beside the gym's back door. Neither of them had firearms in hand, but he had to assume they were strapped. He started to pivot on his feet so he could see both the back door and Cartwright.

"I'm a detective sergeant with IMPD, and this is a police matter," he said, casting his gaze to Cartwright and then to the new arrivals. "Go back inside."

Neither man obeyed his directive. Instead, one reached behind him, presumably for a firearm holstered on his waist.

Despite the low temperature, a bead of sweat trickled into Ash's eye. He wiped it off with the back of his wrist.

"I'm not kidding," said Ash, shifting on his feet and hoping he didn't look as nervous as he suddenly felt. "Back off."

The door squealed again and a third man emerged from the gym. He had buzzed gray hair and a lined, weathered face. Judging by the sweat stains on his T-shirt, he had come out in the middle of a workout. Cartwright's back stiffened and he stood straighter, puffing out his chest and lacing his hands behind his back like a soldier at attention.

"Relax, everyone." Ash glanced over, but the newcomer was already addressing Cartwright. "Detective Sergeant Rashid is a fellow officer. Show him the respect he deserves and answer his questions in a forthright, candid manner."

Cartwright nodded but didn't relax his shoulders. "Yes, sir."

The older man stared at the patrolman for a moment longer before walking toward Ash, a softer expression on his face and his hand extended. Ash shook it; he was too taken aback to do anything else.

"Lieutenant Noah Stuart," he said, introducing himself. "I believe you spoke to one of my detectives this afternoon."

Ash hesitated but then nodded. "His tip led to a raid on a methamphetamine cookhouse."

"Good. I'm glad to hear it," he said, glancing at the three men in the parking lot. Two started going back to the gym, but Cartwright continued to stand at attention, his gaze straight ahead. "If you have further need to talk to my personnel, please do not hesitate to give me a call. We take chain of command very seriously in the Northeastern, and I guarantee that my men will answer every question you have."

Ash hesitated again. "Thank you. If I have any further need to talk to your men, I will contact you first."

"Do that."

Noah said something to Cartwright, and the younger man finally relaxed while the lieutenant went back to the gym.

"Go ahead and ask your questions, Detective. I'll answer them."

Ash coughed, more to give him a moment to think than to clear his throat. Noah Stuart's arrival had thrown him off his rhythm.

"Tell me about the hit-and-run call you took yesterday."

Cartwright led Ash through a story from the beginning to end twice. He claimed he received a call requesting assistance at approximately four in the afternoon, and by the time he arrived at Cassandra's intersection, another uniformed officer had established the perimeter of the crime scene. As he tried to find witnesses to what happened, a couple of detectives he didn't know showed up and ordered him to take Lisa to Child Services. The detectives even gave him information on the victim for the intake form. Cartwright claimed he didn't know what happened after that.

The story was bizarre, but Ash didn't think it was a complete fabrication. Cartwright didn't seem bright enough to create a story on the fly.

"Would it surprise you if Homicide was never called to the scene?"

"We're not morons, Detective. We can handle a hit-and-run investigation."

Most of Cartwright's colleagues might not have been morons, but Ash had doubts about the man personally.

"I know you're not morons, but you didn't answer my question."

Cartwright crossed his arms. "Yeah, it does surprise me, but we can handle the case. If our detectives didn't call Homicide, they had a good reason."

"You think they had good reason to intimidate a witness, too?"

"Why would they? It was an accident."

"One of the neighbors told me some cops warned him against speaking about the case. They said they'd hurt his grandmother."

Cartwright shifted on his feet. "Did it occur to you that he lied? Last I checked, witnesses still do that."

"He's just a kid. He has no reason to lie."

Cartwright shifted again and threw up his hands. "What do you want me to say? I showed up to a crime scene and did my job. Whatever happened after that isn't my business."

"I'm making it your business. If anything happens to that kid, I'll hold it against you personally. If you think I'm bluffing, look up my record."

"I don't need to look up your record, Detective. I've already seen it, and I'm not impressed."

Ash crossed his arms. "Is that supposed to hurt my feelings?"

"No, I'm just calling it like I see it. Like everyone in my precinct sees it. See, we had a meeting about you after you showed up at Detective Walker's house. You want to know what we concluded? You're a loser."

"Your professional opinion means the world to me, so that truly stings."

Cartwright snickered as Ash started to walk away. "Good comeback, Rashid."

Cartwright might have said something else, but Ash wasn't paying attention. All things considered, he knew less about Cassandra Johnson's death now than when he had first started. The day may not have been a complete waste, but it wasn't too far off. If he was going to find out what happened to Cassandra, he was going to have to do better than that.

6

Ash made it to the office at twenty after five, and by that time, most of his colleagues had gone home for the evening. He sat at his desk and wrote notes about who he talked to and what he had done that day. Ideally, his notes would be so detailed another detective could read them and jump into the case without having to backtrack on anything that had already been done. Hopefully involving another detective in the case wouldn't be necessary, though. He preferred to work alone.

He worked for about half an hour before locking the files in the center drawer of his desk. After a bust like the meth house, a lot of detectives would go out to celebrate. Ash felt good about the work he had done, but it didn't change the fact that Cassandra was dead and her daughter was still without her mother. He didn't want to celebrate that; he wanted to forget it. He needed a drink.

Before Ash could reach the bar nearest his station, his cell phone rang. He considered letting it go to voice mail, but he picked it up first to see the caller ID. It was Hannah. The two spoke for only a few minutes, but somehow his need for a drink dissipated slightly after their conversation. They had another guest at home: Cassandra Johnson's mother was there to pick up Lisa, and she wanted to see him before she left.

He skipped the bar for the night and headed home. As soon as he opened his car's door after parking in the driveway, he could hear the rhythmic squeal of a swing and conversation wafting from the backyard. Rather than go through the house, he opened the gate and went directly onto the lawn. The backyard was his home's best feature. It had an oak tree big enough to shade the yard but too large to climb—a welcome feature with his daredevil daughter—and a play set for the kids. Hannah and an older African American woman were on the patio.

"Hi, *Baba*," said Megan, pumping her arms and legs each time the swing slowed along its arc. She skidded her feet on the ground and came bounding toward her father, her arms held wide. Ash reached down and caught her as she flew into his chest. Her arms wrapped around his neck and squeezed tight.

"Hi, pumpkin. How are you?"

"I'm fine," she said, disentangling herself from her father's arms. Ash didn't want to let her go, but he did, and she took a step back, pointing at their guest. "That's Ms. Johnson. She's Lisa's grandma."

"I know. I met Sheila a couple of years ago," he said, patting Megan's upper back and orienting her toward the swing set. "You go back and play with Lisa."

"Okay, *Baba*."

She took off like a sprinter and belly flopped onto the empty swing, her arms spread to the side like wings. The girls resumed whatever game they had been playing before he walked into the yard. Both of them were smiling and laughing. Evidently, Lisa hadn't been told yet what had happened to her mom. Her life was going to change more than anyone probably realized. Ash's father died while his mother was still pregnant with him, but his older sister had been ten. Rana said it took her years to feel safe again. Like Rana, Lisa had a loving family, but the loss of a parent when a kid was so young was going to be hard to overcome.

It had been a while since he last saw Sheila Johnson, but she gave him a hug as soon as he reached the patio. It seemed like she needed that. Once he extricated himself from Sheila's embrace, he sat beside Hannah on their cushioned teak love seat. She leaned against him and handed him Kaden, their son. The baby cooed and smiled. At least Ash pretended it was a smile. He changed Kaden while Hannah started dinner. By the time he got out again, Ms. Johnson was alone on the patio, watching the girls.

"I'm very sorry about Cassandra. She was a good person."

Sheila's lower lip trembled and her eyes were wet, but she blinked back the tears before they fell. "I know. She talked about your family often."

Ash didn't say anything, hoping she would lead the conversation when she was ready.

"Lisa doesn't know yet," she said after a moment's pause. "I'm going to tell her when we get to Seattle. She thinks we're going on vacation."

"We'll pray for you," he said. She covered her mouth and took a breath, her pain evident. It was heart wrenching to see a mother holding back her grief for the sake of her granddaughter, making the questions Ash had to ask even more difficult. "Did someone from the coroner's office contact you yet?"

"Yes. I went to their office as soon as I flew in. Cassandra's flying back with us so she can be buried beside her father."

That was one concern answered; they had their confirmation. It didn't make Ash feel any better.

"I don't know how much the coroner's office told you, but I've been assigned to her case."

She stared at Ash hard. "They told me it was a car accident."

This was going to be awkward.

"It was, but there are extenuating circumstances. I can't get into them right now because it's an active investigation."

Sheila's eyes seemed to darken. "Why didn't they tell me?"

"They probably didn't know. The investigation is still in an early stage," said Ash. "We're not really sure what happened."

She inhaled deeply. "Did someone hurt my baby on purpose?"

"This is an active investigation, so I can't say anything more than I already have. If we determine that someone hurt Cassandra, my department will do everything we possibly can to make sure he's caught and punished. We have one of the best homicide squads in the country, and I promise that we'll do our best."

That didn't console her, but it did seem to take some of the sharpness out of her anger. They talked for about twenty minutes. She didn't know much more about Cassandra's personal life than he and Hannah did, unfortunately. She didn't know if her daughter was seeing anyone new or having problems with anybody. She did mention that the two of them hadn't talked in over a week because Cassandra had just gotten a new job. It had something to do with computers, but Sheila didn't know what. She suggested that he talk to Cassandra's sister, Whitney, if he needed to know more about her personal life. A new potential witness was better than nothing, but not by much.

Normally, Hannah, Ash, and Megan would have dusk prayer before dinner, but they skipped them that night. Sheila and Lisa stayed over for a simple meal. The girls talked quite a bit, but the adults didn't say much. There wasn't a lot to say. Since he still had keys to Cassandra's home, Ash offered to take Sheila and Lisa over to get some clothes before they headed back to Seattle. Megan and Lisa hugged each other before they left. Hopefully it wouldn't be the last time they saw each other.

They took separate cars to Cassandra's home, and by the time they arrived, the sun had been down for over an hour. A television flickered in the Washingtons' home across the street, and Ash saw a group of teenagers smoking on the corner about a block away. The neighborhood wasn't generally dangerous, but few parents dreamed of their children ending up in it, either. Sheila looked disturbed.

"I'll just open the front door and let you get what you need out of the place," he said, already walking toward the front porch. "I'll wait outside if you want me to carry something."

"Thank you," said Sheila.

Ash opened the front door but held his hand across the opening before letting anyone in. The couch cushions were on the floor in the living room; they hadn't been earlier.

"Go back to your car and take a loop around the block," he said, reaching into his jacket for his weapon. His hands tingled with nerves and adrenaline. "If I'm not on the front porch when you get around, call nine-one-one."

"I want to go in," said Lisa. "This is my home."

Ash started to tell her that she needed to go with her grandmother but stopped midsentence as he heard something. Whispers. He waved Lisa and Sheila back with his left hand.

"Get in your car and drive."

Lisa didn't seem to understand, but Sheila grabbed her around the shoulders and hauled her toward their awaiting car so quickly that her feet barely touched the ground. Ash took a breath and a step inside. The house felt icy cold. Few burglars were violent, but that thought did little to stanch the torrents of adrenaline now freely flowing through his system.

"I am an armed police officer. More are on their way. Identify yourselves and lie on the ground with your arms outstretched or I will shoot you."

The whispering stopped immediately, but no identifications were forthcoming. Ash pressed his back to the wall beside the front door and crept forward. He hadn't noticed the floor creaking on his visit before, but it seemed awfully loud now. Anyone listening would know exactly where he was.

He took a couple of breaths, thinking through the situation. There were at least two other people in the house. Chances were they were just a couple of opportunists who saw an empty building and decided to make some cash by robbing it. They'd probably run if they were given the chance. Without backup, Ash would normally let them. Material possessions weren't worth risking his life for. Unfortunately, this wasn't a normal circumstance. He didn't know enough about Cassandra's death to know what in her home was critical to his investigation and what wasn't, and he wasn't willing to let potentially important evidence walk away if he could stop it.

He counted backward from ten to calm himself before starting forward, his weapon held ready in front of him.

The bedrooms, living room, and home office had all been trashed. Thankfully, they were also devoid of persons, which meant his company was in the kitchen. The room wasn't very big, which would reduce maneuverability in a fight. That would keep whoever was in there from using their numbers to gang up on him, but that probably wouldn't help much if they started shooting. He stopped in the doorway of Cassandra's home office and held his breath to slow his heartbeat and calm down. The kitchen was about five feet to his right.

God, let this be a good idea.

The floor creaked as he stepped forward again.

"I repeat, I am an armed—"

Ash never finished the statement. Two figures darted from alcoves in the kitchen. One ran straight to the back door while a second jumped in front of him. Ash raised his weapon, but before he could say anything, the guy in front of him grabbed the barrel and pushed it to the side while simultaneously striking Ash's jaw with an openhanded strike. It wrenched his neck to the side and caused white spots to form in his vision.

Ash staggered back, but his attacker kept pressing forward. He shoved the firearm against Ash's hip and pulled on the stock hard, violently twisting it. Had Ash's finger been inside the trigger guard, it would have been broken and he would have lost control of the gun. As it was, his training kicked in and he squeezed the grip on his firearm with his right hand while simultaneously punching his attacker twice on the temple with his left. The guy released his handhold on the gun and took a step back, giving Ash some breathing room.

Redirect, control, attack, take away. It was a disarming technique they taught recruits in the police academy. His attacker flubbed the takeaway part, but he got the basic movements right. Ash held his firearm in front of him.

"Lie on the ground."

Rather than do as Ash asked, the burglar grabbed a teakettle that had been sitting on the stove and heaved it. Ash blocked it with a forearm, but as he did, his assailant ran out the back door. Without thinking, Ash followed, water dripping from his shirt. The back door started to swing slowly shut before he could reach it, blocking his vision of the yard. He threw it open again, causing it to crash against a bank of kitchen cabinets and rattle the pots inside. Ash could see only one of the men in the backyard, so the other must have already turned the corner somewhere.

He plunged into the chilly evening air, his vision focused on the man in front of him. Cassandra's backyard had a simple concrete patio and grass all the way to a chain-link fence. His first and second steps pounded against the concrete, finding sure purchase, but then his foot found something hard and cylindrical. His legs flew from beneath him and his back thudded to the ground hard enough to knock his breath out. He tried to breathe but could only gasp as a figure in black bent down and picked up the small purple T-ball bat that had tripped him.

Ash looked to his right. He had dropped his firearm in the fall, and it now rested on the grass about five feet away. It was well out of reach.

"Should have been watching where you were going," said the figure. He pulled the bat over his shoulder like a golf club. Before his assailant could bring the weapon down, Ash kicked him on his right kneecap. The man didn't fall, but he took a step back, and that was all Ash needed. With his breath returning, Ash flipped onto his stomach, pushed upright, and charged the burglar, hitting him in the stomach with his shoulder. They went down on the grass.

Ash dug his toes into the dirt, keeping as much pressure as he could on the man's stomach and hips. They writhed on the ground, each trying to get to a stable base and control the other man. It didn't take long for Ash to realize that he was the stronger and heavier of the two, though. He climbed the man's body as if it were a ladder lying on the ground and pinned one of his opponent's forearms to the grass with a knee. Most of the time, that would have ended it right there. Half a dozen officers would have piled on him by that point. Ash was alone, though. Worse, he didn't have his firearm or even handcuffs.

With his right hand pinned, Ash's opponent started to reach to his waist. He was going for the purple baseball bat. That wasn't going to happen. There's a bundle of nerves at the base of the neck, so if you hit somebody hard enough in the right spot, you can disorient him without permanently injuring him. That was the theory, at least; Ash had never done it outside of a gym. He reached his left hand up as high as it would go and elbowed hard. Eventually, the man stopped fighting. Whether that was out of pain or because he was knocked out, Ash didn't know. Either way, he reached to his opponent's waist and felt for the bat. He threw it onto the grass beside his gun before standing and rubbing sweat off his forehead. The man's chest moved, but his eyes were closed.

Before Ash could bend over to retrieve his firearm, he heard the familiar click of a round being inserted into the chamber of a gun. There were two men, after all, and he had taken care of only one. He swallowed and closed his eyes.

Shit.

"I'm a police officer," he said. "You don't want to do this. You kill me, you get a needle in your arm guaranteed."

The gunman pushed his weapon into the back of Ash's head, shoving him forward. Ash pretended to stumble but stopped a couple of feet from his firearm and turned. Like the man he had wrestled with, the newcomer wore a black ski mask over his face and blue polypropylene gloves. They were the same sort of gloves the department handed out to its officers. The guy Ash had fought with a moment earlier slowly wobbled to his feet. He looked like he could stumble at any moment, but he was quickly coming to his senses. There were no official procedures about what to do in that situation, but going for his gun would just get him shot. He stood there and watched as the two men hobbled out of the yard. As they climbed the fence, Ash noticed that both men wore identical black tactical boots. He had worn the same ones when he was on patrol.

Once they were gone, he picked up his firearm and kicked the baseball bat that had tripped him. The gloves, the disarm attempt outside the kitchen, the boots. Ash couldn't be sure, but he thought he had just gotten into a fistfight with a cop.

"Damn it."

Ash walked back inside and looked out the kitchen window. His two assailants were gone. He stayed there for another minute before grabbing a plastic cup that had been thrown onto the floor. He filled it with water and took a drink, trying to put his thoughts in order. No matter how much he thought, though, he couldn't escape one simple fact: Two cops may have broken into a murder victim's home. He didn't even know how to begin to handle that.

He waited for another few minutes in the kitchen to see if the two men he had tangled with would return. When they didn't, he went to the front of the house and flagged down Sheila's car. She parked and opened her window.

"I called nine-one-one, but I'm on hold," she said. "A recording said all the dispatchers are busy."

"That's okay. I've got a direct number," said Ash. He sighed. "Where are you guys staying?"

"The airport Holiday Inn."

"Does Lisa have clothes for the night?"

She looked at Lisa but then turned back to Ash. "There's a department store up the street from the hotel. We can pick up some pajamas there."

"I think that's a good idea," he said, gulping the cool night air. "I'm going to call in some patrol officers and have them check the area out. If you can come back tomorrow, it should be safe then."

"Are you all right?" asked Sheila. "You have a red mark on your face. Do you need me to call somebody for you?"

Ash rubbed his jaw and winced. One of the punches he caught was going to leave a mark.

"Thank you, but I'm okay," he said, hesitating. "I ran into a door when I was chasing people off. It was probably just kids thinking the home was abandoned. That happens in this neighborhood."

That was bull, but Sheila seemed to believe it.

"That's awful," she said. "I didn't know the neighborhood was that bad."

"It's usually not. I'll make sure the place is locked up."

Lisa said something from the backseat, but Ash couldn't hear her. Once she finished speaking, Sheila leaned partially out of the window and lowered her voice.

"She's worried about her cat. I don't think we'll be able to take him with us. Once we're gone, could you call Animal Control and have him picked up?"

He had forgotten about the cat. There wasn't a lot of call for rescue cats at the city's animal shelters, so Animal Control would likely just put it to sleep. That didn't seem fair. Normally, Ash would never take a pet home without talking to his wife first, but this case was an exception. Besides, cats had a special place within Islam. The prophet Muhammad may have even had one.

"How about if I just take him home? I think he'd be a good way for Megan to remember Lisa. I've heard they get along well."

Sheila put her hand on Ash's forearm. "That would be nice. Thank you, Detective."

"Anytime."

Sheila shielded her eyes and wished him a good night before driving away. As he watched the car disappear, Ash tried to figure out what to do. If he had just fought with cops, there was a fair chance they had come from the Northeastern Precinct. One of them might have even been Joe Cartwright; the voice he hard heard during their wrestling match sounded similar, at least. Ideally, he'd call in a burglary, but the call would be routed through the Northeastern, and he didn't know who he could trust there. Maybe he'd find inspiration inside.

Once Sheila's car turned a corner two blocks away, Ash went back to the house. The burglars had tossed the living room. They'd ripped off the couch cushions, overturned a chest full of blankets, and moved the television. They were looking for something, and it must have been small because they opened every single DVD on the shelves. Ash couldn't tell if they had taken anything, but they'd touched everything.

He checked out the bedrooms next. Cassandra's furniture was out of date, but it was constructed of well-polished, solid wood. She probably purchased it at a thrift store, the cast-offs of a family with enough money to care about aesthetics. From what he could tell, every drawer on the dresser had been emptied, and everything in the wardrobe had been thrown onto her bed, including a small jewelry box. Even if Cassandra didn't have much, her jewelry still had some value. The burglars weren't there to rob her, then; they wanted something specific and left everything else.

He left the bedroom and went to the office next. As soon as he stepped inside, he knew it was the real target. Papers and office supplies littered the floor, but the stack of filing boxes and the cell phone he had examined earlier were gone. If he hadn't seen them on his first visit, he wouldn't have known they existed.

He leaned against the desk, papers crumpling under his feet as a pit grew in his stomach. He should have checked out those files when he'd had the chance. No one would have risked coming back to the house unless they were important. Since neither the man he wrestled with nor the other burglar

carried anything out of the house, they either had more partners or they had cleared out the house earlier. Either way, the
documents were probably part of a bonfire by now.

Ash ran his hands through his hair and swore under
his breath. He stayed in the office, looking around for any
documents that may have been missed, but unfortunately,
he couldn't find a damn thing. When he went back to the
kitchen, Garfield, Lisa's cat, was lapping up water from
the floor. Ash didn't bother trying to catch him; instead, he
found a plastic travel crate in a closet beside the kitchen and
put a handful of cat food inside. Garfield must have been
hungry because he walked right in. At least something had
gone right that night.

Once Ash had the cat secured on the backseat of his cruiser,
he slumped into the driver's seat, feeling the weight of the day
press down on his shoulders. He needed to call somebody, but
he wouldn't get anywhere without evidence. They'd listen to
him, but they wouldn't be able to act without more information than he had. Maybe he could convince Michael Washington to talk on the record about the detectives who threatened
him. That'd get some attention, at least. Ash glanced across
the street at his house to see if anyone was up, but the television and house lights had been turned off. Grandma probably
went to bed early; he'd go the next morning.

Ash pulled out his cell phone and glanced at his watch.
It was a little before nine, which meant Kaden would probably be in bed and Megan would be going there shortly. He
punched in his home number. It wasn't easy to gauge her
reaction on the phone, but it sounded like Hannah was okay
with him staying out late again that night. Maybe that was

just wishful thinking, though. She said they'd talk about the cat later.

She put Megan on the phone next, giving him the opportunity to wish her a good night. Kaden was being fussy and didn't want to go to sleep, so Hannah held the phone to his ear. He laughed when he heard his father's voice, which was generally a good sign. One of Ash's recurring fears was that he'd walk into the house one day and pick up Kaden only for the infant to start crying because he thought he was being held by a stranger. It was a common concern among those on call twenty-four hours a day.

He wished Hannah a good night last of all. He told her that he loved her and that he'd come home as soon as he could. She said likewise and wished him luck before hanging up. After calling his family, Ash called Detective Paul Murphy and waited through several rings for him to pick up.

"Paul, it's Ash. You got a minute? I need to talk to you about something."

Paul hesitated. "You think this can wait? I'm at home and Becky's looking at me like I'm a piece of meat. I think I might get lucky, and that doesn't happen too often."

"Thanks for the visual. And sorry for interrupting, but it can't wait. I got a problem and I need some help."

Paul sighed. "You went and pissed off Joe Cartwright, didn't you?"

"Yeah. Is he straight?"

"I think he's married. Aside from that, it's not the policy of the Indianapolis Metropolitan Police Department to inquire as to the sexual orientation of our officers. You got the memo, didn't you?"

Ash closed his eyes and pinched the bridge of his nose. "Yeah, funny. Is he a good cop?"

"I don't know. I never worked with him directly. Personally, I think he's a jerk if that means anything."

"What about Noah Stuart?"

Paul didn't reply.

"You still there?" asked Ash.

"Yeah," said Paul, sighing. "I like you, Ash, but it sounds like you're stepping into something that could get you in some serious trouble. Stay out of Noah's way. He's not a nice man. If I were you, I'd probably consider staying out of Cartwright's way, too."

That was the second time in a day he had been warned off his case. Usually that meant he was on to something.

"You think someone's buying them off?"

"No. At least I don't think so. Noah's unit operates without a lot of oversight in our precinct. They close a lot of cases people around here thought were hopeless. They're good at their jobs."

"Then why should I stay out of their way?"

"You didn't hear it from me, but they can get rough. A lot of their suspects don't make it to trial. Just in the past six weeks, two drug dealers they investigated accidentally fell off the roofs of their apartment buildings. Another guy who beat up his girlfriend accidentally broke every bone in his right hand at a construction site. He wasn't a construction worker, either. Noah and his officers get results, but nobody's asking too many questions about how they do that. You probably shouldn't, either."

Ash stared at his windshield for a moment, thinking.

Noah and his crew weren't just closing cases; they were bury-
ing them. Someone needed to speak for their victims, too.

"Thanks for the advice, Paul. I'll keep it in mind."

"You better."

"Before you go, let me ask one more thing. If I called in a
burglary in the Northeastern's district, am I going to get solid
officers or guys like Cartwright?"

Paul grunted. "There are a couple of dunces in the mix,
but most of the patrol division are good. Watch them, but you
should be fine. Cartwright is in Noah's unit, so he doesn't
go out without the old man's say-so. He won't be on patrol."

"Good. That's what I wanted to hear."

"Good luck out there."

"Thanks."

Ash hung up and called it in. Two patrol officers arrived
within four minutes. While one searched the house, the other
took Ash's statement. He told them the truth, that he'd come
with the homeowner's daughter, and while there, two men
attacked him. He didn't mention his suspicions about Cartwright or the files that had been taken, but at least there'd be
a record of the break-in for the Johnsons' insurance. Since the
front door had been kicked open, Ash drove to the nearest
Walmart and purchased a bracket and padlock to keep the
neighborhood kids from breaking in. As soon as he had the
front door secured, the patrol officers left, leaving another
dark house on a dark street.

Ash went back to his car to think. Cassandra had clearly
been interested in the Thomas Rahal trial, but it went further
than that. She had boxes full of court filings—some of which
were likely confidential—and a history of conversations with

the defense counsel's lead investigator. Now her files had been stolen, she had been murdered, and the investigator she had been speaking to was missing. This was turning into something way beyond a hit-and-run investigation.

Ash drove home and dropped off the cat before calling the dispatcher and requesting Gillespie's home address. Within twenty minutes, he was parked in front of a sprawling story-and-a-half brick home near the Geist Reservoir, a man-made lake on the northeast side of town. None of the home's lights were on. John Meyers said Gillespie was missing, but no one had seen his body yet. Ash wanted to believe he was alive somewhere; hopefully he wasn't alive and at home for the night.

He stepped out of his car and walked to the front door. Unlike the homes around him, Gillespie's lawn was unkempt and the bushes beneath his windows protruded onto the spaces they were meant to beautify. Ash was surprised the neighbors hadn't started complaining yet. Or maybe they had. Maybe they had complained and been ignored so often that they finally snapped and hacked Gillespie into pieces for use as organic fertilizer. That certainly would explain his absence.

Ash pounded on the door and waited, but no one responded to his summons. He took a step back from the porch. Missing persons cases involving adults were tough to investigate. Without signs of foul play, the police usually couldn't even get into the potential victim's house until a neighbor smelled a body. It could be frustrating as hell. Ash wasn't too concerned, though. He was never very big on following the rules.

He walked to his car and grabbed a pair of blue polypropylene gloves from his evidence-collection kit. The department bought them in bulk and handed them out twice a year, so it was nice to get some use out of them finally. Once he had the gloves, he went to the backyard. The grass was slick with moisture, and water seeped through his shoes and socks, sending a chill up his spine. Carl's back door was wood and had a nine-pane window on top, a popular style for home-owners unconcerned about security.

Ash knew a couple of detectives who could pick a dead bolt almost as quickly as someone could open it with a key. He didn't have that particular skill, though, so he checked every window in the backyard to see if any were unlatched. The only one he could find led to a two-car garage with a gray BMW parked in the center. Ash slid the window up and climbed inside. The interior held a smell redolent of lawn clippings and engine oil, while garden tools hung on pegs extending from the walls. A single unlocked door led to the home's interior.

As soon as he stepped into the house, Ash covered his nose, feeling his stomach contort. The place reeked of bleach; evidently Gillespie liked things clean. Once he became acclimated to the smell, Ash checked out the kitchen. Gillespie had simple, Shaker-style cabinets and beige granite counter-tops. There was a pair of plastic bowls beside the back door and deep scratches on the hardwood around them. Gillespie must have a dog; maybe he took it with him wherever he went. Ash left the kitchen and headed to the living room but found nothing of interest; in fact, the entire first floor was a bust. The place was so clean it was almost as if no one lived there.

He filed the thought away and took a set of stairs beside the kitchen. Gillespie had turned the room above his garage into a home office. He had a desk on the far end and bulletin boards on most of the walls. Five of the bulletin boards were empty, but photographs and note cards covered a sixth. Ash wasn't an expert, but he had seen similar pictures before. They looked like surveillance photos of drug deals, probably taken with a telephoto lens a good distance away. Beneath each picture, Gillespie had tacked a note card explaining when the photo was taken, who was in it, and what camera had been used. The dates were all at least three months ago.

Ash walked toward the desk. Like the rest of the room, Gillespie's desktop was spotless. Ash opened the center drawer and found a nine-millimeter Beretta. He checked the magazine and chamber and found rounds in both. Gillespie was locked, loaded, and ready to respond to a threat. Maybe he knew someone was after him. He was about to close the drawer when he noticed a note card tucked in a corner similar to the ones on the bulletin board.

November 14. Nikon F5. N.S. and two unknown subjects conversing.

The date was just a couple of days ago. Ash couldn't be sure, but *N.S.* might be Noah Stuart. Of course, it equally might have been Nathan Smith, Natalia Sackville, or any number of other people whose initials happened to be N.S. The note card alone wasn't going to get him anywhere, so he checked out the bulletin boards again, hoping to find a picture without a tag. Nothing was missing, though. As organized as Gillespie clearly was, something wasn't right.

Ash closed the center drawer and checked out the others. Three of them held general office supplies, while a fourth held old police files. He leafed through them quickly, but the files were all over five years old. They were probably open unsolved cases Gillespie had worked on when he was with the department.

Ash stayed still, thinking. As he did, he noticed something interesting about the desk. It glinted in the moonlight as if it had just been polished. It wasn't the only thing in the house that glinted, either. So had Gillespie's floors, his kitchen countertops, and his cabinets. The house wasn't just clean; it was immaculate. Odd for a home that had a dog.

On a hunch, Ash opened the blinds covering the windows so they allowed as much light into the room as possible. The carpet had lines on it as if it had just been vacuumed. To settle his curiosity, he went downstairs and found a vacuum in the front hall closet. Its bag was brand-new, and the old one wasn't in the trash can.

By itself, nothing in the house was off. Plenty of people kept clean kitchens, and plenty of people liked to have their floors cleaned regularly. When put together, though, the picture became a little unnerving. Either Carl had the best cleaning service in the world, or someone sterilized the home of forensic evidence. Considering what had just happened at Cassandra Johnson's house, Ash leaned toward the latter.

He stopped before leaving the house and said a quick prayer for the family of the man who had once lived there, fearing he was long since dead.

7

Ash arrived home at a little after eleven. The lights were on in both the living room and kitchen. The kids were in bed, but Hannah was awake. He covered his eyes with the palms of his hands and slunk deep into the seat of his car. He wanted a drink, but he'd have to wait until she went to bed. Knowing Hannah, that could be a while. A small one in the meantime wouldn't hurt.

He reached into the glove box and unscrewed the cap on his bottle of bourbon. The first sip was sweet and cold, but the second roared down his gullet, scorching his throat. He sighed and capped the bottle before going inside. The kids had gone to bed hours earlier, but he stopped by their rooms anyway. Each was peacefully asleep. Since he didn't want to wake them up, he stayed in the hallway, watching. Megan was the most rambunctious kid he had ever met, while Kaden was quiet and shy. They couldn't be more different, and yet he loved them both more than anything in the world.

Hannah put her hand on his shoulder while he stood outside Kaden's nursery.

"How did you get that bruise?" she asked, touching the spot where he had been punched earlier. Ash hesitated, trying to think of something quickly.

"A bunch of college girls tried to take advantage of me at work. I had to fight them off to defend my virtue, but one caught me with an elbow. They said they'd respect me in the morning, but I didn't believe them."

"You're not funny, Ash."

"On the contrary, I've been told I'm very funny. I'm sorry you don't recognize it."

"What really happened?"

He grunted. "Some teenagers broke into Cassandra's house, and I got hit by something as I was chasing them off."

"Are Sheila and Lisa okay?"

"They're fine. They went back to their hotel, and I called the police. I'll take them by tomorrow to get some clothes."

"A woman dies, and people break into her house. That's awful," said Hannah, shaking her head. She looked at Ash again. "Put on some pajamas. I'll get you an ice pack."

With two kids in the house, Ash and Hannah rarely had time to spend alone together, so they took it whenever they could get it. He did as his wife suggested and put on some pajamas before brushing his teeth. She made him an ice pack and met him in the living room. The two sat on the couch for the next hour watching the second half of a movie about a giant, man-eating alligator that had taken residence in a lake in Maine. For reasons known only to her, Hannah liked bad movies and even reviewed them on a blog. She gave that movie three stars out of five but said it might have earned three and a half if it had more gratuitous violence. They hadn't spent that much time alone together in weeks. Despite the movie, it was nice.

When his alarm rang at six-thirty the next morning, Hannah was no longer in bed, and Ash heard Megan talking in the kitchen. She must have heard the alarm because she ran into the bedroom and jumped on the bed before he could sit up.

"Hi, *Baba*," she said, patting him on the top of the head. "Your hair looks funny."

Ash yawned and pretended to stretch but then pulled her into a hug. She squealed.

"You'll never become my favorite saying things like that, pumpkin."

Megan shook her head vehemently. "*Ummi* says you don't have a favorite and that you love us all equally."

Ash tilted his head to the side. "I think she just wants you out of the competition."

Megan didn't seem to know how to respond to that because she just stared as her father yawned again. He kissed her forehead and let her go.

"Have you had breakfast yet, sweetheart?"

"Orange juice and yogurt with cereal in it. I played with Garfield this morning, too."

At least Megan liked the cat. Hannah didn't seem to be such a fan yet.

"I'm glad. We'll have prayer in a little while."

"Okay, *Baba*," she said, already sliding off the end of the bed closest to the door.

She ran out, giving Ash a few minutes to take a shower and get dressed. The morning went quickly, mostly because he had a lot planned for the day and wanted an early start. At a little before seven, the family had dawn prayer, and by seven-thirty, Ash had hugged his kids, kissed his wife, and grabbed a cup of her black-as-death coffee.

It was Saturday, but weekends meant little to the workload

in a busy police department. Ash drove in but didn't start working immediately upon arrival. Instead, he went by the break room and poured half his wife's coffee down the drain. He filled the second half of his cup with skim milk from the fridge and dumped in enough sugar to almost form a slurry. It was drinkable at that point.

Two of his colleagues had arrived while he was in the break room, but he wasn't interested in catching up on inter-office gossip, so he simply nodded hello to them before going to his desk. His first order of business was to call Sheila Johnson's daughter Whitney. If Whitney knew more about her sister's personal life than her mom did, Ash might actually be able to get some leads; it'd be helpful for once. He sat at his desk and took out his cell phone, but stopped as soon as he powered it on. He had missed three calls from Julie Sims at Child Services the night before.

He punched buttons until he accessed his voice mail. The first call had come in at just after three in the morning.

"Ash, it's Julie. Call me ASAP."

The second and third calls had come in fifteen and thirty minutes later and contained roughly the same message. Julie wouldn't have called at that time of night unless something was seriously wrong. He swore under his breath and dialed her number.

The phone rang four times before she picked up. Her voice sounded gruff, as if she had been asleep.

"I turned off my phone last night so it wouldn't wake up the kids. I just got your message. What's going on?"

Julie cleared her throat. "How do you know Michael Washington?"

Ash leaned back in his chair. "He's a witness in a case I'm working. I had planned to talk to him today. Why?"

"He was brought in last night."

"Where's his grandmother?"

Julie hesitated. "Their house caught fire last night, and she died from smoke inhalation. I tried to talk to him, but all he'd say was that he trusted you. He wouldn't say anything else. I didn't know what that meant."

Ash was so stunned he didn't say anything. His heart flip-flopped in his chest.

"You there, Ash?"

"Yeah, I'm here," he said. "Can I talk to him?"

"He's going to be out for a few more hours, but I don't think it's a good idea regardless. He was so upset that we had to sedate him for his own safety."

"Damn it," he said, rubbing his face and breathing hard enough out of his nose that his nostrils flared. "I think I got his grandma killed."

"Oh."

"When he wakes up, tell him..." Ash paused. Tell him what? That everything would be okay? That he'd wake up in a few days and everything would be back to normal? Michael already lived with his grandma. There probably wasn't anyone else left to take him. Ash's hands started shaking. "Tell him I'll find out what happened and if..." His voice trailed off. He wasn't even sure what to say. Everything sounded hollow before the words even left his mouth. He sighed. "Just tell him I'll find out what happened. If someone hurt his grandma, I'll make sure they get what they deserve."

"I'm not sure if that's—"

"Just tell him," said Ash, interrupting her. "He needs to hear that someone's doing something. Trust me on that."

"All right," she said. "I'll tell him when I can. In the meantime, good luck, I guess."

Ash thanked her before hanging up. His lungs felt tight as cascading waves of revulsion and rage washed over him. He was beyond upset, and the longer he stayed at his desk, the less oxygen there seemed to be in the room. To keep himself from hyperventilating, he got up and left the building for some fresh air. The chill outside took some of the edge off the anger boiling inside him but did little to dissipate it.

He couldn't prove that Lieutenant Stuart or Officer Cartwright had something to do with that fire yet, but he'd do his best. And if he couldn't prove it to the court's satisfaction, that was too bad for them. Someone was going to pay—in court or out. He paced outside for a few minutes, getting his temper under control. When he reached the point where he could control his voice, he took out his cell phone and dialed IMPD's dispatcher. Ash didn't know anyone in the fire department, but hopefully someone would be willing to help out a fellow civil servant.

The dispatcher connected him to an investigator in the Fire Investigations section of the Indianapolis Fire Department. Unfortunately, the Washingtons' house was still too hot for the arson investigations team to work on, so they didn't have anything. Ash left his name and number, and they promised to call if they found anything unusual.

With that call made, Ash sat on a metal bench beside his building and rested his elbows on his knees. He had too much work to do to sit around, so he swallowed his anger and forced it into a dark corner of his mind for when it would be needed again.

According to his watch, it was twenty after eight. That didn't leave him a lot of time, unfortunately. Stupidly or not, he had told Leonard Wilson that he'd attend a city council meeting that morning in exchange for having police patrols around the Washingtons' house increased. Lot of good that did everybody. Ash had better things to do than attend a meeting, but Wilson could put the screws to him if he skipped it. He didn't need to give someone an excuse to make his life miserable.

Since the city council met in the City-County Building a few blocks away, Ash just walked over. It was a Saturday morning, so sidewalks that would normally be full of men and women on smoke breaks were deserted. That was good. He wasn't in the mood to be jostled by a crowd.

As soon as he arrived, Ash flashed his badge to the officers working the front security gate, allowing him to bypass the metal detectors and the line to get into the building. The city council's chamber was a modified auditorium with desks at the front of the room for the city councilors and chairs in the back for the audience. The floor was bare concrete that sloped downward, so even seats in the back had a clear view of the proceedings. In front of everyone was a wooden podium behind which petitioners spoke. None of the council members had arrived yet, but Susan sat in the front row, a briefcase at her side. Technically, the meeting was open to the public, but aside from a cameraman at the back, Ash had the feeling that he and Susan would be the only audience members. He sat beside her. She didn't look at him at first, but eventually she sighed.

"Why are you here?"

"Because a politician wants to waste my time. Why are you here?"

"It's a monthly meeting with the city council. What are you really doing here, Ash?"

Ash shook his head, brushing off the question. "Leonard Wilson did me a favor, so I'm fulfilling my end of the bargain."

Susan started to ask something, but Leonard's voice boomed from the chamber's entrance before she could.

"Detective Rashid. I'm glad you made it."

Ash looked over his shoulder in time to see the councilman walking toward the two of them, his arms outstretched. If he hadn't known better, Ash would have thought Leonard was going for a hug. Thankfully, he stopped just outside of arm's reach.

"And I'm glad to see you, too, Miss Mercer," he said, turning his gaze to Susan. "You folks can relax for a few minutes. We'll go ahead and get started as soon as everyone arrives." Leonard didn't wait to see how Susan reacted before walking to the front of the room.

She leaned into Ash and whispered, "What kind of bargain did you make?"

Supposedly, he was there to talk about the safety concerns of the Islamic community. Knowing Leonard, though, there was more to it than that.

"I guess we'll find out together, won't we?"

Susan crossed her arms and avoided looking at him even though he sat beside her. They waited for about five minutes for the rest of the committee to arrive. As soon as they did, Leonard pulled his microphone toward him and called the meeting to order. The secretary read the minutes from their previous meeting. He then led a quick discussion of the week's agenda. Leonard called Susan to the podium first.

He flipped through papers before glancing up and smiling at her. "I'm glad you made it, Ms. Mercer. For the record, please state who you are and describe your position with the prosecutor's office."

"Sure," she said, lowering the microphone to her height. "I'm Susan Mercer, and I am Marion County's acting prosecutor. I oversee the office and its staff."

"For the record again," said Leonard, still smiling. "How did you come into this position?"

"The city council appointed me after Jack Whittler's arrest."

Leonard nodded. "To be clear, you were not elected to this position." He said it as a statement rather than a question.

Susan hesitated before nodding. "Correct. The city council appointed me to this position with the unanimous approval of this subcommittee."

Leonard's smile never faltered. "I kindly ask that you answer the question and refrain from making unnecessary commentary. Everyone's time is tight here, so if we can stick to yes or no answers to yes or no questions, that would be appreciated," he said. He leaned forward. "How would you evaluate your performance since being posted to this position?"

Susan coughed, clearing her throat before speaking. "The prosecutor's office has performed admirably, given our resources. Despite losing our prosecutor, our office morale is excellent, and we maintain an extremely high conviction rate compared to other metropolitan areas our size. All told, I would give our office a high rating."

Leonard smiled and pulled a pair of glasses from inside his jacket before picking up a document from the table in front of him. "You said almost the exact same thing in the recent self-performance evaluation you gave to this committee," said Leonard, holding up a document. "You didn't answer my question, though. You are more than just your office. How are you doing?"

"I believe I'm doing well. If I wasn't up to the job, I'd resign."

"That's admirable," said Leonard, nodding and glancing at Ash. "If we called other individuals from your office today, would they agree that you're doing well?"

Ash's back stiffened.

"I believe so," said Susan, her voice stilted.

"Are you sure?" asked Leonard, staring right at Ash. Susan followed Leonard's gaze and glanced back at him. She furrowed her brow before turning back to the city council members.

"Yeeesss," she said, drawing the syllable out. "I think my colleagues would say I'm doing well."

"What would you say if I've heard otherwise?"

Susan looked over her shoulder at Ash again, her forehead furrowed deeply and her face red. At least he knew why Leonard had invited him now. He held his breath to keep himself from saying something as Susan turned back around.

"I would respectfully disagree with that person's assessment and point to our office's conviction rates, budget, and employee-satisfaction surveys."

"Ahh," said Leonard, leaning forward. "And what firm conducted those employee-satisfaction surveys?"

Susan took a deep breath. "I didn't feel the need to hire an outside firm. My assistant conducted the survey and compiled the results."

"Okay. No problem," said Leonard. "Who audits your budget?"

Susan didn't answer at first, but eventually she cleared her throat. "We have our own accountant on staff. He reports to me."

"Okay. That's no problem, either," said Leonard, nodding. Susan started to say something, but Leonard cleared his throat and smiled, interrupting her. "Who compiles data about your conviction rates?"

"The Marion Superior Court maintains the records, but my assistant compiles the data into a usable format for us."

Leonard paused. "Is it fair to say, then, that you have no independent verification of anything you've said?"

"No one has questioned my integrity in the past, so I didn't feel the need to expend the resources to hire an outside firm. You're free to examine our records yourself if you'd like."

Leonard chuckled. "Forgive me if I'm incredulous, but your predecessor was arrested and convicted on corruption charges. Did you not think it prudent to reevaluate your office's procedures in light of the circumstances?"

"It was a judgment call. We have a limited budget. I wanted to spend it on putting people in jail."

"After what I hear, it sure would be nice if we could verify what you're really doing," said Leonard. He coughed before Susan could respond. "Unless anyone else has questions, I'm done with Ms. Mercer."

After Susan's shellacking, the city council seemed to be done with her, too, so Leonard dismissed her about ten minutes after calling her to the podium. She glared at Ash as she walked down the center aisle. Rather than respond, he clenched his jaw and stared straight ahead.

Leonard's voice boomed out once again in short order. "I'd like Detective Rashid to come to the podium if he's able," he said. "I have a couple of things I'd like to ask him."

Ash stood and walked to the podium as Susan exited the room. He forced his lips into a thin line so Leonard wouldn't see his annoyance. The councilman smiled smugly in response.

"Detective Rashid," said Leonard. "It's good to talk to you on record. Please introduce yourself and describe your position."

Ash pulled the microphone toward him. "Yeah. Good morning. I'm Detective Sergeant Ashraf Rashid. I'm an investigator assigned to the prosecutor's office, and I work directly for Susan Mercer."

Leonard nodded. "Let me take a moment to commend you for your public service. It takes a special sort of person to stand up and protect others."

"Thank you."

Jackass.

Leonard leaned back in his chair and put his hands behind his head. "In your opinion, Detective," he said, "what sort of job is Ms. Mercer doing as a prosecutor?"

"What do you want me to say? You scored your points with your constituents and you got a video you can leak to the Internet. Why don't you let me go back to work?"

Some of the counselors shifted uncomfortably, but Leonard hardly slowed down.

"I understand that you have work to do, and I appreciate you coming down here. The sooner you answer my questions, though, the sooner this will be over. So please tell me, Detective, what sort of job is Ms. Mercer doing?"

"Fine," said Ash, closing his eyes and putting up his hands. "She's the best lawyer in the office. She understands trial strategy better than anyone I know, and she's been a generally supportive colleague and supervisor. That's probably not what you wanted to hear, though, is it?"

"I want to hear only the truth," he said, leaning forward and flipping through a stack of notes. "Explain one thing to me if you can. Statistics gathered by third parties indicate that crime in this city—particularly violent crime—is up. Despite that, the number of cases your office brings to trial remains steady. Why is Ms. Mercer allowing so many violent criminals to wander our streets without so much as a trial for their crimes? Tell me it isn't just so she can maintain her high conviction rate."

It was more of an ambush than a question. If he said the cases were thin, it'd make IMPD look bad. If he said that Susan didn't prosecute because she didn't think she could win, he'd make her look bad. Ash wasn't above doing either if it was deserved, but in this case, the situation was more complex than the numbers let on.

"I'm not a mind reader, and I'd rather not speculate as to her motives."

Leonard leaned forward. "I noticed your hesitation. If we turned off these cameras to keep Ms. Mercer from seeing your response, would your answer stay the same?"

"You're an asshole, and I'm done answering your questions."

That got people's attention. Ash heard a gasp or two as well as the noise of chairs shuffling.

Leonard chuckled and straightened his posture. "I apologize for the abruptness of my questions, Detective, and I apologize if I've offended you. I didn't mean to imply anything about you. I think you're an excellent detective, and I admire the work you do. Like everyone on this council, I'm passionate about justice, though."

"The next time this council wants to question me, subpoena me. Fair enough?"

"I hope we don't have to," said Leonard. He looked at his fellow council members. "Unless anyone else has questions, I say we adjourn until next week."

No one had further questions—not surprising, considering Ash's outburst—so Leonard banged his gavel on the desk, ending the meeting. Before Ash left, Leonard hurried toward him, his hands held in front of him.

"I'm having a bad day, Councilman," said Ash. "You probably want to leave me alone."

Leonard dropped his chin, smiling slightly. "I apologize if I've made it worse. That was never my intent," he said. "And I actually agree with you about Ms. Mercer. By all accounts, she's a superb attorney. As a city council member, though, my job is to ensure that she's fit to be prosecutor, and that question is still open."

"So making it look like I sandbagged her was just part of your job?"

"It's part of the game we all play, Detective," said Leonard. "If Susan didn't want to be part of it, she shouldn't have stepped onto the field."

"You're something else," said Ash, shaking his head. He started to turn, but Leonard put his hand on Ash's shoulder, slowing him down. Ash shrugged it off, but he couldn't keep the councilman from following him.

"However you feel about me, we have things to discuss. I'd like to talk to you off the record for a few minutes."

Ash slowed and put his hands in his pockets so Leonard wouldn't see his clenched fists. "What are you really after?"

"I'm only trying to improve the lives of the people of my city, and I want to talk to you about your career. As a minority, do you feel IMPD is doing an adequate job of meeting your workplace needs?"

Leonard had hit a sore spot, and while Ash didn't like him, he had no problem using him.

"My office has four Muslims. We've asked a few times for somewhere quiet for prayer, but so far, the city hasn't obliged."

Leonard nodded. "This city needs minority leadership to address the complaints of its minority populations."

"I'm sure it does. Good luck," said Ash, shaking his head as he opened the chamber door. As soon as he saw the first flash, he knew he had stepped into a trap. Leonard put his hand on Ash's shoulder, smiling as he waved to a pair of TV cameras and numerous photographers outside. Ash tried to duck out of the way, but too many people crowded around him. Leonard leaned close enough that no one else could hear him whisper.

"In politics, perception is reality, Detective Rashid. Remember that, and smile."

Leonard stepped away but kept a hand on Ash's elbow. His gaze panned across the assembled group of journalists.

"Thank you all for coming. For those of you who don't know me, I'm Leonard Wilson. I've been on the city council for about eight years now. Standing beside me is Detective Sergeant Ashraf Rashid, the highest-ranking investigator with the Marion County prosecutor's office and one of the most decorated detectives in IMPD. As Detective Rashid and I were discussing, this city lacks minority leadership. Our elected officials don't understand our minority population or our unique needs. Because of that, I would like to formally announce my candidacy for Marion County's prosecutor. You can find more information about my positions by checking out my campaign's website and Facebook page."

Leonard glanced at Ash before returning his gaze to the reporters.

"I'm announcing my candidacy today because I cannot sit by while my minority friends and colleagues are abused or ignored by the law enforcement community. We must take a stand."

Leonard kept talking, but Ash managed to slip through the crowd. Thankfully, no one tried to stop him and no reporter tried to ask him questions. As soon as he left the building, he pulled out his cell phone and dialed his boss's number. She probably didn't want to talk to him, but he figured it was better to start the damage control early rather than late.

Susan picked up and started speaking before he could say anything.

"I appreciate your call, and I'm listening to your press conference right now on the radio. I'm going to request your immediate transfer out of the prosecutor's office. If you'd like, I will request that the deputy chief of investigations transfer you to a post of your choosing."

"Susan, just—"

"Excuse me, Detective," she said, cutting him off. "I'm speaking. Please don't interrupt me. This isn't personal. I simply do not feel that it is appropriate for us to work together considering your political ambitions. Do you understand?"

"Just wait a minute—"

"All I want is a yes or no, Detective," she said, interrupting him again.

"Then yes, I understand."

"Good," she said. She paused and sighed. "We've worked together for several years. Maybe we're not friends, but I had hoped that you'd come to me if you had a problem. If you wanted to sit for a lieutenant's exam, you would have had my blessing and recommendation. If you had a problem with a coworker, I would have handled it. If you had a problem with me, I would have sat down and talked through it. At this point and after what you and Leonard Wilson did, I don't even know what to say to you."

"Then shut up and listen . . . please."

Susan didn't respond, so Ash told her his side of the story. He went because Leonard asked him to. He didn't know what the councilman planned, and he had no part in it.

"I hate this job," she said. "I'm not a politician. I'm not cut out for this shit."

"What do you want me to do?"

"Nothing, and I am so mad right now that I can't even think straight."

Welcome to my world.

Susan didn't hang up, but Ash didn't know what to say, either. After a moment, he coughed, clearing his throat. "If you transfer me after that press conference, it'll just look vindictive."

"Gee, thanks, Ash. I've always found it helpful when my subordinates—"

He hung up before she could finish. Contrary to what Susan seemed to think, he wasn't paid well enough to put up with shit. It was just before nine, and he already wanted a drink badly enough he was practically shaking. Ash had difficulty remembering it, but there was a time when that sort of craving would have given him pause. He didn't used to drink at all, not even in college. Then he had the worst day of his life, and he decided it was a whole lot easier to forget about the world than try to deal with it. He had his first drink and got drunk for the first time on the same night. After that, he started sneaking a drink or two every time he had a bad day. As the years progressed and as his caseload increased, the victims for whom he was supposed to speak started making appearances in his dreams, and his bad days merged with the good. Alcohol was the only thing he found that could shut them off, even for just a little while.

He wouldn't drink now, though. He wanted to, but a strident voice in the back of his head warned him not to. He had learned a couple of weeks earlier to avoid ignoring that voice because it took a lot of booze to drown it out.

8

Ash walked a couple of blocks to his car, forcing his mind to focus on the case rather than the bars he passed. A big part of him wanted to find Joe Cartwright and beat him with a baseball bat or rubber hose until he admitted setting Michael Washington's house ablaze. He wouldn't be able to do anything with the confession, but having one would make him feel better, at least until the guilt caught back up to him. Neither Michael nor his grandmother would have been involved in the case if not for him, and now Michael's life was ruined and his grandmother was gone. It wasn't right.

Ash was still missing critical pieces of the puzzle, but everything he had seen was connected. Cassandra's murder, Gillespie's disappearance, Michael's house fire, the problems at the Northeastern Precinct. Ideally, he'd call John Meyers at that point and ask him what Gillespie had been working on before he disappeared, but with a big trial looming on the horizon, Susan needed to approve even the most casual conversation with her opposing counsel. Ash didn't think she'd be in the mood to do him any favors anytime soon.

Since the conversation was out, he didn't have many options. Still, he had one. Cassandra Johnson had a sister in Cincinnati. Ash didn't know how close the two women were, but Hannah and her sister shared just about everything with each other. With luck, Whitney and Cassandra had been just as friendly. He got Whitney's address from his notepad and entered it into his cruiser's GPS. His estimated time of arrival was two hours and ten minutes; hopefully it'd be worth it.

Whitney lived in a part of Cincinnati called Over-the-Rhine, and Ash's phone started vibrating as soon as he turned in. After a recent trip to a St. Louis Cardinals game that ended up with them driving through a less-than-safe area, Hannah had installed an app on both of their cell phones that alerted them whenever they entered a high-crime neighborhood. Ash had fiddled with the filters on his so it wouldn't buzz in Indianapolis, but those filters didn't extend to Cincinnati. According to his app, he had just turned into one of the most dangerous zip codes in the United States. Whitney Johnson apparently had a very different life than her sister and mother.

Ash pulled to a stop in front of the District 1 police station and told the lieutenant in charge of the day shift who he was and what he was up to. The lieutenant offered to send patrol officers to pick up Whitney, but Ash declined. Unless there was a security risk, he preferred interviewing witnesses in their homes rather than at a station; people were more talkative if they were comfortable. He left the station about twenty minutes after entering and drove until he found Whitney's address.

She lived in a dilapidated granite building with rounded cornices above the windows. At one time, the first floor held a boutique clothing shop, but only an empty storefront with a few forlorn and naked mannequins remained. Weeds popped out of the cracks in the sidewalk, while the remnants of brown liquor bottles littered the street. The upper floors of Whitney's building weren't much better than the first, but at least the windows were intact.

Ash locked his car before heading to a set of stairs beside the abandoned store. The building's interior smelled musky, and gang graffiti covered the walls. Whitney supposedly lived on the second floor, in apartment 201. Ash knocked hard, but no one answered.

"I'm a police officer, Miss Johnson," he said, pounding on the door with his fist. Flecks of dried, cracked paint fell to the ground like confetti. He held his breath, allowing the dust to settle before speaking again. "Please open up if you're home."

Nothing stirred, so he tried the knob and found it locked. Ash took a step back and peered up and down the hall. The carpet was so stained he couldn't recognize its original color, while the plaster walls were cracked in spots and crumbling in others. The floor sagged visibly. If a building inspector had come through, he probably would have condemned the place. Since Whitney locked her door in that dump, she must have had something worth saving; hopefully she'd be back for it soon.

Ash went back to the street and sat inside his car to wait. He hadn't been sitting there long before his phone started ringing. It was Sheila Johnson. He picked up the phone and waited for her to speak. She hemmed and hawed uncomfortably.

"I'm at Cassandra's bank right now, and I found something you should know about. Some company called Indy

Holdings, Inc., gave Cassandra money two weeks ago. A lot of money."

"How much?"

Sheila paused again. "Twenty-five thousand dollars. It was a wire transfer."

That was a lot of money, especially for someone who had only recently regained full-time employment.

"I appreciate the call," he said. "I'll ask someone in our white-collar crime squad if he knows anything about that company. Maybe we'll get lucky."

Ash heard Sheila breathe, but she didn't say anything for a few seconds.

"Do you think my baby was killed for money?"

"I don't know. I'll do my best to find out, though."

"I know you will. Thank you, Detective."

Sheila hung up after that, and Ash immediately called Karl Sharma, a prosecuting attorney who specialized in embezzlement, bankruptcy, and insurance fraud. Karl hadn't heard of Indy Holdings, Inc., off the top of his head, but he promised to look into it and see what he could find.

Ash settled in to wait again. About half an hour later, he noticed a young girl pushing a stroller toward his car. He'd never seen her before, but he recognized Whitney at a glance. She was younger than Cassandra, but she had the same high cheekbones and thin, angular face. Unlike her sister, her arms were so thin they almost looked like twigs, and her face was emaciated.

Ash opened his door and stepped out. As soon as he did, Whitney stopped walking and leveled her gaze at him, her mouth hanging open and a hand on her hip. Her scowl was severe and angry.

"What do you want, Five-O?"

The inexpensive but serviceable suit, the Crown Victoria, the telltale bulge of a firearm against his chest, eyes that never seemed to stay in one place too long. Most people who hadn't been through the criminal justice system missed those things, but the signs were there for those who knew to look. Whitney had apparently spent some time around the police. Ash looked up and down the street. Aside from her and her baby, he was alone. He shielded his eyes from the sun.

"I'm Detective Sergeant Ash Rashid with the Indianapolis Metropolitan Police Department. Have you talked to your mother lately, Whitney?"

She stiffened. "That ain't none of your business."

The attitude didn't bode well for his interview, but he tried to keep his voice even nonetheless.

"Have you heard about your sister?"

Whitney's baby started crying, so she reached into the stroller and moved something around.

"Will you shut up?" she asked, looking at the child. She sighed exasperatedly before looking back at Ash. "Cassandra's dead. Why do you care? You hittin' it or something?"

Ash took a moment to process the question. "I wasn't sleeping with your sister if that's what you're asking. I'm investigating her death."

"Then shouldn't you be out investigating?"

"I am, and I'd like to talk to you about her."

Whitney eyed him warily before nodding. "All right," she said, turning toward her building. Once Whitney reached the stairs, she grabbed her baby but left the stroller on the street as if it were worthless. Having just purchased a new stroller for Kaden, Ash knew they weren't cheap and Whitney's hardly looked used. She leaned on the handrail as she climbed the steps. He thought she was drunk at first, but her voice wasn't slurred, nor could he smell alcohol from where he stood. Of course, in that hallway, he couldn't have smelled much of anything except mold and urine.

He picked up the stroller and carried it with him upstairs. Something that valuable left on the street would be gone before he could tie his shoes. There was no point in Whitney losing it if she didn't have to. When they got to the apartment, Whitney stared at him again, confusion evident in her face.

"Who are you again?" she asked.

"I'm Detective Sergeant Ash Rashid with the Indianapolis Metropolitan Police Department," he said. "I'm investigating your dead sister."

"So you're a policeman?"

She had already forgotten who he was; this really wasn't going well. Ash clenched his jaw and nodded. She handed him the baby and then began rooting through her purse for her keys. Even after she opened the door, though, she didn't make a move to pick up her kid. That was convenient because Ash didn't plan on handing him back. The boy's clothes were dirty, he had scrapes and cuts on his cheeks and forehead, and his diaper was obviously soiled. Ash cradled him as well as he could, but the poor kid couldn't have been comfortable.

He followed Whitney inside. Like the neighborhood, the apartment had seen better days. The front room had a couch, a coffee table, and a flat-screen television big enough to rival some small movie theaters. At least he knew why she locked her door.

"Do you have clean diapers for your son?" he asked.

Whitney flopped onto the couch and focused on the baby as if she had never seen him before.

"He's fine," she said with a wave of her hand. "I'll get more soon."

"Whatever," said Ash. "You stay there."

"Where are you going? How do I know you're not a child molester or something?"

It was nice to hear she cared about her kid's welfare.

"I'm taking him to his bedroom so you and I can talk. Stay on the couch."

She didn't need the command. She may have been mouthy, but her eyes were blank and uncomprehending. Ash took the baby to the home's only bedroom. The room was small, but nothing in it looked dangerous. That was something. He put the baby in a Pack 'n Play before going back to the living room. Whitney was still on the couch, her head tilted back and her breathing heavy. Ash took out his notebook even though he doubted she'd be able to tell him anything important.

"Are you with me, Whitney?"

She turned her head toward him. The drugs she had taken dilated her pupils until very little iris remained in either eye. Ash crossed the room and slapped her lightly on both cheeks until she focused.

"What are you doing?" she asked.

"Asking you questions. Tell me about Cassandra."

Whitney shrugged. "Nothing to tell. The bitch is dead. Had it comin'."

"Why do you say that?"

Whitney shrugged again. "Why are you all up in my

face?" she said, suddenly animated. She took a swing at him, but Ash pulled back and shoved her shoulders hard. She fell back into the couch.

"Please don't do that again. Why did your sister have it coming?"

Whitney scowled. "Because she thinks she's all that," she said, shaking her head. "Like she's better than me or something."

"Did you guys talk much?"

"Sometimes."

Very helpful.

"Did she ever mention if she was having problems with anyone? Maybe at work?"

Whitney put up her hands. "I don't know," she said. "It ain't like we friends or nothing. She sends me money for Jermaine, but that's it. She doesn't even visit."

"Is that where you got the TV?"

Whitney didn't answer.

"What about boyfriends? Did Cassandra have a boyfriend?"

She smirked. "Cassandra doesn't know how to keep a man happy. Besides, every time I talk to her, she's always talking about Lisa. Lisa did this. Lisa did that. It's like the brat's taking over her life."

That's what happens to good parents, but Ash didn't think it was appropriate to mention that.

"Did she have money problems?"

"I don't know. We didn't ever talk about that."

Whitney's pupils narrowed as whatever substance she had taken wore off. Her son's whimpers from the bedroom grew louder.

"Your son's name is Jermaine?" he asked. Whitney nodded. "How old is he?"

She had to stop and think for a second. "About six months. Why?"

Ash ignored her question and walked to the bedroom. Jermaine was still in the Pack 'n Play where Ash had left him. He picked him up and smiled. The boy stopped fidgeting and leaned his head against Ash's shoulder as he carried him to the living room. Whitney hadn't bothered moving from the couch, nor did she bother acknowledging either of them.

For the second time in his career, Ash considered just taking a kid and leaving. The first time had been at the scene of a domestic dispute when he was still a uniformed patrol officer. A young woman had been beaten up by her boyfriend in front of her infant son, Tyrone. From the police reports Ash saw, it was a fairly regular occurrence. Looking back, he should have searched her apartment, picked up Tyrone, and left. There had been liquor bottles on the counter, dead cockroaches on the floor, cigarette butts mashed into the carpet. It hadn't been a fit environment for anyone, let alone a newborn.

Instead of calling Child Services or taking Tyrone, though, Ash did what he thought was the right thing. He gave Tyrone's mother the number of a battered women's shelter downtown. One call, and they would have picked up her and Tyrone without asking a question. Volunteers would have even packed her stuff so she wouldn't lose anything. She promised to make the call, but she probably tossed the number as soon as Ash left.

He arrested Tyrone's mother two years later, after he'd

been promoted to the homicide squad. Tyrone had died of exposure after his mother dumped him in the park with her garbage in the middle of winter. Apparently his crying had interrupted his mother's attempts to entertain the same boyfriend who had beaten her up years earlier. Ash had his first drink after the funeral. The liquor didn't make things easier; it just made things easier to forget. He wasn't about to relive that mistake, though, not when he could do something about it. He shifted Whitney's baby from one arm to the other. Jermaine fussed at first, but Ash rubbed his back, shushing him.

"All he ever does is cry," said Whitney, shaking her head. "Give him to me. I know how to shut him up."

"I think he'll quiet down on his own. I've got an infant myself, and he cries all the time, too. How do you manage to shut yours up?"

"Hold his nose shut. He learns."

There's something to be said for an interview subject willing to take bait dangled right in front of her. Ash was glad he was holding the kid.

"By holding his nose shut, you're not teaching him anything. You're suffocating him. Infants are obligate nose breathers. Anatomically, they can't breathe through their mouths well. Do me a favor and stay on the couch. I'm taking Jermaine into protective custody because you've proven to me that you pose a serious and immediate danger to his health."

"What do you mean?"

"I'm going to call the local police precinct and Child Protective Services, and they're going to take him into protective custody for his own safety."

"They ain't going to take my baby."

"Maybe, maybe not. It's not your choice, though. Stay where you are and do whatever they ask you."

She tried to stagger upright but fell backward before she could. "Whatever. He ain't worth it."

Ash balanced Jermaine on one hip and walked to the hallway for some privacy. He didn't know the phone number of the lieutenant he had spoken to earlier that afternoon, so he called the nearest police station and introduced himself to the watch commander. After hearing the basics of the story, the officer agreed to send a patrol vehicle by the house and contact the Hamilton County Jobs and Family Services office. Ash stayed in the hallway with the baby to wait, but he kept an eye on Whitney most of the time. She didn't move from the couch.

The officers arrived in about ten minutes. They talked to Whitney in the front room for a few minutes, but it didn't take them long to figure out she was high. It also didn't take them long to spot a modified cigarette lighter on an end table beside the couch. The lighter's butane regulator had been removed, causing the flame to burn significantly larger and hotter than in a normal lighter. A modified lighter may have had some legitimate use, but most people who had them used them to light crack pipes. If nothing else, the possession of drug paraphernalia gave the officers probable cause to secure a search warrant for the rest of the apartment.

A social worker from Child Protective Services arrived about an hour later. Like most of the men and women who worked in those sorts of offices, she probably had fifty or a hundred cases open on any given day, limiting the amount of work she could do for specific cases. Ash introduced himself and told her about what he had seen so far. She hardly reacted, even when he told her about Whitney's method for quieting her child. Of course, she probably heard similar stories several times a week.

While Ash was talking to the social worker, a patrol officer came by with a signed search warrant. It didn't take them long to find drugs. Whitney kept a fairly large Baggie of a white rocklike substance in the bottom of a coffee can above her refrigerator. A field test was positive for cocaine. Apparently she had used the money her sister gave her for more than just a TV. The penalties for the possession of crack were stringent in Ohio, so she would likely be away for a while. Hopefully it'd be long enough for her to get into a drug treatment program in prison.

By that time, Ash had seen enough to know that Jermaine wouldn't be going back to his mother immediately. He would likely be placed with a foster family, but whether that would help the situation was anybody's guess. Some foster families were fantastic. They provided stable homes where a kid could have a healthy, normal childhood, even if for just a few months. Other foster homes were just as bad as the homes from which the kids were taken in the first place. That was the system, though, and as miserable as it was, it was the best the world could come up with. Before leaving, Ash patted Jermaine's back and prayed the city would soon find someone decent to watch over him.

When he got back to his car, he pulled out the bottle of bourbon he had purchased two days earlier and twisted off the cap. There wasn't a lot left, but it'd be enough.

His hands shook as he twisted off the cap.

"Detective Rashid?"

He startled, almost tipping the bottle over as he set it on the seat beside him. It was the social worker he had met inside.

"Yeah?" he asked, stepping out of his cruiser.

She hesitated. "Sorry if I startled you," she said, holding up a tabbed manila folder. "I need you to sign my report. I forgot inside."

"Of course," said Ash, reaching into his pocket for a pen. He signed the paper on the cruiser's trunk and handed the folder back to the social worker. She wouldn't meet his gaze.

"Jermaine is a tragedy, but there are better ways to cope than with alcohol. I know some people in Indianapolis who can help. I can make a recommendation if you need to see someone."

Evidently Ash hadn't been as fast with the bottle as he had hoped.

"I appreciate your concern, but I'm okay."

She probably heard excuses like that quite often. It didn't seem to move her.

"Are you sure?"

No.

"Yes. I'm fine. Thank you."

She stayed for another minute, her eyes locked with his until her cell phone started ringing. At first, Ash thought she'd ignore it. He didn't know if he wanted her to or not. Eventually, though, she wished him well and turned around. His throat and face felt warm. He shouldn't have been angry, especially considering he didn't even know who he was angry at, but he was. When he was sure the social worker was gone, he picked up the bottle again and took two swigs, emptying it.

He had spent his entire adult life fixing other people's

mistakes only to walk into the same sort of situation over and over again. It felt pointless.

He threw the empty bottle into a Dumpster beside a nearby apartment building and glanced at Whitney's building. When Jermaine went to sleep that night, he'd do it in a cold hospital bed surrounded by strangers. He'd wake up the next day wrapped in unfamiliar sheets, and he'd call out for comfort that would never come. Worse, it'd likely be for nothing. Knowing the family court system, he'd be back with Whitney as soon as she got out of jail, only to be abused and ignored again. As long as the lawyers and bureaucrats had the proper papers filled out, though, it'd be considered a job well done. It didn't even seem worth it anymore.

9

It was nearly time for afternoon prayer, so Ash used the GPS in his cruiser to search for the nearest mosque. It was a mile and a half away. In many Middle Eastern countries, it's common to see entire busloads of people praying on the side of the road at prayer times. Ash wasn't a fan of praying in public, though. Almost ten years ago, he had a five-hour layover in an airport in the South while flying home from a continuing education conference. When afternoon prayer time came, he went to the on-site interfaith chapel and prayed. Before he could finish, two airport police officers, having received complaints from other passengers, dragged him to his feet and placed him in custody for suspicious activity. It was one of his more humiliating experiences. Since then, Ash sought privacy for prayer.

The mosque served a small community, but there were eight men and four women inside. Not bad for a prayer time when most men and women were still at work. To that community, Ash was a complete stranger, but they welcomed him and treated him like one of their own. It was comforting and familiar. They prayed together, and he left about twenty minutes later, the heat of his anger gone.

*   *   *

Ash's cell phone rang when he was still seventy miles from home on I-74. It was late afternoon, and the sun was so low it blinded him every time he looked in the rearview mirror.

He felt better than he had in the parking lot of the hospital, but he wasn't in the mood for a conversation. He let the phone go to voice mail before looking at the caller ID. The caller had blocked his name, but the number belonged to a department-issued cell phone. At least it wasn't Susan Mercer.

He drove for another ten miles or so before pulling off at a rest stop on the side of the highway. None of the parking spots near the welcome center were available, so Ash pulled to the end of the lot and parked in the shade cast by a ginkgo tree. The closest car was four spots down, far enough away that no one could hear his conversation. He opened his windows and allowed a cool breeze to air out the cabin before hitting a button on his phone to make the call.

"This is Detective Ash Rashid. I got a call from this number just a few minutes ago."

"About time you called back."

Ash's shoulders dropped and his momentary sense of calm dissipated. The voice belonged to Mike Bowers, the lieutenant in charge of the homicide squad. Objectively speaking, Bowers had a good head on his shoulders and a feel for homicide that few other officers possessed. Unfortunately, he was also a colossal dick who'd burn his own grandmother at the stake to close a tough case. Ash respected the guy's ability and tenacity, but Bowers had damn near gotten him and his family killed a year earlier during an investigation into a series of murdered teenagers, one of whom was Ash's niece. He had a hard time forgetting or forgiving that.

"I assume this isn't a social call. What do you want, Mike?"

"Oh, you know. Peace on Earth, goodwill toward men. Things like that. I'd also like you to tell me about Carl Gillespie."

Ash drummed his fingers on the steering wheel. "Did you find his body?"

"Maybe. Did you kill him?"

"No," said Ash. "Where'd he show up?"

"He's doing the backstroke in a canal near Military Park."

Without major bodies of water in the area, IMPD rarely had to handle floaters, something for which Ash was grateful. The water scrubbed trace material and fibers from the body, eliminating one major source of evidence. Almost as bad, if a body was found in a lake or river, the current could carry it for miles before someone found it, making it damn near impossible to find the original dump site. Floaters, in short, sucked.

"You sure it's Gillespie?" asked Ash.

"Well, I'm not going to take a swim to check his wallet, but it's him."

Ash had hoped to be a little further along in his investigation into Cassandra before he had to start looking at Gillespie seriously. Evidence didn't wait, though; he would just have to wing it.

"I'll be there in forty-five minutes."

"I'm so excited that you're coming to join us," said Bowers. "I do love—"

Ash hit the power button on his phone, ending the call and interrupting Bowers midsentence. It looked like his long day was going to turn into a long night.

*   *   *

Military Park was a fifteen-acre plot of grass and trees on the White River canal near IUPUI, the city's major university. When they first started seeing each other, he and Hannah met there a couple of times on their lunch breaks, so he knew the place well. If he had gone on any other evening, Ash would have seen couples and families strolling along the canal walk to its south. Not surprisingly, though, the park was empty that night; corpses tend to keep the tourists away.

He jogged down the paved walking trail toward the canal. The trees blotted out many of the nearby buildings. By the time Ash neared the water, he couldn't even hear the traffic over the sound of a man-made waterfall. A light breeze carried the sweet, crisp scent of black walnuts, pecans, and decaying leaves. It was a nice place to spend a fall evening. He had asked Hannah to marry him on a night like that on a bench about two hundred feet away.

He walked down a hill toward the canal. A number of uniformed police officers meandered on the limestone pathway surrounding the canal, while two representatives from the coroner's office stood to the side talking to each other. As Ash walked, one of the uniformed officers took notice of him.

"This is a crime scene, sir. You'll have to come back some other night."

Ash pulled back his jacket, exposing the badge on his hip. "I'm Detective Sergeant Ash Rashid. I'm looking for Mike Bowers. You seen him around?"

The officer studied Ash's face before tilting his head and speaking into the microphone attached to his shoulder. Eventually, he pointed to a lone figure leaning on one of the waist-high light pedestals that illuminated the pathway. Ash thanked the officer and walked over.

Bowers was a hulk of a man. He wasn't tall, but he was almost as wide as a refrigerator, and he looked as if he could bench press a Buick. Ash had gotten into a minor fistfight with him a year ago, and while it hadn't turned out well for either of them, Bowers had been the least battered of the two. He nodded a greeting when Ash drew close.

"You guys pull Gillespie out yet?" asked Ash.

"We were waiting for you to get here. Hope you brought your waders because I'm sure as hell not going in."

Ash turned his gaze to the canal. "You're not afraid of a little water, are you?"

Bowers pressed his lips into a thin line before answering. "No. I'm afraid of the homeless people who use the canal as a toilet. I'd like to avoid contracting dysentery if I can."

The fear was probably reasonable. Ash glanced back at the squad of officers securing the crime scene.

"You ever handled a floater before?" he asked.

Bowers nodded. "A few. Pulled a body from the Geist Reservoir a couple of months back. Never even got a name on him."

"Then you know we're not going to find any forensics on this guy," said Ash, nodding toward the patrol officers. "What do you say we send a probie?"

Instead of answering, Bowers took a step up the hill. "Hey, Barnes," he shouted. The group of uniformed officers near the canal stopped talking, and one, the youngest of the bunch, stepped forward. The poor kid probably didn't even shave every day yet. "Get some waders from the coroner's van because you're going for a swim."

The officer pointed to his chest, his eyebrows raised. Bowers nodded slowly before making a shushing motion with his hand. Probationary Officer Barnes nodded and headed back up the hill from which Ash had just come. Neither Bowers nor he said anything until the kid came back wearing a pair of black rubber gloves and galoshes that went nearly to his armpits.

"I don't suppose you have any witnesses," Ash said, watching as the kid and a representative from the coroner's office in a similar outfit dipped their feet into the canal. The waterway was only a couple of feet deep, but the water was so dark he couldn't see the bottom. Of course, the canal contained so much litter and pollution, he probably wouldn't have been able to see the bottom even in broad daylight. Bowers held out his arms and turned in a circle.

"Do you see any witnesses?" he asked. He paused and cocked his head at Ash. "Susan Mercer told me to call you when Gillespie showed up. How'd you know he was going to swan dive his way to hell, anyway?"

"Educated guess," he said. Bowers raised his eyebrows incredulously, and Ash shrugged. "I knew he was missing, and his name came up in a case I'm working. Didn't take much thought."

"If his murderer's name comes up, I'm sure you'll give me a call."

"You'll be the first."

Bowers and Ash walked closer to the canal's edge. Gillespie floated near the far side. He had looked better. His skin was so pale that it was almost translucent, and he looked bloated. Somehow, the corpse had gotten its hand caught in a grate covering a drainage passage, holding it in place. Ash couldn't see any obvious wounds, and there didn't appear to be blood in the water, but the man was definitely dead.

"So how are you handling this?" he asked, watching as Officer Barnes and the technician from the coroner's office arrived at the body. Barnes tried to free Gillespie's hand but had little success.

Bowers shrugged. "I've got four uniforms knocking on doors, but there's not much here aside from some condos a couple of blocks away. I've also got a detective typing up a warrant for Carl's house. We'll go there once we're done here," he said, looking from Ash to Gillespie's body and back. "How's our friend tied into your case?"

"I'm not sure yet. I found—"

"This guy's really hard," shouted Officer Barnes from the canal. "I don't know if that's important."

Bowers turned, a scowl on his face and his hands on his hips. "You're supposed to be collecting evidence, Barnes," said Bowers. "You're not giving him a hand job. Unless you see lipstick on his johnson and you know the hooker it's from, I don't want to hear it."

"That's not what I meant, sir," said Barnes, his voice wavering as his teeth chattered. "This guy's really hard. Like all over."

"He's right, Lieutenant," said the guy from the coroner's office. "His body is rigid."

"That's why he's called a stiff, gentlemen. Now get him on a back brace and pull him out."

Bowers didn't seem interested in resuming their conversation, so Ash merely watched as Officer Barnes freed Gillespie from the grate and then helped secure the body on a bright red backboard. The two men in the water pushed up on their end while the officers assembled on the side of the canal took the weight and pulled until the body was on dry ground. Almost immediately, another representative from the coroner's office began taking pictures of the corpse. Eventually, he handed his camera to a nearby officer and put his hand on Gillespie's throat.

"He's cold."

"No shit," said Bowers, pulling his jacket tight around him. "It's fall, and he's been in the water. What are you seeing as far as a potential cause of death?"

"Nothing yet," he said, running his hands from Gillespie's neck to his ribs. "His entire body is very cold."

"Check his liver," said Ash, glancing at Bowers. "It'll give us a better estimate of his core temperature."

The techs were already a step ahead. One took a foot-long thermometer with a barbed end out of his bag while a second technician made a slit in Gillespie's side with a scalpel. The first tech then pushed on the thermometer hard enough to penetrate Gillespie's muscle tissue. He stared at the dial for a second and then lit it with a flashlight to read it better. When he pulled the probe out, not a single drop of blood fell to the ground.

"Thirty-two degrees," he said. "Your victim is an ice cube."

Ash looked at Bowers. The lieutenant looked confused.

"How cold do you think it is out here?" Ash asked.

"Forty, forty-five, maybe."

Nobody said anything for a second, so Ash took the initiative.

"We should start checking out local restaurants and ask to see their freezers. We might even want to see if any refrigerated trucks have been stolen."

"We should," said Bowers. "It's going to be a waste of time, though. We pulled him out of the water, so there aren't going to be fibers on him. We're not going to have witnesses around here, either, and with Gillespie frozen, we won't have an accurate time of death. Whoever whacked him knew what he was doing."

"And you doubt he'd be stupid enough to keep him in a freezer nearby."

Bowers looked at the building across the canal. "The Indiana State Museum might have a camera or two pointed in this direction, so we might get lucky, but I doubt it. I'm thinking our hitters are long since gone."

Bowers waved over a nearby officer. "Give me your radio," he said.

The officer handed him a coal-black two-way radio.

Bowers hit the CALL button. "This is Lieutenant Mike Bowers. All units on canal detail, report back to Military Park for new assignments."

He and Ash waited about thirty seconds before a shaky voice squawked a message in response.

"Uh, sir. We found something in some condos north of your position. Our squad cars are out front."

Bowers put the radio to his lips. "And what did you find?" he asked, glancing at Ash, an impatient scowl on his face.

The officer hesitated. "We think we found the killing room, sir." The speaker paused again, his voice cracking. "It's like a horror movie."

"This is an open channel, so watch your mouth, Officer," said Bowers, sighing. "We'll be right over. And whatever you do, do not go in."

"No problem."

IO

Ash followed Bowers's cruiser for about half a mile until they arrived at an upscale condominium development near the canal. A wrought-iron fence surrounded the complex, presumably having been designed to keep the riffraff out. If the scene was as bad as the reporting officer implied, it would pull double duty and keep the reporters away. Ash parallel parked on the street outside the fence while Bowers parked crookedly in the center of the development's only gate, blocking the entrance.

Ash got out of his car and joined Bowers at the front of the lieutenant's Crown Vic. A pair of uniformed officers stood outside a three-story brick town house about thirty feet away. Both looked a little green and both swayed unsteadily on their feet. So far, none of the nearby residents had exited their homes, but that would change soon enough.

"I hate probies," said Bowers, getting Ash's attention again. "One of them puked on the steps. He didn't even make it onto the grass. Now we're going to have to walk through that all night."

Ash squinted and saw a fresh pile of vomit on the ground.

"Pull them off the post. We can put one of them on the

logbook and the other on crowd control. I'm sure you've got more experienced officers who can knock on doors."

Bowers shot his eyes around the complex. As expected, a couple wearing pajamas had just stepped out of a nearby town house.

"That's probably smart," he said, cupping his hands around his mouth and directing his voice to the uniformed officers. "Hey, new guys. Get over here and try not to puke on anything."

While Bowers castigated and then reassigned his officers, Ash went to his car and grabbed two pairs of gloves and shoe covers from his evidence collection kit. Bowers was examining the condo's front door when Ash joined him again. There were no obvious tool marks on the door frame or lock, and none of the windows around it were broken. Someone knew what he was doing to get inside. The two men snapped on gloves and slipped the covers over their shoes before Bowers pushed open the front door.

As soon as Ash saw the home's interior, his stomach felt like he had just jumped off the side of a building. Neither he nor Bowers said anything; they just stared, not moving. It wasn't hard to understand why the first men inside had puked.

"Christ," said Bowers, his breath low as he drew the syllable out. The entryway was big enough to hold a baby grand piano, two enormous potted plants, and a curving staircase that led to the second floor. The floor might have been hardwood, but it could have been tile; it was too hard to tell beneath the blood. When the officer called in the scene and said it was something out of a horror film, Ash thought he had been exaggerating. He wasn't.

Ash reached into his jacket and withdrew his firearm before taking his first step inside. The slipcovers over his shoes stuck to the congealing blood, leaving footprints wherever he walked. The room was two stories tall and round with cream-colored walls and a chandelier hanging from a chain. Blood covered the floor, but no splatter clung to the walls or ceiling. Likely, the victims had been killed elsewhere and then dragged into the front room to bleed out.

Ash adjusted his grip on his firearm and took another couple of steps. Despite the amount of gore on the ground, the place didn't smell. Whatever had happened had occurred recently, and judging by the amount of liquid on the ground, it involved multiple victims.

Ash looked back over his shoulder at Bowers. The lieutenant had stepped inside the room with his firearm held at his side, his face pale. He nodded at Ash, silently telling him to proceed. A short hallway led to a small half-bath beneath the stairs. Blood had seeped beneath the door, but, like the front room, none clung to the walls or ceiling. Nothing had happened in there.

They went to the kitchen next. The room was roughly half the size of Ash's house and had a two-story wall of glass overlooking the White River. Blood splattered the mahogany cabinets, granite countertops, and walls from floor to ceiling. Ash pointed his firearm to what might have been arterial spray on the glass backsplash above the stove.

"We've likely got our kill spot."

Bowers never turned his head and instead focused on the wall of the adjoining sunroom. Ash followed the lieutenant's gaze. He had to squint to make it out, and even then he had difficulty seeing it in the moonlight, but someone had written a message on the far wall. Ash felt his stomach twist in knots as the two walked toward it.

"'Long is the way, and hard,'" said Bowers. "What the hell does that mean?"

Ash ignored the question and walked forward to get a better look. The letters had been written with a black marker in long, even strokes. The department didn't have a handwriting expert, so they'd probably have to contact someone at the FBI for analysis. To Ash's untrained eye, though, nothing about the letters themselves stood out. He looked back at Bowers.

"'Long is the way, and hard, that leads from Hell into the light,'" he said, completing the part of the quote that hadn't been placed on the wall. "It's from *Paradise Lost,* by John Milton."

"And you just know that?"

"I passed high school English."

"Yeah, right. How'd you really know that?"

"My mother had a PhD in English literature and wanted my sister and me to understand Western culture. *Paradise Lost* was a bedtime story."

"That's kind of a morbid bedtime story. What'd your dad read you?"

Ash glanced at Bowers. "He was murdered by one of his students before my mom even knew she was pregnant with me," he said, looking back at the writing on the wall. "Gillespie wasn't killed here. Whoever killed him was methodical and didn't want to get caught. This is something different. This is..." He paused, trying and failing to form the words he wanted to say. "It's messed up, whatever it is."

"Agreed," said Bowers, looking around the room. "There might be survivors, though, so let's keep going."

The two men searched the rest of the house, but they didn't even find bodies, let alone survivors. The blood and gore were confined to the first floor, most notably the kitchen. Ash didn't think they needed to find bodies to know where the homeowners were, though. The average person carried a little more than a gallon of blood in his body; they had four to five times that much in the kitchen and entryway.

By the time they got outside, Ash and Bowers's communication had been reduced to grunts and gestures. Ash wouldn't admit it aloud, but the scene unnerved him. In the course of his career, he had seen dozens and dozens of bodies in person and probably hundreds more in photographs. It was different to see puddles of blood in real life, though. Ash was so absorbed in the scene that he didn't notice the news vans lined up on the street outside the complex until the reporters started shouting questions. Even then, he didn't pay them much mind. He followed Bowers back to his car. The lieutenant reached into his jacket and pulled out a pack of cigarettes, his hands shaking slightly.

"I've been trying to quit," said Bowers after lighting up and staring at the glowing red ember at the tip of his cigarette. He put it to his lips and drew heavily again. "Some nights make it harder than others."

Ash looked back at the condo. The evidence collection team seemed antsy to do something. That would probably change as soon as they stepped through the door.

"Have you ever seen anything like this before?"

Bowers blew out a lungful of smoke. "No. I appreciate you

going in with me, but I'm not going to lie. I want you off this case. We have a lot of work here, and some of my guys need it bad. You go home and kiss your wife. I'll owe you one."

There were thirty or forty townhomes within the gated community and at least ten times that many apartments in the surrounding blocks. It'd take a lot of man-hours to knock on all those doors, so Ash couldn't blame Bowers for wanting the case. Indianapolis had a fifty-million-dollar deficit, and while the city hadn't started laying off cops yet, it had cut overtime pay. A lot of people depended on that money to pay their mortgages and their kids' college tuition bills. A case with media attention, though, meant the money would flow again, at least for a little while.

"You don't owe me anything. I don't want any part of this. I've got enough to do."

Bowers evidently recognized Ash was sincere about not wanting anything because he turned and started barking orders at anyone who would listen. Ash flagged down the uniformed officer with the crime scene logbook.

"You heading home, Detective?" he asked. Ash signed his name and the current time in the box the officer indicated.

"Back to the office for some paperwork," he said, glancing up. "Do your family a favor. Never sit for the detective's exam. Trust me."

The guy chuckled, apparently thinking he was kidding.

"Have a good night, Detective Rashid," he said, looking at the signature Ash had scribbled onto the clipboard.

He grunted and nodded before heading back to his cruiser. The news crews must have realized they weren't going to get much by shouting at Mike Bowers and the rest of his team through the fence, so they had surrounded Ash's car.

He said "no comment" to every question they asked. Most took the hint and left him alone, but one leaned against his car with her arms crossed. Kristen Tanaka. She called herself an investigative journalist, but mostly she read from a tele-prompter for one of the TV stations in town. Ash had heard rumors that she'd do a whole lot more than read if a detective gave her an exclusive story, but he hadn't tested it. Besides, Hannah probably wouldn't approve.

"Is it true there are multiple bodies inside?"

Ash looked around. The other reporters were slinking off, giving them a moment of privacy.

"Who told you that?"

"I have a source."

He took a step back and looked at her truck. Kristen's cameraman held something that looked a little like a metal bowl with a giant Q-tip protruding from the center. It was a parabolic microphone. Guys in IMPD's narcotics squad used them to record whispered drug deals from two or three hundred feet away. Kristen had probably been able to hear everything he and Bowers had said to each other.

"No comment. Please get off my car. I'm tired, and I've had a long day. I'm sure you know what that's like."

"What are you going to be doing downtown? Typing up a warrant?"

"Get off my car," he said again. Ash took a deep breath and forced a smile to his lips. "Please."

"The press has a right to be here."

Ash stared for another moment before turning and wav-ing over one of the officers on the perimeter of the crime scene. The young woman who answered his summons was probably the smallest uniformed officer he had ever met. She couldn't have been over five-two and couldn't have weighed much over a hundred pounds even with her utility belt on. She wasn't intimidating physically, but at least she was armed.

"You have a right to be at the scene, but you don't have a right to be on my car. Please get off or this officer will place you under arrest for impeding me in my official duties."

Tanaka looked the officer up and down. She didn't look impressed, but at least she stood up.

"Why are you trying to silence the press?"

"If you had been paying attention, you'd know I'm not trying to silence anyone. I'm just not answering your questions. There's quite a big difference."

"We have a right to know what's going on, Detective Rashid."

Ash stepped around her and opened his door. "Maybe you do, but waste somebody else's time. I've got work to do."

Kristen may have said something in response, but Ash ignored her and closed his door. He didn't drive off immediately. Instead, he closed his eyes and leaned his head back. His plan was to write out some notes in his office and then hit the first after-hours bar he could find. Getting sloshed would be a suitable way for his day to end.

Traffic was relatively light, so the trip downtown took only about ten minutes. He pulled into the city government parking lot at a little after one in the morning. With the budget deep in the red, basic maintenance around the city was no longer a priority, and normally bright streetlights had been allowed to go dark. Ash pulled his jacket tight and stepped out of his car and into the gloom.

During the day, the parking lot was full to capacity with several hundred vehicles. Now it contained a dozen cars, almost all of which were old and rusted. Since he didn't want to get mugged, Ash hurried toward his building. He almost made it, too. With the sidewalk still twenty feet away, though, he heard footsteps behind him.

"Put your hands on your head but do not turn around."

Ash swore under his breath but didn't move his hands from his waist. The nearest building was about two hundred feet to his left, and the nearest car was probably thirty feet behind him. Without cover or backup, he didn't have a lot of options if someone started shooting.

"I'm an armed police officer. Why don't you take a walk before someone gets shot?"

"We know who you are, Detective Rashid."

He furrowed his brow.

Detective Rashid?

Before he could puzzle through the statement, the footsteps behind him increased into a sprint, and Ash dove to the right, whirling to face his assailants. He saw three men in black ski masks. None of them carried guns, but each held some sort of black sling. Ash had taken several self-defense courses offered through the police department in the last few years, but the techniques he had been taught focused on safely subduing suspects with the help of one's fellow officers. Rarely did his classes focus on one-on-one combat, and even more rarely did they focus on three-on-one combat. Without help, he was in pretty serious trouble.

He reached into his jacket for his firearm, but before he could pull it out, one of the assailants closed the distance between them. Ash put up his hands, but the guy still caught a glancing blow to his head with the sling. Whatever was in the sling was firm, but somewhat yielding. The blow was enough to knock Ash back a step, but it wasn't enough to knock him out. A couple more, though, might. His best chance was to take out one of his attackers hard and fast and hope to scare off the others.

He lunged forward as if he were going to tackle the man in front of him, but instead of ramming his shoulder against the man's midsection, he stood up at the last moment, ramming his head against the underside of the guy's jaw. It was a bit like coldcocking someone with a bowling ball. Ash heard and felt the guy's teeth crash into each other as his jaw snapped shut. His body went limp, and Ash could see blood dribble down his chin even through the ski mask.

With one of his attackers down, Ash whirled around to face the other two. His hope had been that they'd run away after seeing him level their compatriot, but that wasn't happening. They circled him. He could probably handle himself reasonably well against one, but not both of them. He lunged at one of the men and immediately felt a blow to the back of his head. His vision flashed white, disorienting him. Ash put his hands up, but he caught another shot from behind, this time to his neck.

He staggered to one knee, and then they were on him simultaneously. Pain exploded up and down his spine as one of the men kicked him in the lower back. He might have been hallucinating, but it sounded as if the other one warned his partner to take it easy. Unfortunately, no one else seemed to be having the same delusions as Ash because he received a couple of more shots to his kidneys and head before the beating ceased. A pair of arms rolled him onto his back.

He grimaced as one of the masked men bent and reached into Ash's jacket for his firearm. Ash closed his eyes and prayed for his kids and wife, thankful that he'd at least be sober on his way to the afterlife. The gunshot he expected never came, though. The masked man pulled back the slide on the Glock, ejecting the round from the chamber before removing the magazine. He pocketed the ammunition and threw the weapon on the sidewalk before kicking Ash's knees hard.

He lost track of time after that. Eventually, he heard a shrill whistle, and his assailants froze. Before leaving, one of the men bent down and held his face so close to Ash's that he could feel breath on his cheek.

"Cassandra Johnson is gone. Drop it or we burn your house next. This is your only warning."

The men turned and ran, leaving him huddled on the ground and bleeding from his nose. He caught his breath while a fresh set of legs walked into his field of vision. Unlike the men who had attacked him, these were shapely and wore fishnets. A very attractive young woman with a low-cut top and a sleek, black skirt knelt beside him. She put her hand on his shoulder and helped him sit up. He breathed hard for a few minutes, trying to get his bearings before looking at the woman again. A belief in angels was one of the six Articles of Faith in Islam, and many Muslims believe that every man and woman has two guardian angels, one for the day and one for the night. If Ash had known his guardian angels were that attractive, he might have tried to meet them sooner.

"Are you all right?" she asked. "I'm going to get a cop. There's a police station up the road."

Ash ran his tongue across the front of his teeth. They were all there.

"Don't bother," he said, reaching to his belt for his badge.

He held it up and winced as pain shot through his side. His hero took a step back and pointed at the ground about ten feet away.

"There's a gun over there."

"It's mine," he said, shifting his weight. Ash pulled himself upright on a nearby streetlight. His head felt light and he was dizzy, but he could stand with support. He leaned against the lamppost, gasping as his rib cage, back, and head throbbed. The young woman leaned down and picked up a long black sock. She handed it to him.

"They hit you with this," she said. Ash held the sock by the toe and watched as a cracked and broken potato tumbled out. The girl frowned at it, confused. "Who hits somebody with a potato?"

A cop.

Ash shrugged as if he didn't know. He never had the need to use one himself, but he knew a couple of people who talked about using potatoes in socks as improvised, nonlethal weapons before the department started issuing Tasers. They were good for crowd control on college campuses and at sporting events because they would hit hard enough to knock somebody senseless, but, unlike a nightstick, they wouldn't crack a skull or cause permanent damage.

Ash waited for another moment for his balance to return before pushing off from the light post and standing more or less straight.

"Thank you for your help, miss," he said, grimacing as he shifted his weight. He spoke again when the pain subsided. "If you'd like, I can walk you home and make sure you arrive safely."

She looked him up and down before taking a short, hesitant step back. "I just live up the street. I think I'll be okay. Besides, I have my whistle. I'm sure you'll come after me if you hear it."

She held out a silver whistle for him to see. Hannah had a similar one she received at a rape prevention course taught at the local YMCA. That was a little sad, really. Ash was less than a block from a major police department, and yet he had been saved by a girl with a whistle. She left a moment later, but he stayed by the lamppost, trying to catch his breath. Paperwork was definitely out; his head hurt too much. He had just been beaten up by police officers and warned against investigating a murder further. It was disturbing to say the least. He rubbed his temples, hoping to squeeze out a headache.

I've really got to get a better job.

II

None of the lights in the house were on when Ash arrived home. Every part of his body hurt, but so far he didn't have any major signs of a concussion. With a little sleep, he'd probably be back to normal. Unfortunately, he knew before even entering his house that the sandman wouldn't visit anytime soon. He had managed to hold off the desire earlier, but he needed a drink. It felt like an itch in the back of his throat that he couldn't scratch. He had finished his only bottle of bourbon earlier, but he checked the glove compartment anyway, as if hoping God would bestow upon him some sort of alcoholic miracle. Apparently God wasn't an enabler, though, because no divinely gifted bottle greeted him from inside.

He slammed the glove compartment shut. His grocery store had a limited beer selection and it was open twenty-four hours a day, so at least he could get something. He put the keys in the ignition but stopped turning his wrist when the light in his bedroom popped on. Megan probably woke up when he pulled into the driveway and went to the master bedroom. She did that sometimes when he came home late. Kaden had pretty good ears, too, though, so maybe he had started crying. Either way, Hannah would hear the car's engine if he tried to leave.

Eventually, he reached for the door handle and noticed for the first time that his fingers trembled. He stared until the shaking subsided. That was new. As soon as he regained control of himself, Ash opened his door and felt the cold, early morning air hit him in the face. His breath came out as frost and the hairs on his face stood at attention. He wasn't drunk, but his head felt light and his body felt sluggish. He must have been hit harder than he realized.

He went through the kitchen door and locked it behind him, tiptoeing so he wouldn't disturb anyone. Hannah was in Kaden's nursery. She whispered that *Baba* was home before she resumed singing a Persian lullaby that her mother had probably sung to her. Ash didn't speak Persian, so Hannah could have been singing about anything in the world. It sounded nice, though.

He walked to their bedroom and sat listening. Hearing her sing the kids to sleep did more to put his world right than any drink ever could. When she finished, he vaulted up, kicked off his shoes, and pulled off his shirt so she wouldn't think he had been eavesdropping. He stretched and yawned in a vain attempt to seem nonchalant when she walked through the door. As soon as she saw him, Hannah covered her mouth and stopped moving.

"Am I that ugly?"

Hannah walked toward him, her eyes moist. Ash looked at himself in the mirror. He had several red and purple welts on his chest and rib cage, and one of his cheeks was swollen. Hannah had been a nurse for a number of years, so she knew how to check someone for injuries. She put her hands on his rib cage, feeling for breaks. Ash tried not to gasp, but he did anyway as his wife probed his sides. She jumped whenever he twitched.

"What happened?"

He started and stopped speaking twice before settling on a story. "It was barbecue day in the cafeteria at work, and you know how some of those guys get..." He couldn't finish the joke. "It was just something at work. Everything is okay."

She looked at her feet. "You always do that, you know? Every time something like this happens, you shut down or you make a joke."

"I don't want to worry you, especially for something unimportant like this."

Hannah closed her eyes, her shoulders rising and falling as she breathed.

"This isn't about worrying me. It's about you being reckless," she said, opening her eyes again. "When other people come home at night, they have dinner, they watch TV, and they play with their kids. When you come home—if you come home at all—I bandage you up and make sure your ribs aren't broken. That's not normal."

"I know it's not normal," he said. "But can we talk about this tomorrow? I'm exhausted, and I've got to get up early and go to work tomorrow. It's not a big deal."

Hannah jabbed one of the bruises on his rib cage with the index and middle fingers of her left hand. Ash gasped hard enough that he lost his breath; it felt like he had just been punched by an NFL linebacker. He leaned against the bed.

"You still think this isn't a big deal?" she asked. "If you were hit just a little harder, you'd have broken ribs and a broken orbital socket instead of bruises and a black eye. As is, your hundred-twenty-pound wife can double you over in pain with two fingers."

Ash breathed heavily before slowly dropping onto the bed.

"I'm sorry, then."

"What are you sorry for?" she asked.

"For getting hurt."

She jabbed at his side again, this time not quite as force-fully. It still nearly took his breath away.

"I'm not upset that you were hurt. I know what you do for a living, and I know you can get hurt at work. I'm upset because you're an idiot. Other people in your department don't come home like this, only you. I want to know why."

"I get the same cases other people do, and I do the same sort of job. I've got bad luck, I guess."

Hannah's eyes narrowed. "In the past eighteen months, our daughter was kidnapped by a drug dealer, your colleagues broke down our front door and arrested you, and now you were beaten up so badly you look like you got into a car accident. That's more than just bad luck. What are you doing?"

His bad luck theory did sound kind of shallow when she put it like that. He started to say something about the city's decreased budget and IMPD's need to do more with less, but that wasn't true, either. He waited until he could breathe easily before speaking.

"I don't know anymore. Sometimes I feel like I look for trouble."

Hannah blinked but didn't say anything for a moment. "What do you mean?"

He paused as his mind flashed to cases long since closed but never forgotten. He swallowed the memories back before standing up and shutting the door so their conversation wouldn't wake the kids.

"I went to Whitney Johnson's house this afternoon—she's

Cassandra's sister. Whitney was messed up. I mean, she was really messed up."

"Go on."

Ash swallowed. "Her son is a little older than Kaden. I picked him up because he was crying, and as soon as I did, I wanted to walk out and take him somewhere she couldn't ever find him again. If you're willing to let your infant sit in his own filth because you don't want to buy diapers, you don't deserve him."

Hannah's eyes softened. "What'd you do?"

Ash sighed. "The only thing I could. I called the police, and they arrested Whitney for possession," he said. "And that's the problem. I get up every morning, and I walk through the worst shit humanity can throw at me, and I'm supposed to forget about it on the drive home and pretend that nothing is wrong. I don't know if I can do that anymore. I'm getting tired of it."

"What do you want to do, then? Do you want to see a counselor? There might be somebody at work."

Ash chuckled, but there was no humor in it.

"We've got a whole counseling department, but they're worthless. You go to a counselor, and you sit in his office and talk about how you feel for an hour. I already know how I feel. I'm pissed off all the time, I'm hurt, and I'm disappointed. The worst is that I don't even know who to blame." Ash paused. "Cassandra Johnson was run down like some kid's lost dog. I can't stop thinking about that. She raised Lisa the best she could, she worked hard, she made a life for her family, and now she's dead. I don't know how to deal with that anymore. I just don't."

"Maybe you can take some time off. You can play with

Kaden in the day. You can take Megan to school. Maybe things will seem better if you get away from work for a while."

"I wish I could, but I don't have time." Hannah started to speak, but Ash gently squeezed her hand. "Thank you for listening, and I love you, but we need to go to bed."

"We'll talk again later, then."

"Sure."

They stayed on the end of the bed for another moment, not saying anything else. Eventually, Ash put on his pajamas and got beneath the covers. Hannah fell into bed beside him and shimmied until her back was pressed against his stomach. He wrapped his arms around her.

"You don't smell like alcohol tonight."

He had been naive to believe she didn't know about his drinking, but it still hurt to hear.

"I didn't drink anything."

"Promise me you'll quit."

"I'll do my best."

Ash slept until about nine the next morning, several hours later than he was accustomed to sleeping. He was called to prayer five times a day, once at dawn, once around noon, once in the afternoon, once at sunset, and once in the evening. The times change by a few minutes during the year, so he had an app on his cell phone to remind him of the proper prayer times. That app rather politely let him know that the sun had risen well over an hour ago, indicating that he had missed *salat al-Fajr*, dawn prayer, by the same length of time. While Ash may not have been the most pious man in the world, prayers were still a big part of his life. He hated skipping them.

He ignored his throbbing ribs and washed up in the bathroom before beginning the movements. Praying now wouldn't make up for what he had missed, but it felt right nonetheless. Unfortunately, as soon as he rolled up his prayer mat, the world came crashing back into focus.

The welts he had seen on his chest and back the night before had turned purple, and abrasions had formed on his palms where he had hit the asphalt. A small bruise had appeared under his right eye; it was likely the first sign of a world-class shiner. At least his attackers hadn't broken his nose. All in all, he had gotten off lucky with superficial injuries that would heal without leaving a mark. Hopefully he could avoid getting more.

Ash called out for Hannah or the kids, but no one answered, so he went to the kitchen. Hannah had left a note on the coffeemaker to let him know that she had taken the kids to the park so he could sleep in. She had even left him a pot of coffee. He glanced at the stainless-steel carafe and shuddered, knowing what was inside. He poured a cup anyway and sat down to think.

The people who had attacked him the night before went out of their way to avoid injuring him permanently. What's more, they knew he was armed, but they hadn't taken his gun. Both were out of character for street thugs. He didn't want to believe it, but the more he thought, the more the assessment he made the night before seemed correct. He had been attacked by cops. In Ash's time in the department, he had seen maybe a dozen legitimately bad cops, and none of them would have given him a warning; if he had gotten in their way, they would have shot him from behind as he crossed the parking lot. The guys who jumped him were up to something entirely different, and Ash didn't have a clue what they were doing or why.

He took a sip of coffee, trying to puzzle things out. Nothing fit, though. He had no idea what was in the files taken from Cassandra's house; he had no idea why someone would want Cassandra or Gillespie dead; he didn't even really know how or why the two of them knew each other. He was no further along than he had been when Konstantin Bukoholov showed up in his backyard three days ago, and it was starting to wear at him.

Ash finished his coffee, hopped in the shower, and then got dressed. With Gillespie's death confirmed, he figured he might as well see what Bowers had. He went back to the kitchen, grabbed his cell phone, and called Mike Bowers. Somebody picked up because Ash heard voices in the background, but before he could say anything, the call was disconnected. He tried again, but the call went straight to voice mail.

Asshole.

Rather than give up, Ash called the home number of Eddie Alvarez, hoping one of Bowers's detectives would be able to fill him in.

"Eddie, it's Ash Rashid. What's going on?"

"The usual. I'm getting the family ready to go to Mass. What can I do for you?"

"I'm trying to talk to your boss, but he keeps hanging up on me. You know where he's at?"

"You talkin' about Mike Bowers?"

"That's him."

Eddie clucked his tongue a few times. "Last I heard he's at a scene by some condos on the White River."

"You haven't heard anything about Carl Gillespie, have you?"

"Just that we pulled his body from the canal," said Eddie. "It's a shame he's dead, but he's low priority for now."

"He's retired IMPD. How can he be low priority?"

"You seen the news?" asked Eddie. "Kristen Tanaka's saying we've got a serial killer on our hands. Called him the White River Slasher. The city's going nuts."

"I've been out of the homicide loop for a little while, so correct me if I'm wrong, but don't you need multiple bodies over a period of time to have a serial killer?"

"As long as I'm getting overtime pay, Kristen Tanaka can call it whatever she wants."

Even when she wasn't sleeping with anyone, Tanaka still managed to screw him over.

"Are you going into work today?"

"I hope so," he said. "I'd like to get a couple of weekend hours in."

"If you hear anything about Carl Gillespie, give me a call."

"Will do. Later, Ash."

Eddie hung up the phone. With Bowers ignoring his calls, Ash's best way forward was out. Susan Mercer wouldn't like it, but he used an app on his phone to find the business line of John Meyers and Associates. Most private offices would be closed on a Sunday morning, but Meyers was going to trial in less than twenty-four hours on the Thomas Rahal case. He'd be in. A perky-sounding receptionist picked up the phone before the first ring ended. She put him on hold as soon as he introduced himself, and he waited for about ten minutes more for Meyers to answer.

"I've only got a few minutes, but what can I do for you, Detective?"

"I wanted to send my condolences. Carl Gillespie died too young."

"So he is dead."

Meyers's voice sounded tired.

"I assumed someone had told you."

"I'm not family, so I'm not on the list. Where's his body? My firm will take care of the funeral arrangements."

"I'm not handling the case, so you'll have to call the coroner's office. I wondered if you could tell me about Gillespie's relationship with Cassandra Johnson, though."

"I'm afraid I can't."

"Can't tell me because you've never heard of her, or…" Ash let his voice trail off, hoping Meyers would answer.

"I have heard of Ms. Johnson, but I can't say anything more about her."

"I've heard she was a secretary. Was she in your office?"

Meyers paused for another moment. "She's not on my payroll."

It was a classic lawyer's answer. Technically true, but completely unenlightening.

"Did she work for you or not?"

Meyers clucked his tongue, not saying anything. "I think you should come to my office. If you're trying to discover what happened to Carl, I have evidence you need to examine."

Ash rubbed his brow. The clock on his microwave said it was nearing ten, which meant he had already wasted an hour. He didn't know how much time he had to spend following up on leads that might not go anywhere.

"And this isn't something we can do over the phone?" asked Ash.

"You need to see this in person, Detective. Trust me."

Ash sighed.

"All right. I'll be over in about twenty minutes."

John M. Meyers and Associates occupied the entire thirty-eighth floor of an office building about a block away from the prosecutor's office. Ash didn't know how many associates Meyers actually had, but they must have done well to afford the real estate. One of his friends from law school had started his own practice after graduating and said the rent on his office ran somewhere around fourteen hundred a month for eight hundred square feet in a lousy neighborhood. Meyers had at least ten times that amount of space in one of the most expensive buildings in town. Crime does pay for some people, evidently.

He took the elevator to Meyers's floor. Mahogany paneling covered the walls, but the furniture was metal and leather. Everything in the place looked expensive, including the very attractive receptionists behind the front desk. Ash ignored them for the moment and memorized the faces of two men in business suits waiting in the lobby. They may have been sales reps or attorneys, but he figured anyone else requiring a Sunday morning meeting with a defense attorney was worth studying.

Once the suits noticed him, Ash walked to the front desk

and leaned against the counter. "I'm Detective Sergeant Ash Rashid with IMPD. I'm here to see John Meyers."

"Do you have an appointment?"

"He asked me to come over. It's about Carl Gillespie."

She smiled at him. "How is Carl? I haven't seen him for a few days."

Ash wasn't quite sure how to respond at first. Maybe Meyers was waiting to tell the staff all at once.

"He's been better. That's really about all I can say right now."

"If you see him, wish him well for us. Can I get you a cup of coffee while you wait for Mr. Meyers?"

Again, Ash wasn't quite sure how to respond. He had spent his entire career in the public sector, and in that time he had met hundreds of office assistants and receptionists. Most were as surly as drunken sailors who hadn't been laid in months, and none had ever offered him a cup of coffee.

"Sure. Coffee would be nice."

The receptionist smiled and winked at him before picking up the phone and requesting someone send coffee service to the lobby. He was truly a stranger in a strange land. He sat at one of the leather chairs opposite the two men in suits he had spotted earlier. Within about a minute and a half, a young woman carried an earthenware coffee cup to the lobby. Maybe something could be said for the private sector after all.

John Meyers showed up ten minutes later. Ash had never seen him out of a suit before, but he now wore a pair of jeans and a blue striped Oxford shirt. Sundays must be casual. As soon as he drew close enough to shake Meyers's hand, Ash noticed that the whites of his eyes were very slightly streaked with red and he smelled peaty, a decent scotch if Ash had to guess. Apparently lawyers and police officers grieve in similar fashion. Ash followed him past the wall separating the lobby from the office space in back.

"Thank you for coming," he said. "And I'm sorry for the wait. I just learned of an incident involving one of my long-term clients. I had to send one of my associates to take care of it."

Aside from the bloodbath at the condo, nothing major had been reported the night before. Whatever his client had done couldn't have been too serious. "DUI or possession of narcotics?"

Meyers glanced at him, his brows drawn together. "I'm sorry?"

"DUI or possession?"

"DUI," said Meyers, shaking his head as if to clear it. "He called his wife and asked her to call us. She refused, so he spent the night in the drunk tank."

"That's a bad weekend."

"There have been a lot of those going around."

They stepped past the wall separating the lobby from the rest of the floor, giving Ash his first behind-the-scenes look at John Meyers and Associates. The individual offices were separated by glass partitions with black privacy shades, while a common space with tables and chairs dominated the center of the room. Everything was chic and modern. Despite it being a Sunday, staff members ambled from office to office, more often than not talking into cell phones. The room may have lacked the historic charm of IMPD's headquarters, but it had a functioning climate-control system, and that counted for a lot. Ash tried not to look impressed.

They eventually stopped beside an office on the far side of the room. Gillespie's name was etched in neat script on a brass plaque beside the door. Unlike the other offices nearby, the room was dark and its privacy blinds had been drawn. "This is Carl's office. Please try to be respectful."

Ash gave the door a once-over, not quite sure what Meyers wanted him to see. "What do you want me to see?"

"Take a closer look," said Meyers.

Ash obliged and knelt down. "I don't see anything interesting."

"Keep that in mind," said Meyers, opening the door and exposing an office with thick, beige carpet and floor-to-ceiling windows overlooking Monument Circle. It was the very heart of the city. Evidently Carl Gillespie's post-law-enforcement career was going well; he had one of the best offices on the floor. Ash walked inside and felt his feet sink into the plush carpet. The room was roughly twenty by twenty, making it bigger than his first apartment in college. Gillespie had either done a lot of things well or had found skeletons in Meyers's closet the older lawyer wanted to keep hidden. Ash leaned toward the latter.

"I'm not really seeing anything," said Ash.

"Just keep looking," said Meyers. "I want to see if your reaction is the same as mine."

"Sure," said Ash. Gillespie's furniture matched the mahogany woodwork in the rest of the office. He walked around the desk in the center of the floor and pulled out Gillespie's chair. There were scratch marks on the wood. Ash looked at

Meyers for some reaction, but the lawyer didn't even blink, apparently content that Ash would find whatever there was to find.

Ash pushed the chair aside so he could get a better look at the furniture. Whoever scratched the desk focused on the center drawer, the only one with a lock. Ash tried to pull it open, but the drawer slides were off, causing the side of the drawer to dig into the wood.

He stopped and looked up. "Is this what you wanted me to see?"

Meyers nodded. "Yeah. And before you open it, don't bother. It's empty," he said. He pointed to the rest of the furniture in the room. "So are his file cabinets and the bookshelves."

Two offices connected to his case had been robbed so far, but this was a new twist. Anyone who could break a window and climb inside could rob a house, but it took a lot more to rob a busy workplace, especially one like Meyers's office. He probably had lawyers and paralegals in his office twenty-four hours a day, so a thief would have to be inconspicuous enough to get past not only building security, but also the office staff. He'd also have to get inside Gillespie's office without marking the door or drawing attention to himself, which meant he probably had a key. It sounded like an inside job.

"Has anyone stopped showing up to work in the past day or two?"

"I thought it may have been one of my employees, too, but they're all accounted for," said Meyers, already turning to leave the room. "I do have something else to show you, though."

Ash had been reluctant to follow him earlier, but now

Meyers had his full attention. They walked the length of the office but stopped at the receptionist's desk in the lobby. Meyers called the building's chief of security, Keith Silberman. Evidently Silberman had been waiting for the call because he stepped off the elevator within thirty seconds. He wore a black suit, a white Oxford shirt, and a bright red tie. After a round of introductions, Ash took Meyers aside so he could speak to him in private before leaving.

"Carl Gillespie was killed for something he did in this office. I'm not asking for specifics, but give me a name. What case was he on before he died?"

Meyers considered before answering. "Thomas Rahal."

"And what did Cassandra Johnson have to do with that case?"

"I'm sorry, but I can't say."

Ash flicked his eyes toward Silberman. The security chief stared at them and shifted his weight impatiently. Ash ignored him.

"I understand your privacy concerns, but both Cassandra and Gillespie are dead. I respect your duty to your clients, but bodies are starting to stack up. Was Cassandra a witness, a client, or something else? You can at least tell me that."

"I appreciate your position, Detective Rashid, but I've said all I can. Carl was a friend of mine. Believe me, I want the people who killed him caught as badly as you do. I'm not willing to violate my clients' confidence to do that, though."

Meyers wasn't explicit, but he had given part of an answer at least. An attorney's client roster is only confidential in rare circumstances, and Ash doubted they were in one. That meant Cassandra wasn't a client, and Meyers was covering for someone else. He stared at Meyers, hoping he'd say something else, but the lawyer kept his mouth shut. Eventually, Ash thanked him for his time and headed out of the office with Silberman following a few steps behind.

As soon as they stepped into the elevator, Silberman used a key to access the service panel below the rows of buttons that led to the building's various floors. He pressed a normally inaccessible red button, and the elevator shot downward fast enough that Ash had to grab the rail bolted to the elevator's silver walls to keep from falling.

Silberman nodded at him. "Our elevators take some getting used to. Before we slowed them down, going from the top floor to the basement felt like the Tower of Terror ride at Disney World. The kids in the day care on the second floor loved it."

Ash gripped the handrail and did his best not to look uncomfortable. While he didn't have a problem with heights, he wasn't a big fan of falling from them either, and it felt deceptively like that's what they were doing. He shifted his weight.

"My daughter would love this. Why are we going to the basement?"

"Mr. Meyers wanted you to see some of our surveillance video." Silberman paused and tilted his head to the side. "You're Ash Rashid, aren't you?"

"Yeah. Have we met before?"

Silberman resumed staring at the electronic display showing their descent. "No, but I saw you in the paper last year. You arrested Jack Whittler, right?"

"Something like that."

Truthfully, Ash hadn't arrested anyone. He saw Jack Whittler, the former prosecutor, at an illegal card game hosted by Konstantin Bukoholov and then told a couple of FBI agents he happened to run into. They arrested Whittler a few days later. The department's public relations team had made it look like Ash was part of a multiagency, anticorruption task force, but in actuality, he just got lucky. As far as he could tell, he had used his lifetime's allotment in that case.

The elevator slowed to a stop at a sub-basement three floors below the lobby, and the doors opened onto what Ash could only surmise was a bomb shelter. A concrete hallway ran for fifty or sixty feet in front of him with rooms jutting off to the left and right. Silberman exited and Ash followed behind, his footsteps echoing in the enclosed space. Someone had posted pictures of a hot-air balloon race on the walls, but rather than brightening the place, the cheery, colorful imagery seemed to enhance and magnify the gloom.

They passed three closed doors before coming to a large, open room with a dozen flat-screen video monitors attached to the front wall. The lights were muted and low, but despite being several floors underground, the air smelled fresh. It must have been pumped from the surface. Silberman walked inside first, but Ash followed closely. Two men monitored the video feeds. One wore a guard's uniform, while the second wore a black T-shirt and a pair of jeans.

"Bring up the footage on John Doe," said Silberman. The man in the T-shirt spun around and nodded before scooting his chair to a nearby computer terminal. Ash couldn't see what he did, but the video shifted to a split-screen view of the building's lobby. It was evening in the image, so it wasn't a live feed. A moment after the video showed up, a man stepped into the frame. He pushed a janitor's cart and wore a pair of light blue coveralls and an Indianapolis Colts cap that cast a shadow over his features.

Ash watched but grew increasingly impatient as little interesting happened. "I presume this is going somewhere important."

"You'll see in a minute," said Silberman, his lips thin.

Ash crossed his arms and waited but didn't say anything else. Someone had edited the video because the picture shifted from camera to camera, following the Colts fan around the building. He took the main elevator to Meyers's floor and walked straight inside, never giving the security cameras a clear shot of his face. Ash would have attributed that to bad luck and poor camera placement, but his movements were too deliberate. Whenever he approached a camera, he'd hunch his shoulders over, duck his head, and stare at his cart of supplies, thereby obscuring his face. Once, he even took off his hat, ostensibly to wipe sweat off his forehead, but in the process, he blocked his profile from a camera hidden behind a planter—he knew where the cameras were.

"Is the rest of the film like this?"

"Yeah. We never even got close to a clear shot. We don't have cameras in Mr. Meyers's office, but we suspect this is the guy who broke in. Nobody even thought to stop him because he dressed like one of our janitors, and he seemed to know where he was going."

Ash's first thought was to suggest Silberman hire competent security people in the future, but he held back.

"When was this taken?" asked Ash.

"Two nights ago."

The same day Cassandra Johnson was run down.

"I'm going to need a list of everyone who knows where your cameras are. I'd also like a copy of this footage."

"I guarantee that no one on my crew did this. Everyone on my staff is former IMPD or sheriff's department."

"Any of them from the Northeastern Precinct?"

Silberman paused for a second. "A few."

That's what Ash expected. "Good. Fax the list to the prosecutor's office. And while you're at it, I'll need your contact information in case I need to call you."

"Of course," said Silberman, reaching into his jacket and pulling out a silver carrying case for business cards. He took one off the small stack and handed it to Ash. "Anything else?"

Ash put the business card in his wallet and then looked at Silberman. "You said you worked with some guys out of the Northeastern. You know Noah Stuart, by chance?"

Silberman brightened and nodded. "Yeah, he's tight with a couple of my guys. Comes by maybe once or twice a week."

"The next time you see him, can you let him know that I was here and that I hope to run into him in a parking lot sometime soon? It's an inside joke. He'll know what that means."

Silberman raised his eyebrows. "Um, sure."

"Thanks."

Ash left the basement, leaving behind a clearly confused security chief. At least no one could accuse him of running away from a fight.

12

It was a few minutes after noon by the time he made it outside, and his eyelids were starting to droop. On most days, a walk outside would have revived him, but after his evening the night before, he wanted something a bit stronger. He walked to a coffee shop near Monument Circle and ordered four shots of espresso and enough steamed milk to fill the largest to-go cup they had. The resulting drink wasn't quite as strong as Hannah's coffee, but it was a close approximation. Ash took the drink outside and sat at a cast-iron table on the sidewalk to think.

Bells from a nearby church rang, and well-dressed people milled about on the sidewalk. Christ's Church Cathedral must have just let out. Ash smiled at the churchgoers who acknowledged his presence but he ignored the rest, letting his mind wander. Every thought he had kept drifting back to one conclusion: Northeastern police officers murdered Carl Gillespie and Cassandra Johnson because they discovered something about the Thomas Rahal trial.

The theory fit the evidence, and yet it didn't make sense. Thomas Rahal shot and killed a Northeastern police officer in front of half a dozen witnesses. The arresting officers found a literal smoking gun in his hand. There was nothing for Gillespie or Cassandra to find. Ash sat thinking long enough for his coffee to grow cold and bitter. He choked it down before standing and heading toward his office. Susan Mercer wouldn't like it, but they needed to talk. On a normal Sunday, she'd be at home. This close to trial, she'd be preparing for her case. She might even sleep in the office that night. Ash took the elevator to her floor and walked to her office. Her door was open, but Ash knocked on the frame anyway.

"It's open."

As soon as he opened the door, Susan dropped the papers she had been holding and leaned back in her chair. She crossed her arms.

"You look terrible. Why does your face look like that?"

"My father was a pious but ugly man. It's not my fault." Susan raised an eyebrow. Ash's mom had done the same thing when he was a kid and made up a story in order to avoid getting in trouble. He considered telling her the truth but dismissed the idea. If he told her he had been beaten up by men he suspected were cops, she'd turn over the entire case to Internal Affairs. He wasn't ready for that yet, not until he found out what was going on. "I fell down the stairs. What do you want me to say?"

Susan picked up her papers, shaking her head. "You hung up on me the last time we spoke on the phone."

"Must have been a bad connection," said Ash, speaking quickly. "Did you hear that we pulled Carl Gillespie's body out of a canal last night?"

Susan nodded.

"Did you also hear someone broke into John Meyers's office and stole Gillespie's files?"

Susan laced her fingers in front of her and shifted in her seat. "No, I didn't hear that. How did you hear it?"

Ash cleared his throat and looked over Susan's shoulder at the window behind her. The news hadn't said anything about rain, but the sky was darkening.

"John Meyers told me."

Almost all the color drained out of Susan's face.

"We're going to trial tomorrow morning. Please enlighten me as to why you saw him without bothering to tell me first."

At least Ash's instincts weren't off; that was about the reaction he had expected.

"You remember the hit-and-run case I told you about on Friday? It's branched off in an unexpected direction."

Susan blinked, but her aggressive posture didn't soften. "Explain this unexpected direction."

Ash pointed to a well-worn, file-covered chair in front of Susan's desk. She nodded, so he moved the papers and sat down.

"I told you before that Carl Gillespie and Cassandra John-son, the hit-and-run victim, spoke on the phone at least half a dozen times. When I went to Cassandra's house on Fri-day afternoon, I found a file box full of documents from the Rahal trial. Since that time, someone broke into her home and removed the files. Since then, we've found Carl Gillespie's body and discovered that someone broke into his office and stole his files on the Rahal trial. Think about that. Cassandra was investigating the Rahal trial, Gillespie was investigating the Rahal trial, and now they're both dead and everything they've discovered has been stolen."

"Did you ask John Meyers about Cassandra?"

"I did. He claimed privilege."

She exhaled through her nose and nodded. "With Gillespie dead, Meyers will request a continuance in the Rahal trial. This is going to ruin my whole week."

Ash tilted his head to the side. "If Meyers asks for a continuance, don't fight it. Something is wrong with your case. I've got two bodies connected to it so far. That's a problem."

Susan narrowed her gaze. "Don't go there unless you've got something better than a hunch. Thomas Rahal murdered a police officer. I'm going to make sure he gets a needle in his arm for it. Of all people, you should appreciate that."

Ash's shoulder twitched involuntarily, causing an ache to spread across his chest. Susan was right about part of that. A couple of years back, he and an old partner tried to serve a high-risk felony warrant on a murder suspect, but before they reached his house, the suspect opened fire on them with a hunting rifle. Ash was hit in the shoulder, but his partner was shot in the neck. Even if they had been in the best hospital in the world, there wasn't a damn thing the doctors could have done.

"If Rahal murdered a cop, I'll put his lights out myself. Delaying the trial for a week won't hurt your case, though."

Susan leaned forward. "I know this isn't your field, so I'll explain things using small words. I have a jury. If I allow John Meyers to delay our trial on the very first day, some members of the jury will be upset because we wasted their time. Others, though, will start to question why we're delaying things. They'll think my case is weak and judge it before I've even started. In short, it will hurt my case."

"What do you want me to do, then?" asked Ash, crossing his arms. "Pretend I didn't find anything?"

"No. I want you to keep investigating your two victims.

Something is wrong, but it's not with my case. I've got five witnesses—all police officers—who saw Thomas Rahal shoot Officer Ryan Dixon, I've got forensic evidence that backs up their accounts, and what's more, I've got a signed confession. Rahal murdered Ryan Dixon, and I'm going to make sure he pays for that. End of story."

"If the case is so clear, why are Cassandra Johnson and Carl Gillespie dead?"

Susan shrugged. "I don't know. Maybe they were sleeping together and someone didn't like it. Maybe they were extorting money from someone and their mark got tired of paying. Maybe their deaths are just a coincidence. It could be anything. Your job is to figure it out."

"If you're so confident in your case, let me look at your files. If there's nothing in there, you've got nothing to lose."

Susan started to say something, but then she caught herself. "I don't have time to argue with you. If you want information, talk to Charity Lewis. She knows as much about the case as I do."

"Thank you."

Ash turned to leave but stopped when he heard Susan clear her throat.

"I've been thinking about what happened at the city council meeting yesterday. For the good of your career, you should request a transfer. I'll sign off on wherever you want to go, but if you stay here, Leonard is going to draw you into his campaign. You don't want that."

"Where would I go?"

"I've heard the vice squad will have an opening for a sergeant soon. If you want, you could even sit for a lieutenant's exam. You've got enough years on the job, you've got the educational background, and you'd have my recommendation. One of the lieutenants in Homicide is going to be promoted to captain within a year, so you could apply for his position. I'd recommend you for it, and I bet he'd be willing to recommend you, too."

"I went to law school because I wanted to become a prosecutor. You know that. You steered me in that direction, and I wouldn't have done it without you. Now you're telling me that's not going to happen?"

"Maybe in a couple of years. It's gotten political now, though. If I hire you, it'll look like I'm trying to buy you off. It'll make you look bad, and it will make me look bad. If I transfer you, it'll look like punishment. I need you to do this for yourself."

Instead of answering, Ash stood. "This isn't politics. This is bullshit, and you know it."

"Yeah, it is, and you can complain about it or you can work with the system. That's up to you."

"Doesn't sound like I have much of a choice."

"No, you don't."

He walked toward the door, but stopped before going out. "I'll think about it."

"Make up your mind soon, or I'll have to make it up for you."

He said he would and then shut the door. Decisions about his career would have to wait; he had work to do. He hadn't worked with Charity Lewis much, but he knew her in passing. She was in her early thirties and had dyed blond hair with brunette roots. She had a lilting, Southern accent, which was more than a little disarming and more than a little charming. Juries liked her, especially the men. She smiled when he walked toward her cubicle, exposing even, white teeth.

"I was just about to grab some lunch. What can I do for you, Detective?"

"I'm looking into a few things possibly related to the Thomas Rahal case. Susan said you know the evidence."

She pushed her chair back from the table and crossed her legs, exposing a large swath of tanned skin. Maybe male jury members liked more than her accent.

"Sure, I've got a few minutes."

"I'd like a rundown of the entire case."

Charity's smile faltered. "Did you clear this with Susan?"

He nodded. "She gave me your name."

Charity glanced at her watch. "I hoped to get lunch."

"I'll buy you a sandwich."

They went to a deli nearby. Charity had pastrami on rye, and Ash had grilled cheese with tomatoes and pesto. Somebody must have ordered a BLT because the entire room smelled like bacon. Islam forbids the consumption of pork products because pigs are unclean animals, but even still, Ash loved the smell. He had accidentally eaten a slice at a greasy spoon diner when he was a teenager. It might have been the greatest gastronomic experience of his life; the turkey bacon he ate on a regular basis was a pale imitation. Nothing in the world would make Ash leave his faith, but sometimes he wished God had given pigs a better sense of cleanliness.

After eating, Ash pushed aside the empty basket that had held his sandwich and took a pen and notepad from his pocket. Charity straightened and took a sip of water before nodding at him to begin.

"So tell me about the Thomas Rahal case."

Charity wrapped the second half of her sandwich with the butcher paper in which it had been packaged before answering.

"How much do you know?"

"Pretend you're talking to someone who attends the same mosque as the suspect and has avoided the case as much as possible."

"Sure," she said, drawing in a breath and composing herself. "From the beginning, the Rahal case was simple. Detectives from the Northeastern Precinct heard reports of Mr. Rahal selling drugs out of his home, so they utilized their network of confidential informants to make three separate narcotics purchases on three separate occasions. They used these drug buys to secure warrants for Mr. Rahal's arrest and a search of his residence."

Ash shifted, nodding and writing notes. He didn't want to doubt the case, but the facts didn't sit well with him. Every religion, including Islam, was full of hypocrites, but Rahal wasn't one of them. He went to Friday prayer; his family took part in community activities; he even participated on the mosque's outreach committee. Drug dealing didn't fit. Ash tried not to let his incredulity show, but it likely came through anyway. Charity took it in stride.

"I need names. Who made the drug buys?"

Charity paused and rooted through a bag she had brought with her. When she looked up again, she had a paper in her hand.

"The same CI made each buy. I don't have his name, but

he was listed as confidential informant number zero-eight-one-four. We don't plan to call him to the stand."

Ash wrote the information down.

"So far, so good," he said, clearing his throat. "Who filled out the affidavit for the search warrant?"

"Lieutenant Noah Stuart of the Northeastern Precinct."

Noah and his buddies certainly kept busy. He wrote the information down.

"Please go on."

Charity nodded before continuing. "Once the warrant was secured, our team entered at approximately one in the morning on July twenty-first and cleared the home room by room. Officers found Mr. Rahal hiding under his daughter's crib in the nursery. They ordered him to surrender, but he refused. He then fatally shot Officer Ryan Dixon with an unregistered semiautomatic handgun. Believing Mr. Rahal held his infant daughter hostage, our officers backed off.

"At that point, we contacted Mr. Rahal's wife, who worked in the housekeeping department of a bank downtown. Officers drove her from her work to her home at which point she convinced her husband to surrender. Those officers then brought Mr. Rahal back to the station where, after being advised of his rights, he confessed."

Ash leaned back. If the case was as straightforward as Charity presented it, Meyers wouldn't have taken it on. He'd earn publicity, but he'd lose the trial. She was holding back on him.

"During the search of the home, did our officers find any drugs?"

Charity nodded. "We found two ounces of marijuana and thirty-two oxycodone pills."

Ash wrote down the amounts and leaned back in his chair. "So he's a drug dealer, but he's only got about two hundred bucks' worth of weed and maybe three hundred bucks' worth of pills?"

Charity nodded. "We suspect he flushed the rest of his stash after the police announced their arrival but before they stormed the building."

"What did Mr. Rahal confess to?"

Charity's eyes swept up and to the left. "We have a transcript somewhere," she said, her voice drawn out and slow. "But I believe he admitted to lying in wait in order to murder a police officer. I don't remember the exact language he used, but that was the gist of it. Two hours after he confessed, we charged him with murder in the first degree with aggravating circumstances."

"So you're going for the death penalty."

"It was Susan Mercer's call, but I agree with it."

"Okay," said Ash, reserving judgment until he had more facts. "Does tech services have the video of the interrogation and confession?"

Charity shook her head. "We're not focusing on the interrogation and confession videos," she said. "Judge Haller ruled in a pretrial motion that they were unduly prejudicial, so she excluded them. Instead, we're focusing on the transcripts. I can get you copies if you want."

Ash had to give credit where it was due; juries love confessions. Having the confession video excluded was a major legal victory. Maybe Meyers actually was worth whatever he charged.

"How'd Meyers get the confession pulled?"

Charity faltered. "Susan motioned to have the video excluded," she said.

"Oh?" said Ash, cocking his head to the side.

Charity shifted in her seat. "Mr. Rahal was in pretty rough shape by the time he was brought in."

Ash leaned back and crossed his arms. "Let me guess. He resisted arrest."

"Yeah," she said, her voice low.

Ash blinked and shook his head, annoyed. He wasn't against a rough interrogation in principle if it got the right information, but it was bad business in actual practice. If a judge saw a suspect come into his court with broken fingers and bruises on his face, he'd throw out the interrogation, he'd pressure IMPD to investigate the officers involved, and he might even let the suspect walk free. It was stupid. At least the officers involved hadn't lynched Rahal on the front lawn. That was progress, Ash supposed.

"Even though it's not in the trial, I want the video. I assume tech services has it?"

Charity shifted again. "They've had technical problems," she said. "The video and all backups containing it were deleted from the county's servers."

Like every detective, Ash had heard the rumors. The right amount of money to the right tech in the IT department could make anything from the department's servers disappear, no questions asked. As often as he had heard that, though, he hadn't heard of it actually happening. Maybe John Meyers had taken the case for a reason.

"Do you get the sense that you're missing something?"

Charity shook her head. "None whatsoever. Mr. Rahal and his infant daughter were the only people in the home at the time of his arrest, and several officers saw him shoot Ryan Dixon.

Even if he was treated roughly—and I'm not saying he was—
Mr. Rahal is as guilty as they come. You can count on that."

"I'm going to need to talk to Rahal. Are we holding him
downtown?"

"Yeah, but there's no way John Meyers will let you talk
to him."

Ash pulled his cell phone from his pocket and started
thumbing through the list of recently made calls. He found
Meyers's number.

"You'd be surprised at how persuasive I can be," he said,
waiting through two rings before someone picked up. Charity
looked incredulous, but Ash ignored her. Meyers must have
told his receptionists to expect his call because they patched
him to their boss's office as soon as he introduced himself.
Within three minutes, he had the meeting set up. Meyers was
busy prepping for the trial, but he agreed to send one of his
associates to supervise the interview in two hours. When he
hung up, Charity raised her eyebrows, smiling smugly.

"Is Meyers going to let you talk to him?"

"Yeah," said Ash, sliding out of the booth. "I'm going to
meet one of his junior associates in two hours."

The smile slipped from Charity's lips. "You're serious?"

Ash put his phone back in his pocket. "I tried to tell you.
I'm very persuasive."

"I need to prepare," said Charity, all traces of merriment
gone from her face. "I need to be there. This is my case."

Ash was pretty sure it was Susan's case, but he didn't want
to argue the point.

"Good luck, and I'll see you then. In the meantime, I've
got work to do."

13

Ash left the diner and started walking to IMPD's headquarters. Charity and Susan may have been confident
in their case, but if it were as simple as they thought, Cassandra Johnson and Carl Gillespie would still be alive. They
were missing something, and while a two-hour break before
his meeting with Rahal wasn't much, it was still too much
time to waste. About halfway to his destination, Ash took
out his phone and dialed Mike Bowers's office to see if the
lieutenant was in. Thankfully, he was, so Ash jogged the
rest of the way.

Bowers had a private corner office on the third floor of
IMPD's headquarters. He didn't have much of a view, but at
least he had windows. Ash didn't even have walls. When he
arrived, Bowers sat behind his desk, writing a report. Ash
coughed, getting his attention from the doorway. The lieutenant glanced up and dropped his pen before nodding to
one of the chairs in front of his desk.

"I heard you were looking for me," he said.

Thanks for calling me back, then.

"How's that mass-murder-in-the-condo thing going?"

Bowers grunted. "Found out our condo is the builder's
model, and every high-end real estate agent in town has

access to it. Haven't found a single clear print in the whole place. It's a dead end so far."

"You find the victims yet?"

Bowers nodded, his gaze focused above Ash's shoulder. "Close the door."

Ash did as he was asked before taking a seat on one of the chairs in front of Bowers's desk.

"I've got the lab working nonstop on the case, but they're backlogged, and DNA results will take a couple of weeks," he said. He paused and ran his hand across his scalp. "I think the blood was a prank."

"What do you mean?"

"You heard me," said Bowers, shaking his head. "We've found six distinct blood types in the house so far. That's not a family—it's a dance club."

"And you don't think you have six victims?"

Bowers shook his head again but didn't meet Ash's gaze.

"Got a report this morning that a bunch of kids stole a cooler of blood from a blood drive at a church in Zionsville yesterday. I've wasted almost two hundred man-hours on a goddamn high school prank. What kind of sick kids break into a condo, throw blood all over the walls, and pretend to be serial killers? Who does that?"

"You talked to them yet?"

"Little shits lawyered up as soon as one of my detectives started asking questions."

Neither Bowers nor Ash said anything for a moment.

"Have you done anything else on Gillespie yet?"

Rather than answer, Bowers thumbed through papers on his desk and pulled out a folded stack of blue carbon paper.

"Search warrant for his house."

Ash unfolded the papers and read the first few lines. It looked like IMPD's standard warrant for searching a victim's home. The language was straight boilerplate; the detective requesting the warrant just filled in his name and qualifications, the location to be searched, and the probable cause. He folded the papers and put them down.

"When are you guys going?"

Bowers glanced at his watch. "As soon as I get all my guys together."

"I'll meet you and secure the home's exterior," said Ash, already standing. He almost reached the door before Bowers cleared his throat, getting his attention. Ash turned so he could see him.

"I trust you'll stay out of the house."

"Do you think I'm stupid enough to go into a murder victim's home without backup?"

Bowers leaned forward, resting his elbows on his desk. "You really want me to answer that?"

Ash knew he walked into that one, so he probably deserved the response. He didn't leave, though.

"What if the blood wasn't just a prank?"

Bowers smiled wistfully and leaned back. "We'd have a psycho on our hands, and happy days would be here again."

"I didn't mean that, either," said Ash, shaking his head. "Think about this. Ever since you found the condo, the Gillespie investigation has pretty much stopped. What if that was the point?"

Bowers stared at him for about fifteen or twenty seconds before tilting his head to the side and furrowing his brow.

"Are you guys bored in the prosecutor's office?" he asked. "I've heard rumors, you know. Do you guys sit around, thinking shit like this up all day? If so, I have paperwork you can fill out. I can give you some work if you need it."

Ash shook his head and started out. "Thanks, Mike."

He took the elevator downstairs and walked to his car. He had already been to Gillespie's house once, so he had little difficulty finding it again. Unfortunately, he wasn't alone when he arrived. There was a marked police cruiser on the street out front and an unmarked Dodge Charger in the driveway. Probably having heard Ash's car, Lieutenant Noah Stuart and two uniformed officers walked from the backyard to the drive as Ash parked. They stopped walking when they saw his car.

As the men came closer, Ash recognized one of the uniformed officers as Joe Cartwright, but the other was a stranger. Cartwright had a limp. That didn't prove that he had been on the receiving end of a kick in Cassandra Johnson's house, but it didn't help his case much, either. Whether they had been involved in his beating or not, Gillespie's home was a crime scene, and police officers from a neighboring precinct had no business being there. It was Ash's job to secure the scene, and he sure as hell was going to do it.

He stepped out of his car and pulled his firearm from its shoulder holster.

"This is an active crime scene. What are you doing here?"

"I might ask you the same thing, Detective," said Noah, putting his hands to the sides so his men would stop.

"I'm doing my job. Identify yourselves for my report."

"You know who we are, Rashid," said Cartwright, taking a step forward. "Why don't you grow a pair and put that gun away? We can settle this as men."

"Three against one is probably fair considering the

competition, but I think I'll stick to doing my job. Nice limp, by the way."

Cartwright took another limping step forward, but Noah put a hand on his shoulder to hold him back.

"We're not here to cause trouble," said Noah. "Carl Gillespie was one of my sergeants fifteen years ago, and I came by to see if I could help with the investigation into his death."

"I'm sure Gillespie would appreciate that. If you tell me the new guy's name, I'll make sure my report mentions you. Lieutenant Bowers will keep you informed."

"Like I said before, you know who we are," said Cartwright. "We're here to help. We look out for each other in our precinct. I wouldn't expect you to understand."

Ash ignored Cartwright and nodded toward the sole officer he didn't recognize.

"Who are you?"

The officer looked to Noah before answering. "Patrick Dixon."

The voice was vaguely familiar, but Ash couldn't quite place it.

"Any relation to Ryan Dixon? The guy Thomas Rahal shot?"

Dixon's back stiffened and his nostrils flared as he exhaled. "He was my older brother."

After hearing it again, Ash recognized the voice. Dixon had threatened Ash and his family in IMPD's parking lot the night before.

"I'm sorry about your brother. It's a tragedy whenever an officer dies."

"Thank you."

"No problem," said Ash, tilting his head to the side and looking back to Cartwright. "I can't blame you for watching out for your own. If someone even tried to hurt my family, I'd put a bullet in him without a second thought." Ash panned his gaze over the officers before settling on Dixon. "I'm sure I'll see you guys later."

Ash couldn't tell if Dixon or the rest of them picked up on his message, but he had a hard time believing they hadn't. He wasn't subtle. The officers piled into their cars and left the scene, giving Ash a moment alone. He felt more numb than anything else, like his brain just gave up and stopped trying to process everything he was feeling rather than try to focus on any specific emotion.

He holstered his firearm and sat in the front seat to wait for Bowers and the rest of his crew. They arrived in a caravan about ten minutes later. Bowers parked behind Ash's cruiser on the street while the evidence technicians and other uniformed officers parked wherever they could find space. Ash considered telling the lieutenant about the early arrivals but decided against it. He didn't want to bring anyone into his investigation until he figured out who he could trust.

While Bowers and his team searched the house, Ash stayed outside and watched the neighbors. Most left after watching for a few minutes, but one stayed on the edge of Gillespie's lawn. She was in her late thirties and had brown hair and a trim figure. She fidgeted when he started toward her, but she didn't walk away.

"Did you know Mr. Gillespie?" he asked, nodding toward the home.

"I, uh, yes . . . well, not really. Not well, at least." She licked her lips. "Is he okay?"

"Unfortunately, no. We found his body last night, and we're trying to piece together what happened."

She took a step back and flinched as if something had hit her.

"Are you okay?" he asked.

She swallowed and nodded, so Ash got out his notebook and started an interview. Her name was Lynn Meister, and she lived two houses down. When he pressed her on her relationship with Gillespie, she said they barely knew each other. Judging by her reaction to his death, there was more to it than that, but Ash wasn't ready to push it yet.

"Did you see Carl often?"

"He was a neighbor, so I saw him get his mail almost every day. Sometimes we'd talk, but not all the time."

"When was the last time you saw him getting his mail?"

"Maybe a week ago."

"Are you married?"

Lynn stuttered before answering. To her, it probably seemed like a random question. It was, but it was also calculated. Everybody lies. It's one of the few truisms of police work. He didn't think Lynn had anything to do with Gillespie's death, but she'd still lie to him to protect her husband, her kids, herself. A random question every now and then prevents a witness from being able to anticipate a line of questioning and think of answers in advance. It may not have been able to keep someone from lying to him, but it usually made the lies easier to spot.

"Yeah."

"What's your spouse's name?"

"Isaac Meister. He's an attorney."

"If he's anything like the lawyers I know, he's probably at the office a lot." She nodded, but there wasn't a lot of enthusiasm behind it. Ash smiled again, hoping to reassure her. "I work in the prosecutor's office, and some of my colleagues sleep more often in their offices than they do at home."

"It's what you have to do if you want to become partner. Or whatever prosecutors want to do."

"That it is," said Ash. "So you saw Carl get the mail about a week ago. Is that the last time you saw him?" Lynn didn't respond either verbally or otherwise. "It's important that I get an accurate timeline. When was the last time you saw him?"

Ash waited for about a minute. Lynn wouldn't meet his eyes, and when she spoke, her voice was soft.

"Three days ago."

"Was he alone?"

Ash waited for even longer than he had a moment earlier, but she didn't respond. He'd come back to it.

"How about you tell me about your husband," said Ash. "Does Isaac get along well with Carl?"

She flinched again. If Ash hadn't known earlier, he did now. Lynn and Gillespie were more than just neighborly, probably quite a bit more. Ash didn't want to push a woman who had lost someone she cared about, but he needed information.

"I don't know if Isaac and Carl have even met," she said, her voice low. "They both work a lot."

"Really? That's surprising since they're both in the legal profession. The legal community here is relatively small, so I bet they knew a lot of people in common."

She shrugged but kept her eyes averted from his. "I wouldn't know. He's never mentioned him before."

Ash nodded and pretended to write it down. "And by that, you mean Carl never talked about your husband?"

"Yeah. I mean no," she said, sighing. "They never talked

about each other. Either of them. Your question was confusing."

"I'm sorry about that. Let's go back to something I asked earlier, though. Was Carl alone the last time you saw him?"

Ash waited for maybe fifteen seconds for her to answer. She didn't.

"If this is too difficult for you, I can visit Isaac at work and talk to him. Maybe he'll remember your sighting of Carl three days ago. Maybe you mentioned it in your sleep or something."

Ash smiled as if he were joking. A tear slid down Lynn's cheek.

"I'm sorry if I'm upsetting you, but I have to ask questions," he said. "I think deep down you want me to ask them, too. If you didn't, you could have gone inside like the rest of your neighbors. You're here because you have something to tell me. Was Carl alone the last time you saw him?"

She looked at her feet. "We were together."

"What time was this?"

She inhaled deeply. "Maybe eight or nine. I don't remember. Isaac wasn't home yet."

"And that's the last time you saw him?" She nodded. "Did you try to talk to him at any other time? Did you, maybe, give him a call on Friday or Saturday?"

"I stopped by on Saturday morning to surprise him while Isaac was playing golf. Carl didn't answer, though. I assumed he spent the night at work. He does that sometimes."

"Okay," said Ash. "Have you seen anyone else at his house lately? Maybe a police car like mine?"

Ash pointed out his unmarked cruiser, but Lynn shook her head.

"I saw a white van in his driveway on Friday morning. He has a cleaning lady, so I assumed she got a new car."

That van may have belonged to the people who killed him. Ash pressed her for details, but she didn't catch a license plate number or see the driver. She did mention that it didn't have windows, though. That would at least narrow the possibilities somewhat.

"Tell me about Carl himself. How's he been lately?"

"Fine."

"Did he ever talk about work?"

"Sometimes, but not often."

"When he did talk about things, what did he talk about?"

"Sometimes he talked about cases if he had a good day. He told me about a drug-trafficking case his boss just won because Carl found out the prosecution's lead witness lied about something. I don't know what."

"Did he ever mention Thomas Rahal?"

"Yeah," she said. "He's been worried about the trial."

"Was he worried about losing?"

She nodded. "Carl was honest about who he worked for. He knew most of his clients were guilty, so his goal was always to find something that would give them the best plea deal. Rahal was different, though. He was scared. Carl thought he was innocent."

"Did Carl actually use the word *innocent*?"

She nodded. So Carl really did find something. It sure would have been nice if he'd shared that something with others. Ash continued talking to Lynn for another five minutes or so, but she didn't know much else. Eventually, Ash tucked his notebook back inside his jacket.

"Okay. I appreciate your help," he said, reaching into his

back pocket for his wallet. He withdrew a business card and handed it to her. "If you remember anything else that you think might be helpful, anything at all, give me a call."

Lynn bit her lower lip. "Just find out what happened to him."

Ash said he'd do his best, then walked to the house and signed in with the officer Bowers had posted on the front porch. The home was as he had left it. Clean, empty, and lifeless. He followed a plastic tarp to the kitchen. Bowers stood beside the back door, watching a forensic technician dust the counter for fingerprints.

"Have you found anything?" asked Ash.

Bowers sighed before shaking his head. "Nada. This place is cleaner than Buckingham Palace," he said. "Someone's been here, but we've got nothing. When we find these guys, I think I'll hire them to clean my bathrooms at home."

"Find any signs of a break-in?"

"Nothing at all. I think we found where Gillespie's corpse was stashed, at least. He's got a walk-in fridge full of beer in the basement. Somebody cranked the temperature down, and everything is frozen inside. Someone tried to claw through the insulation on the door, so I'll have the coroner look at Gillespie's fingers later."

Ash hadn't checked the basement. He wondered if Gillespie had been there when he broke in a few days ago.

"Any blood or prints in the freezer?"

"None that we can find yet. What'd the broad next door say?"

Ash considered for a second. If he said Lynn had been having an affair with Gillespie, Bowers would find her husband, drag him downtown, and interrogate him until a lawyer showed up. In the process, he'd ruin a marriage, embarrass a family, and make a fool out of a woman who had lost someone she cared about. Worse, it'd just be a waste of time. Carl wasn't killed for sleeping with the wrong woman; he was killed for doing his job. Ash coughed to cover his momentary hesitation.

"She wanted to give me her phone number. I tried to let her down gently."

"She looked hot. You should have taken it," he said, already turning his attention back to the kitchen. "Make sure you sign out before you leave."

Ash nodded and glanced at his watch. He had a meeting with Thomas Rahal in half an hour, but he wasn't sure what to expect anymore. Police officers were among the most cynical, grizzled people on the planet. Despite twenty years on the job, Gillespie thought Rahal was innocent. And now he was dead, his home and office had been robbed, and every speck of evidence he'd collected was gone. Ash's case may have started as a simple hit-and-run, but it was more than that now. It was something else, and if he didn't figure out what, a potentially innocent man would pay the price.

14

IMPD didn't have many holding cells downtown, and it usually reserved the few it did have for inmates on trial. Thomas Rahal was a special case, though. The county jailer had tried putting him in the general population at the Marion County Jail, but that hadn't gone very well. Rahal was an Arab, so the street gangs didn't know what to make of him. Jail was never a pleasant place to be, but without a gang to watch his back, no one helped him keep the predators away. Rahal's fellow inmates roughed him up a couple of times and took his soap and toothbrush. Ash was just glad he hadn't been stabbed in the shower. To keep him safe, the jail transferred him to the holding cells atop IMPD's headquarters. It wasn't the Hilton, but at least he wouldn't be beaten while having lunch.

Ash met Charity in the lobby, but she was on the phone, so he left her there and went ahead of her to the jail. After he'd been searched half a dozen times by half a dozen people, an officer led him to a small interrogation room with painted cinder-block walls, a steel table bolted to the ground, and linoleum tile flooring. Had there been a lumpy mattress on the table, it would have reminded him of his dorm room at Purdue University.

He pulled out a folding chair from beneath the table and sat down to wait. Rahal arrived first. He was thin to the point of being emaciated, and his skin was yellowing as if he were jaundiced. He had traded the navy sport coat and khakis he usually wore to Friday prayer for an orange prison-issue jumpsuit. Purple welts covered his forearms and Ash noticed cuts on his hands and knuckles. They looked like defensive wounds; life evidently hadn't been going well for him lately.

He looked at Ash with hopeful, pleading eyes. "*As-Salamu Alaykum*," he said, extending his hand. *Peace be upon you.* It was the polite greeting used by Muslims around the world.

"*Wa-laikum as-Salam.*"

May God's peace be upon you, too. Ash didn't think he had ever wished someone peace in an interrogation booth before. There really is a first time for everything. Rahal sat down and gestured toward the seat across from him.

"Are you here to take me home?" he asked. He spoke the Arabic of a native Iraqi. Ash had grown up hearing a different dialect, so it took him a moment to figure out what Rahal asked.

"No, I'm a detective, and I'm here to talk to you," Ash answered in English. "One of your attorneys is on her way."

Rahal nodded, his chest rising and falling as he cast his gaze to his hands. They trembled.

"I've seen your family at the mosque. I assumed Imam Habib had sent you."

The Imam had contacted Ash a couple of weeks ago to see if he'd be willing to visit Rahal in jail and make sure he was doing well. Until that afternoon, though, he'd refused. As far as Ash was concerned, Rahal was just another suspect in another detective's case. A visit would have been inappropriate. It also would have pissed off his colleagues, something he preferred to avoid if at all possible. Rahal continued staring at his hands.

"The food here is *haram*. Lunch is always ham sandwiches, and breakfast is always sausage or bacon. I don't know what I can eat."

"The kitchen staff probably doesn't know what a *halal* meal is. They should have a vegetarian meal, though, and you should be able to eat that. If the jail refuses to give you what you need, tell your attorney. He'll straighten things out. If not, I'll make some calls."

"Thank you."

They sat in silence for the next few minutes, waiting for Rahal's attorney to arrive. The jailer let her in a few minutes later. She hadn't gone to the same law school as Ash, but she looked so young that she had to have been a first- or second-year associate. It was surprising that Meyers let her out of the office alone. She wore a sleek green dress and had red hair past her shoulders. She didn't introduce herself, but she looked like Daphne from *Scooby-Doo*.

"I hope you haven't been talking to my client without me present, Detective," she said, laying a black briefcase on the table.

"Your client has been having some difficulties in jail. I don't care if he's a Christian, a Jew, or a Muslim—he shouldn't be forced to eat something prohibited by his religious beliefs. You should have called Marion County's jailer and ensured they had proper meals and protection for him."

Daphne's back straightened. "We've been preoccupied with saving his life. Perhaps if your jail were properly staffed, Mr. Rahal's well-being wouldn't be such an issue."

"And perhaps the skies will open, men will lay down their arms, and peace will finally reign on earth. It's probably not going to happen. You've had clients in jail before, so you know what it's like. You should have prepared him better. If you want, I'll call the jailer on your behalf to ensure your client is given proper meals."

Daphne's nostrils flared as she exhaled. "I'll make the calls," she said, looking at Rahal for the first time since walking into the room. She looked back at Ash. "Are you done posturing now?"

Ash forced his shoulders to relax. "I assume you know why you're here," said Ash, crossing his arms.

"I'm here to keep you from trampling on any of my client's rights again," said Daphne, opening her briefcase and pulling out a yellow legal notepad, a small voice recorder, and a pen. She looked at Ash, her lips straight and her face stern. "Let's go over the ground rules. Mr. Meyers and I are extending this meeting to you as a courtesy. As such, we reserve the right to end it at any time. Furthermore, any questions about our trial strategy are off-limits. Okay?"

"Yeah. Of course," said Ash, flipping through his notebook for a blank page. As he did that, Charity walked into the room, breathing hard. She looked frazzled at first, but she regained her composure quickly and sat beside him, nodding hello to everyone. "Since we're all finally here, I'd like to get started. As I'm sure everyone knows, I'm working a special investigation for the prosecutor's office, and as part of my investigation, I'm interested in hearing Mr. Rahal's recollections of what happened during his arrest and the events that led to his arrest."

Daphne coughed before Ash asked his first question.

"Since we're sharing, what case are you working on, Detective?"

Normally, Ash would have answered her without hesitation, but the bickering had him annoyed already.

"That's confidential. If he deems it necessary, I'm sure your boss can fill you in," he said, glancing at her but quickly looking back at Rahal. "So tell me about the night you were arrested."

Rahal shrugged. "Men broke into my house in the middle of the night and arrested me. I don't understand what else you want to know."

Ash nodded. Rahal may have been innocent like Gillespie thought, but no one would learn anything new unless Ash pressed him.

"Let's just slow down a bit," he said. "You murdered a police officer. How'd that happen?"

Rahal drew his eyebrows together and cocked his head to the side, obviously confused. "I didn't murder—"

"Detective Rashid is trying to trick you into saying something you shouldn't," said Daphne, interrupting her client and turning to Ash. "Tone down your rhetoric or I will end this meeting forthwith."

"You should call your boss before you make threats. My presence here is as much a favor to him as it is part of my investigation."

Daphne glared without saying anything. Ash took a breath, thinking through his next question.

"Let's start at the beginning," he said, speaking slowly but building up speed as the line of questioning coalesced in his head. "Do you work, Mr. Rahal?"

"I was a painter."

"Art?" asked Ash, surprised.

"Bridges. I work for the Department of Transportation."

"So you work during the day."

"Day or night," he said. "It depends on the job."

"Okay," said Ash, pretending to write the information down. "Did you work on the day you were arrested?"

Rahal nodded. "From seven in the morning to three-thirty in the afternoon. I came home at four."

"Did you stop off for a drink with your coworkers before going home?" Ash asked.

"I don't drink alcohol," said Rahal, his eyebrows drawn together, confused. "It is *haram*. You know this."

"Marijuana is *haram* as well, and yet the police still found some in your home."

"Don't say anything, Thomas," said Daphne, looking to her client. She looked back at Ash, her eyes boring into his skull. "This is not an interrogation, Detective. I expect you to conduct this interview in a cordial, professional manner."

"Of course," said Ash, not taking his eyes from Rahal's. "I apologize for my rudeness. Does your wife work, Mr. Rahal?"

"She cleans at a bank from eleven at night to seven the next morning."

"So she was home when you came home from work. What did you do after coming home on the day of your arrest?"

"It was still light, so we took A'ishah for a walk. After that, we had dinner and prayers."

"And A'ishah is your daughter?" Ash asked. Rahal nodded. "It's a pretty name. My wife and I almost named our daughter that." Ash paused for a second, thinking. "Let's fast-forward. Your wife went to work, at what, around ten-thirty?"

Rahal nodded.

"And you were alone with your daughter?"

He nodded again.

"What time did the police come?"

Ash could get that information in a report, but he wanted to hear Rahal's recollections.

"It was late. I went to bed after my wife went to work, so I was asleep when they came."

Ash leaned forward. "Did you open the door when the police announced themselves?"

"I was asleep. They just came in."

Ash glanced at Charity, but she just rolled her eyes and leaned forward. "Our team pounded on Mr. Rahal's door so loud his neighbors woke up. He didn't answer, so they broke the door down."

Rahal shrugged and looked at the table. "If you say so."

Daphne started to speak, but Ash held up his hand, stopping her. His eyes never wandered from Rahal's.

"If you didn't hear the police announce themselves, you didn't hear them. That's fine, and that's all you have to say. I want your story, not what a bunch of lawyers tell you to say."

"Oh, please, Detective," said Daphne, interrupting him. "If you think I'll allow you to—"

"You'll have your chance to speak in court, Counselor," said Ash, talking over her. "This is my interview, and I'm conducting it with your boss's permission. Unless you want to be unemployed in the worst legal economy in decades, I'd suggest you let me do my job."

The threat was mostly empty, but Daphne got the point and shut up. Ash looked back at Rahal.

"Men came into your house, and you didn't hear them announce themselves. What did you think was happening?"

Rahal seemed to stare through him, remembering. His eyes took on a glassy appearance. "Someone broke into a home in my neighborhood last year and shot a man. I didn't know what was happening. I thought..." His voice trailed off.

"You thought these men wanted to hurt you," he said.

Rahal nodded. "Yes," he said. His voice cracked. "I ran to A'ishah's room and took her from her crib. She was crying, so I put my hand over her mouth to keep her quiet. We hid under her crib before the men came to the nursery. They wore black boots like the men in Iraq wore."

They were probably combat boots. Rahal paused to gather his breath. Ash took the break to glance at Charity. Her face was emotionless, but he noticed worry in her eyes. She had good reason to be worried. Rahal seemed credible and sincere. Ash doubted he'd take the stand, but he'd be a hell of a witness if he did.

"At what point did you get a gun?" Ash asked.

Rahal looked at his hands. "I kept it in a locked drawer of my nightstand. I took it as soon as they broke down the door."

"So you hid under the bed with your daughter and a handgun," said Ash. "How did the police find out you were in the room?"

Rahal took a deep breath. "A'ishah. I took my hand off her mouth so she could breathe, and the officers heard her crying. They started screaming at me to give her to them."

"And you refused?"

Rahal nodded, tears in his eyes now. "Of course. They kept shouting, though. I thought they were going to hurt her, so I told them no. I told them I would call the police. One of the men bent down and tried to reach for her. I don't know what happened next. I heard a bang and saw the flash."

"Did you shoot him?" asked Ash.

"I don't think so."

The "I-didn't-pull-the-trigger" defense probably wouldn't fly, but the story was interesting and convincingly told. Of course, Susan would eviscerate it. She'd say Rahal heard the police announce themselves, so he grabbed his daughter and hid under her crib. If hiding didn't work, she'd say he intended to use his daughter as a hostage and hope to negotiate his way out.

"What happened after the policeman was shot?"

"Someone pulled out the body, and the men left. I put A'ishah back in her crib and called Fatima, my wife."

"Why didn't you call the police?"

"I was scared," said Rahal. "Fatima convinced me to call nine-one-one. The person I spoke to told me to leave A'ishah in her crib and surrender to the men outside. I didn't, though. When we moved here, my contact at the U.S. Department of State said people might try to hurt me for what I've done, that people from Iraq might still come after me. I thought we were safe inside. I stayed in the nursery and tried to clean the blood from the carpet. Then Fatima called and said she was outside. She told me to leave A'ishah in her crib and come out. I trusted her, so I did."

That part of the story would likely be the heart of Meyers's defense. He'd say Rahal was so accustomed to an oppressive, violent dictatorship that he didn't know to trust the police. Depending on the makeup of the jury, it might even work. At the very least, it would gain him some sympathy at sentencing.

"What happened after your arrest?" asked Ash. "Did the police search your house?"

Charity leaned forward and put her hands up, stopping Rahal from speaking. "Whatever allegedly happened to Mr. Rahal after his arrest has been excluded from the trial by the judge. There's no point in going over land already amply plowed."

"Just because you found a judge willing to exclude evidence of torture hardly means it's irrelevant," said Daphne.

"You're bitter because you lost," said Charity. "Get over—"

"Let's keep this professional, please," said Ash, interrupting Charity before she could finish her thought. "We're not in court, so I'd like Mr. Rahal to speak. Is that okay with you two?"

Both attorneys glared at him, but Ash had grown up with a single mother and a significantly older sister; he was accustomed to women glaring at him. He nodded to Rahal, encouraging him to speak.

"Someone tied my hands behind me and led me to a van. It didn't have windows, so I couldn't see anything. We stopped in a warehouse full of cars. Someone pulled me out and tied me to a chair." Rahal paused. When he spoke again, his voice was higher and strained. "They took turns hitting me."

"Oh, please," said Charity, shaking her head. "I have sworn statements from five officers that describe you resisting arrest. They had to subdue you in the back of a van. That's how you got bruises, and that's why you were Tased."

Ash raised an eyebrow at Charity, but she apparently didn't have anything else to say. He fixed his gaze on Rahal again.

"Do you remember the color of the van?"

"It was white."

Just like the one Lynn Meister reported seeing outside Gillespie's house.

"How long did this continue?"

Rahal looked down at his hands. "I don't know," he said. "It felt like a long time."

"Did they Tase you?"

"Yes," said Rahal, nodding. "They threw water on me first, but then they shocked me. I passed out after that. I don't know what happened."

"I'll tell you what happened," said Daphne before Ash could say anything. "Thomas went into cardiac arrest. Your fellow officers tortured my client."

Charity shook her head, not saying anything.

"My understanding is that you confessed," said Ash. "When did that happen?"

Daphne looked at her client and nodded.

"I woke up in a room like this one," he said, casting his gaze about the conference room. "They had washed off my face, but I had a hard time breathing. They said if I admitted hiding under A'ishah's crib so I could kill them, they'd take me to the hospital. I didn't know what they would do to me if I told them no. Where I grew up, you would disappear if you didn't do what the police told you. I didn't want my daughter growing up without a father, so I read their paper aloud and signed it. A camera recorded everything. After that, they took me to the hospital."

It was an interesting story, but it didn't advance Ash's

investigation. Rahal's rough treatment after arrest notwith-standing, his trial was going to be pretty swift. He may deny pulling the trigger, but the state had enough evidence to put him away.

"What about the drugs they found in your house?" Ash asked.

Rahal looked to his lawyer. She leaned forward.

"Like the firearm, we stipulate to the drugs. His mother-in-law has terminal cancer, and she stays with them at times. The drugs were hers to manage her pain."

Ash looked at Rahal, his eyebrows raised. "We have wit-nesses who say you're a drug dealer. One of our confidential informants even bought drugs from you."

Rahal shook his head vigorously. Before he answered, though, Daphne put her hand on his shoulder, stopping him. She laced her fingers together on the table.

"We stipulate to the drugs found in Mr. Rahal's home, not the drugs the police allegedly bought from him. Mr. Rahal's mother-in-law kept a small amount of marijuana in his home for its antinausea properties as well as a small quantity of oxycodone for pain. Both were legally prescribed and pur-chased in Colorado. There were no other illegal drugs in the home, nor is there evidence that Mr. Rahal has ever had other illegal drugs in the home."

Ash nodded, not really sure who to believe.

"Okay. The jury can decide that, then," he said, staring at Rahal and hoping he'd say something. "Anything you want me to tell the Imam or our community?"

Daphne stood, her hands in front of her. "Not a word," she said, glancing at her client. "This interview is done. I don't believe my client has anything else to say."

"Pray for me," said Rahal, ignoring his attorney's advice. "And pray for my family."

Daphne muttered something and called for a guard to escort Rahal back to his cell. Within two minutes, Ash and Charity were alone.

"Did you get what you needed?" she asked.

He sighed. "I don't know," he said, leaning back in his chair. "If this case is as simple as it seems, why wouldn't Meyers ask for a plea deal?"

Charity hesitated before answering. "Probably because he'd lose all the publicity," she said, her voice suddenly getting stronger. "Our case is solid. Our evidence is tight, our witnesses are convincing, and we've got the forensics to back it up where needed. We've got him."

"How many murderers have you prosecuted?"

Charity leaned back. "Half a dozen," she said. "Susan's prosecuted ten times that."

"Does Rahal seem like the sort of guy who would use his infant daughter as a shield in order to murder a cop?"

Charity hesitated again. "What I think doesn't matter," she said. "I have to look at the evidence, and it says Mr. Rahal hid beneath a bed and willfully killed a police officer. No one is arguing that."

Charity was right. Ash couldn't ignore the evidence, but he didn't think they had a complete picture yet, either. The interrogation room had a single door; it was as much of a dead end as his interview had been. Before leaving, he looked at Charity.

"Good luck with your trial."

He didn't say that she probably needed it.

15

Ash made it to his office by midafternoon. He had a better idea of the weaknesses in Susan's case—and there were many—but none were real game changers. Some might affect the sentence Rahal received, but they wouldn't keep him out of jail. He called Susan Mercer anyway and asked her to reconsider her decision about delaying the trial. She didn't blow him off, but she didn't give his request much thought, either. Until he found something that could be proven in court, she wasn't going to change her mind. Unfortunately, that didn't leave him with much time. If Rahal was innocent and still went to jail, the game was over. He could appeal the decision, of course, but he'd have to survive state prison first. Based on his experience in the county jail so far, Ash didn't think that was likely.

He sat at his desk and locked his firearm in the center drawer so it wouldn't weigh down his shoulders. To find whatever Carl Gillespie and Cassandra Johnson had stumbled on, he needed to think like them. He didn't know enough about Cassandra to do that, but Gillespie had been a cop, and Ash knew how cops thought. Had he been in Gillespie's position, he would have started with the search warrant for Thomas Rahal's home. If the warrant had a flaw, the entire case could be in jeopardy.

Ash flipped through the notes he had taken during his discussion with Charity Lewis. She said the search warrant was justified by a series of drug buys by a confidential informant. That was standard operating procedure when trying to arrest a low-level dealer. In a normal case, the narcs would have Rahal arrested based on those buys, and then they'd offer him a deal for testifying against the people from whom he bought drugs. They'd then go out and arrest Rahal's supplier and try the same thing on him. The strategy rarely worked once they started getting to the top of the supply chain, but it was a good way to round up midlevel pushers and wholesalers.

He pulled out his cell phone and called David Lee. The detective picked up on the second ring. If the background noise was any indication, he was watching football.

"What's going on, Ash?"

"They give you the day off after your meth bust?"

"Sort of," he said. The sound from the football game disappeared as Lee, presumably, muted the TV. "No OT, no David Lee. That's what I told my lieutenant yesterday. You want to come by and catch a game? Mom got a big box of tube socks from Korea. I'm sure she'd be willing to share a pair with you."

Lee was a first-generation American with parents as eccentric as any Ash had ever met. His mom collected socks and gave them out for special occasions. She even gave Ash some on his last birthday. Why she chose a pair adorned with Christmas trees was anyone's guess, but Ash made a point to wear them to the department's holiday parties.

"Your mom is a generous woman, but this isn't a social call. I need to talk to a confidential informant your unit works with."

Lee grunted. "Which upstanding citizen would that be?"

Ash scanned his notes until he found the correct entry. "All I've got is his ID number: zero-eight-one-four."

He grunted again. "Did you consider calling accounting? With his ID, they could pull his contact information for you."

Ash's cell phone began beeping midconversation, so he pulled it away from his ear and glanced at the screen. According to his prayer app, he had just missed *salat al-Asr*, afternoon prayer. He sighed and put the phone back to his ear.

"I would call them, but I'm in a time crunch and they're not in today."

"All right, all right...," said David, his voice trailing off. "He's not one of mine, so let me make a call and see what I can find. I'll call you back in a few minutes."

"Thanks."

Ash hung up and skimmed through his notes again. Nothing immediately jumped out at him, but that wasn't surprising. If the problems with the case were obvious, Susan Mercer would have seen them. David Lee called back about fifteen minutes later.

"I don't know him, but our database lists your CI as a guy named Swimmer. Real name is Kevin Terrel. We don't have much info on him in our official database, but he supposedly hangs out on East Forty-Ninth near the Monon Trail."

Ash nodded and wrote the information down. The Monon Trail was an asphalt walkway that passed north and south through town. At one time it had been a railroad, but the railroad company abandoned it in the late eighties. The city paved over the old tracks, and now parts of it were popular with bikers and joggers. Unfortunately, the unpopular part of the trail traversed some shady sections of town. Several joggers had been mugged, and a couple of people had even been shot on it. It didn't surprise him to hear that a drug dealer hung out there.

Ash closed his notebook. "I owe you one, buddy."

"Don't thank me yet. Swimmer's file has a do-not-contact tag on it."

Ostensibly, a do-not-contact note on a CI's file meant just that. Don't contact the guy without talking to his handler first. More than likely, Susan or Charity had put the tag on the file when they filed charges against Rahal. Hopefully they hadn't sequestered him somewhere.

"I won't mention your name."

"Please don't, and don't forget us little folks when you and your buddy Leonard Wilson take over the prosecutor's office. I saw you on the news. Before I let you go, let me ask you a serious question. When you stabbed your boss in the back, is it true she fell on one knee and said '*Et tu*, Ash?' That's the rumor going around."

Ash didn't say anything for a second. "Is that a Shakespeare reference?" he asked.

"Yeah," said Lee. "I'm a man of many talents."

"Good for you. Listen, though, I've got to go. Thanks and see you later."

Lee wished him luck before hanging up. Ash grabbed his firearm from his desk and made sure he had a full magazine before standing. It was time to meet and greet.

*　　*　　*

Swimmer's neighborhood was one of the worst in town. There were no sidewalks, and most of the houses were small clapboard buildings with peeling paint. Many had rusted chain-link fences and grass so long it would cover the average person's ankles. Aside from being ugly, it also had one of the highest violent crime rates of any neighborhood in the city. The situation was bad enough that most of the churches had even left years ago.

Ash drove for about ten minutes before finding a group of boys smoking under an old oak tree in front of an abandoned home. Most of them wouldn't even be shaving for another four or five years, which meant they were too young to possess real criminal records or be truly afraid of the police. Ash pulled off on the side of the road and parked with one set of tires on the asphalt and the other on the grass. The boys simply stared at him.

As soon as he got out of his car, he held up his badge.

"What do you want?"

One of the boys, probably the oldest, stood up. His hair was so short he was almost bald, but he had the wisps of a goatee on his chin. He and Ash stood roughly the same height, but age hadn't begun to fill in the boy's muscles yet. A high school football or basketball coach would be happy to see him in a couple of years, but for now he was just a kid. Ash clipped his badge to his belt before looking back at the group.

"I want to see some ID. Make sure you guys are old enough for those cigarettes."

Baldy lowered his gaze. "Don't you have something better to do than bother us?"

"Of course I have better things to do. Now show me your IDs. And if any of you try to slip me something fake, I'm not going to be happy."

Baldy looked back at his friends and shrugged. "What if we don't have IDs?" he asked. "You gonna arrest us or something?"

"I'm going to take you home and tell your mothers about the cigarettes."

A couple of the boys dropped their cigarettes behind their backs and looked around as if he wouldn't notice.

"You don't even know our moms," said Baldy. "You ain't going to take us home."

Ash looked past Baldy and counted the boys. According to the most recent census, the most common surname among African American families in the city was Williams. There were enough boys under the tree to field a football team, so the odds were fair.

"I'm looking for a kid with the last name Williams."

The boys shifted, and Baldy looked back at one of his friends. "What do you want Andre for?"

"I don't want him. His mom does, and she won't stop calling."

All the boys dropped their cigarettes and stopped talking. A heavier boy stepped forward. He was at least six inches shorter than Baldy, but his hair made him seem taller.

"So are you going to tell my mom what I've been doing?" asked Andre.

"That depends," said Ash. "I'm looking for somebody named Swimmer. You guys know where he is?"

The boys whispered to each other. Eventually, Baldy nodded to Ash as if the group had come to an agreement.

"We might. What do you want with him?"

"I want to talk to him. Tell me where he is, and I'll leave
you alone. You won't even see me again. Sound good?"

Baldy looked back at his friends. A couple of the boys nodded, imploring their leader to continue.

"All right," he said, turning to face Ash. "Swimmer's
working up by the trail."

"What sort of work does he do?"

Baldy shrugged. "You know," he said. "Business."

Drugs.

"Good," said Ash. "What's he look like?"

Baldy held out his arms. "He's fat."

Very descriptive.

"Okay," said Ash, yawning. "Thanks for your help. Before
I leave, everybody stand up and turn out your pockets."

Baldy leaned back and squinted. "For real?"

Rather than answer, Ash simply raised his eyebrows. The
boys did as he asked and emptied their pockets. It turned out
better than he had expected. He found two packs of cigarettes among them, but no drugs, liquor, or weapons. It was
a refreshing haul. Before leaving, he made them drop all the
cigarettes he had found in their pockets and grind them into
the dirt with their feet. They weren't pleased about that, but
their lungs would thank him one day.

Ash got back in his cruiser and drove for about five minutes until he found a parking spot along the trail. There were
enough people milling about to discourage muggers, but the
drug dealers were still there. He walked until he found a
heavyset, middle-aged man sitting by himself on a bench

nestled between two trees beside the asphalt. Ash sat next to him and looked around, but the drug dealer ignored him.

"Are you Swimmer?"

He looked at Ash up and down. "I am," he said. "And who can I thank for our introduction?"

Ash pulled his jacket past his hip, exposing his badge. "A mutual friend."

Swimmer's back stiffened. He looked away. "Put your badge away, Detective," he said, speaking under his breath. "Don't you know how to set up a meeting?"

Ash pushed his jacket back over his hip. Swimmer's street accent had disappeared rather quickly.

"Who are you?"

"Someone you're pissing off," he said. "Who sent you here?"

"Nobody sent me. I heard you were a confidential informant on a drug buy a couple of months ago. What's the deal?"

Swimmer brought his hand to his face and covered his mouth. "You know where West Park is in Carmel?"

"I can find it."

"Good. Meet me in an hour," he said, glaring at Ash. "If anyone from IMPD ever pulls this shit again, we'll cut you out of every investigation we've even thought about doing together. Do you get me?"

"Yeah," said Ash, his voice low with surprise. "I get you."

Swimmer stormed off, leaving Ash alone on the bench. Apparently Swimmer had a do-not-contact note in his file for a reason. He stayed on the bench long after Swimmer left, pretty sure he had just stepped into something he shouldn't have.

*　　*　　*

West Park was halfway between two suburbs on Indianapolis's north side. Ash pulled inside and parked beside a play-
ground with a bright blue tornado slide that ran in and out
of an old grain silo. Swimmer sat on a bench, glaring as Ash
got out of his car. They were the only people in sight. He sat
beside the big man but kept a hand near his breast in case he
had to get to his firearm quickly.

"Who are you, Detective?"

"My name is Ash Rashid. I'm a detective sergeant with
IMPD. I'm investigating Thomas Rahal, and your name
came up in my search."

Rahal's name didn't seem to register because Swimmer's
eyes still smoldered.

"What idiot told you to contact me?"

Ash stood up. "Nobody, okay?" he said, feeling his own
temper rise. "You were listed on an affidavit in support of a
search warrant. I'm following up. Who are you?"

Swimmer pulled a wallet from his back pocket and flipped
it open, exposing a gold badge with an eagle on top. Ash felt
his heart sink into his feet. He was a DEA agent.

"I've spent eight months working this city. That's eight
months away from my wife and kids. You think I like hanging around with drug dealers all day? Or dressing up like a
goddamn pimp? If the wrong guy saw me talking to you,
I'd be burned, and that'd be eight months of my life wasted.
Do you understand? I missed teaching my son how to ride a
bike. I missed my daughter's fourth birthday. Can you make
that up to me?"

"Had I known who you were, I never would have contacted you."

Swimmer continued to stare, his jaw working. "What do you want?"

"You purchased drugs from Thomas Rahal. Those drugs were listed in an affidavit in support of a search warrant. I needed to talk to you to see if that was real."

Swimmer shook his head. "Did you read my CI file?"

Ash knew what Swimmer was getting at, so he didn't want to answer. After about a minute of awkward silence, Swimmer raised his eyebrows expectantly.

"It said not to contact you," Ash said finally.

"And you did anyway."

"Yes."

Swimmer's nostrils flared as he exhaled. "I work for the federal government, asshole. Do you think I went undercover for eight months to make street pops?"

"You were listed on an affidavit for a search warrant. I didn't contact you for fun."

"I don't care why you contacted me," said Swimmer. "And I'm only going to say this once. I don't buy drugs from street dealers, but even if I did, I wouldn't turn that evidence over to IMPD. If you show up in my neighborhood again looking for me, I'll file complaints against your department, your unit, and you. By the time I'm done, you won't even be able to get a job scrubbing toilets at the police academy. Got it?"

Swimmer stormed off before he could say anything else. Not that there was anything else to say. Ash stayed still to think. If Swimmer didn't make the drug buy, the search warrant for the Rahal home was completely bogus. That didn't make sense, though. Without evidence of a crime, the police would have no reason to show up at Rahal's door and drag him out of the house. And not only had they shown up, they lied and claimed an undercover DEA agent gave them probable cause for their warrant. Something was seriously wrong.

At the same time, even if the judge presiding over Rahal's murder trial knew the search warrant for his apartment was fraudulent, she wouldn't throw out the case. She might throw out the pills and marijuana, but she'd let the shooting stand. What's more, a bad warrant didn't prove Rahal's innocence. Gillespie and Cassandra Johnson wouldn't have been killed for discovering a bad warrant. They found something else.

He walked back to his cruiser. The meeting was a mistake, but it confirmed the case against Thomas Rahal was seriously flawed. With Susan still intent on bringing him to court, things were going to get ugly.

16

Ash got back in his car at just after five, and he felt a dry itch in the back of his throat. He had promised Hannah that he would do his best not to drink again, but from the moment he touched his door handle to the moment he sat down, he couldn't stop thinking of a bar he had seen on his way into town. He had memorized its location without conscious thought. The scariest part was that he knew he wouldn't enjoy the drinks or the company and he'd leave feeling terrible about himself, but he still wanted to go. That wasn't the sort of thing a casual drinker did.

Had Ash's life been a made-for-TV movie, the epiphany would have been accompanied by joy and fulfillment. If anything, it made him feel worse. He ran his fingers through his hair and pulled out his cell phone. His fingers trembled as he dialed his home number. Hannah picked up quickly.

"Hey, honey," he said.

"Ashraf?" she asked.

Ash nodded even though she was fifteen or twenty miles away. "Yeah, it's me. I'm on my way home. I just wanted to let you know."

"Good. I'm making fish for dinner."

"I'm glad. I'll be there as soon as I can. Love you."

"I love you, too, honey."

The conversation was short, but Ash's hands stopped shaking about halfway through it. He had an easier time staying out of bars knowing his family expected him. Once that call was completed, he dialed Susan Mercer's personal cell number.

"I found something you're not going to want to hear."

She sighed. "Go on."

"The search warrant for the Rahal's home is FUBAR. The confidential informant specified in the affidavit never made the drug buy Noah Stuart claimed he did. The whole reason to go to the house was a lie."

Susan didn't respond for a moment.

"I'd like to talk to this CI in person. Is there any way you can run him down to my office?"

"That's going to be a problem. He's not in the talking mood, and I can't force him. He's an undercover DEA agent."

"Excuse me?" said Susan.

"Swimmer, CI number zero-eight-one-four, is a DEA agent, and he did not make a drug buy."

"Tell me this is a joke."

"No joke."

"Damn," said Susan, sighing audibly. "I'll call Judge Haller and John Meyers to let them know we've found an error in the documents we submitted and plan to correct it as soon as we can. Thanks for finding this. It might save our asses at trial."

"You're not going to file for a continuance?"

"Not unless I have to," said Susan. "As long as the search team went to Rahal's home in good faith, the status of the warrant isn't germane to the murder trial. If needed, I'll drop the drug charges against him, but problematic warrant or not, he murdered a police officer. Ryan Dixon is dead because of Thomas Rahal. Nothing else matters."

"You might be able to prove that he killed Dixon, but that's a big step away from proving that he murdered him."

"You want to tell that to Ryan's parents?" she asked. "Their son is dead because he was doing his job. Thomas Rahal killed him because he was a police officer. Nothing you've found changes that."

Ash rubbed his brow and sighed. "What are you going to do?"

Susan softened her voice. "I'm going to find out what happened with the warrant and correct it. Charity will call Noah Stuart and find out who really should have been listed on the affidavit, and once we have that, we'll make him available to the defense. That should mollify the judge."

"You shouldn't dismiss this that easily. I think it's important."

"I'm not dismissing it, and I agree. It is important, and I appreciate your call. I'm going to spend the rest of the night following up on it. If we find that this is more than a paperwork error, we'll deal with it appropriately. You have my word."

"I'll keep looking, too."

"Sure. Now, I've got to go. You've given me a lot of work to do."

Susan hung up before he could say anything else. Well, at least she talked to him. That was better than it might have been. Ash stopped by the grocery on his way home and picked up a premade bag of salad and two small bouquets from the store's floral shop. They weren't much, but he thought Hannah and Megan would like them.

As soon as he opened his car's door at home, Megan called out from the backyard. Ash couldn't see her, but judging by the squeal, she was on the swing set.

"Hi, *Baba*!"

"Hi, pumpkin," he said, grabbing his packages from the backseat of his cruiser.

"I'm going really high."

"I can imagine," he said, closing his door. "I'm going inside. Don't jump out."

"I won't."

He walked into the kitchen and found vases for the flowers he purchased while Hannah tended to Kaden in the nursery. When she came out, he held a vase with six roses in his right hand and a vase with a small bouquet of yellow and white daisies in his left.

"Did you break something?" she asked.

"Only a string of hearts on my way to you," he said.

She rolled her eyes and then took the flowers and laid them beside the sink. Unlike most nights, she didn't step away immediately after kissing him hello. Instead, she kept her face near his. He realized later that she was smelling his breath for alcohol. He'd have to get used to that. Apparently satisfied, she laid her hand flat on his chest.

"Kissing is gross, *Ummi*."

Megan walked through the back door and slammed it shut behind her. Hannah patted Ash's chest and took a step back.

"It's not gross, honey," said Ash, bending to look

Megan in the eye. "When you get married, I'm sure you'll enjoy it."

"I don't want to," she said, shaking her head and looking entirely too serious for someone who had just spent the last few minutes on a swing set. "Boys are dirty."

"Good attitude," said Ash, standing up. "Go wash your hands, please."

Megan nodded and ran to the bathroom, giving the adults a moment of peace.

"I'll get back to dinner if you take care of the kids," said Hannah.

"Sure."

Megan came back in the room a moment later, her hands dripping on the floor. At least she had washed them. She sat at the breakfast table and motioned for her father to sit across from her. When he did, she leaned forward conspiratorially but didn't modulate the volume of her voice. She still didn't quite grasp the concept of a secret.

"You're famous, *Baba*."

"Yes," said Hannah. "We saw you on the news."

Ash looked from Hannah to Megan and then back. "What was I doing?" he asked.

"It was a story about Leonard Wilson," said Hannah. "It showed the two of you together."

Ash grunted and looked at Megan.

"I'm not famous. I'm infamous. There's a difference."

She scrunched up her face. "What do you mean?"

"Don't worry, pumpkin," he said, standing and pushing his chair back with his legs. "We'll watch the *Three Amigos* sometime. You'll see."

The evening went pretty well. Hannah, Megan, and Ash

had prayer before dinner. It was Ash's turn to feed Kaden that night. They had started giving him baby food a couple of weeks ago, but so far their success had been limited. He liked sweet potatoes, but nothing else yet. Ash tried feeding him carrots, which went about as well as he had expected. Most of the food ended up on Ash's shirt and Kaden's bib, but the baby had a couple of mouthfuls. Ash cleaned him up and held him for a little while after dinner. He was a great baby, and Ash loved him dearly, but he also thanked God for blessing the world with birth control every time he saw him. Two kids were enough.

Hannah and Ash put Kaden to bed around seven, while Megan stayed up for another hour and watched part of a documentary on penguins. By then, Ash wasn't paying much attention. His mind was back on the Thomas Rahal trial. Eventually, he left the living room and went to the backyard so he could think in a quiet environment.

Thomas Rahal lived a simple but decent life. He had a young family and a long future ahead of him. If he wasn't dealing drugs—and Ash seriously doubted he was after his conversation with Swimmer—why would the police raid his home? That didn't make sense. There had to be something else going on.

He went back inside and searched through the stack of phone books they kept in the kitchen until he found a directory his mosque published every other year. The Rahals lived in an apartment building on the east side of town; it was about a fifteen-minute drive away. There was plenty of time to check the place out before the sun set. When he got back to the living room, Megan and Hannah sat beside each other on the couch, a book spread between them. The book was about a little girl from Iraq whose wicked stepmother forces her to do all the household chores and only allows her to eat dried date leaves. It was one of Megan's favorites because she could read most of it by herself.

Ash coughed, getting their attention. "I've got to go back to work and check on a few things."

Megan closed the book and jumped off the couch before running into his legs at full force.

"Good night, *Baba*," she said.

He tousled her hair while Hannah stared.

"Are you really going to work?" she asked.

"Yeah. Susan is going to trial tomorrow morning on a case, and I want to check up on a few things."

"If that's what you're doing, then."

She probably thought he was going to a bar, and he couldn't blame her. It'd take time to earn her trust again; at least he had managed to come home sober. He kissed both his wife and daughter before heading out.

Ash parked in the lot beside the Rahals' apartment complex and grabbed a police-issue Windbreaker from his trunk before walking toward the buildings. The Rahals' front door had a dent in the center, but the wood frame surrounding it was fresh and unpainted. The house numbers were nowhere to be found. They must have fallen off when IMPD's SWAT team beat down the door. He almost knocked but ultimately decided not to. The family might have some information, but he doubted they'd be happy to see him.

He skipped their apartment and checked out the apartments to their immediate right and left. Both were empty, which wasn't terribly surprising. Ash couldn't imagine many people wanted to live next door to a family that had recently gotten into a gunfight with the police. Rather than give up and go home, he walked around the side of the building and came across a man about his own age sitting on a lawn chair beside a dark apartment. His eyes were closed and his shoulders slumped. It looked like he had a medical textbook in his lap. Ash cleared his throat, and the guy startled, blinking rapidly.

"Sorry to wake you up, but I'm Detective Sergeant Ash Rashid with the police department. You have a minute to talk?"

The med student stretched and yawned. He had dark features and straight black hair. He could have passed for Italian or Greek, but if Ash had to guess, he had some Persian or Arab in his family tree.

"Sure, I can talk," he said. "But can you keep your voice down? My wife and kids are asleep inside."

"Of course," said Ash, lowering his voice. His interviewee's name was Isaac Klein, and he and his family had moved into the complex about a year earlier. He had two kids, including an infant boy the same age as Thomas Rahal's daughter, A'ishah. The two families knew each other well. All in all, he was bright, polite, and open; he was everything Ash could want in a potential witness. After a few minutes of introduction, Ash took his notebook from his pocket.

"I'm investigating a couple of cases related to one of your neighbors. What can you tell me about drugs in the area?"

"Very little. This isn't the best neighborhood, and there are drugs around here, but my family stays out of it as much as we can. We leave them alone, and they leave us alone."

"What about in this complex? Are there any problems with drugs here?"

As soon as he said it, Isaac's entire demeanor changed. His eyes narrowed, he crossed his arms, and a scowl formed on his face.

"I think it's time for you to leave, Detective."

That was unexpected. Ash looked around quickly to see if anyone was listening.

"If you're worried about retribution for what you tell me, I'm very discreet. I can keep your name private."

"What's wrong with you people? You think that if you keep coming, I'll change my story?"

"I'm not asking you to change anything," said Ash. "I'm just here to talk to you, to find out what your story is."

"That's what the last detective said right before he threatened my kids."

Ash put his hands up. "I've got kids of my own," he said. "I'm not about to threaten yours."

The angry glare stayed on Isaac's face. "What do you want? I don't know anything."

"You probably know more than you think, and you can start by telling me who threatened you."

Isaac shook his head. "Why? So you can tell him I talked? I don't think so."

"Tell me this, at least. Were you threatened by a uniformed officer named Joe Cartwright or a plainclothes lieutenant named Noah Stuart?"

Isaac stared at him, apparently trying to get a read on him. "Noah Stuart. I remember because my little boy asked if he had an ark in his backyard at home."

"Okay," said Ash. "Do you have any relatives nearby?"

"My mother-in-law lives in Franklin."

"As soon as you're done talking to me, I want you to get your stuff together and go there. Don't tell anybody."

Isaac raised his eyebrows. "You're serious?"

"Yeah. You're not the only witness Noah and his men have threatened."

"What happened to the others?"

"They're dead." Isaac's face paled and he started to turn away. Ash grabbed his bicep before he could. "I still need to talk to you. Noah threatened you because he thinks you know something. What did he say to you?"

Isaac ran his hands through his hair. "He wanted me to say that I saw people come out of Thomas Rahal's house all the time, that I thought he was dealing out of his apartment. I can't believe this."

"Was he?"

Isaac shook his head, his eyes narrow and confused. "What?"

"Was Thomas Rahal dealing drugs?"

"No," said Isaac, pacing now. "His wife babysat my kids. I wouldn't leave my kids with a drug dealer. And he sure as hell wouldn't shoot someone without damn good reason. He's from Iraq, you know. I think he's seen enough people shot."

"Would your other neighbors agree?"

"How the hell should I know?" asked Isaac. "Look, I've got to go. I can't handle this right now."

Ash put his hand on his chest before he could leave.

"If you answer my questions, I might be able to put Noah and his whole crew in jail. I can't do it without you, though."

Isaac started to speak, but then stopped himself. "Fine.

Just make it quick," he said. "I don't know what anyone else would say. You'd have to ask them."

"I will. Can you tell me about the apartments beside the Rahals'?"

He stuttered something before taking a deep breath. "One of them has been empty since I moved in two years ago. The guy who lived in the other one moved out right after Thomas was arrested. I didn't know him."

"Do you know his name at least?"

"Andrew something. He kept to himself mostly."

"Mostly?" asked Ash.

"Yeah," said Isaac. "He had women over sometimes, but I think they were hookers."

Ash made a note to call the apartment's manager and see what he could discover about the neighbor. He kept Isaac talking for a few minutes, but he didn't get anything new out of him. Eventually, Isaac went inside and Ash started to walk back to his car. He hadn't meant to frighten Isaac or his family, but he'd rather do that than attend their funerals. He had gone to enough of those.

It was a little after nine when he arrived at his car. His investigation wore at his gut. Everything he found led to something else. After four days of work, he still hadn't even found the starting point, the single event that set everything else into motion and put what followed into context. It was out there somewhere, but until he found it, he was as lost as he was when he took Lisa home from the Child Services office. At least he had a pretty good idea that he was going in the right direction.

He sat down and grabbed his cell phone. Bukoholov had blown off his questions on Thursday, but Ash wasn't going to take silence for an answer this time. The old man would either talk to him on the phone or he'd talk to him from a jail cell. Ash dialed and waited for him to pick up.

"How are Thomas Rahal and Cassandra Johnson connected?"

"I wondered when you would call me again."

"What do you know?" asked Ash.

Bukoholov paused. When he answered again, his voice sounded almost pensive. "What do you know, Detective Rashid?"

"I think some of my colleagues have been less than honest lately, and when I started investigating, they threatened to burn my house down. I also think you've been holding out on me."

"Rest assured that your family is in no danger. I have men watching your house at this moment."

Ash paused and ground his teeth.

"You knew what would happen if I started investigating."

"I had an idea, and I took precautionary measures to protect your wife and children. I knew you could take care of yourself."

"You son of a bitch," said Ash. "Don't you think I deserve to make decisions about my family's safety myself?"

"Sometimes people like me—and you, incidentally—have to make hard decisions that affect other people. Unfortunately, I can't often concern myself with what those people deserve. I have to deal with the world as it is. If you can't understand that, perhaps you're not the man I thought you were."

"This isn't over."

"I don't suspect it is," said Bukoholov. "If you want

information about your case, though, come by my club. I'll tell you what I can."

Had Bukoholov been in reach, Ash would have punched him.

"If you knew something about this case, why didn't you tell me sooner?"

All traces of merriment disappeared from Bukoholov's voice by the time he answered.

"I thought that would be obvious, Detective. You wouldn't have believed me. Now, please, do as I ask so we can keep an undeserving man from going to prison for the rest of his life."

"Fine. I'm on my way."

17

Bukoholov's club had a gray limestone facade and marble columns in front. At one time, it had been a Masonic temple. Ash didn't know much about the Masons, but he doubted they'd be thrilled by the building's current use or owner. It was architecturally interesting, at least. There weren't a lot of buildings downtown that he could say that about. Rather than park on the street and fight his way through the crowd inside, he swung around the block and nosed his cruiser into the back alley. Little light penetrated the shadows cast by the nearby buildings, making it seem as if he were driving into a cave.

Ash parked beside a Dumpster and heard something scurry away as he opened his door. Probably rats. The alley ran for about a block in both directions, and it stunk like garbage and urine. As far as he could tell, he was alone. The last time Ash had been in the club, Bukoholov had hosted an illegal, high-stakes card game in one of the back rooms. If he still held the games, Bukoholov would have kept guards outside to protect the VIPs as they entered and exited the building. Maybe a crumbling regional economy was hurting more than just the city's budget.

Ash straightened his shirt and reached into his jacket for

his cell phone, intending to call Bukoholov and ask him to open the back door. As he did that, he heard a noise from the other end of the alley. He stopped moving for a second and looked to his right. There was something coming toward him, but his brain refused to process the image at first.

It was a car.

His legs locked at the knees as his brain finally caught up with his senses. The engine screamed louder, and the gray sedan slammed into a heavy plastic trash can about forty feet away. Black bags and garbage flew everywhere.

"Shit."

Ash vaulted onto the hood of his car, but not quick enough. The car plowed into his cruiser in a wrenching scream of metal striking metal. He pulled his legs back, but his left foot thumped into the speeding car's window, spinning him around like a top. The back of his skull crashed into the front window of his Crown Vic hard enough that lights flashed in front of his eyes as if he had just had his picture taken by thousands of cameramen at once. He grabbed his windshield wipers to prevent him from sliding off his car, while the sedan that struck him careened around the corner at the end of the alley, its tires screeching. Ash stayed on the hood until he felt his limbs again. He preferred the numbness.

He could move his left foot, so the ankle wasn't broken. That was about all the good he could say, though. He allowed gravity to pull him off the hood of the car, but he fell over as soon as he tried to stand. Sitting on the ground gave him a good view of his cruiser, at least. Deep furrows had been dug into the metal from the rear quarter panel all the way to the hood, while the plastic side-view mirror hung from a thin cord. The technicians in Vehicle Services weren't going to like that.

Ash hadn't seen the man who tried to hit him, but his car left dark gray paint embedded in his cruiser. He stayed on the damp, piss-smelling ground for another few minutes before trying to wrench the driver's door open. Despite straining his shoulders, it didn't budge. He pulled himself up using his car as a handhold and stood with most of his weight on his right foot. Through trial and error, he found he could put a little weight on his left foot without screaming in pain, but he couldn't walk on it.

He shuffled to the passenger's side of the car and sat down, his head feeling light and dizzy. In his present condition, driving was stupid, but staying in the alley and calling for assistance was even more stupid. Bukoholov was the only person who knew he'd be there. Ash couldn't understand why, but the old man had just tried to kill him. He wouldn't fail a second time, which meant Ash needed to get the hell out of there while he still could.

He grabbed the steering wheel, pulled himself into the driver's seat, and then put the key in the ignition. His muscles twitched and his vision was blurry. He blinked several times, trying to focus; it helped some, but not much.

Ash didn't try going home. Instead, he drove to the nearest hospital. It was a Sunday night and traffic was light, allowing him to avoid hitting anyone. He pulled to a stop under the glass awning in front of the Indiana University Hospital and took out his phone. Bukoholov said he had men watching Ash's house; given what had just happened, he needed to make sure his family was safe. He called IMPD's dispatcher and requested they send officers by his house to check the place out.

After that, he stumbled through the hospital's front doors. The nurses seemed to think he was drunk, so they kept shouting at him to fill out a form. For some reason, he couldn't understand what that meant. He reached to his belt for his badge to show them he was a cop, but before he could, someone saw his firearm and started screaming.

He couldn't remember what happened next except that a pair of security guards who seemed intent on smothering him tackled him. He blacked out after that. It wasn't the best trip he'd ever had to the emergency room.

Ash woke up the next morning in a hospital bed. His mouth felt dry, and his vision was blurry, but he was still alive; that usually signified that his night before wasn't too bad. He pushed a button on a remote control attached to the bed and lifted the top portion of his body upright. His sister and brother-in-law sat on chairs on the far side of the room. Nassir's head was tilted back and his chest rose and fell rhythmically as he slumbered. Rana stood up and walked toward the bed, wringing her hands. She put her hand on Ash's forehead as their mother had done when they were children.

"I'm glad you're awake," she said. "You looked terrible last night."

Ash tried to speak, but his mouth felt as if it were full of cotton balls. Rana handed him a glass of water from a stand beside the bed.

"Thank you," he said after taking a few sips. "Is Hannah here?"

Rana's shoulders rose and fell, and she looked at her feet before speaking. "She was pretty upset when she called last night. I don't think she wanted to see you."

The painkillers pumping through Ash's system must have been stronger than he thought. He sat up.

"I don't understand."

Rana took her hand from Ash's forehead before speaking. "Some patrol officers went to your house last night. You apparently called them in." Rana took a step back from the bed. "Were you drunk?"

Ash shut his eyes and sank deeper into the bed, not saying anything.

"Ashraf?" asked Rana.

"No. I was as sober as I am now. I was hit by another car."

Rana nodded slowly. "Hannah told the police you were probably drunk. The dispatcher thought so, too, from your call."

"I wasn't," he said, sighing. "Did Hannah say if the police found anybody at the house?"

"No."

Unfortunately, that didn't mean much. If Bukoholov had men watching his home, they probably had a police radio in their car. They would have known exactly when the patrols went by and what they were looking for. Hopefully the knowledge that officers were there would be enough to keep Bukoholov's men away. In the meantime, he had work to do. He pulled the blanket off his feet, but even with the drugs the hospital had poured into him, his ankle throbbed with pain.

"What time is it?"

Rana looked at her watch. "Twenty to eight," she said.

"Hannah's taking Megan to school. I'll call and see if she can come down. We'll talk about this together as a family. We're here for you, and we love you."

Ash closed his eyes. He didn't have time for an intervention. Rahal was going to trial in forty minutes. He opened his eyes and held his breath before swinging his legs off the bed. With the initial shock of pain out of the way, movement was more manageable. The hospital staff had put a thick fabric boot over his foot, but no cast. Hopefully nothing was broken. As if sensing his intent to leave, Rana put her hands on his shoulders and held him back.

"Just stay in bed for now. You tore some ligaments in your ankle, and you were hit on the head pretty hard. The doctors want you here for observation. Besides that, someone from your department is supposed to come at nine to talk to you. Hannah will wait."

The drugs must have loosened Ash's hold on his emotions because his face started to grow warm as his temper built.

"Hannah can wait, but court won't. I've got to go. Where are my clothes?"

Rana pressed his shoulders into the bed harder. "You are as stubborn as when you were a kid. You're not going anywhere."

Ash looked across the room. Nassir, his brother-in-law, was stirring, but his eyes weren't open yet. He looked back at his sister.

"If you don't let me up, I'll arrest you for obstructing a police officer. I'm not kidding, Rana. I have to get to court before my boss does something stupid."

She opened her mouth to say something but stopped when Nassir coughed.

"Let him go," he said. "He's an adult."

Rana wheeled around to face her husband. "He might be an adult, but he's also my little brother, and he's acting like a child."

They kept arguing, giving Ash a moment to clear his head. He moved his feet and stretched before feeling a breeze run across his skin. Rana and Nassir's conversation stopped instantly, but neither looked at him.

"If you're going to leave, you should put on some pants," said Nassir. "We brought you a bag."

Ash covered his legs with the bed's blanket. "Thank you."

Rana sighed and pinched the bridge of her nose. Ash did the same thing when he was exasperated, making him wonder where they had both learned it. Likely from their mother.

"Just don't do anything stupid."

She probably didn't know how big that request was. He promised her he'd do his best, though. She and Nassir left, leaving him alone to get dressed. He couldn't put much weight on his foot, so even getting off the bed took a while. He found a duffel bag of his clothes beside the chair on which Nassir had slept and then dressed in the room's en suite bathroom. He would have preferred to wear a suit to court, but Rana and Nassir had brought only jeans, boxer shorts, and a polo shirt. They'd have to do.

He grabbed the jacket he'd worn the night before as well as his keys, wallet, and badge. He had been tackled by the hospital's security guards the night before; hopefully they had his gun. If not, he had a whole new set of problems to deal with it. He made a final sweep of the room with his eyes but then limped outside when he couldn't find anything else. The hospital was a busy place. Ash used a handrail on the wall for support until he came across a pair of aluminum crutches leaning beside a door frame. They were roughly his size, so they'd do. He paused to look around but didn't see anyone with a limp. Hopefully the crutches wouldn't be missed.

It was a lot easier to walk once he had support. He stopped by the hospital's security desk to inquire about his firearm. The supervisor recognized him from the paper, but unfortunately, a lieutenant from Internal Affairs had already come by for his firearm. At least it was safe. Ash would make some inquiries at work when he got back.

He left the hospital by ten after eight and flagged a cab a few minutes later. The trip to the courthouse didn't take long. Lawyers, protesters, and police surrounded the building, while blue sawhorse barricades created a small patch where members of the media could congregate and broadcast without being harassed by the crowds. Ash paid the cabdriver with a credit card and hurried onto the sidewalk.

A couple of people holding signs proclaiming Thomas Rahal's guilt stared as Ash shuffled across the concrete, but none turned their vitriol toward him. As one of the relatively few Arab men in the area, he found that refreshing. He stopped and leaned on a sawhorse beside the media's enclosure. Leonard Wilson was being interviewed by one of the local TV stations. He nodded a cursory hello to Ash between questions but thankfully didn't try to include him in the discussion. He and Susan may not have always gotten along, but she was still a decent boss and an honest lawyer; that was a rare combination in Ash's experience. At the very least, she was the lesser of two evils in the race, and Ash didn't want to become any more involved with the other if he could help it. That didn't preclude him from listening, though.

"Thomas Rahal is innocent. Let me repeat: Mr. Rahal is innocent. Whether John Meyers can prove that in court, I don't know, but Susan Mercer never should have brought this case to trial. This is about politics, plain and simple. Ms. Mercer wants to seem tough on crime, and she may even win her case, but it will be a miscarriage of justice of the first degree."

Leonard spoke rapidly and gesticulated wildly to punctuate his points. He kept talking for another ten minutes, but Ash tuned him out. He may have looked more like a Southern Baptist minister than a politician, but if the delivery of his speech was any indication, he was more than capable of stealing an election. Several members of the crowd around Ash even nodded their heads in agreement when Leonard arrived at his talking points.

Even completely apart from the delivery, the content wasn't bad, either. As long as John Meyers put on a plausible case, Leonard could stick by his guns and say an innocent man had been convicted. That wouldn't win over too many converts to his position, but it would solidify Leonard's base. If Rahal was found not guilty, though, it would be one hell of a blow to Susan's election chances.

"That's quite a bold statement, Councilman. What do you have to back up your claim that Mr. Rahal is innocent?"

Leonard held his hands in front of him, smiling. "I'm afraid I can't divulge any information at this time. I'm sure it will come out during the trial. Now if you'll excuse me, I have some people to see before it begins."

Leonard slipped past the reporters and walked toward

Ash. He turned and hobbled away before the politician reached him. Leonard had done enough to damage his career; they didn't need to talk to each other again.

As expected, the line to get through the security checkpoint inside the courthouse was a nightmare. Amid the potential jurors, witnesses, and gallery members, Ash recognized several lawyers, detectives, and even homeless people likely trying to find somewhere warm to stay for the day. It was a hodgepodge of social class, ethnicity, and temperaments in a hot, confined area. Ash was amazed there hadn't been fistfights yet.

He held up his badge and went through the security gate without having to wait. The courthouse's interior was significantly less hectic than the lobby. Few courtrooms would be in session yet, so people milled about everywhere. Ash walked to the largest courtroom in the building but didn't recognize anyone in the crowd outside. According to a clock in the hallway, it was twenty to nine. Susan should already be here.

He felt his pockets for his cell phone, but he must have left it in the hospital. Since a phone call was out, he shuffled toward the door. Unlike the staid, wood-paneled courtrooms on television shows, the interior had drywall painted a flat white, while the furniture was light oak veneer over particleboard. Ash flashed his badge to the bailiff and walked toward the prosecutor's table. Susan scowled at him, but he could tell her heart wasn't in it. Had she been really mad, the skin beneath her eyes would have twitched. Her features softened when he drew near.

"I heard about your accident. We ordered flowers sent to your room this morning," she said. She looked at John Meyers. He didn't acknowledge her but instead stared at Ash quizzically. Ash tried to ignore him. "Sit down. You look like you're about to fall over."

Ash took a seat in the first row of chairs behind the prosecutor's table. He straightened his leg to take the pressure off his foot and looked at his boss.

"I never pictured you to be the flowers type."

"I wanted to ignore you, but I was outvoted," she said. "What are you doing here?"

"I came to cheer on my boss in a big case. In my infirm state, I think that should be worth at least a few days off."

"After last night, you deserve it. Charity talked to Lieutenant Stuart about the affidavit. He transposed two numbers in his informant's ID number. It was an honest mistake. We got the right information to John Meyers and Judge Haller, and she's going to let the charges stand as long as we make the confidential informant available to Meyers this afternoon and tomorrow for deposition. Haller might give him a short continuance, too, if he asks for it."

"Noah Stuart is a snake. He's up to something, so you shouldn't believe him."

"This is one of the strongest cases I've ever prosecuted, Ash. I've got almost half a dozen extremely credible witnesses to the shooting, Rahal's fingerprints on the firearm, a signed confession, and a city looking for a conviction. You've made your feelings about Noah Stuart very clear. You've also made it clear that you can't prove he's done anything wrong. Has that changed?"

"I can't prove anything yet, but—"

"Until that changes, I don't want to hear it. If you find something concrete, I will listen to every word you have to say and consider it. Until then, stay out of my hair."

She was still stuck on her case, and maybe she was right to be. When she discussed it, it sounded solid. There was more, though. There had to be.

"Good luck."

"Thank you."

Ash would have left, but at that moment, a uniformed bailiff led Thomas Rahal into the room. To Ash, he looked healthier than he had a day earlier, but poor eyesight may have just been one of the residual effects of his head injury from the night before. At the very least, Rahal seemed to have a little more energy. Hopefully that meant he had been able to get a couple of meals that didn't feature pork.

Judge Ann Haller came in right after Rahal. Haller was new to the bench, and if the lack of wrinkles on her face and neck were any indication, she couldn't have been more than forty. She had a long career ahead of her, so Ash thought it was in his long-term interests to avoid upsetting her now by slipping out in front of her.

The day started out swiftly with the judge introducing herself before turning the stage over to Susan for her opening statement. Ash watched his boss for a little while, but he also watched the jury. There were seven women and five men plucked from all layers of society, and they all seemed riveted by the story Susan spun. Ash had heard the information before, but Charity Lewis's rendition had been dry and lifeless; Susan was a storyteller.

Rahal, according to Susan, was an underemployed immigrant who sold drugs as a side job to support his family. He was a criminal, but he may not have been a bad guy, she explained, until he picked up a gun, hid under his daughter's crib, and fired at a police officer. By doing that, he put himself outside the law and its protections. He declared war on his adopted society, and for that reason, Susan asked the jury to find him guilty of all charges brought against him. The statement was eloquent, impassioned, and clear. By the time she finished speaking, at least three jurors were nodding and one went so far as to frown at Rahal.

Meyers stood up and spoke next. His opening statement was just as impassioned and just as clear as Susan's, but he made no broad pronouncements that his client was innocent and gave no outlines of a strategy to prove the trial was a farce. He focused on reasonable doubt and a man who had been rushed to trial. Meyers wouldn't admit it, but his case was weak. His trial strategy seemed to center around taking potshots at Susan's case and hoping for the best. That might be good enough to keep Rahal off death row, but he needed more for an acquittal. He needed an alternative theory of the crime that made as much sense of the facts as Susan's theory.

Despite everything Ash had found, Meyers wasn't the only one still in the dark.

He left at the break after opening statements. Susan would call her first witness in fifteen minutes, and, unlike celebrity trials that went on for days, she'd probably be done by Wednesday. That didn't give him much time. The court-house was about a block from his office, so he considered walking straight to work. With his foot in the state it was, that probably would have taken him several days. Moreover, he hadn't been home all night, and after wallowing in a dank alley, he wanted to take a shower. His coworkers would prob-ably appreciate that as well.

He took a cab home. Hannah went grocery shopping on Monday mornings, so the driveway was empty when he arrived. Ash paid the cabdriver, went inside, and called his wife while he sat at their breakfast table. Hannah picked up on the second ring.

"Hey, honey," said Ash. "I just wanted to call and tell you that I'm home."

Ash had hoped his wife would be pleased to hear he was home and free from permanent brain damage or other debilitating injuries. Instead, she sighed exasperatedly.

"We'll talk about that later. You're not going to believe where I am right now."

"The checkout line at Walmart?"

She paused. "No," she said, sounding more than a little perturbed. "I'm in the principal's office at Megan's school."

Ash sat straighter. "Is she okay?"

"She won't be when I'm done with her."

Ash grimaced. Despite it being early in the semester, Megan had already visited the principal's office more times than he cared to remember. Usually she was accompanied by Lisa, but no more, obviously. Megan was a good kid and she had a good heart, but she was one of the few Muslim kids in school, which led to misunderstandings. On the first day, some of the other kids made fun of her for calling Ash *Baba* instead of *Dad* or *Daddy*. There had also been incidents in the cafeteria, but nothing serious yet. Ash had been the only Muslim kid in school when he was young, too, so he was sympathetic. At least Megan hadn't gotten into fistfights like he had.

"Did she yell at the other kids for eating with their left hands again?"

"I wish," said Hannah. "After morning recess today, Megan was disruptive in class, so Mrs. Clardy had to ask her to quiet down more than once. After the third time, Megan climbed on top of her desk, put her hands above her head, and then brought them down in an X motion over her crotch while shouting, 'Suck it.' Where does a six-year-old even learn to do something like that?"

Unfortunately, Ash knew exactly where Megan had learned to do that. He wasn't sure how she was introduced to it, but she loved professional wrestling and watched it on nights when Hannah was at yoga class. In some strange way, he could understand her interest. The villains of professional wrestling were unabashedly bad, while the heroes were almost always virtuous and good. Moreover, everyone got his come-uppance in the end. It probably reinforced the worldview he and Hannah were trying to instill in her. Ash didn't think he'd score too many points mentioning that, though.

"Is she with you now?"

"Yes. And I already told her you'd want to talk to her."

Hannah handed Megan the phone before resuming a discussion with the principal, giving him a moment of private conversation with his daughter.

"Hi, *Baba*," she said, her voice small. "I think I did something bad."

"That's what I hear. Do you remember what I told you about professional wrestling?"

Megan hesitated for a second. "Never tell *Ummi*."

Ash paused. "Yeah. What else did I say about professional wrestling?"

Megan's voice was smaller still. "Don't do what the wrestlers do."

"That's right," he said. "I know it's not fun to listen to Mrs. Clardy, but she's your teacher. You have to do what she tells you. Do you understand?"

"Yes, *Baba*," she said. "Are you mad at me?"

Ash considered his answer for a second. "I'm disappointed in you, but I'm not angry."

"Oh," said Megan, her voice thoughtful. "Am I in trouble?"

"Yes," he said. "You're in big trouble."

"I thought so."

Megan put her mother back on the phone. Hannah and Ash didn't talk for long, but they agreed to bar Megan from watching television for the next two weeks. That seemed like the start of a fair punishment, at least. With his family taken care of, Ash leaned back in his chair to think about the case.

He had enjoyed only modest success so far, but he hadn't known where to look. Now he had a starting point: the search warrant. Noah Stuart had worked hard to get faulty paperwork in order, and Ash wanted to find out what he could about it. Technically, a search warrant and its various filings are public records, so he should have been able to go to the county records building and pick them up. In actuality, though, a records search wasn't that easy, and he needed more information than he currently had.

Ash considered his options and then called Susan Mercer's office and waited for her secretary to pick up.

"Pam, it's Detective Ash Rashid. I know Susan's in court, so I need you to check something for me."

"I heard about your car accident. Are you okay?"

"I've been better," he said, answering honestly. "I need some information for the Rahal case, though. Do you remember when the warrant for the search of Thomas Rahal's home was approved?"

Pam clucked her tongue. "Is this for Susan?"

Ash hesitated. "Yeah. I'm just double-checking something for her."

"Okay," said Pam. "Give me a second."

She put him on hold for two or three minutes while she found the information he requested. The date she eventually gave him was a little over four months ago. She also gave him the case number. Ash wrote the information down and thanked her before hanging up. It was time to see what other problems he could find with the Rahal case.

18

Since Ash's car had been impounded after being run into behind Bukoholov's club, he could have gone by Vehicle Services and requested another. That'd require filling out more paperwork than he thought was worthwhile at the moment, though, so he called a rental place and asked what they had available. They offered him an American-made luxury monstrosity or a Japanese econobox, which would likely double as his coffin if he got into an accident. Based on his track record with vehicles in the past week, Ash chose the monstrosity and bought extra insurance. The rental company said they'd pick him up in about an hour, giving him time to shower and change before starting his day.

The city kept criminal court records in either the basement of the City-County Building or in a city-owned warehouse near the airport. Hopefully the information he needed was recent enough to still be downtown. Once he picked up the car, he drove to the City-County Building and parked on the street about half a block away.

It was a workday, so dozens of city workers sat outside smoking and, more often than not, catching up on interoffice gossip. Ash stopped by a coffee shop about a block away and purchased a plain black coffee and a sweet espresso drink with caramel sauce and whipped cream. The barista was even nice enough to give him a cardboard holder so he could carry them while on his crutches. He put a couple of bucks in her tip jar; it's the little things that make life easier.

Once he had the drinks, he shuffled back to the City-County Building and took the elevator to the basement. The county record's office was sparsely decorated and its lobby had cinder-block walls painted baby blue. The air smelled musty, making a trip there almost feel like going to the library. Ash walked to the counter at the head of the room and smiled at the clerk. She stopped typing and smiled in return.

"The coffee shop on Pennsylvania gave me a free sample if you'd like one."

The clerk shook her head. "I'm afraid I'm not allowed to accept tips or gifts, but thank you."

Ash removed his badge from his belt and laid it on the counter. "I'm not allowed, either, so I'd be eternally grateful if you helped me destroy the evidence by drinking a cup of my free coffee. I've got straight black coffee and some sort of caramel drink."

The clerk hesitated but then took the caramel espresso and nodded toward him. A cup of coffee was almost nothing in the world of bribes, but even a little courtesy usually went a long way.

"Thank you, Detective," she said, taking a sip. She pulled the drink away from her and stared at it a second later. "This is good. What can I do for you?"

"I need to see a search warrant and its accompanying affidavit filed in July. Is that still available downtown?"

"It should be. If not, I'm sure we can find it. Do you have the case number and date it was filed?"

Ash took out his notepad and read her the information, which she entered into her computer. It took her a moment, but eventually she furrowed her brow. She looked at him again.

"I've got good news and bad news. The good news is we do have your search warrant and all accompanying documentation. The bad news is that a judge ordered everything sealed, so I can't give it to you."

Ash leaned against the counter, taking the weight off his injured foot. "Can you give me a copy of the order sealing the documents?"

"Sure," said the clerk, nodding. She typed something on her computer before grabbing her coffee. "I'll be right back."

The clerk disappeared into the records room. Generally speaking, the only people who ever went back there were other clerks, but Ash had been given a tour about a year earlier. Had he known what was inside, he probably would have stayed in the lobby. The room was simply a large, open space with row upon row of gray metal filing cabinets. He didn't know the place's history, but he was reasonably sure no one had ever had fun in it. Had there been a chair in the middle, it would have been a great place to put a kid for time-out.

As soon as the clerk came back, she handed Ash a still-warm photocopy of the order to seal the affidavit. He skimmed. Lieutenant Noah Stuart of the Northeastern Precinct declared under penalty of perjury that he believed allowing the public to view the affidavit would damage an ongoing investigation and reveal the identity of at least one undercover police officer. It was standard language for an ex parte order to seal the documents in a narcotics case.

Ash flipped the document around and slid it toward the clerk. "Can you read the judge's signature?"

She squinted and picked up the paper. "I believe that's Michael Garibaldi," she said. "He doesn't write—he scribbles."

Ash turned the paper toward him and wrote the name below the judge's signature.

"I haven't heard of him," he said. "Is he new?"

"Oh, no," said the clerk, shaking her head. "He's been on the bench since the early seventies, but normally he only works cases involving juveniles. We've been getting a lot of documents from his office lately, though. Must be that time of year."

"Yeah, it must be," said Ash, jotting the information down. Garibaldi was a superior court judge, so he certainly possessed the authority to issue a search warrant. Ash was surprised he hadn't heard of him, though. The average criminal wasn't very big on respecting other people's time, so he didn't stop committing crimes at the end of a regular workday. Because of that, the court system had a rotating schedule that kept a judge on duty twenty-four hours a day for emergencies; somehow, Garibaldi was able to stay off the rotation. Ash wasn't sure what that meant. "You don't know where his office is, by chance, do you?"

"Sorry, I don't. It's probably upstairs somewhere."

Ash nodded and grabbed his coffee. "Thank you for your time," he said, stuffing his notebook into his jacket pocket. "I appreciate it."

"And thank you, Detective. It's not every day I get treated to a coffee for doing my job."

Ash winked at her and put his finger to his lips before heading to the elevator. The City-County Building was a utilitarian, twenty-eight-story glass and steel block that had been built sometime during the Kennedy administration. It wasn't a blight on the city's skyline, but it didn't do much to beautify it, either. Unfortunately, it was also so large and so poorly laid out that only people who traversed its halls on a regular basis knew how to get anywhere. Ash spent ten minutes in the lobby looking through the building's directory before he found the number for Judge Garibaldi's office. By that time in the morning, the building was clearing out as people went to lunch. Hopefully he could catch Garibaldi's clerk before he or she left, too.

He took the elevator to the sixth floor and stepped into a hallway a little nicer than he had expected. The gray carpet wasn't plush, but it lacked holes or other signs of significant wear. Unlike his own building, he didn't have to take off his jacket or bundle up with a scarf to feel comfortable, either. That showed where law enforcement ranked in the city's pecking order.

Judge Garibaldi and his staff had a corner office suite at the end of the building. Ash knocked on the oak door and waited for someone to respond, but no one did. The door was unlocked, so he stuck his head inside to see if anyone was home. The overhead lights were off, and the window blinds were drawn, shading the interior. Bookshelves carrying legal texts covered every wall, while an Oriental throw rug covered the floor. A young woman sat behind a desk in the middle of the floor, yawning and rubbing her eyes.

"Can I help you?" she asked, opening her eyes wide. She squinted at him. Ash didn't know her name, but he had seen her before. "I know you. Aren't you the guy who called Professor Ruiz's daughter a prostitute last year?"

Ash shifted his weight on his crutches. "It wasn't my finest moment, but yes."

She perked up immediately. "I'm Sarah Baird. We graduated the same year. If you're here looking for a job, Judge Garibaldi already has a full staff of clerks. Sorry."

She probably said that a lot. The legal market was always competitive, but with the economy on the ropes, law firms and the big government agencies had hired fewer new attorneys than usual in the past few years, making the market tougher than many attorneys had ever seen. Thankfully, Ash didn't have to worry about it. Like death and taxes, crime occurred no matter what anyone did, guaranteeing him a job for the foreseeable future.

Ash pulled back his jacket, exposing his badge. "I'm employed, but thank you," he said. "I'd like to talk to Judge Garibaldi about a warrant he signed a few months ago. Is he in?"

Sarah pulled a stray strand of her brunette hair past her ear. "Yes, but he's unavailable right now."

"When will he be available?"

She glanced at her watch and shrugged. "He usually wakes up in twenty or thirty minutes."

Ash thought it was a joke, but she looked serious.

What is this, naptime?

"Maybe you can help me, then. I'm interested in a search warrant the judge signed in July. It's sealed, but I need to see it."

Sarah opened her mouth to say something, but then she broke eye contact and stared at the desk, fidgeting.

"It's not our office's policy to discuss warrants without the judge present. Perhaps if you know the detectives involved, you can talk to them."

The judge had the first and final say on all warrants, so it was a sensible policy. Ash thought there was more going on than it seemed, though. Sarah almost looked nervous. He flicked his eyes to the door leading to the judge's private office.

"Are you all right?" he asked.

She straightened. "I'm fine, but I'd prefer if you come back later when Judge Garibaldi is available."

He leaned on his crutches and took a step back from the desk before putting up his hands, purposely exposing his wedding ring. The legal profession was better than it had once been, but it was still something of an old boys' club. Even though she had been in the profession for only a limited amount of time, Sarah was probably accustomed to being hit on and propositioned by other attorneys.

"I'm a detective, and my visit is purely professional. We can leave the door open if you'd like, but I do need to talk to somebody."

She shook her head and closed her eyes. "I'm not worried about being seen. I've been out of work since May, and I'm sure I don't need to tell you how hard it is to pay student loan bills. I need this job. I can't do anything to jeopardize it."

"I'm not sure that I'm following," he said. "I just need to see a warrant and its supporting affidavit. That's all. I am a police officer, and I'm involved in an investigation. I can have someone call to verify my employment if you'd like."

Sarah caught and held his gaze. Eventually, her eyes softened.

"Can you meet me outside the City Market in about ten minutes?"

The City Market was an indoor farmer's market just across the street, making it a popular lunch spot for city employees. Ash looked at his watch. It was about twenty to noon, so the market would be busy as hell.

"I'll see if I can get some seats."

She nodded and began tidying up her desk while he left the building. The sky was cloudy, and the temperature was in the low fifties, limiting the appeal of sitting at the market's exterior tables. That's what Sarah wanted, though, so that's what they would do.

Ash crossed the street at the nearest light and sat on a metal bench bolted to the sidewalk to wait. Several people smiled at him as they passed. Most were probably just trying to be friendly, but a good number drifted to the edge of the sidewalk and sped up as soon as they saw him. That was the price to pay for being an Arab in the Midwest, though. They probably didn't even consciously realize they were shying away from him, so he wasn't too bothered by it.

Sarah came down on schedule and waved at him from across the street. Ash took out his notebook and flipped pages until he found a clean one. When Sarah sat down beside him, she held her head higher and her breathing seemed easier.

"Are you okay here?" he asked. "We can go inside if you'd like."

She took a quick look around before turning to him. "It's fine. I don't see anyone I know," she said. "I know you might have to report some of the things I say, but I'm only going to speak on one condition. Keep my name out of anything you write. You can call me a source or whatever, but I don't want this coming back on me."

Ash furrowed his brow. "If you're about to confess to a crime, I will have to arrest you. We're both attorneys, but our conversation isn't privileged."

"I know, and I haven't done anything wrong. I don't think Judge Garibaldi has, either, at least not intentionally."

Ash's hands tingled. The conversation wasn't what he had expected, making him think he was about to either discover something important to his case or step into the middle of something he had no business being involved in. With his luck, it would be both.

"Okay. Tell me what you can."

Sarah shifted on the seat and turned so her shoulders faced Ash. "Judge Garibaldi is brilliant. When he's on, he's like a walking legal encyclopedia. When I interviewed for this clerkship position, we talked about a law review article I had written, and he knew more about the subject off the top of his head than I did after a year of study. He was smart. He was charming. He was funny. He was like a better-educated version of my grandfather. Do you know what I mean?"

Ash hadn't ever met either of his grandfathers, but he nodded anyway as if he knew exactly what she meant.

"I'm sensing there's a 'but' coming."

She nodded. "Yeah. His court hears cases involving juveniles, so he likes to keep up with trends among teenagers. About a month into my job, he got a case involving a bunch of kids from Carmel who used Facebook to plan parties where they would get drunk and smoke pot. Judge Garibaldi thought Facebook was a physical book kids would pass around to each other at school, so I had to explain it to him before he came to a decision on a motion."

Ash nodded and jotted a few notes, not sure what she was implying.

"Okay. I'm with you so far."

"Good. Here's the problem: Judge Garibaldi has his own Facebook page. I checked. It hasn't been updated for a while, but he's Facebook friends with his grandkids and his son and daughter. He even published an article last year about the privacy rights of adolescents in a digital world. He knew what Facebook was, but he forgot."

Ash shifted his weight and furrowed his brow. "What are you getting at?"

"Facebook isn't the only thing he's forgotten. His office has been in the same spot in the City-County Building for twenty years, but he couldn't find it two weeks ago. He tries to cover up his memory lapses, but he gets confused at least once a day. I talked about this with my fiancé, who's a neurology resident at Methodist Hospital. He thinks Judge Garibaldi might have dementia or early stage Alzheimer's disease."

Ash tilted his head back and looked up at the gray sky, understanding Sarah's trepidation to speak. If the judge's mental condition became common knowledge, every case he had worked on for the past ten or fifteen years would have to be reviewed and possibly retried. It would cost an already cash-strapped county millions. It might not reflect well on the judge's law clerks, either, for letting him keep working without making a bigger fuss.

"Is this why he isn't on the call list with the rest of the criminal court judges?"

Sarah started to nod, but then stopped. "Yeah, but it

doesn't stop people from seeing him. Detectives still come to him when they need things signed. We think they take advantage of him."

That might have explained the uptick in Garibaldi-signed documents the record's room saw, too.

"Who's *we*?"

Sarah looked away. "Me, the judge's former clerks, and a few others. Judge Garibaldi is a good man, but he doesn't want to admit what's happening to him. If a detective comes in with an affidavit for a search warrant and a story about how the judge already promised to sign it, then he'll sign without reading it. I've seen it happen. He doesn't want to seem like a fool."

"Can't the courts do something?"

"The court has done something. The judge supervising the criminal courts has taken Judge Garibaldi off the on-call list, and he's limited the number of cases he presides over. He's also filed a notice with the Judicial Qualifications Commission of the Indiana Supreme Court, but their investigation will take time. Judge Garibaldi has given forty years of his life to this court. No one will remove him without proper deliberation."

The judge's deteriorating mental abilities would be disastrous for the court, but they weren't his primary interest. Something she said stuck out to him, though.

"You said detectives are taking advantage of him. Do you have anyone specific in mind?"

"I've seen several come, but I don't know any of their names. If I saw them again, I might be able to point them out."

"Is the name Noah Stuart familiar?"

Sarah shrugged. "Yeah. I've heard that name before, but I don't know where. He's a lieutenant, isn't he?"

"Yeah," said Ash. Her recognition wasn't proof that Noah was up to something nefarious, but it helped. "I'm looking for one affidavit in particular. It involved a search of Thomas Rahal's home. Does that ring a bell?"

"Did Judge Garibaldi sign it?"

Ash nodded.

"I know Thomas Rahal's name because he's on trial, but I don't remember anything else about the case. If Judge Garibaldi issued the warrant, we have the documentation. It won't be in our office, though. We're digitizing our file system and have outsourced it to a legal staffing firm. They have everything but our most recent files."

Of course it wasn't accessible. Nothing he ever wanted was available. Ash flipped to a clean page in his notebook.

"What company is that?"

"Professional Staffing Services. I think they're in Fishers."

He wrote the name down and leveraged himself upright with his crutches, feeling his injured foot throb once again as blood rushed into his legs.

"Okay. Thanks for your time. Are you going to be by this afternoon in case I have to see you again?"

"Until four or so," she said, reaching into her purse and pulling out her wallet. She took out a cream-colored business card and handed it to Ash. "That has my cell phone number and e-mail address on it if you need to reach me."

"Thanks," he said, slipping the card into his pocket. "Good luck with the judge."

Sarah stayed on the bench as he walked away. There were

two or three dozen judges in the county who could issue arrest and search warrants; if Noah needed a warrant issued, he could have gone to any of them. He wouldn't have gone to Garibaldi without reason. What that reason was, though, God only knew.

Ash stood and started walking back to his office, but stopped before arriving. An overweight, middle-aged man stepped out of a bar down the street, a broom in one hand and a cigarette in the other. He nodded and threw the butt of his cigarette on the ground.

"You coming in for a round, Detective?"

Ash didn't recognize the guy, but he must have been a regular in his bar if he knew Ash was a detective. Hannah had reason to be worried about his drinking, apparently. He sighed, wondering if he was a regular at other bars and didn't realize it.

"Not today," he said. "Too much work to do."

"This weekend, then. And hey, saw you on the news. Good luck with Representative Wilson's campaign."

Ash relaxed some. Maybe he wasn't a regular after all; maybe he was just a familiar face from TV.

"Thank you," he said, glancing at his watch. The barkeep took the hint and began sweeping his front stoop. With his proximity to so many office buildings, he probably did a brisk business. He wouldn't remember one customer. Ash's drinking wasn't that bad; it was a problem, maybe, but it wasn't a disaster.

It was just after noon, so Megan, assuming she wasn't in trouble, would likely be at recess, while Hannah and Kaden would probably be at home. Knowing they were safe did a lot to make his day more tolerable. He found an empty bus bench nearby and sat down to think through his situation. Fishers was at least a half-hour drive, so he didn't want to make the trip if he didn't have to.

He pulled out his cell phone and used the built-in browser to look up Professional Staffing Services. As soon as he had the company's number, he called the office and waited through six rings before the voice mail system picked up. Apparently they weren't open on Mondays. Ash left a voice mail with his name and cell number, but he doubted anyone would call him back anytime soon. Few businesses jumped when a detective asked to see their records. More than likely, he'd get a call from the company's legal counsel sometime the next day telling him to piss off until he got a search warrant. Maybe he'd get lucky, though.

He walked back to his office and joined two office mates in noon prayer before settling into work at his desk. He doubted it would help, but he wanted to find Rahal's neighbor if he could. He got the phone number of the apartment's leasing office from the Internet and called. A woman picked up quickly.

"Fairview Properties, can I help you?"

"This is Detective Ash Rashid with the Indianapolis Metropolitan Police Department. I'm calling about one of your previous residents. He lived next to Thomas Rahal."

"You'll have to show me a court order before I can talk about our residents. We don't release private information unless ordered to do so."

Ash shifted in his seat. "I'm investigating two separate homicides, and I just need his name. I don't need to know about his rental history or anything private. Just a name."

"You think Andrew killed somebody?"

Ash took out his pen and shrugged even though no one was around to witness it. "What do you think?"

"He was a creep who liked looking at me. I just turned nineteen, and he was like fifty. It was gross."

"What was Andrew's last name? You're not the only person who thought he was a creep. I need to check him out."

She hesitated. "I should call my manager."

"It's just a name. It's in the phone book."

He heard keys click as she typed.

"Andrew Rutkowski."

"Did he give you a forwarding address?"

"I'm not supposed to tell you these things without talking to my boss first."

"I can get his address by calling the post office, miss. I'm asking you to save me a little time. These aren't state secrets."

She muttered something under her breath before typing on her computer again. "He didn't leave a forwarding address when he left, and he owes us two months' rent. Anything else? Maybe you want me to add you to his Christmas card list?"

Snarky teenage girls. In another seven years, Ash would have one of his own. He didn't look forward to it.

"That's it," he said, writing the information down. "Thanks for your time."

She hung up immediately. Ash stretched and yawned before opening the department's felon database. Andrew Rutkowski had a record, but it was uninspiring. He had a couple of convictions for trespassing, two convictions for possession of marijuana, and one conviction for possession of a schedule II substance. The specific drug wasn't listed, but it was probably crack or cocaine.

In the last decade, Rutkowski had spent about eighteen

months in and out of the county correctional facility. He was
last arrested two years ago for misdemeanor solicitation of a
prostitute. Unfortunately, he didn't seem to commit crimes
with anyone in particular, nor did he stay in one spot for very
long. The arrest record didn't give Ash much to go on, and it
didn't give him a current address.

Ash opened a Web browser next. The Internet was one of
the best investigative tools the department had, especially for
crimes involving teenagers. Common sense eludes some people
as soon as they sit in front of a keyboard. People who usually
would never talk about drug deals or other illegal activities suddenly become chatty. Hopefully Rutkowski was equally stupid.

Ash Googled Rutkowski's name and clicked on the first
link in the results. The story was from a newspaper in Gary,
Indiana, a formerly thriving industrial town south of Chicago. He read the title and skimmed the article, feeling his
gut twist. Eventually, he pushed himself back from the desk
and swore under his breath.

Rutkowski was dead. Two weeks ago, a bunch of kids found
his decaying corpse hanging from an I beam in a shuttered steel
mill. Ash scanned for follow-up articles but didn't find anything.
Cassandra Johnson, Carl Gillespie, and now Rutkowski. Knowing anything about Thomas Rahal was a hazardous proposition.

"Shit."

He spoke loud enough that several detectives around him
looked up from whatever they were working on. Each of
them had been in Ash's shoes before, though, so they smiled
and went back to their work without saying anything. Eventually he picked up the phone and called the information
desk at Gary's police department. It took some arm-twisting,
but the dispatcher called the detective assigned to Rutkowski's

case on Ash's behalf and left a message. Ten minutes later, that detective called Ash's office phone.

"What can I do for you? I'm off the clock."

Ash heard the distinctive clack of billiard balls striking each other and a low murmur of conversation in the background. It was early afternoon, but the detective was in a bar. So far, Ash's day had been free of alcohol cravings, but he had a hard time ignoring that familiar sound.

"Detective Rashid?"

"Yeah, sorry," said Ash, shaking his head and focusing. "I'm calling about Andrew Rutkowski. I wondered if you found anything."

"His case is still open pending new developments."

Translating that, he had nothing and didn't plan to waste more time on it unless something else came up.

"In your investigation, did you come across the names Thomas Rahal, Cassandra Johnson, or Carl Gillespie?"

The officer paused for a second. "No, what's this about?"

"I think your vic was murdered for knowing something about a case I'm investigating. Have you found anything at all?"

"No," he said, his voice brightening. "But it sounds like Indianapolis may have jurisdiction on this."

"Unless our jurisdiction extends all the way to Gary, he's yours. Thanks all the same, though."

"Yeah, whatever," said the detective, his voice sounding dejected once again. Ash wrote down the detective's number before hanging up and rubbing his eye sockets. Four days and his investigation into Cassandra Johnson was going in circles at best. He ran his fingers over his eyelids to the bridge of his nose. This had to end soon or they weren't going to have any witnesses left.

19

Whether consciously or not, Ash parked half a block from a downtown pub he and a lot of cops frequented. No one expected him for a while, so he had time to go in and grab a drink. The pub made its own crackers, so he'd even have something with which to soak up the alcohol in his stomach. He started walking without thinking but stopped as soon as his hand pulled open the door and a cloud of smoke billowed out. He'd never get the smell out of his clothes, and as suspicious as she was, Hannah would probably be able to guess where he had been as soon as he stepped through the door at home.

He let the door fall shut before closing his eyes. "I'm an asshole."

He took a step back from the bar. He was beginning to think like some of the teenagers he had picked up when he'd been a patrol officer. They would carry around changes of clothes, cologne, and dryer sheets to keep their mothers from knowing they had spent the entire night smoking marijuana. It wasn't normal behavior for an adult. Besides, getting caught wasn't even the real problem; he could get around that easily enough. He could tell Hannah he interviewed a witness in a bar or that a suspect wanted to smoke during an interrogation.

Both happened on the job. If she wanted confirmation, Ash could even call David Lee or one of the other detectives he knew to cover for him. Lee was a good guy, and he'd do it without skipping a beat. Ash's family deserved someone better than that, though. He stared at the door for another moment, his entire body feeling heavy.

Two days. Ash had gone two days without a drink, and he already felt miserable. He wasn't sure how other people did it. Eventually, he turned and walked toward his rental car. It was early, so the drive was quick. Two cars cut him off, one so close he had to swerve into another lane to avoid being hit, but he didn't have the energy to stay mad. By the time he made it home, he could barely keep his eyes open. When he got in, he hugged his wife, played with Kaden, and then fell into bed.

Megan woke him up a few hours later by jumping on the bed when she came home from school. His head felt clearer after his nap; the drugs the hospital had given him earlier that morning must have been wearing off. Despite a throbbing foot, Ash threw Megan over his shoulder and carried her to the backyard, where he watched her play for another hour. They probably would have stayed out longer, but Megan coughed intermittently and Ash didn't want her to get ill.

Eventually, the family had prayer and then dinner. Hannah had made lamb stew with rice. He tried to feed Kaden, but the baby was more interested in pulling his chest hair than eating squash. At least Kaden didn't vomit on him. That always made an evening better. He went down at about seven, and Megan followed an hour later. Ash and Hannah stayed up for an hour after that, talking. They didn't do anything special, but it was one of the best nights he had spent with her in a long time. Ash realized as they went to bed why it had seemed so nice: it was the first night he had been home and sober in at least a month.

As Hannah turned off the light, Ash lay in bed, staring at the ceiling. "I haven't had a drink in two days. It's been hard."

Hannah reached over and grabbed his hand and squeezed. "Let's make it two more."

Ash's alarm rang at a little after seven the next morning, but he hit the snooze button twice before swinging his legs off the bed. Despite having nothing to drink the night before, his head pounded as if he had gone out on a weeklong bender. He blinked and rubbed his temples, hoping the fresh blood flow would alleviate some of the pain. It didn't. At least his foot wasn't screaming at him anymore every time he put weight on it. That was something.

Ash stayed for about a minute, waiting for his daughter to come bounding into the room as she usually did when his alarm rang. Apparently he wasn't as interesting as he once had been, though, because she stayed wherever she was, giving him a few minutes of privacy to shower, shave, and get dressed.

When he got out of the shower, Hannah sat at the breakfast table, typing something on their aging laptop. Neither child was in the room. Ash left his crutches against a wall in the kitchen and pulled out the chair opposite her and sat down, expecting to hear crying or the pounding of tiny feet running toward him. Nothing.

"You finally did it," he said. "You put the kids up for adoption so we can live the rest of our lives in quiet wedded bliss."

Hannah finished whatever she had been typing and then closed the laptop, ignoring his attempt at humor.

"Megan was coughing this morning and her chest sounded congested, so I'm keeping her home from school. It sounds like bronchitis. I'll take her to Dr. Prior's office as soon as I can. Kaden may be coming down with the same thing because he sounded congested, too."

Having spent most of her working career in a pediatric hospital, Hannah would know what a respiratory infection sounded like. It was too bad she didn't work anymore because she would have been able to get free samples of medicine from the hospital. Even with health insurance, drugs were expensive; add the copays from the kids' doctor appointments, and they'd be three hundred dollars in the hole for the day. There was nothing he could do about it but complain, though.

"Well, at least Megan won't get in trouble for doing more professional wrestling moves if she's sick."

Hannah squinted at him. "What do you mean about professional wrestling moves?"

Shit.

Ash coughed into his hand to cover his initial pause. "That thing in class when she jumped on the desk. I asked a guy at work about it. He said a bunch of professional wrestlers do it."

Hannah shook her head. She moved her lips, but no sound came out at first. "It's her uncle Jack, you know," she said. "He lets her watch whatever she wants when she visits."

Ash's shoulders relaxed. "Yeah, it must be Jack. Can you believe the nerve of that guy? I'll call him and ask him to make sure he puts on kid-friendly programs."

"And tell him if Megan comes back doing more of that, I'll do some pro-wrestling moves on him."

"I will," said Ash, standing. He poured half a mug of coffee from the pot Hannah had made earlier but stopped when he put it to his nose. It smelled...good. He furrowed his brow and sipped gingerly. The coffee was smooth and nutty.

"Sorry about the coffee," said Hannah, standing and waving. "I'm out of our usual stuff, so I had to get this at the grocery store. I ordered more beans on the Internet."

Ash looked at his cup wistfully. Some things are just too good to last.

"I can live with this for a while," he said. "No hurry."

"Don't worry. I know how you like your coffee, so I paid extra for expedited shipping. We won't be out too long."

"Great," said Ash, forcing himself to smile.

They had dawn prayer, and Ash checked on the kids before leaving. Megan looked a little paler than usual, and her breathing sounded raspy. Kaden was asleep, so Ash didn't wake him up. He didn't usually sleep that late, so he was likely sick, too. It was never fun to be ill, but it seemed worse with young children. Kaden couldn't even tell them what was wrong. Hopefully whatever they had would be short-lived.

He left his crutches in the kitchen and kissed Hannah on his way out the door. Neither Susan nor John Meyers were the sort of attorneys to grandstand before cameras or prolong a trial beyond what was necessary. As soon as Susan rested, Meyers would pound the prosecution's case, attack witnesses, and present an alternative theory of the crime, but he'd finish within two or three days. That didn't leave Ash much time to complete what he started.

He drove to his office and went by Susan Mercer's floor to let her know he had come in for the day, but she and Charity were already busy discussing their trial. Both women said hello but quickly went back to work. That was just as well; he didn't have anything new to tell either of them. By ten after eight, he was back in his car, driving toward Professional Staffing Services, one of the firms the county had hired to help digitize old court filings. Their office occupied half of a stucco-covered strip mall on the outskirts of Fishers.

Ash parked in the lot and looked around. The grass around the complex was longer than it should have been, and road noise echoed against the buildings nearby. He walked to the staffing service's front door. His foot wasn't well enough that he'd go running anytime soon, but it didn't hurt quite as much as it had the day before. If he managed to avoid being run over again, he'd be back to normal in a couple of weeks or so. It'd be nice.

As soon as he stepped inside, Ash covered his nose. The lobby smelled like an ashtray. That combined with the close quarters and haphazard furniture placement made it uncomfortable to say the least. He nodded to a pair of African American women in wool business suits at the other end of the room before walking to the pass-through window that served as the front desk.

Instead of having a full-time receptionist, Professional Staffing Services had a bell and a RING BELL FOR SERVICE sign. A temporary staffing agency that wouldn't hire its own temps to man the front door didn't fill him with confidence, but he rang the bell anyway. The woman who answered his summons was petite and had shoulder-length brunette hair. She didn't smile at him or bother saying anything; instead, she thrust a clipboard into his hands and walked away.

"Excuse me, miss," said Ash. "I need to talk to somebody."

She turned around, a scowl on her face. "We're busy. Fill out the form, and we'll get back to you when we're available."

Ash stared for another moment, having rarely seen such rudeness outside of the post office or the Bureau of Motor Vehicles. His stare, evidently, wasn't as commanding as it had once been, because the surly receptionist disappeared into a maze of file cabinets behind the partition without saying another word.

Ash glanced at the clipboard. The receptionist had given him an application for temporary employment. He dropped the clipboard on the counter and rang the bell twice before removing his badge from his belt.

When the receptionist came back, her eyes were narrow and her face was red. She started to point at the door but stopped when Ash waved his badge. He pressed his lips into a thin line.

"I didn't realize you were a police officer. What can I do for you?"

Ash put his badge back on his belt. "You can start by introducing me to your supervisor."

She stood straighter. "I'm afraid Jonathan is busy right now. I can take a message, though."

"Sure," said Ash, leaning against the counter. "I'm Detective Sergeant Ash Rashid with the Marion County prosecutor's office. Please inform Jonathan that if he values doing business with the city of Indianapolis, he'll come and see me shortly. I'll wait here in the lobby."

Ash wasn't empowered to limit contracts for the city, but he could bullshit with the best of them. Hopefully the receptionist wouldn't see his bluff for what it was.

"I'll be right back, sir."

She hurried back, and Ash turned around in time to see the two women still remaining in the lobby smiling at him.

"It's hard to get good help," he said.

"It is," said one of the women.

Ash sat down near the door. Times had evidently been tough on the temporary staffing industry because the upholstery on his chair was so thin he could see the foam cushioning beneath. Since he was going to be there for a few minutes, he took out his cell phone and opened a video game he had installed for Megan a few weeks ago. Destroying wooden and stone structures with kamikaze birds was a waste of time, but it kept him from thinking about the nearest bar. When the receptionist came to the window again, a middle-aged man wearing a sweater vest over a maroon long-sleeved shirt stood behind her. She cleared her throat and Ash paused his game before looking up.

"Sergeant Rashid?" asked the man, holding his arm past the through window. Ash stood and shook the man's hand. "I'm Jonathan Glasgow. Let's head to my office and talk."

"Yes, let's," said Ash, already walking toward the door that led deeper into the office. Like the records rooms beneath the City-County Building, Professional Staffing Service's office was a large open room with a maze of filing cabinets in the center. Jonathan led Ash past row after row of nondescript gray cabinets until they came to the far end of the room. A dozen men and women fed documents into machines that looked like high-speed copiers, while another dozen men and women reviewed documents on computers nearby.

"They're optical character recognition scanners," said

Jonathan, pointing to the machines. "Our team members scan documents just like at a copy machine, but instead of printing the document, it's sent to a computer. A computer program reads the file sent by the scanner and extracts the semantic content. It's like reading a paper aloud and typing it into a word processing program. We even have staff members who proofread the digital copies we make. Eventually, we'll digitize every search warrant and affidavit filed by your department in the last ten years."

Ash wasn't sure that was such a good idea. It wouldn't hurt the department to have digital copies of those sorts of documents, but it wouldn't help much, either. It would be a huge boon for lawyers and reporters, though, and Ash didn't like the idea of empowering them more than he had to.

"That's great. I'm here to see an affidavit the city sent over."

Jonathan reached an office door in the middle of the bank of scanners but paused before opening it. "And the city doesn't have these files?"

Ash forced himself to smile. "I wouldn't be here if they were available elsewhere."

Jonathan nodded and opened his door. "We'll see what we can do."

Jonathan's office was a small, windowless room with familiar looking white cardboard filing boxes stacked everywhere. He sat behind an oak desk and moved a mouse beside his keyboard.

"I need the date your affidavit was filed, and I'll see what we've got."

Ash took his notebook from his pocket and flipped to the appropriate page to find the date. He read it aloud and Jonathan started typing as Ash sat on a stack of file boxes. It wasn't the most stable seat in the world, but it beat standing. Besides, if he fell, he could probably sue. He might even put his law degree to use; it'd be nice to get some value out of that.

"We've got a slight problem," said Jonathan, removing his glasses and rubbing his brow. "It seems one of our workers has misappropriated some boxes of files. She hasn't been back to work since."

Story of my life.

Ash rubbed his sinuses and held his breath for a ten count. "Okay," he said, his eyes closed. "What was this worker's name? I'll visit her at home and reappropriate your files."

Jonathan looked at his computer for confirmation and then looked back at Ash. "Her name is Cassandra Johnson. I can give you her address if you'd like."

Ash's mouth opened slightly of its own volition and he sat straighter. "Cassandra? She worked here at one time?"

"Yeeess," said Jonathan, drawing the syllable out while nodding slowly. "She was one of our data processors."

Things were clicking for the first time. The cardboard file boxes in Jonathan's office looked familiar because Cassandra had the same ones.

"What files did she take?"

Jonathan turned back to his computer and typed. "As best we can tell, Ms. Johnson took three boxes, all of which contained search warrants and affidavits filed in the third week of July of this year. I apologize for the inconvenience. When Ms. Johnson comes in, I can have our receptionist call your office."

"Ms. Johnson was murdered last Friday, so she won't be coming in. And I'm pretty sure she took four boxes of files."

Jonathan looked momentarily stunned, but whether that

was due to his clerical error or Cassandra's death, Ash didn't know. He reached for his keyboard again.

"I'll have to look into that."

"Good idea," said Ash. "Were the files Cassandra took digitized before she took them?"

"Our records say no."

Ash was tempted to ask if those were the same set of records that claimed Cassandra stole only three boxes, but he held back. He had enough work to do without getting into a fight. He stood, but his ankle hurt enough that he almost sat down again.

"Thanks for your time. I'll give you a call if I need anything else from you."

He was about to turn and leave the room when he saw a piece of paper on Jonathan's desk. From the part he could see, it was a memo about employee compensation for snow days. Ash pushed aside a Lucite paperweight and picked it up, tapping the letterhead with his index finger.

"Indy Holdings, Inc.?"

Jonathan nodded. "That's our parent company. We're locally owned and operated. That's part of the reason why the city hired us."

Ash sat down again. Jonathan hesitated, but then took his seat behind the desk as well.

"Something wrong, Detective?"

"Tell me about Cassandra Johnson again."

The office manager's Adam's apple dipped and rose as he swallowed. "I've told you everything I know."

Ash smiled and then snickered. Jonathan tittered nervously.

"I've got a feeling that you're going to be very popular tonight," said Ash.

"I don't understand," said Jonathan.

"Oh, sorry. Silly me." Ash closed his eyes and patted his forehead with the palm of his right hand as if he had forgotten something. "Sometimes I think I've got a screw loose. You're going to be very popular in jail tonight."

The nervous smile slipped off Jonathan's face. "Why would I be in jail?"

"Because you're lying to a detective and obstructing an investigation," said Ash. "I don't like liars."

Jonathan's shoulders rose and fell as he breathed. "What do you want to know?"

"After Cassandra died, her mother checked out her finances. Your parent company wired twenty-five thousand dollars to her bank account two weeks ago. That's a lot of money for a temporary office worker. What was it for?"

Jonathan shook his head slowly. "I don't know anything about that."

"Do me a favor and stand up, then," said Ash. "I'm going to pat you down before I arrest you."

Jonathan opened his mouth in an O shape, but he didn't move.

"Seriously. Get up," said Ash. "You can either walk out of here with me, or I can call for backup and have them drag you out of here kicking and screaming."

"The money comes from higher up in the company. I don't know anything about it."

Ash leaned forward so his palms were on the desk and his face was only about a foot from Jonathan's. "That's not going to keep you out of jail, but it's a start. Keep talking."

Jonathan wet his lips. "If one of our employees finds an irregularity in the paperwork we're scanning, I send it to my

boss. I don't know what happens to it after that, but sometimes the employee who finds the error gets a bonus in his
next paycheck. Usually it's a couple hundred bucks."

"What sort of irregularity did Cassandra find?"

Jonathan shrugged, his mouth still hanging open. "I don't
know. She gave me some files, and I put them in an envelope
and sent them along. Two weeks later, she stopped showing
up to work. I'm sorry, but that's all I know. I'll give you—"

Jonathan continued babbling, but Ash tuned him out so
he could think. Before he only had suspicions about Cassandra's
death, but now he had proof. She found someone's secret and
then she died for it. It wasn't much to go on, but he had a trail
of bread crumbs. Now he needed to find out where they led.

Ash left Professional Staffing Services and headed downtown
to the records room of the City-County Building. If anyone else had a copy of the files Cassandra stole, they would.
When he arrived, sweat almost instantly started to bead on
his forehead; apparently the county had decided to finally
turn on the heat. Like the last time he visited the office, the
records room was empty save the clerk behind the counter.
She smiled as soon as Ash walked up.

"You're walking a little better today," she said.

"Thank you," said Ash. "My foot feels better."

"I guess the coffee shop was out of free samples this morning," she said, winking at him.

Ash forced himself to smile a little broader despite the
frustration that had welled in his gut.

"Afraid so. I need a big favor. I need to get into your
archives."

The smile slipped from her face. "It's against our policy to allow anyone into the stacks," she said. "If you tell me what you're looking for, though, I'd be happy to get it."

Ash leaned against the counter. "I'm not sure what I need, but I know you have it."

She shifted in her seat, an uncomfortable, tight smile on her lips. "I'm afraid I can't help you, then, Detective. Maybe you can talk to my supervisor. Her office is on the fourth—"

Ash held up his hand, interrupting her. "I'm investigating multiple homicides, one of whom was a records clerk," he said. "That clerk died for having files that came from this department."

Her lips moved but no sound came out. Finally she said, "Someone in my office died?"

"Not your office, but a temporary worker the city hired. The people who killed her also killed a former police officer. This office is the only place left that has the information I need, which means you and your coworkers might be the next targets. I need to see your files to stop anyone else from being hurt."

The clerk took a step back from the counter, her face pale. "You really think they'd come after us? We're just doing our jobs."

"Yes, but you're also sitting on something important. I don't know if they'll come after you, but it wouldn't surprise me given their history."

She broke eye contact with Ash and looked at the counter. "If I let you back there, I could lose my job."

"If I'm caught, I'll tell them I snuck in when you went to the restroom."

She didn't take her eyes from the counter, but she nodded.

"You'll never find anything without help. We have too much information to sift through."

"I'm looking for every affidavit filed in support of a search warrant in the third week of July of this year."

The clerk typed something into her computer and then glanced at Ash again. "Aisle four, cabinet Eighteen-B. You can't tell anyone I told you, though."

"I wouldn't consider it," said Ash.

She nodded and stepped away from the counter before shuffling toward the heavy steel door that led to the archives. Ash followed her and stared into a room so dark and warm it was like looking into the vestibule of Hell. The clerk flicked on a light switch, and row after row of overhead lights popped on in quick succession. As he remembered, the room was roughly the size of a football field and had long rows of filing cabinets that stretched from the front to the back. Each cabinet was backed against another, forming eight well-labeled rows like shelves in the library.

Ash rubbed sweat off his brow with the back of his hand. "Is it always this hot in here?"

The clerk nodded. "We're right on top of the boiler, so it's hot in here in the winter. Unless you need anything else, I'll leave you to it."

"You've done more than enough. Thank you," said Ash, looking over his shoulder. The clerk's lips moved as if she were going to say something, but she looked down at her feet and left before speaking another word. Ash had never liked twisting arms, especially on someone who had gone out of her way to help him, but sometimes his job didn't leave him much choice. He made a mental note to send her a box of chocolates or maybe coffee when he had the chance.

As soon as she left, Ash focused on the room's contents. Each row of cabinets was labeled with a number and each side was labeled either A or B. He walked to the fourth aisle and searched until he found cabinet 18B. Like every other filing cabinet in the room, 18B was thin steel painted a utilitarian gray. He pulled open the top drawer.

Ash thumbed through a couple dozen files, getting an understanding of the organizational scheme. Unfortunately, the first drawer he looked in turned out to be a bust. Nothing.

The middle drawer was a little more interesting because it contained the warrant and all accompanying documentation for the search of the Rahals' home. He knew the papers were bogus, so he didn't pay much attention to them beyond noting that they had been signed by Judge Garibaldi and seemed to have been processed correctly. They were proof of fraud, perhaps, but they didn't prove Rahal was innocent. He pulled the papers and set them aside so he could look at them later. More than likely, he'd just turn them over to Internal Affairs and let them have at it. They were good at paperwork. Ash thumbed his way through the rest of the drawer without anything jumping out at him.

Two down. One to go.

He sighed and closed the middle drawer. His heart sank as soon as he opened the bottom. Five files. Must have been a slow week. He pulled out the drawer as far as it would go and sat beside it so he could rest his foot and examine the files closely. The first two were standard affidavits filed by the narcotics squad. Nothing special there. The third, though, was curious. Ash pulled it out and furrowed his brow. It had the same date, the same address, and most of the same facts as the fraudulent affidavit filed by Noah Stuart. What's more, both documents had been signed by the same judge. They were for different apartments, though, and that wasn't the only interesting thing. Ash closed the drawer and leaned against the cabinet across from the one he had just searched.

Carl Gillespie called Rahal innocent. After seeing the files, he might have been right. Ash closed his eyes and banged his head against the steel of the cabinet behind him. He was reasonably sure he had just found out why Cassandra died.

"Shit."

20

Ash grabbed both files. Once she saw the information he found, Susan would have to drop her case. Unlike most lawyers, her job wasn't to act as an advocate for whatever side happened to pay her salary; her job was to seek and foster justice, something she generally took quite seriously. He left the records room and turned the light off behind him. The clerk he had spoken to earlier was outside, arranging a stack of documents on the front desk. Ash coughed so she'd know he was behind her. She turned. Her lips were thin and flat, but her brow was furrowed and her face was red.

"Did you find what you need, Detective?"

"Unfortunately," said Ash, nodding and holding up the files he had taken. "I'd be very grateful if I could get a copy of these."

The clerk took them from his outstretched hand. She went to a copy machine in another room, while he hobbled around the desk and sat down in one of the chairs in the waiting area. His ankle practically sang in relief. The clerk came back a few minutes later and handed him some still-warm copies. She didn't look him in the eye or say anything; she just went back to reordering her files. He should have expected that. She probably had little to say to the man who strong-armed her into doing something that, had she been caught, would have gotten her fired.

Ash took the elevator upstairs and left the building. It wasn't quite noon yet, so Susan still had a long day in court. With luck, he'd catch her when court recessed for lunch. He hurried, knowing he had a limited window of opportunity. The building that contained Ash's cubicle and Susan's office was only about two blocks from the City-County Building, so he made good time.

Since he doubted she would stop by her office on her limited lunch break, Ash took the elevator to his own floor and stopped by Bertha, his aged battleship of a desk, to check his messages and make some calls. Curiously, he found two legal-sized envelopes propped against his monitor with his name, unit, and rank printed where an address should go. He pulled out his chair and sat down before tearing open the flap of one.

Detective Rashid:

As you may know, a supervisory position has recently opened with IMPD's Community Relations team for which you have been nominated. After a careful evaluation of your performance in the prosecutor's office under Susan Mercer, IMPD's administration has made the decision to transfer you immediately to this squad. Henceforth, you will report to Lieutenant Aleda Tovar.

We recognize that you will need some time to settle into your new position, so you will be placed on leave for a period of not less than one week. Because this is a lateral move within the department, your salary will remain unchanged.

If you have questions, please do not hesitate to ask. I value your service.

Deputy Chief,
Sylvia Lombardo

Susan said she would transfer him, but he hadn't expected it so soon. She probably saw the opening and put his name in for it right away, thinking it would be a good assignment. Most of his colleagues probably thought it was. A community relations officer talked to kids about the dangers of drug use, helped organize Neighborhood Watch programs, taught people how to avoid being victims. In his day-to-day life as a detective, Ash was rarely thanked for the work he did. After a tough trial, a victim or a family member of a victim might shake his hand, but that was it. As a community relations officer, kids would cheer when he walked into an auditorium and adults would shake his hand and thank him for setting up programs in their communities. He'd get a lot of the goodwill the police department generated, but he wouldn't have to do much of the heavy lifting to acquire it. Most guys would have jumped at the assignment.

That wasn't what he wanted, though. He liked being in the field; he liked chasing down bad guys. It was who he was, and he didn't want that to change. Unfortunately, he also didn't have time to deal with it at the moment.

In the off chance the second envelope contained a retraction of his orders, he opened it as well. Unfortunately, it was just a note from the lieutenant in Internal Affairs who had picked up his firearm at the hospital. He wanted to talk about the accident, but he didn't seem too insistent on seeing him quickly. With luck, that meant the department wasn't investigating him for misconduct. It wasn't much consolation, but it was something.

He put the second letter back on his desk before going to the elevator and punching the button for Susan's floor. A few of the prosecutors sat at their desks having lunch, but most were still in court or out at the various restaurants near the courthouse. Susan's door was closed and the windows beside it were dark, but Pam sat at her desk with an accountant's ledger in front of her. She looked up as Ash walked toward her, a weak smile on her face.

"I'm afraid Susan isn't in, Detective Rashid."

"Has she come back for lunch?"

Pam's lips straightened and she exhaled before speaking. "She hasn't, but I don't believe she'll be in today, either. If you'd like to talk with her, I can set up an appointment next week after the Thomas Rahal trial."

"That's not going to work. I need to talk to her today, the sooner the better."

"I don't know if that's going to be possible. She plans to call her last witness in the Rahal trial this afternoon. After that, I think she and Charity are going to start working on their closing statement. They don't expect John Meyers to take long to present the defense."

"Can you call her and tell her that it's an emergency? She might take your calls."

"I'm sorry, Ash. She didn't give me a lot of wiggle room. Unless it's life and death, she's asked me not to call."

"It is life and death."

Pam hesitated, but then picked up her phone and called

Susan's cell. As expected, she didn't pick up, but hopefully she'd at least check her messages when court recessed for lunch.

"Thanks," he said.

"I hope everything is okay," said Pam.

"It will be as long as Susan calls me back."

"I'll try to get her to do that."

"That's all I can ask for."

Ash left the office and returned to his desk. Susan would call when she received his message; he was pretty sure about that. No matter how stubborn she was, she wasn't an idiot. In the event she didn't call, though, he needed a backup plan. The official channels were out. No matter what reports he filed with IMPD, it was too late to stop the trial without Susan Mercer's say. The media was also out. Even if he could get a story published, no judge in the world would stop the trial for unsubstantiated reports in the newspaper. That didn't leave him with many options. He did have one, though: The prosecution wasn't the only legal team on the case. Torpedoing a criminal prosecution wouldn't win him too many friends, but it would work.

Ash took out his phone and dialed his boss's cell phone. It went straight to voice mail.

"Susan, give me a call as soon as you get this. I've found something about the Rahal trial that you have to hear about. Call me. This isn't a joke." He paused, trying to think of something that would stress the importance of his call. "Rahal isn't a murderer, and I can prove it in court. Call me back."

He hung up the phone and prayed that she'd take his message to heart.

*   *   *

There was more to his investigation than merely the warrant, so Ash spent most of the rest of the afternoon on the phone and in the field shoring up details with potential witnesses and other parties involved with the case. He finished at about three and spun around in his chair a few times, knowing it would likely be his last time to sit in it. Unlike some of his colleagues, Ash didn't keep much in his desk. He had been meaning to get pictures of his family, but he never had time to sit down for a photographer.

He opened the center drawer and pulled out a drawing of their family Megan had given him a couple of weeks ago. She forgot to include her little brother, but she was six and he could forgive her for that. While he planned to take everything he could with him, that drawing was the only thing he actually cared about. He grabbed a box from the employee break room and filled it with old case files, a coffee mug full of pens, and two paperbacks he never got around to reading. It wasn't much by which to measure a career, but it was what he had.

Court usually let out at sometime between four and five, so Ash called Susan every fifteen minutes after four. He got her voice mail every time. Twice, he went up to her office, but each time, Pam merely shook her head, indicating that she hadn't come in or called. He should have just gone to the courthouse. At half after five, he called John Meyers's office. In contrast to Susan, his secretary put Meyers on the phone quickly.

"Detective Rashid. I don't have a lot of time right now, but what do you need?"

"Here's the deal. I found something that proves Thomas

Rahal didn't murder anyone. I'm going to give this to Susan Mercer as soon as I'm able and try to convince her to dismiss the charges against your client. If I can't, though, are you going to be around this evening?"

"What'd you find?"

"It would take too long to explain over the phone. Are you going to be around?"

"I'm going to be preparing for trial. Of course I'll be around."

"If I can help it, you're not going to go to trial. I'm going to drive by Susan's house and force her to listen to me. If I can't find her, I'll stop by your office and give you everything I have."

Meyers became quiet. "If you've found something that exonerates my client, you have a moral and legal obligation to give it to me. I expect you to live up to that."

"I will. I'm going to try to talk to Susan first, though. If I can convince her to drop the charges, it will save everyone trouble."

"I'll be waiting for your call."

Meyers hung up, and Ash ran to Susan's floor again. Pam was just getting up to leave.

"Has Susan called you back yet?"

"Not yet, and she hasn't been in, either. I don't know where she is."

Ash felt his shoulders drop. "I'm going to go by her house. If she calls you, please call me immediately. Day or night, it doesn't matter."

"I will."

Ash walked to the elevator and hit the DOWN button about eight times before it finally arrived. Everything seemed to be going too slow for him at the moment. He had been to Susan's house only a few times in the past, but his car almost seemed to go without his input. She lived in a two-story Craftsman bungalow near Broad Ripple Village, a very popular historic neighborhood north of the downtown area. Ash rang the doorbell and then kept hitting it until he heard the locks start to open. Susan looked annoyed when she opened the door, but that shifted to confusion when she saw him.

"Ash? What are you doing here?"

"You should really check your phone for messages."

"I turned it off once Charity and I finished our presentation this afternoon in court. We're working on our closing statement." She paused and then crossed her arms. "This isn't about transferring you, is it?"

"No. I found something about your case."

"We've already gone over—"

Ash held up a hand, stopping her from finishing whatever she was going to say.

"Please listen to what I have to say before you make up your mind."

Susan stared at him appraisingly. "If you're wasting my time, I'm going to be very upset."

"I'm not. I promise."

"Then come in," she said, turning and walking inside.

Ash followed her in and shut the door behind them. Susan's home was clean and had white wainscoting along the walls in the front entryway. She walked quickly down the hall without waiting or saying anything further to him. Charity Lewis was sitting at a large oak table in the dining room when they arrived. She squinted at Ash for a moment, surprised to see him.

"Ash says he's got something important for our case."

Over the next half hour, Ash led them step-by-step through everything he had found. Susan's initial skepticism quickly dissipated as he laid out his case. When he finished speaking, neither Susan nor Charity said anything for at least a minute.

"First of all, we need to verify these affidavits you've found," Susan said, glancing at Charity. "Get on the phone with John Meyers's people. Tell him that new evidence about his client has come to light and that we'll be filing a motion for continuance as soon as we can. See if you can get in touch with Judge Haller's clerk, too, to let her know what's going on."

Charity nodded and pushed her chair away from the table. When Ash and Susan were alone again, he sat down.

"Meyers already knows you have new evidence about his client. He's going to expect to see it tonight."

"How does he know anything about this?"

"When I couldn't find you this afternoon, I called him. I didn't give him details, but I told him that I found something that could help his client."

Susan narrowed her gaze. "That's the second time you've talked to my opposing counsel without talking to me first."

"I found exculpatory evidence that will keep an innocent man from going to prison. I have a moral and legal obligation to share it with him."

"Rahal isn't innocent, Ash. Nobody's innocent. You've been a detective long enough to know that."

"Maybe he's not, but he didn't murder Ryan Dixon."

"Rahal hid under a bed and killed Ryan while he was discharging his duties. If not murder, what would you call it?"

"I'd say there were extenuating circumstances that you've ignored."

"They don't matter, Ash. A police officer is dead. That's the only thing that matters."

Ash wanted to say she had an unusually shallow view of what matters, but arguing wouldn't get him anywhere. Eventually, Susan sat down opposite him at the table.

"Would you be here if Thomas Rahal were an atheist?"

"What does that matter?" asked Ash.

"Just answer the question."

Susan stared at him, unblinking.

"Yes. Thomas Rahal happens to be a Muslim. I don't care. He could be a Muslim, a Jew, an atheist, a Zoroastrian, or whatever. It doesn't matter. I'm here because the evidence says he didn't murder anyone."

Susan sighed and looked at the table.

"I think you're closer to this case than you realize. You're not looking at it clearly. Noah Stuart and the men under his command screwed up. There's no denying or excusing that. What's important, though, is that a man who put his life on the line to protect other people is dead. Thomas Rahal hid under a bed and shot him for doing his job. I can't excuse that no matter what the circumstances are."

Ash wanted to respond, but before he could, Susan shifted her gaze to a point behind him. He turned and looked over his shoulder at the entrance to the dining room. Charity walked in, slipping a phone into her pocket.

"Am I interrupting something?" she asked, looking from Ash to Susan.

"Don't worry about it," said Susan. "We're just talking."

"Well, I just called Shelly Flynn at John Meyers's firm," said Charity. "If we file a motion for continuance, they plan to fight it. He wants to go to court."

"Then we'll fight just as hard. Go to the office and start drafting our motion," said Susan. "Keep it short and request a two-day continuance. Say we've recently learned of a significant and unanticipated change in the status of the evidence of the case, a result of which is that we're not adequately prepared for trial. And furthermore, argue that two additional days with which we can prepare will enable a fair trial for all concerned. Haller's big into trial fairness."

Charity hesitated, but then nodded and grabbed a brown leather purse from the dining room table. Ash didn't say anything until he heard the front door open and close.

"Judge Haller is going to deny your motion," said Ash. "The defense is ready, and they had just as much time to prepare as you."

"Thank you for your astute legal analysis, Ash. Get out of my house unless you have something constructive to say."

Ash grabbed his briefcase. "I'm going to John Meyers's office to tell him everything I told you. He will use it in court."

She smiled at him, but there was no warmth in it. "He's going to use you in court, too. Don't forget that part."

"I couldn't stop him from putting me on the stand even if I wanted to. He'd subpoena me, and you know it."

"There's a big difference between being subpoenaed to testify on behalf of the defense and volunteering."

"Yeah. One is the right thing to do, and the other is wrong."

Susan closed her eyes and shook her head. "Just get out of my house."

Ash wanted to tell her that she was making a mistake, but Susan already knew what he had to say. He went through the front door and pulled it shut behind him, unable to shake the feeling that he was shutting the door on a lot more than just his boss's home. It was nearing seven in the evening, and he wanted nothing else than to go home, read his kids a story, and go to sleep. He still had a lot of work to do, though, before he could do that. He pulled out his cell phone and dialed John Meyers's office. The receptionist answered before the first ring finished.

"This is Detective Ash Rashid with the Indianapolis Metropolitan Police Department. Tell your boss that I'm on my way."

Daphne met him in the lobby as soon as Ash walked into the building. She didn't say anything; she just led him to a conference room beside Carl Gillespie's old office.

"I'm glad you could make it," said Meyers as soon as Ash walked into the room.

"Yeah, me too," said Ash. "I've got quite a bit to go through, so let's get going."

For the second time that evening, Ash laid out everything he had found, including the affidavits he had secured from the County Records department.

"Carl said he found something, but he never told me what," said Meyers. "How long has Susan Mercer been sitting on this?"

"She wouldn't sit on evidence," said Ash. "I found out this afternoon, and I told her as soon as I could. Now I'm telling you. Your client didn't murder anyone, and you've got proof."

The older lawyer put his hand to his forehead, his fingers trembling. He looked at Daphne.

"Tell Julie to bring us coffee service for three. We have a lot of work to do."

Ash shook his head. "*You* have a lot of work to do. I don't. I'm going home to tuck my kids into bed."

"Is tucking your kids into bed that important, Detective?" asked Daphne.

"Yes."

Daphne looked like she had a quick retort, but Meyers cleared his throat, stopping her from saying anything. "That's fine. You go home, tuck your kids in, and then come back. We'll order dinner and start fresh."

"I'm not coming back," said Ash. "I've shared everything I have with both you and Susan. Now it's your job to do the rest."

"No, it's *our* job. I need you to testify tomorrow morning."

"I don't think so. I've pissed off my boss enough. Besides, I'm not even on your witness list. Get one of your own investigators to present the information."

"My only investigator is dead. Your colleagues made sure of that. The least you can do in return is to prevent those same colleagues from perpetrating another tragedy."

Ash shook his head. "Susan won't allow it. She'll claim I'm not on your witness list, she'll claim my investigation is privileged work product, and after it all, she'll probably push to have me fired."

"If she fires you, we'll sue. I'll represent you pro bono," said Meyers. "You came to me with this because it was the right thing to do. Do the right thing again and testify in court on behalf of an innocent man. Let me worry about getting you on the stand."

"Susan is as smart as you are, and she knows everything you know. She'll verify the information I gave her and drop the charges."

"And what if she doesn't? Thomas Rahal is an honest-to-God good person. Do you know how rarely I get to say that about my clients?"

Ash looked at the table. "Do you understand what I lose if I do this? I might as well turn in my badge. I'll be a pariah."

"Do you understand what Thomas Rahal will lose if he's found guilty?"

When weighed against a man's life, his job didn't seem all that important. He shifted in his seat.

"If she doesn't drop the charges, I'll testify. I expect you to have my back, though. Susan will object to me at every opportunity, and she'll attack me on cross. I'm going to need you to defend me."

Meyers exhaled deeply. "I will. Thank you," he said, glancing at Daphne. "Let's take a break. We'll start fresh when Detective Rashid comes back." He looked at Ash. "Is that okay with you?"

"Yeah."

"Great," said Meyers. "I'll see you in a little while."

Ash left the building and drove home. When he reached his neighborhood, he drove through it several times to see if anything was out of place. The only thing out of the ordinary was a pair of patrol vehicles parked near his house. Apparently the dispatcher took his request the night before seriously; at least his family would be safe. Both kids were in bed when he arrived. As Hannah had suspected that morning, Megan's doctor diagnosed her cough as bronchitis. With antibiotics, she'd hopefully be okay in a couple of days.

Hannah made him a turkey sandwich while he checked on the kids. Megan hardly moved even when he adjusted the blanket so it covered her chest. Hopefully her illness would be short-lived. Kaden was a little more lively than his sister. He started crying as soon as Ash walked into the room. Ash picked him up and held him until he fell back asleep. After that, he sat down beside Hannah at their breakfast table.

"So I've got big news. I might have a lot more free time with you and the kids after tomorrow."

Hannah inhaled deeply enough that Ash could see her shoulders rise and fall.

"Were you fired?"

"No. Not yet, at least. I think I might have to testify for the defense at Thomas Rahal's trial."

She looked at the table, breaking eye contact. "Is he guilty?"

"No."

She didn't say anything for a moment, then: "If you get fired, what do we do?"

"I don't know. I could probably get a job with a defense attorney, either as a lawyer or an investigator. I think we'd be okay."

"I could go back to work, too, I guess," she said, looking at the table. "I think Yasmina and Jack would be willing to watch Kaden during the day. It could work."

"My sister would probably help, too."

She remained silent for another moment before looking at him. "Then do what you need to do. We'll figure it out."

"There's one more thing. I've managed to upset a couple of people in my investigation. Until I can put them in jail, there are going to be some squad cars by the house."

She closed her eyes and shook her head. "You can't have a normal day, can you?"

"You'll be safe. No one will try anything as long as they're here."

"So you tell me. Eat your sandwich."

Ash did as his wife asked and finished dinner. He was back at Meyers's office at twenty after nine and stayed until well after midnight practicing his testimony. One of Meyers's employees even whipped together a slide show of pictures and documents to illustrate Ash's points, something that likely would have taken a public-sector employee an entire week. By the time he left the office, his voice was hoarse from speaking. Hopefully that would get better overnight because he had a lot to say.

21

Ash arrived at his building at seven-thirty and immedi-ately went to Susan Mercer's floor. Much to his surprise, she was actually in her office. She and her staff must have gotten in early to prepare. As soon as he stepped inside, she stood from her desk.

"Shut the door, Ash."

He did as she asked. "Is everything all right?"

She nodded. "Charity went by the City-County Build-ing this morning and verified the affidavits you showed me. They're genuine."

"I told you they were."

"And I didn't doubt you," she said, pointing to the chair in front of her desk. Ash took a seat, and Susan leaned against the desktop, her arms crossed. "We're going to proceed with the trial."

"Did you even consider the evidence?"

"Yes, I did. I also thought about what Rahal did. No mat-ter how badly Officer Dixon and the rest of his team screwed up, someone needs to speak for him. Until I leave office, that's me."

"And you've made up your mind?"

Susan started to say something but then stopped. She

appeared momentarily rattled, something Ash had never seen in his boss before. That disappeared, though, and was replaced by a familiar, hard-edged resolve.

"My little brother is a police officer. My ex-husband is a police officer. My friends are police officers. I stayed up all night thinking. If one of you were killed in the line of duty—I don't care the circumstances—I'd fight for you until I didn't have anything left. It wouldn't be right if I didn't do the same for Ryan Dixon."

Ash swallowed. "Maybe it wouldn't," he said. "John Meyers is going to call me to testify this morning. This isn't going to end well for you."

"We'll see," said Susan.

As soon as Ash turned to leave Susan's office, he felt a weight pressing against him. Aside from Charity Lewis, none of the other attorneys in the office knew the first thing about what he was going to do that morning, but he couldn't help but feel they were staring at him nonetheless. It was likely his imagination, but he didn't feel welcome in that building anymore.

He walked to the courthouse. CNN was already filming a group of protesters when he arrived. Ash couldn't read their signs in the morning glare, so he didn't know what they were protesting against, but they seemed jovial. He kept his head down and walked slowly toward the building, his stomach churning. Once he got inside, he found a quiet corner outside the courtroom and waited. Susan came in at twenty to nine, and Meyers arrived shortly afterward. They didn't head to the courtroom; instead, they walked to the judge's chambers directly beside it. Evidently her clerk had received Susan's motion for continuance. The lawyers stayed in there until about nine-thirty, half an hour past the time court was set to convene. Ash couldn't hear what was said, but it evidently hadn't gone well for Susan because she stormed out before anyone else, her face bright and angry.

Ash stayed where he was; it was better to let her calm down on her own. Since court was running late, the spectators were already inside. The bailiff shut the doors and called court to order as soon as Judge Haller sat down. Once that happened, Ash, along with a number of other spectators who hadn't been able to get seats, crowded around the door so he could hear the events inside. The judge started the day by thanking the jury for their continued service—not that they had much choice in the matter—and apologizing for the delay. She turned the trial over to Meyers, and he called Ash to the stand first thing. That explained why Susan had left the judge's chambers in such a huff. Haller had not only ruled against her motion, but it also seemed that she was going to let Ash testify. That wasn't going to do much for his boss's mood.

As soon as Ash took a seat, the bailiff swore him in, and Meyers started asking simple questions about Ash's qualifications and experience. He had been on the police force for thirteen years, but he had spent most of that time as a plainclothes detective in various divisions and units. He had several commendations and letters of meritorious service to his name. Generally speaking, those who knew him regarded him as a gifted investigator. Susan, to her credit, didn't object to his answer.

Meyers thumbed through a stack of documents on his desk before asking the judge for permission to approach the witness. It was granted, so he handed Ash a copy of the forged warrant supposedly justifying the search of Rahal's home. As Ash pretended to read the paper, Daphne used a court-supplied video screen and projector to show a scanned image of the document to the jury.

"I wondered if you could tell me what you discovered about this document labeled 'People's Exhibit B.'"

"Sure," said Ash. "This is the warrant the prosecution alleges gave police the right to search Thomas Rahal's home."

Ash glanced at the defense table. Rahal was wearing the same suit he had worn on the opening day of trial, but he looked almost haggard now. There were bags under his eyes and stubble on his chin. His eyes held the biggest change, though. The hope Ash had seen earlier was gone; he looked like a man on death's doorstep.

"You worded your answer in a very interesting way. Did you discover a problem with it?"

"Yeah," said Ash, shaking himself out of his momentary pause. "The warrant was signed and issued by Judge Michael Garibaldi four days after the search of Mr. Rahal's home was conducted and Officer Dixon was shot."

Susan shot to her feet again. "Sidebar, Your Honor."

The judge covered her microphone with her hand so the jury wouldn't hear what she had to say before motioning Meyers and Susan forward. Even straining his ears, all Ash heard was a lot of impassioned whispering. Eventually, Susan stormed back to her seat and Meyers resumed his questioning.

"How do you know this warrant was issued four days after Officer Dixon was shot?"

Ash took a deep breath. "Because Judge Garibaldi's clerk maintains an accurate and meticulous record of every warrant her office issues. I'm sure she'd be willing to testify to that."

Actually, Ash was confident she wouldn't be willing to testify, at least not willingly. Meyers could subpoena her if needed, though.

"We might bring her up later. In the meantime, are you saying the police went to Mr. Rahal's apartment without a valid warrant?"

"Not at all. I'm merely suggesting it wasn't the warrant submitted to this court."

Meyers stopped pacing. "I don't understand. Are you saying the document the prosecution introduced earlier in this trial is a fraud?"

"Yes and no. The warrant the prosecution introduced was signed and issued by a superior court judge, but it wasn't the warrant the officers actually took when they searched Rahal's home. It couldn't have been."

Meyers nodded and crossed his arms as he resumed pacing the courtroom. "And what did you do after discovering that the warrant given to this court was problematic?"

"I searched for other warrants that might have displayed similar problems."

"Did you find anything?"

"Yes. I found what I thought was another warrant for Mr. Rahal's, but it turned out to be a warrant for a neighbor's home."

Susan objected and claimed that the line of questioning was irrelevant to the events in question. After some pleading, the judge gave Meyers leeway to ask his questions. He thanked her before continuing.

"It's interesting that you found another warrant, but let's clarify something. What do you mean by 'a neighbor's home'? Mr. Rahal lived in an apartment. By neighbor, do you mean he lived in a nearby apartment, in the same complex, down the street? What exactly did you mean, Detective?"

"I mean they lived right beside each other."

"Your Honor," said Meyers. "I'd like to take a moment to introduce Defense Exhibit C on the video screen."

"Granted."

The image on the projector shifted to one Ash had taken with his camera phone in front of the Rahals' home the day before. It showed two doors, side-by-side and separated by an interior wall.

"To clarify, Detective Rashid, this is an image of Mr. Rahal's apartment and the neighboring apartment?"

"Yes," said Ash, leaning into his microphone.

"That's very helpful, thank you," said Meyers. "Tell me, though. How do you tell which apartment is which?"

"The Rahals' home is the one with the giant dent on it from the search team's battering ram," said Ash. The jury and audience tittered. "In all seriousness, it is quite difficult. A police report filed by the apartment complex's management said that six months ago, thieves stole every bit of scrap metal from the complex they could, including copper gutters and the copper numbers that used to be beside each apartment."

"The doors are almost exactly alike. I bet they get a lot of each other's pizza orders," said Meyers, smiling. The jury smiled back, although some looked a tad uncomfortable doing so. Meyers may not have been explicit, but he made the point well. Ash glanced at Rahal again. His eyes were closed, but his lips were moving. Praying by the looks of things. "Let's talk about this warrant you found. Was there anything interesting about it?"

Susan shot upright. "Objection, Your Honor. The warrant

to which Mr. Meyers is referring was not included as part of his pretrial discovery package. He can't start introducing more evidence at this time."

Meyers turned to the judge and put up his hands defensively. "I only learned about the warrant last night. It was remarkably well hidden. Ms. Mercer received it before we did."

The judge leaned back in her chair and stared at Ash. "I want to hear this, so I'll give you a little latitude. Please don't make me regret it."

Susan shook her head and sat down while Meyers nodded. "Thank you, Your Honor," he said. "May I approach the witness?"

Haller nodded, and Meyers grabbed a stack of papers from his desk before handing them to Ash.

"This document labeled Defense Exhibit D, is it the warrant you found?"

Ash, again, pretended to read it. "Yes, it is."

"When you read this the first time, did anything stand out to you?"

"Yes," said Ash. He leaned forward and spoke clearly into the microphone. "It was a no-knock warrant."

"And what is that?"

"Objection, Your Honor," said Susan. "I fail to see the relevance to this line of questioning."

"Overruled," said the judge, her voice sharper than it had been a moment earlier.

Ash looked at the judge and nodded before continuing. "It might be best to describe what a no-knock warrant is in terms of what it's not. When executing a standard search warrant, a group of officers visit a location to be searched and then announce themselves loudly so everyone on the premises knows police officers are entering the building. A no-knock warrant allows officers to breach a building and detain its occupants without first announcing who they are or why they've come."

"What do you mean by 'breach'?"

Ash took a breath. "Typically, officers will break the door down with a battering ram. Depending on the situation, they might use flash bangs or other very loud, nonlethal explosives as necessary to ensure the safety of the officers involved."

"That sounds scary," said Meyers.

"It is, and it's designed to be so. The hope is that any individuals in the home will be so shocked by the sudden entrance that they don't have time to destroy evidence or grab weapons."

"I see. Have you ever participated in the execution of a no-knock warrant, Detective?"

"Yes," said Ash, nodding. "On February nineteenth of last year, I, along with a search team, executed a no-knock search warrant on a home on the north side of Indianapolis. Six officers were involved with the search. The first officer blew the home's dead bolt with a breaching shotgun, while the next five officers rushed into the home with their guns drawn. I entered the home last and helped subdue the home's occupants."

The longer he testified, the quieter the room became. Jurors who had been taking notes earlier had stopped and stared with a mix of fascination and horror on their faces.

"How were those occupants?"

"We found three men in the home. One tried to run out the back door, but officers positioned in the home's backyard subdued him quickly. Another tried to get to a gun with which to defend himself, but officers subdued him as well. The third lay on the ground, urinated his pants, and begged us not to kill him. He thought we were members of a rival gang."

Meyers nodded. "That sounds like a truly terrifying event for everyone involved. Tell me, Detective Rashid, the no-knock search warrant you found for Mr. Rahal's neighbor, was it properly filed?"

Ash looked around the courtroom before answering. Rahal sat straight, a tear on his cheek. His wife, sitting directly behind him, had one hand on his shoulder and another covering her mouth.

"Yes, it was."

"Did the officers find anything in that search?"

Ash nodded. "Yes. The officers who conducted the search returned the signed warrant to Judge Garibaldi's office and indicated that they discovered thirty-two oxycodone pills and approximately two ounces of marijuana."

Meyers flipped through some pages on the legal notepad he held. "That sounds awfully familiar. Could you describe the contents the police found during the search of Mr. Rahal's home?"

Susan stood again, but she almost seemed as if she were merely going through the motions now. "Objection, Your Honor. This information has already been entered into the record."

"Overruled," said the judge, not missing a beat. "Please answer, Detective Rashid."

"According to the warrant returned to Judge Garibaldi's office, the police discovered thirty-two oxycodone pills and approximately two ounces of marijuana in Mr. Rahal's home."

Meyers let the silence drag on after Ash spoke.

"That's quite a coincidence. The same number of pills, and the same amount of marijuana was found in both homes. Have you gotten in touch with Mr. Rahal's neighbor to ask him about this amazing coincidence?"

"I have tried to contact Mr. Rutkowski, but he was found hanging from a rafter in an abandoned steel mill in Gary, Indiana. As of yesterday afternoon, his death has been ruled a homicide."

Susan stood again. "Sidebar, Your Honor."

The judge agreed, so the lawyers went to the judge's desk and spoke for a few minutes. The judge listened to both sides without making any indication of where she stood on whatever issues the two lawyers were discussing. Ash leaned back in his chair and let them go at it. Eventually, everyone sat down and the judge looked directly at the jury.

"Please strike the witness's previous statement from the record. It should not be considered part of this trial, nor should it be part of your deliberations."

Having the previous statement stricken was a blow, but not a big one. They had gotten across the point: Something was seriously wrong with the case against Thomas Rahal, and those who knew that ended up dead. Meyers skipped a number of questions on their script about Cassandra Johnson and Carl Gillespie and looked Ash directly in the eye.

"One final question, Detective. You spent five years as a homicide detective, so you're familiar with the concept of premeditated murder. Speaking hypothetically, if the police had made a mistake and breached the wrong apartment, and if Mr. Rahal shot one of those officers in the process, do you believe he committed murder?"

"If strangers broke into an individual's home with guns drawn, never said who they were, and demanded the homeowner hand over his children, I think most people would shoot without hesitation and be justified every time. So, no. Mr. Rahal may have shot an officer, but he did not commit murder."

The members of the gallery were talking to each other loud enough after Ash's statement that the judge had to bang her gavel to bring the courtroom back to order. Susan poured a glass of water from a glass carafe on the table in front of her and took a drink, while Meyers looked at the judge.

"That is all I have for this witness, Your Honor," he said. "Thank you for indulging me."

The judge nodded and looked to Susan. "Your witness, Counselor."

Susan stood, swaying on her feet as if she were a drunk walking home.

"Due to unexpected evidence introduced in Detective Rashid's testimony, I respectfully request the court grant a twenty-four-hour recess so the prosecution may verify the facts as presented."

The judge laced her fingers together and stared at Susan. "I'd rather not slow this trial beyond its present speed, but due to Detective Rashid's testimony, a recess is prudent. We are hereby adjourned until nine tomorrow morning."

She banged her gavel, and members of the gallery began speaking as the bailiff led the jury out. Ash focused on Thomas Rahal. He and his wife hugged each other, crying. It was a little early to celebrate, but Ash had done what he could. He stood up and shook Meyers's hand as he left. His eyes caught Susan's, but she looked away before he could get a read on her.

He left the courthouse through a side entrance reserved for prisoners and law enforcement officials, avoiding the mass of reporters and protesters on the front steps. He'd feel good about himself if he kept Rahal from going to jail for a crime he didn't commit, but the goal had always been secondary to finding out who killed Cassandra Johnson and Carl Gillespie. He still had work to do, but thankfully he now had some help. Both the no-knock warrant and the standard search warrant he had discussed in court had been drafted by Noah Stuart. If things had gone according to plan, Mike Bowers would have taken him into custody that morning on suspicion of murder charges.

A uniformed officer in a black-and-white patrol vehicle drove Ash to IMPD's headquarters and let him out in front of the building. Bowers was in his office on the second floor.

"You've been busy this morning," said Bowers, nodding to a chair in front of his desk. "Your testimony has already made the news."

"Yeah. I thought it might," said Ash, staying in the doorway. "Did you pick up Noah Stuart?"

"We did," said Bowers, nodding and standing. "And he's agreed to cooperate fully. We've got him in interview room B. I wanted to wait until you arrived to talk to him."

"Good. Let's see what we've got."

Ash followed Bowers out of the office and to an interview room nearby. Unlike the interrogation rooms, the interview rooms were on the exterior of the building and had a bank of windows overlooking the city streets. A heavy, rectangular table dominated the center of the room, and a flat-screen television hung from a bracket in the corner. Noah sat watching a reporter interview Leonard Wilson. Ash hadn't intended to watch the news, but he stopped anyway, picking up the story midstream.

"... is innocent. This goes beyond mere politics. Even Jack Whittler, as bad as he was, never prosecuted a man he knew to be innocent. I'm not speaking as a candidate here. I'm speaking as the chairman of the city council's Public Safety Committee. I may have to step aside from my committee position in the future, but mark my words: There will be hearings. As a society, we cannot allow our elected officials to abuse their power in this fashion. And let me just go on record and say thank God for people like Detective Ash Rashid. If he hadn't been—"

Ash walked around the conference room table and turned off the television so he wouldn't have to hear any more grandstanding. Noah blinked as Ash pulled out a chair and sat down. The lieutenant seemed strangely calm. He didn't fidget or have other nervous tics, and he didn't balk and look away after catching Ash's gaze. That didn't bode well for his interview.

"Before you say anything," said Ash, "I want to make sure you understand your rights. You don't have to talk to me, and you can leave at any time. Moreover, you're not under arrest yet. As you probably know, we also have hidden video cameras recording this interview. Do you understand?"

Noah leaned forward. "I've been in this department since you were probably in diapers. I think I understand my rights by now."

"Do you want an attorney brought in? We can call the union."

Noah looked at Lieutenant Bowers. "We've already gone over this, Sergeant, but for your sake, I'll say it again. I waive my right to remain silent, and I recognize that you can use what I say in court. I also waive my right to counsel. Is that clear? If not, Mike already has a release I signed when he brought me in."

Ash looked at Bowers. He nodded.

"Okay, then," said Ash. "Cassandra Johnson. Tell me what you know about her."

"I ran her down with a car Friday afternoon."

Ash almost jumped. He coughed to cover his momentary surprise and grabbed a pen from his jacket. "Is that a joke?"

"I hid in the shadow cast by a house behind hers until she was in the middle of the intersection. I floored the accelerator and hit her as she walked across the street. To make sure she was dead, I backed over her twice."

It took Ash a moment to process the remark. He closed his eyes, trying to think of what else to say. "What kind of car were you driving?"

"A navy blue Ford Crown Victoria. I stole it from a state police lot in Vigo County near Terre Haute."

Ash and Bowers looked at each other knowingly. The murder never hit the papers; Noah was giving them information that only someone involved with the death would know.

"Why did you kill Ms. Johnson?" Ash asked.

"I think you know the answer," he said. "I don't know how, but she found out about the warrant I secured for

Andrew Rutkowski's apartment. I couldn't let that become public knowledge, so I ran her down to shut her up."

Ash leaned forward. "Why couldn't you let that information become public?"

Noah's eyes narrowed angrily, and he crossed his arms. "I don't expect you to understand, but Officer Ryan Dixon died under my command because I made a mistake. Once that became public knowledge, the man who killed him would get a slap on the wrist at best. Ryan was a good cop and a good man. I don't care if we went to that camel jockey's house by mistake. He used an illegal firearm to shoot one of my officers, and anyone who does that deserves what he gets."

"Rahal and I aren't that different, you know? We go to the same mosque. We believe most of the same things. We have similar skin tone. If you call him racially charged names, you're sort of calling me the same thing."

Noah stared right at him. "Yes, Sergeant, I know that."

"Okay, just making sure," he said, scooting back from the table to give himself a moment to think and get back on his rhythm.

"How did you discover Cassandra knew about your original warrant?"

Noah tilted his head to the side. "Lieutenant Carl Gillespie told me. Like I told you a few days ago, I supervised him when he was still a sergeant. Seems he ran into Cassandra during an investigation. Regrettably, I had to kill him, too. It was for the good of my precinct."

"How did you kill him?" asked Ash.

Noah shrugged. "It was easier than you'd probably expect. Carl asked me over to discuss things. As soon as I got to his house, I used chloroform to knock him out and then I dumped him in the walk-in freezer in his basement. When it was convenient, I took him out and threw him in the canal near Military Park."

Noah had the thin, wiry frame of a long-distance runner. He was fit, obviously, but he didn't look strong enough to throw a grown man over his shoulder and carry him up and down stairs by himself.

"What about Andrew Rutkowski, Thomas Rahal's neighbor?" asked Ash. "Did you kill him, too?"

Noah leaned back in his chair and looked up at the ceiling as if he were thinking. "Yeah."

"How'd you do it?" asked Ash.

Noah stared at Ash before shrugging. "Hit him a couple of times with a baton and then strung him up."

"By yourself?"

"Yes. I murdered all three individuals alone. They deserved it."

"Okay," said Ash, closing his notebook. "I'd like you to sit tight here for a little while. Do you need anything? Coffee? Soda?"

"I'm fine. Thank you, Sergeant."

"Good deal," said Ash, sliding his chair beneath the table. "You know where the TV is. Lieutenant Bowers and I will be back soon."

Bowers and Ash left the room one after the other and shut the door behind them. As soon as the lock clicked, Ash leaned into Bowers.

"Does he expect us to believe this?"

"Carl Gillespie, God have mercy on him, was a fat man. He was probably pushing two hundred and fifty pounds.

I don't know how big Rutkowski was, but I doubt a single person could have pulled him up. Noah's involved, but he's covering for his men."

"Yeah, but why?"

Bowers looked at the door to the interview room. "Have you ever lost somebody you supervised?" Ash shook his head. "I haven't, either, but Noah's lost at least two officers in the last two years. That's got to eat at him. I think he's trying to make up for that."

"What do you want to do, then?"

Bowers scratched his forehead and shrugged. "Noah has almost thirty years on the force, and he's probably interrogated more people than you've ever met. He knows every trick and technique we do. We could try to sweat him out in an interrogation room, but he's been through enough investigations to know what cards he's holding. He's not going to tell us anything."

"Maybe we should do something he doesn't expect, then," said Ash.

"You got something in mind?" asked Bowers, his eyebrows raised.

"Maybe we should let him go."

Bowers chuckled. "Releasing a man who's admitted to several murders certainly would be unexpected."

Ash held up his hands. "That's not what I had in mind. If Noah isn't going to talk to us, we shouldn't waste our time with him. His partners won't have any idea what's going on, though. We can keep him in custody but put the word out that we've released him for cooperating with us. The way this department talks, his partners will hear about it almost as soon as we start spreading the rumors. I'm willing to bet that they'll go after him. When they do, we'll arrest them."

Bowers considered for a moment. "It's going to be a pretty big tell if he's sitting in jail somewhere. Somebody's going to notice him."

"Then we put him in a hotel with people we can trust."

Bowers scratched the back of his neck. "It's risky. If Noah's partners are willing to kill him, they're going to be willing to do the same to us."

"True, but they're not going to be expecting us. We need to get them off the street or this whole situation will repeat. If we let them go, we'll have a new Cassandra Johnson, a new Carl Gillespie, and probably a new Noah Stuart. Only next time, they'll be more careful."

Bowers seemed to think for a moment. "If this goes bad, it could be very bad."

"You're right, but Noah isn't going to confess, and right now, his crew is probably burning every piece of evidence they have about what they've done. This is the only way we're going to get them."

He sighed. "We're going to need a lot of people to do this safely, and that's going to get some notice. We'll have to move people around from existing assignments. How many people are watching your house right now?"

"Just a pair of squad cars, I think."

"We'll leave one there, then, and assign two additional officers to watch Noah Stuart at the hotel. I think I'll also assign a pair of officers to watch the Rahals' apartment just in case."

"Who's going to be watching Noah's house?"

"You, me, and hopefully four to six other officers. I'll ask for volunteers from patrol."

Ash played through the scenario in his head. It'd be risky, but it could work.

"If you make tactical arrangements, I'll tie up some loose ends on the Rahal trial."

"Sure."

Bowers went to his office and Ash found an unoccupied desk in the homicide squad's bullpen and called Susan Mercer's office on his cell phone. Pam picked up quickly.

"This is Ash Rashid. I know Susan is busy, but tell her that Lieutenant Noah Stuart admitted his team executed their no-knock warrant on the Rahals' apartment by mistake. Tell her also that Noah has confessed to murdering Cassandra Johnson, Carl Gillespie, and Andrew Rutkowski."

That ought to get a response.

Pam's breath was heavy. "I'll tell her right away," she said. "Do you want to wait on the line, or would you like me to call you back if she wants to talk?"

He rubbed his brow and yawned. His lack of sleep the night before was starting to catch up to him.

"I'll wait."

Pam put him on hold, and he listened to elevator music for the next five minutes. Eventually, the line clicked and Ash heard his boss's voice.

"Did you see the jury after you finished testifying? Two of them were crying. I think you won the case."

"Nobody won, Susan. We all lost."

"Not true. Leonard Wilson has already been on TV to talk about what a bad job I'm doing. This one hurt."

"Your next big trial will be better."

"There's not going to be a next one. I'll finish out my term, but I'm dropping out of the primary race."

Ash hadn't been thinking about politics for a while, so it took him a moment to figure out what she was talking about.

"Losing was a setback, sure, but—"

"Don't try to console me. I'm done. I'm not a politician, and I never was. You didn't mean to, but you..." Her voice softened so it was nearly below Ash's threshold of hearing. "It's over, okay?"

"I'm sorry."

"Me too."

Susan hung up, and Ash stayed in his chair. For whatever faults she might have had, she was a good prosecutor. It was a shame that the skills required to win an election were almost diametrically opposed to those possessed by people who actually deserved to hold elected office. Susan would land on her feet, though; there was no doubt in Ash's mind about that. She could enter private practice; she could teach; she could retire. The real loser was going to be the city. God help them if Leonard Wilson became prosecutor.

Ash didn't have time to dwell on such thoughts, though. He had a long day and night ahead of him.

22

S ince he was probably going to be up all night, Ash went home and straight to bed. Unfortunately, his mind wouldn't shut up long enough for him to get to sleep. Noah had lied about the details, but Ash believed he had been truthful about one thing: The case was about revenge. Thomas Rahal killed a cop during a botched search, and the cop's buddies wanted him to pay for it. The story made sense, but it was the only thing that did. Ash hadn't just stumbled on the case or been assigned to it; Konstantin Bukoholov had asked him to investigate. He wouldn't have done that without good reason, which meant Ash still didn't know every player on the field.

He got up at about three in the afternoon. Megan had stayed home from school again, but after taking fast-acting antibiotics, she felt well enough to be up and about. The two of them played a bowling video game on the family's Nintendo Wii while Kaden watched from his Pack 'n Play and Hannah exercised at the YMCA. It was a welcome break from the rest of his week.

By half after six, he and the rest of the family sat down to a quick dinner. He liked sitting at the same table as his family, but his mind was only half focused on the meal.

Bukoholov had no reason to involve himself in the investigation. He didn't profit from Rahal's trial or the investigation. He didn't learn anything new; he didn't eliminate a competitor. He didn't get anything out of it. Despite everything Ash had learned, they were still missing something vital. That was disturbing, but he'd figure it out when he could. At the moment, he had bigger issues to worry about.

He left the house at seven-thirty and drove downtown. Thankfully, Hannah's new supply of her coffee hadn't arrived yet, so before leaving, she gave him an eight-cup thermos full of the hazelnut coffee he had liked so much a few days earlier. He met Lieutenant Mike Bowers and six uniformed officers in the city government parking lot. Two deputies from the Marion County sheriff's department were already guarding Noah at a hotel by the airport. The plan was to have four officers covering Noah's house, one at the Rahals' home, and one at Ash's home just in case somebody tried going after his family. With luck, the officer at Ash's house would stay long enough to scare off the delivery guy before he brought over Hannah's resupply of her black-death coffee blend.

Bowers dealt out the assignments and the teams left simultaneously. Ash rode with Bowers. He didn't look forward to six hours in a car with the man, but despite the homicide squad's involvement, Ash still considered the case to be his. He intended to see it through to the end.

They rode in silence and parked in the driveway of a home for sale about a block and a half from Noah's. Bowers had borrowed an unmarked Chevy Impala from the motor pool. It wasn't IMPD's standard vehicle, so hopefully they wouldn't be noticed. Ash slunk low in his seat and opened his thermos of coffee to wait. Since Noah was in custody, his house was empty. Bowers had gone in earlier and turned on his TV and a few lights, though, so it looked occupied.

"Coffee?" asked Ash, holding his thermos up.

"Thanks, but no. My kids gave me an ulcer."

Thankfully Ash's kids weren't old enough to worry him too much yet. He poured a cup and capped the thermos before settling back into his seat. Neither spoke for the next two hours. The police radio, though, sputtered a constant stream of quiet chatter. Eventually, it, too, blended into the background noise around them.

"I've got shots fired near Forty-Ninth and Pennsylvania. Immediate assistance requested."

Both Bowers and Ash shot upright. It was a quarter after one in the morning, and most of the windows in the homes around them were dark. The intersection was only three or four blocks away. It was a residential neighborhood, so it was likely some kind of domestic dispute. The two patrol vehicles that had accompanied them and parked at the other end of the street put on their lights and sped off. Bowers turned on his car and looked as if he were going to do the same, but Ash opened his door before he could.

"Wait just a second," he said, stepping out. The night was chilly, and the moon cast long shadows on the grass. Ash held his breath and blocked out everything around him but the sound. He heard sirens in the distance and road noise from a relatively busy street nearby, but that was it.

"You see something?" asked Bowers, stepping out of his side of the vehicle.

"No. And I don't hear anything, either," he said. "If there's something going on at Forty-Ninth and Pennsylvania, we should hear it." Ash reached into his jacket and felt his firearm but didn't take it out of the holster. Internal Affairs still had his service piece, so he was stuck with his backup, a lighter nine-millimeter. "Let's swing by Noah's house. I've got a bad feeling."

"Sure."

As soon as Ash sat down again, Bowers put the car in reverse and inched out of the driveway. The street was long and straight, so as soon as their car cleared the landscaping, Ash could see for three blocks in either direction. Nothing moved. Despite that, he couldn't shake the unsettled feeling that had taken residence in his gut. Noah's men hadn't left much to chance when they killed witnesses before. Chances were they wouldn't leave any now, either.

Bowers accelerated slowly. Trees dotted the landscape, casting shadows over bicycles, basketball hoops, and sundry other objects. Ash strained his eyes to see something out of place. He almost told Bowers to just circle the block and go back to the driveway when he saw something out of the corner of his eye. Movement.

"They're on the porch," he said, throwing open his door while the car was a house down from Noah's. Bowers braked hard, and Ash jumped out, his firearm in hand. "Lie on the ground. Now."

The men on the porch hesitated for a split second and then opened fire. Ash ducked behind the front wheel well as rounds dinged against the cruiser. He couldn't see Bowers, but hopefully he had gotten down before the first volley hit. The cruiser's door panels were lined with Kevlar, but the windows were standard safety glass. Ash's heart pounded hard and his breath came out in bursts.

The shooting stopped as quickly as it started. Ash popped his head up in time to see two figures running in opposite directions from the porch. His ears rang with the sound of gunfire, and two of the cruiser's windows had been shattered. There was a thin trail of blood above one of Bowers's eyebrows, probably a cut from falling glass. For a split second, neither he nor Ash moved.

As if on cue, the gravity of the situation seemed to hit them both simultaneously. Ash jumped back from the car and pounded on the roof, letting Bowers know he was clear. The lieutenant didn't waste time and roared off after one of the runners while Ash sprinted after the other.

Lights popped on in nearby houses as the residents became alert to whatever was happening in front of their homes. Ash could hear sirens somewhere distant and coming closer. He'd have backup eventually, but that didn't help if his suspect got away. The grass and buildings blurred as Ash sprinted, but he hardly noticed. For a while, it felt like he was gaining, but then something happened. The foot he had injured a few days ago felt weak. It didn't hurt exactly, but it couldn't support his weight like it should. He kept sprinting anyway, the distance between him and the man he was chasing widening.

The neighborhood ended abruptly at a major intersection. The streetlights were so bright they blinded him after the relative darkness of the neighborhood. Ash felt his lungs and legs burn, but neither he nor his quarry slowed. The runner reached the intersection first. Time seemed to slow. At that time of night and in that part of the city, the streets were relatively empty. Unfortunately, for a certain class of reckless asshole, that turned them into drag strips.

"Stop."

Ash saw the collision coming long before it occurred, and unlike his chase with Michael Washington, he was powerless to stop it. A midsized SUV barreled through the intersection at seventy or eighty miles an hour. The driver slammed on his brakes, but he was still moving too fast to avoid the collision. The runner's legs hit the bumper, while the rest of his body slammed into the window. He spun over the top, his legs and arms thrown to the sides by the force, and landed on the ground, unmoving.

The driver, along with everyone else on the road, screeched to a halt. By the time he arrived at the intersection, Ash already had his phone out. He dialed IMPD's dispatcher. The victim was Officer Joe Cartwright. Ash wedged his cell phone between his head and shoulder as he felt Cartwright's neck for a pulse. It was thready and growing weaker. As he pushed aside the collar on Cartwright's shirt, he noticed a crucifix dangling from a silver chain.

The dispatcher finally answered, and Ash took a breath, calming his heart.

"I have an officer down at the corner of Fifty-Second and Meridian. I need ambulance service immediately." He hesitated for a second. "And find a priest."

The dispatcher said something in response, but Ash dropped his phone and warned the civilians from nearby vehicles to stay back. Lieutenant Bowers, followed by a marked cruiser, drove up a few minutes later with their lights and sirens blaring. Bowers's tires had barely stopped screeching when he jumped out of the car.

"Get in, Rashid."

"What's going on?"

"Noah escaped. Get in the car, now. We'll talk on the way."

Ash still hadn't caught his breath after chasing Cartwright, but the lieutenant's tone was urgent enough to get his attention. As soon as his ass touched the seat, Bowers floored the accelerator, pushing him back into the vinyl and shutting the cruiser's door with the momentum. Ash remained silent, trying to get his bearings in the vehicle. They were speeding west down Fifty-Second, but where they were going, he didn't know.

"How'd we lose him?"

Bowers shrugged. "Somebody screwed up. One of the deputies went for a smoke break, and Noah overpowered his partner. He took the deputy's firearm and then nabbed the other."

"So he's armed now. What about Thomas Rahal?"

"They hit his house just like they did here. Somebody made an emergency call, so the squad car we had watching the apartment complex bugged out. Officers Patrick Dixon and Jim Haines then tried to break in, but Fatima Rahal shot them point-blank with a twenty-gauge shotgun. Blew a hole right through Dixon's chest cavity, but the shot ricocheted off something and then hit Haines in the neck. Haines could live, but Dixon is gone."

That hit Ash like a physical force. He sat up straighter. "Shit. Is she okay?"

Bowers looked over and accelerated hard enough that Ash felt himself pressed against the seat again.

"She's fine, but we lost radio contact with the officer we put on your house."

Ash's mind didn't process the statement and time seemed to stand still. Then everything in the world seemed to hit him at once.

"Fucking move."

Bowers didn't need the encouragement. He whipped their Chevy around turns hard enough that Ash felt the rear wheels slip several times. Even still, Bowers kept his foot on the gas throughout. Frenzied drivers hurried to get out of their way, one even going so far as to pull his truck onto the sidewalk. Ash barely noticed. He kept playing scenarios in his head. Even if the officer assigned to watch his house went inside to use the bathroom, he should have kept his radio or his cell phone. Ash leaned forward in his seat, silently willing the car to go just a little faster.

They covered the seven miles to Ash's home quickly and entered his neighborhood about five minutes after setting out. There were a couple of cars parked on the side of the road Ash didn't recognize, but he couldn't see anyone running. He wasn't sure if that was good or bad.

Ash threw his door open as Bowers started to slow in front of his house. As soon as it stopped, Ash vaulted out and stumbled on the uneven ground. He caught himself before falling and sprinted toward his kitchen door. The house was dark and the neighborhood was quiet. There was a marked patrol car in his driveway, but despite all the noise Ash was making, no one came running.

He ignored the squad car and rammed his shoulder into the kitchen door, half expecting it to give. The wood splintered and popped, but the dead bolt held. Rather than break through, he grabbed his keys but his fingers were shaking so much he couldn't unlock the dead bolt. Sweat poured down his face.

Come on, come on, come on.

He held his breath, hoping that would steady his hands.

Before he could put his keys in the lock, though, the kitchen light popped on and the door opened. Ash was blinded. Eventually, the blurry shape in front of him solidified into his wife. She scowled at him, a baseball bat held at her side.

"What are you doing? You scared me half to death."

The strength left Ash's legs in a rush, and he leaned against the door frame, panting.

"Sorry."

Ash heard footsteps behind him, but Hannah didn't seem frightened, so he didn't bother turning his head.

"He's alive, but—" Whatever Bowers had to say was stopped short. He paused for a second. "Hi, Mrs. Rashid. Didn't mean to wake you up."

She sighed exasperatedly. "Can you tell me what's wrong with my husband?"

"I'm not sure if I have that kind of time."

Ash looked at Bowers, confused. "Did you find Noah?"

"He's gone. The officer I put on your house is unconscious and tied up with duct tape, but he's alive."

"Can someone tell me what's going on?" asked Hannah, crossing her arms.

Ash used the side of the house to steady himself as he stood up. "How about you put on some tea? This may take a while."

23

Trueto her word, Susan stuck with the trial to the end. Within an hour of having the case handed to them, the jury found Rahal guilty of reckless homicide, a lesser offense inherently included in the murder charge. Judge Haller sentenced him to two years in prison, the minimum amount of time for that level of felony. Rahal lost his job, his apartment, and, since he committed an aggravated felony for immigration purposes, his visa. Unless he found a hell of an immigration lawyer, he'd be deported as soon as he finished his sentence. Everybody lost all the way around. Maybe that was justice, but it left a bitter taste in Ash's mouth.

He had almost three months' worth of vacation days stored up, so he took the next two weeks off to spend with his family and sort out his life and career. His new position with the community relations team would begin as soon as he got back. It wasn't the job he wanted, but he'd live with it. As soon as Child Services told him he could, Ash visited Michael Washington in a home for boys on the city's west side. He was grateful to hear that the police had gotten the people who killed his grandmother, but that wouldn't make up for the loss. Michael didn't have a lot of family left, just a mom who was in and out of drug treatment centers and an older brother in the Marines. Ash told him that he'd try to visit once a week. With everything going on in Michael's life, he'd need a steady friend. Ash couldn't do much, but he could do that.

Aside from the changes at work, life returned to normal, mostly, and somehow, he managed to stay sober. The experience was scary and new.

As the days passed, more details emerged about the events surrounding Officer Ryan Dixon's death. Six officers mistakenly served the no-knock warrant on Thomas Rahal's home, but only five made it out. Those five agreed to do whatever it took to ensure that someone paid for Dixon's death. They tried to convince Andrew Rutkowski, the real target of their original search warrant, to remain silent about what he knew. Unfortunately, the conversation turned violent and Rutkowski died in their custody.

According to Detective Dennis Walker, Rutkowski's death changed things. It was as if something snapped in all of them, and they threw out the rulebook. They convinced a judge to issue a warrant they knew to be fraudulent and tried to make Rutkowski's death look like a suicide. If it hadn't been for the county's attempt to digitize its old files, no one would have seen a thing.

Cassandra Johnson found both the original and fraudulent warrants, though, and contacted Carl Gillespie. Gillespie then contacted his old colleague Lieutenant Noah Stuart to find out what was going on. Noah and the rest of his team killed them both to shut them up. Noah and Patrick Dixon stole a car from a police impound lot in Terre Haute, Indiana, and used it to run Cassandra over. They then handed it to two hapless idiots so high on meth that they couldn't walk straight. They had no idea what they had been given.

Gillespie was easier. Noah Stuart, Patrick Dixon, and Joe

Cartwright went to his house, chloroformed him, and then locked him in the walk-in fridge in the basement. It was so well insulated, the neighbors didn't even hear him screaming for help. To cover it up, Joe Cartwright torched a house to keep Michael Washington from talking to the police about Cassandra's death. He even paid some students in Zionsville to steal a cooler full of blood from a blood drive and splash it around an apartment in Indianapolis in an effort to tie up the police force.

When Ash started investigating, they tried to shut him up, too. They threatened him, they beat him up, and finally they followed him one night and tried to hit him with a car when he went to see Bukoholov. The old man had nothing to do with Ash's accident. It was twisted street justice, and it left him feeling ill.

All six men who mistakenly searched Thomas Rahal's home paid for their mistake. Ryan Dixon, Patrick Dixon, and Joe Cartwright died, but they may have been the lucky ones. Officer Jim Haines survived, but barely. He lost so much blood after being shot by Fatima Rahal that he was effectively brain dead. Noah Stuart disappeared completely.

Dennis Walker was the only one to survive unscathed. Mike Bowers picked him up running from Noah's house, and in the coming week, he pleaded guilty to a litany of charges to stay off death row. He even admitted that he went to Lieutenant Stuart's home with Joe Cartwright to commit murder. Walker would never see daylight again. Noah, wherever he was, was running, something he'd be doing for the rest of his miserable life. They'd find him eventually, and he'd get what he deserved, too.

The case was over, except for one thread. Konstantin Bukoholov, the man who had tipped him off to Cassandra's death in the first place. Two days before he was set to go back to work, Ash made an appointment to meet the old man in Military Park. When he arrived, Bukoholov was already sitting down on a bench overlooking the canal. It was a blustery December morning, but there were joggers and sightseers near the water.

"Mr. Bukoholov."

"Please, call me Kostya," said Bukoholov. "It's what my friends call me."

Ash dropped a business-sized envelope on the bench beside the older man.

"There's a receipt in the envelope for the donation you made to the Marion County Food Bank."

Bukoholov picked up the envelope and looked at the document inside. "Four thousand six hundred and fifty dollars," he said. "I'm usually more generous than that."

"I had some expenses," said Ash. "That's what was left of the money you gave me a few weeks ago."

"That was for you and your family. I assumed you needed it."

Ash crossed his arms. "We don't."

"Then why are you here?"

"I thought we could talk." Bukoholov moved the envelope Ash had put on the bench, and Ash sat down. "Before she died, Cassandra Johnson was paid twenty-five thousand dollars by a company called Indy Holdings, Inc. Do you know the name?"

Bukoholov looked straight ahead. "Of course," he said. "I'm the company's only shareholder."

"Took two lawyers the better part of a week to figure that out. We wouldn't have even gotten that far if I didn't know you owned the Lucky Bastard."

Bukoholov turned to look at him, an eyebrow raised. "The Lucky Bastard?"

"Blue-collar bar a couple of blocks southwest of Lucas Oil Stadium. I met you there last year."

The old man smiled wistfully and nodded. "I remember now. You took my nephew there after you shot him. I didn't realize I still owned that place."

"One of your companies does, at least."

"Thank you for that trip down memory lane, Detective," said Bukoholov, pushing on his knees to help himself stand. "If all you're interested in is conversation, I have business to attend to. Perhaps I could meet you in a bar some night."

He started to walk away, but Ash cleared his throat before the Russian got very far.

"I know you're funding Leonard Wilson's political campaign. Your accountants weren't very clever about hiding that."

Bukoholov stopped and looked over his shoulder. "I'll have to talk to them about that. Last I checked, though, it's not a crime to exercise my citizenship."

"Of course not," said Ash. "It must be nice to own a temporary employment agency with city contracts, though."

The old man turned around. His skin was wrinkled, but his eyes were narrow and his gaze was focused and tight. "I have a lot of businesses, and I'm very proud of the work I do for this city."

"Professional Staffing Services isn't just a normal business for you, and we both know that. It gave you access to the court system's confidential files. With a little bit of work, you could find the real names of confidential informants, the identities of undercover officers, transcripts of sealed grand jury testimony, all sorts of things. You could even find out when misguided officers file fraudulent paperwork."

"My patience is wearing thin, Detective Rashid."

"I'll make this simple, then. Cassandra found two problematic search warrant affidavits while working for your company. You paid her twenty-five thousand dollars to share them with Carl Gillespie. Gillespie contacted Noah Stuart to see what he had to say about them. Noah and some of the men under his command killed them both to keep them quiet."

The corners of Bukoholov's lips crept upward into a smile. "You have quite an imagination. Why would I do any of that?"

"Because if Cassandra and Carl Gillespie revealed those documents during the Rahal trial, the case would blow up on live TV. Susan Mercer, despite whatever other faults she may have, is a hell of a prosecutor. If she lost a case like that, though, there's no way she could win the primary. Without someone from the other party running, Leonard Wilson would win next fall's election, and the biggest drug wholesaler in town will have a friend in the prosecutor's office."

Bukoholov shook his head, allowing the smile to slip from his lips. "Walk with me."

"I'm fine here."

Bukoholov glanced to his left, and Ash felt a heavy hand on his shoulder.

"That's not a request," he said, already walking toward the canal. Ash stood and looked behind him. The Hulk and another one of Bukoholov's goons smiled back. Ash hurried to catch up with the old man. "My employees are like my family. I contacted you when Ms. Johnson died because

I knew you would do everything you could to make sure she received the justice she deserved."

Ash felt the muscles of his chest and back quiver, practically begging him to lash out at the old man.

"You almost got my family killed."

"I would never willingly let harm come to your family. They were safe. I had my own people watching them."

Ash glanced at the men behind them. "If they were watching my house, they should probably stick around and talk to the police. We're still looking for Noah Stuart."

"You'll never find him. He's gone."

"You know that for a fact?"

Bukoholov shrugged. "Did you know that if you stick a body in a cast-iron bathtub and cover it in lye, it will be gone in a week?"

"Is that what you did to Noah?"

Bukoholov waved him off. "I didn't do anything to anyone. I'm merely pointing out that human beings are fragile and any number of things could have happened to him. Maybe he fell into a bathtub full of lye, maybe he's sitting in a bar in Mexico right now, or maybe he became so guilt stricken over what he did that he killed himself. You'll never know, so you might as well stop wasting your time searching for him. Just some advice."

That was likely as close as Ash would get to a confession. If Bukoholov had killed Noah, the body was gone. Ash probably should have felt something, but he didn't. The world was better off without him.

"If you ever come to my house again, I'll kill you, bodyguards or not. Stay away from my family."

The old man smiled. "I've always liked your bravado, but

you're not a murderer. Trust me when I say you don't have it in you."

"You have no idea what I have in me. If you put my kids in danger again, I will put a gun to your head and pull the trigger. That's not bravado."

The smile slipped from Bukoholov's lips. "Hopefully we'll never have to test that," he said, regaining his cold, dead stare. "Leonard Wilson will offer you a job in his administration when he's sworn in next year. The pay will be roughly double your present salary, and I think you should take it. It will be good for both of you. Someone needs to ensure he doesn't stray too far from the path of righteousness."

"Yeah, right. What would you get out of that?"

"You keep an eye on him, and I get an eye on you. We both win," he said. "As always, I enjoyed seeing you. Give my best to your wife and children."

"Go fuck yourself."

Bukoholov laughed before walking toward the park's exit. Ash stayed at the canal's edge, watching the reflection of activity around him in the water. He was a gray figure at the precipice between black and white, a thin, wavering line that was neither entirely one nor the other. Maybe he stepped over that line sometimes, maybe he was a little rougher than he should be, and maybe he was a little more aggressive than he should be. As long as the world had men like Bukoholov, though, that's what was needed and he wasn't going to change.

He drove home and met his family in the backyard. Megan was jumping into and scattering a pile of leaves Ash had raked a week earlier, while Hannah gently pushed Kaden on the baby swing on the play set. As soon as Megan saw him, she stopped running and put her hands to her sides.

"*Ummi* said I could do it," she said. "I can't get in trouble."

"You're not in trouble, honey," said Ash. "Keep playing."

"Okay."

She started running again, although her enthusiasm at first seemed a little dampened. Nevertheless, she managed to scatter in roughly two minutes what had taken him almost an hour to rake just a few days earlier. He needed another project anyway, though. While Megan played, Ash walked toward the play set and sat on the swing Megan usually used. It felt a little tight on his considerably bigger backside.

"How have the kids been?" he asked.

"Megan's been...well, she's been Megan. Kaden has been good, though," she said. "How was your meeting?"

"It's over. That's about all the good I can say about it."

Hannah nodded. "My sister called. She and Jack offered to take Kaden and Megan for the night. I thought we could go to the art museum. This is the last weekend for their summer film series. They're showing *Batman*."

"Is it one of those things we can bring food to?"

"Yeah. We could have a picnic if you wanted."

Ash shrugged. "I was also thinking we could run by that Turkish bakery that has those almond cookies I like."

"Only if you promise not to eat them all in the car."

"I don't know if I can make that promise. What the stomach wants, the stomach wants."

Hannah patted his midsection. "Believe me, I know."

Ash sucked his stomach in and sat straighter. Before he could think of a response, though, Kaden started fussing and

Hannah turned to pick him up. Despite her efforts, the baby squirmed and kept fussing until she finally handed him to Ash. He promptly sneezed in Ash's face and relaxed.

"He's still a little congested," she said, handing him a tissue. "I have some good news, though. Leonard Wilson called while you were out. He wants to talk to you about a job in his administration if he's elected next year. That's what you wanted, isn't it? A full-time job in the prosecutor's office?"

Ash wiped his cheek off with the tissue. "I think I've got all I want here."

ACKNOWLEDGMENTS

The author would like to thank the following people for their invaluable assistance bringing this book to market:

Many thanks to Mitch Hoffman at Grand Central Publishing and Jade Chandler at Little, Brown UK. Your editorial expertise and patience with a still relatively inexperienced writer are truly appreciated.

Thanks also to Robert Gottlieb and the entire staff at Trident Media Group. Thank you for your enthusiasm and belief in my work. I would also like to thank Mark Gottlieb and Erica Silverman for providing editorial feedback on early versions of my manuscript. You helped me see things in the manuscript that I didn't see before, and for that, I am very appreciative.

Finally and most important, thanks to my family and friends. Your patience and support have allowed me to follow a dream I've had for many years. I couldn't have done this without you.

ABOUT THE AUTHOR

CHRIS CULVER is the *New York Times* bestselling author of the Ash Rashid series of mysteries. After graduate school, Chris taught courses in ethics and comparative religion at a small liberal arts university in southern Arkansas. Between classes, he wrote *The Abbey*, which spent sixteen weeks on the *New York Times* bestsellers list and introduced the world to Detective Ash Rashid.

Chris has been a storyteller since he was a kid, but he decided to write crime fiction after picking up a dog-eared, coffee-stained paperback of Mickey Spillane's *I, the Jury* in a library book sale. Many years later, his wife, despite considerable effort, still can't stop him from bringing more orphan books home. The two of them, along with more houseplants than any normal family needs, reside near St. Louis, where Chris is hard at work on his next novel.

**DON'T MISS THE FIRST ASH
RASHID NOVEL**

When his niece's body is found in the guest
home of one of Indianapolis's most wealthy
citizens, Ash defies orders and launches an
investigation. But if he doesn't solve the
case fast, his niece won't be the only family
member he has to bury....

Please turn this page for an excerpt from

The Abbey.

I

I hated doing next-of-kin notifications. Most people guessed why I was there as soon as they opened the door. They put on airs of fortitude and strength, but almost all fell apart in front of me. I could see it in their eyes. They looked at me and knew something, too. I'd go home afterward as if nothing was wrong. I might hug my family a little tighter than usual, but the world would go on for me without much of a hiccup. Most hated me for what I had to do, and I couldn't blame them. My Islamic faith told me that drinking to escape their stares was an abomination in the sight of God, but I didn't care as long as it helped me sleep without dreams.

I pulled my department-issued Ford Crown Victoria to a stop beside the mailbox in front of my sister's house and took a deep breath, stilling myself as a familiar anxiety flooded over me. I knew as soon as I had volunteered for the duty that I was going to have one of those nights I'd need to forget, but it took that moment for it to become real. It tore at my gut like barbed wire.

I opened my car door. My sister and her husband lived in a 4000-square-foot historic home that could have comfortably housed my entire extended family. As a resident of the poorer, smaller neighborhood next door, I was glad that it didn't. My brother-in-law Nassir smiled and put his hand on my shoulder when he opened the front door but stiffened when I didn't return the gesture.

"What's wrong?" he asked.

"We'll talk in a moment," I said. "Where's Rana?"

"In the kitchen," said Nassir, leaving his hand on my shoulder a moment longer. "Come in."

I walked in, and Nassir shut the door behind me. The house's first floor was typical of well-kept historic homes. The woodwork was straight and clean, with a rich patina that could only come from eighty years of polishing, and the rooms were open and bright. Nassir half-led and half-pushed me down the home's main hallway to the kitchen in back. Rana was in front of a gas stove large enough to have been at home in the kitchen of a Las Vegas strip hotel. The air smelled like garlic and yeast.

"Ash," she said, smiling at me. "I thought you and Hannah were going out tonight."

"We were," I said. "I need you both to sit at the table. We need to talk."

Nassir and Rana did as I asked. In return, I broke their hearts as gently as I could.

Nassir and Rana had taken the news about as well as anyone could expect. They hadn't cried in front of me, but they told me they wanted to be alone. If I went home, though, I'd have to tell my wife why I canceled our wedding anniversary plans. I didn't think I had the strength or stomach for that yet. Instead, I drove to my office. It wasn't my case, but I had enough friends in my department that I had a stack of eight-by-ten photos and notes on my desk when I arrived. They made my stomach turn.

I read through the timeline quickly. The call had come in at six in the evening. The caller reported the presence of a prone female, approximately sixteen to eighteen years old, in the guest home of one of Indianapolis's most wealthy citizens. The first officer on the scene checked her pulse but found nothing. He called in a probable homicide, and that's when the gears started moving. Within half an hour, five forensic technicians were documenting the scene, and Detective Olivia Rhodes was interviewing potential witnesses.

I flipped through the photographs. Each picture was numbered and had a written description. The first few were wide-angle shots of the scene. The photographer had snapped pictures of a kitchen with light maple cabinetry and a living room with a television, lounge chairs, and pool table. A vase of calla lilies rested on the counter beside the stove. They were my niece's favorite flower; my wife and I always sent them to her on her birthday.

Rachel, my niece, was in the center of the room. Her skin was pale, indicating that her blood had already begun to pool beneath her, and her arms were pressed against her sides like a supine soldier at attention. I stared at the picture for a moment, my stomach twisting. She didn't deserve that.

I skimmed through the next few pictures. The photographer had snapped more shots of the kitchen and living room. They were helpful for orienting someone in a crime scene, but not particularly interesting to me. I stopped when the photographs started focusing on my niece. The photographer had started with wider shots of her placement and then continued by photographing her closely from her head to her feet. She had no obvious external injuries, nor could I see puddles of blood around her. That was comforting. Unfortunately, I knew without even reading the crime scene report that her body had been staged.

I turned through the stack of photos until I found one focusing on Rachel's neck. She wore a light-blue polo shirt with an open collar. I couldn't see ligature marks on her neck, but the bottom button on her shirt had been popped off, leaving a pair of strings in its place. The detective in charge might not have thought much of it, but that wasn't like Rachel. She was as meticulous about her clothes as anyone I had ever met. She wouldn't have worn that shirt until she had a new button sewn back on.

I shifted on my seat and flipped through a few more pictures until I saw one focusing on her waist. Rachel wore a denim skirt with buttons instead of a zipper in front. The buttons were misaligned, though, so the skirt would have ridden uncomfortably against her abdomen. She wouldn't have done that to herself.

I continued turning over photographs until I saw one I couldn't explain. It looked like a shot of the carpet. Puzzled, I scanned through the notes that accompanied the photographs until I found the appropriate one. The photographer had tried to capture track marks. I looked at the picture again, straining my eyes until I saw two long strips where the carpet's nap was flattened in one direction. Rachel had been dragged in there with her feet dangling behind her.

I could feel bile rise in the back of my throat.

I stared at that picture for a moment, thankful I hadn't seen it before going to my sister's house. Since I had come right from home, I hadn't been able to tell her much about her daughter's death. That was probably good.

The rest of the pictures focused on something odd, a glass vial full of a brownish-red liquid. The technician's notes said someone had found it on an end table in one of the bedrooms. It was roughly the size of a cigar, and when the technician picked it up to catalog it, the liquid inside coated the glass like cough syrup. There was pink lipstick on the rim that appeared to be a match to Rachel's.

What were you into, honey?

My desk phone rang, startling me. I glanced at my watch. It was after ten, well past my regular hours, so I doubted it was a casual phone call. I picked it up.

"Rashid," I said. "What can I do for you?"

"Yeah, Detective Rashid. This is Sergeant Hensley at IMPD downtown. Olivia Rhodes brought in somebody in your niece's case, and I thought I'd give you the heads-up."

I nodded. Hensley was an old-school watch sergeant and had been on the force before we had civilian oversight committees or cameras in every room. When he was my age, interrogations had included rubber hoses and phone books. I envied him. Justice may not have been pretty, but shit got done.

"Suspect or witness?" I asked.

Hensley chuckled.

"Fuck if I know," he said. "They don't tell me anything. If you want, I could do some poking around."

I almost snickered. Hensley was as well connected in our department as anyone alive. He probably knew exactly who Olivia brought in and why, probably before she even entered the building. He wanted a handout.

"Don't bother," I said. "When'd she bring him in?"

"Just walked by my desk."

If they had just walked by the front desk, I had at least twenty minutes to get over to IMPD. While I was still officially a detective, I was on a permanent investigative assignment with the Prosecutor's Office, so I shared office space with the prosecutors about a block from the department's downtown bullpen. In another year, I'd hopefully finish law school and be done with the department completely. I still loved the work, but I could only see so many bodies before I became as broken as the victims I investigated.

"Appreciate the call, Sergeant," I said. "I'll be over in a few."

I hung up before Hensley could respond and grabbed my tweed jacket. My shoulder ached dully when I twisted my arm inside. I was thirty-four and generally too young to have arthritis, but I had been shot with a hunting rifle four years earlier while serving a high-risk felony warrant. I was the lucky one; my partner had been shot in the neck and bled out before paramedics could stabilize him.

The concrete outside my building radiated pent-up heat from earlier that day. My throat was dry and scratchy. One of my favorite bars was just a block away, and for a brief moment, I considered stopping. I decided against it, though. The station wasn't far, and I could probably find someone inside willing to give me a pick-me-up if I needed it.

I reached the building quickly. IMPD's downtown station was at least fifty years old, and it smelled musty. The front lobby was large and clad in white marble polished to a mirror shine by footsteps. A middle-aged couple clung to each other in the waiting room. They were well-dressed and looked nervous. My guess was that they were picking up their delinquent kid for his first DUI. That happened a lot. I'd see them again.

I walked to the front desk. Sergeant Hensley sat behind it, reading *Sports Illustrated*. He dropped his magazine and looked at me with green, rapacious eyes.

"You look like shit, Rashid."

"Feel like it, too," I said, reaching over the counter for a sign-in sheet. I scribbled my name and rank. Detective Sergeant Ashraf Rashid. I had been named after my father, although I hadn't ever met him. He had been a history professor at the American University of Cairo, but one of his students shot and killed him before I was born. Apparently that kid's family took grades seriously. The remnants of my family immigrated to the U.S. shortly after that.

I pushed the sign-in sheet toward Hensley and pulled out my wallet. I took out two twenties and put them on top of the counter.

"I think I missed your kid's last birthday. Buy him a football for me."

Hensley slipped the money in his pocket and smiled.

"I'm sure he'll appreciate this," he said. "Detective Rhodes is in interrogation room three with Robert Cutting."

If Hensley thought that earned him another payoff, he was wrong. I thanked him and headed toward the elevators to the left of the desk.

The homicide bullpen hadn't changed much since I had left it. Unlike most regular office buildings, IMPD didn't have individual offices. At least not for peons like me. It had desks in open rooms. The administration justified the arrangement by arguing that separate offices would impede communication on sensitive investigations. In actuality, I'm pretty sure they were just too cheap to spring for the extra materials when they last renovated the building.

I weaved my way through desks and columns of file folders. The interrogation rooms were designed to be oppressive and to give a suspect the feeling that there was no escape. They were cramped, they had no windows, and the airflow inside them was carefully regulated depending on the interrogator's mood. If a suspect looked around before going in, he'd even see a well-labeled express elevator that went directly to the holding cells on the top four floors of the building.

I walked until I came to interrogation room three. The door was shut, but Detective Olivia Rhodes stood outside, cup of coffee in hand. She nodded at me when I drew close. Olivia was a good detective. I had been in homicide for six years before being transferred to the Prosecutor's Office. I spent one of those years as her partner. From what I had heard earlier, she fought to be assigned to my niece's case. I liked her.

"I thought you might be up," she said, turning down the hallway. She opened an unmarked door beside the interrogation room and held it for me. "Come on."

Police interrogations have come a long way in the twelve years I've been on the force. Our station no longer had the infamous one-way mirror overlooking the interrogation room. Instead, we had a sophisticated set of hidden video cameras and microphones around the room. Everything was recorded from the moment a suspect walked inside to the moment he walked out. I had heard those recordings could disappear if the right person got the right incentive, but I had never taken advantage of that. It was nice to know the option was there if I needed it, though.

Olivia turned on a flat-screen monitor attached to the wall. The picture showed a kid in jeans and a blue T-shirt. He had curly brown hair and one of his arms was handcuffed to the wall, keeping him upright. He stared at the steel table in front of him, apparently unaware that he was being filmed.

"Is this Robert Cutting?" I asked.

"He goes by Robbie," she said. "He's your niece's boyfriend. Was your niece's boyfriend, at least. I appreciate you doing the next-of-kin notification."

"That's no problem," I said. "The kid have a lawyer yet?"

"Meyers," she said. That figured. John Meyers was one of the best defense attorneys in town. "He's on his way in."

"Did the kid ask for him?"

Olivia shrugged.

"Sort of. Nathan Cutting called him, and Robbie agreed to use him. I think we can nail this kid, so I'm not going to push and try to talk to him before Meyers comes in."

"What do you think you have?" I asked.

"You've seen the crime scene photos?" she asked.

I nodded.

"Upper-class victim without signs of trauma or injury," she said, slipping her hands through her blond hair and securing it in a ponytail. "I think she overdosed and Robbie tried to cover it up."

I shook my head.

"Rachel wasn't on drugs," I said.

"You sure about that?" asked Olivia.

"Yeah. She's got a scholarship to play tennis at Purdue next year, and her high school tests randomly to make sure the kids aren't doping. My sister would have said something if Rachel wasn't clean."

Olivia bit her lower lip.

"We'll see how things go, then," she said. "You hang around here. I'm going to wait downstairs for Meyers to show up and get this started."

Olivia left shortly after that. I sat and waited, staring at the monitor. Robbie looked thin and awkward. Appearances could be deceiving, but I doubted he was Islamic. That wouldn't sit too well with Rana and Nassir, which might have been part of his appeal to my niece.

I leaned back in my chair, wishing I had thought to grab a cup of coffee on my way in.

Olivia returned about five minutes later with John Meyers in tow. Meyers looked as if he was in his fifties. He wore a lustrous blue suit and carried a soft leather bag over one shoulder. He sat at the table in the interrogation room beside his client while Olivia sat across with a file folder in front of her. The microphones inside were sensitive enough that I could hear the clatter of the metal buckles on Meyers's bag strike the steel table.

"Okay, so why don't we get this started," said Olivia. "For the record, it's eleven in the evening on August nineteenth, and this is Detective Olivia Rhodes interviewing Robbie Cutting. Sitting in on this interview is Mr. Cutting's lawyer, John Meyers. Is that correct?"

Robbie mumbled "Yes," but didn't meet Olivia's gaze. I took a closer look at him then. He had bags under his eyes, and he swayed as if he were being buffeted by wind. He looked lost.

"Good," said Olivia. "Right now, this is an information-gathering interview. I'm trying to figure out what happened. You're not under arrest, but I can use what you tell me here in court. Just to be clear, you don't have to say anything, and you're free to leave at any time. Do you understand these rights, Mr. Cutting?"

Robbie looked up, hope in his eyes.

"Does that mean I can go?"

Meyers reached over and squeezed his client's shoulder.

"We can leave now, but we should answer Detective Rhodes's questions first," he said. "The sooner we get the questions out of the way, the sooner you and your parents get your lives back on track. Okay?"

Robbie nodded for Olivia to continue. She smiled at him.

"Tell me about yourself. You're in high school?"

"I'm a senior, but I take mostly college classes."

Robbie's voice was so soft that even that short answer seemed labored. I shifted, unsure what to make of his apparent anguish.

"Any thought about where you're going to college yet?"

"Purdue. With Rachel."

Olivia and Robbie went back and forth for a while. His shoulders relaxed and his answers became more verbose the longer Olivia questioned him. She was a good interviewer. She established rapport and common ground before diving into her questions. More than that, she listened sympathetically to Robbie's answers. If I didn't know her better, I would have thought she actually cared about him.

"Okay," said Olivia after a few minutes of conversation. "What was your relationship to the victim?"

Robbie looked down.

"She was my girlfriend. I've been with her for about two years."

I paused for a second. My sister hadn't mentioned Rachel had a steady boyfriend. I doubted she knew, making me wonder what else Rachel had been hiding.

"What can you tell us about her death?" asked Olivia. I leaned forward, resting my elbows on my knees.

"Rachel came over at four this afternoon while my mom and dad played golf. She's not very good at math, so I was tutoring her. We did that for a while and then we played a video game."

That at least sounded like my niece. She played with my family's Nintendo Wii more than my daughter did.

"Okay," said Olivia, nodding. "What happened after you guys played a game?"

Robbie looked down again.

"Rachel got sick in the bathroom. I don't know what happened. Then she died."

"So she puked and then she died. And you have no idea why."

Robbie didn't answer, so Olivia opened the file folder in front of her and began to pull out pictures. They were probably the originals of the ones of which I had copies. She laid them in an array in front of Robbie. His lower lip quivered, and his lawyer put a hand on his shoulder.

"I think we're done here," said Meyers. "If you have any need to question my client further, I expect you to call me at my office."

Meyers stood, but Robbie didn't move.

Olivia pressed one picture under Robbie's gaze. It was a

headshot of my niece. Her eyes were closed, and rigor had contracted her face into a grimace.

"I bet she was a pretty girl," said Olivia. "At one time."

"She is pretty," said Robbie, a tear streaming down his cheek. "I loved her."

"This interview is over," said Meyers, his voice strained. "Get these cuffs off my client. Unless Robbie is under arrest, we're leaving."

Robbie still didn't move. Meyers said the interview was over, but it wasn't his call. If his client didn't want to take his advice, there was no reason for Olivia to stop.

"Look at her, Robbie," said Olivia, tapping the picture she had slid toward Robbie. "If you don't tell us what happened, we're going to cut her open, we're going to photograph her, and then we're going to put her on display. Is that how you want to remember her?"

Robbie didn't say anything, but another tear slid down his cheek. Olivia continued.

"We haven't found the girl's underwear, and I know you redressed her. If you don't tell us what happened, this girl you supposedly loved will be forever known as the bimbo who died with her pants down in your bedroom. Is that what you want?"

I winced. I'm not a prude, nor am I naive. Rachel was seventeen and had apparently been dating the same boy for two years. Of course they were having sex. Rana wouldn't see it like that, though. Hopefully we'd be able to keep that detail out of the papers.

"Don't say anything, Robbie," said Meyers. "Let me handle this."

For a moment, I thought Robbie was going to take his lawyer's advice, but then his lips started moving. No sound came out for a few seconds.

"She wasn't supposed to die," he said. His voice was so soft I almost didn't hear it above the ambient room noise.

"No, I'm sure she wasn't," said Olivia, matching Robbie's voice. Meyers rubbed his brow, his eyes closed. Olivia ignored him. "What happened? Did you have some kind of accident?"

Robbie closed his eyes, his lips moving before he spoke.

"Rachel was a Sanguinarian."

"I'm sorry?" asked Olivia.

"She drank blood. She drank part of a vial of blood. That's when she started puking. Then she died."

Robbie didn't say anything after that. I took a deep breath. As a detective, I'd been to more death scenes than I cared to remember, thirty-four of which had turned into criminal homicide investigations. Even with all that experience, this was my first vampire. I doubted Hallmark made cards to commemorate the occasion.

"Okay," said Olivia. "Let's start at the beginning and go from there."